THE ALEXANDRIA SEMAPHORE

ROBERT SOLÉ was born in Cairo in 1946. He moved to France at the age of 18. He has combined his career as a journalist with that of author, and works for *Le Monde*.

JOHN BROWNJOHN is one of Britain's foremost translators from the German and the French.

Also by Robert Solé in English translation

Fiction

THE PHOTOGRAPHER'S WIFE

BIRDS OF PASSAGE

Non-fiction

THE ROSETTA STONE

Robert Solé

THE ALEXANDRIA SEMAPHORE

Translated from the French by
John Brownjohn

THE HARVILL PRESS
LONDON

First published with the title *Le Sémaphore d'Alexandrie* by Editions du Seuil, Paris, 1994
First published in Great Britain in 2001 by The Harvill Press

2 4 6 8 10 9 7 5 3 1

This edition has been published with the financial assistance of the French Ministry of Culture

First published in Great Britain in 2002 by The Harvill Press,
Random House, 20 Vauxhall Bridge Road, London SW1V 2SA

Random House Australia (Pty) Limited, 20 Alfred Street, Milsons Point,
Sydney, New South Wales 2061, Australia

Random House New Zealand Limited, 18 Poland Road, Glenfield,
Auckland 10, New Zealand

Random House South Africa (Pty) Limited, Endulini, 5A Jubilee Road,
Parktown 2193, South Africa

The Random House Group Limited Reg. No. 954009
www.randomhouse.co.uk

A CIP catalogue record for this book is available from the British Library

ISBN 1 86046 968 X

Papers used by Random House are natural, recyclable products made from wood
grown in sustainable forests; the manufacturing processes conform to the
environmental regulations of the country of origin

Designed and typeset in Centaur at
Libanus Press, Marlborough, Wiltshire

Printed and bound in Great Britain by
Bookmarque Ltd, Croydon, Surrey

THE ALEXANDRIA
SEMAPHORE

May 1885

I love the early summer at Alexandria. The season, which has yet to begin, seems filled with promise. All is possible, all is still in the lap of the gods. I'm like the infatuated boy I used to be, feverishly waiting for Sunday to come round.

Relations and friends will be arriving one after another in a few days' time, complete with luggage, silverware, servants, and rapidly growing children. In Cairo at this very moment, attractive young women and girls I've never met are getting their summer outfits ready. I'm aroused, even now, by visions of their bare feet surreptitiously glimpsed on the beach.

"You're thirty-five, Maxime, and you've a good position. High time you got married," Aunt Angéline told me last month between two taps of her fan. "Leave it to me, I'll find you a regular little beauty."

Indefatigable Angéline, the human hurricane! She's due to arrive next Tuesday. Poor Mahmud's nerves are already on edge.

For the time being, however, we live in peace. The only sounds are those of the sea and the cicadas at nightfall.

I arrived at the villa ahead of everyone, just as I did last year – a ritual that never fails to enchant me.

The little train that conveys me to Ramlah seems to operate for my sole benefit. The lone cabby at the deserted station greets me with a gap-toothed smile, as if we had parted only yesterday. He heaves my bags aboard, cracks his whip loudly, and off we go.

The emaciated horse ambles along sandy roads flanked by fig trees. Stupefied by the sweltering sun, we have to ascend a small dune without getting stuck. And then, quite suddenly, the sea unfolds before us, a blue-green expanse fringed with foam. A gentle breeze caresses my cheeks. I shut my eyes and fill my lungs.

My heart pounds violently as we pull up outside the villa. The gate squeaks — it always has. The closed shutters are streaked with rust and the drive is carpeted with parched, luxuriant plants that crackle underfoot. It's time the wooden balconies and upstairs rooms were repainted, I tell myself. I shall pick out a pale pink for Nada — her favourite colour.

In August last year my father went for a swim in the sea. What a stir *that* caused! The whole of Fleming Beach buzzed with comments.

"If Dr Touta bathes at the age of seventy-three," exclaimed Nassif Bey's widow, "the sea must *really* be good for one's health!"

The next day, several gentlemen ventured into the water up to their thighs. Even the ladies moistened the hems of their gowns, uttering little shrieks as they did so. Exhausted but delighted, they spoke of it all evening on the terrace of the Miramare. Papa smiled to himself. I know him: it's his way of continuing to minister to the welfare of others.

This summer promises to be even livelier than last. The three Dabbour families have rented a house at Bulkeley and Albin Balanvin has taken a room at the hotel. On the other side of the dune, workmen are busy putting the finishing touches to Rizqallah's palatial villa. Even Boctor is said to be coming to spend a few weeks beside the sea . . .

In town, elaborate preparations to enliven our summer evenings are in progress. It seems that concerts, pantomimes and operettas are to be staged in the garden of the French consulate. The trees will be illuminated by electricity. Not wishing to be outdone, the British have built a band-stand a little further away, in the Place des Consuls. We shall, I suppose, be privileged to listen to the band of the Devonshire Regiment, which has pitched camp beside the sea, near Mustafa Pasha's mansion.

The khedive's arrival in Alexandria is set for 28 May. A triumphal arch has already been erected at the mouth of Franc Street — the first of many, no doubt. The Europeans have formed a reception committee, and the native dignitaries are planning to do likewise. How glad I am to be here, away from all that commotion!

Every morning, as soon as I awake, I gently open the shutters. If the sea is glassy, my heart leaps. I put on my bathing costume and run down to the water's edge.

I give my thoughts free rein as I float on the unruffled water with my arms outstretched. Everything surfaces in my mind, good years and bad, Nada, Ismailia . . . And everything takes me back to that January in 1863. How could I ever forget my first visit to Alexandria? Twenty-two years have gone by since then. Twenty-two years already . . .

PART ONE

The Place des Consuls

I

It was dark by the time we reached Alexandria. I didn't see the sea, nor the Place des Consuls of which I had heard so much. Outside the station my father dived into the first available cab and asked the cabby to whip up his horse. Setting off at a jog trot, we rode through the ill-lit streets to Nassif Bey's house.

My only contact with the unseen city was a warm breeze, so gentle as to be almost imperceptible. The air was filled with an unfamiliar, exciting smell.

"Seaweed . . . " Papa murmured.

Dr Nassif Bey wasn't at home, but he'd left my father a message asking him to come at once to Palace No. 3. We set off right away. In the darkness, gigantic trees stretched out their branches towards us in a rather unnerving manner.

The heavy gates of the palace were open, and two rows of sputtering torches led to the pavilion to which the viceroy had been taken. The cab set us down in the midst of a small crowd of nurses, relations, friends and courtiers who were bustling to and fro in the utmost confusion.

Nassif Bey tugged my father by the sleeve. "Thank you for coming," he said. "Have you brought my stethoscope?"

His stethoscope, left behind in Cairo the previous week and sent for by telegram, suddenly acquired immense importance in my eyes. After all, my father's colleague was one of Sa'id Pasha's six or seven personal physicians. I was not to know that the sovereign's family, having no faith in native doctors, had summoned every European practitioner in Alexandria to his bedside, and that the sick man's condition was thought hopeless in any case.

"The urine looks bad," Nassif Bey said in a low voice. "Sugar and albumin . . . It's in there, if you'd care to see it."

I followed them with sundry strangers trailing after us. No one seemed to be controlling access to the viceroy's room, which was lit by numerous candelabra. I stopped short after a few steps, overcome with panic. I should never have come even this far, I told myself. What would I say if someone questioned me? That I was Boutros Touta's son? How many people here knew who Dr Touta was?

The ill-ventilated room gave off an unpleasant odour of vomit and wilting flowers. Sa'id's bulky form reposed on a heap of mattresses. It was, of course, my very first sight of the viceroy, and his squint made my blood run cold. I turned and beat a hasty retreat.

My father emerged from the room a few minutes later. He seemed surprised to see me, as if he had forgotten my existence. Nassif Bey joined us in the passage soon afterwards. He jerked his head in the direction of three weasel-faced men in black, who were conversing in a corner. It took me some time to gather that they were the informants of Isma'il Pasha, the crown prince.

My father's colleague had insisted on putting us up for the night, so we waited for him to leave. He kept greeting people and moving from room to room, however, and Papa himself chatted with various people unknown to me. Tired out by the journey and all this excitement, I ended by sinking down on a bench. All that prevented me from falling asleep, no doubt, were the goings-on of the three men in black. From time to time, one of these hawk-eyed spies would insinuate himself into the sickroom, then come back and bring the others up to date. I sensed that each of them was poised to dash to the telegraph office, eager to be the first to acquaint his lord and master with the glad tidings . . .

It was a little after midnight when I awoke with a start, roused by a woman's lingering cry. Sa'id Pasha was dead. Everyone hurried out into the neighbouring rooms, and the palace officials met at once to draft a telegram to the crown prince. The latter summoned them to Cairo by the next train.

The pavilion had quickly emptied. We rejoined Nassif Bey in the garden, now deserted save for a few of the dead man's closest companions, who were weeping in silence. The sea air was growing cool. We put on our overcoats and boarded a victoria drawn by two horses. Alexandria looked sinister that moonless January night.

Nassif Bey's house, like those of all good Alexandrians, faced away from the sea. Papa was given a handsome room at the front. I was accommodated more modestly on the other side. Next morning, on opening the shutters, I got a shock: the bay, with its many sailing ships, lay spread out before me in all its majesty, and the air was filled with the ever-present scent of seaweed.

At breakfast Nassif Bey told us that the viceroy was already buried. The interment had taken place at dawn, almost in secret, on orders from Cairo. It only goes to show what a fantasist my Aunt Angéline is when she claims we walked at the head of the funeral cortège, cheek by jowl with princes, ulamas, and consuls-general! Still, if one had to edit all Aunt Angéline's half-false or wholly fictitious stories . . .

"After we left last night," said Nassif Bey, "a dust-covered carriage came bowling into the courtyard of Palace No. 3. It was Ferdinand de Lesseps, who had hurried over from Suez when he heard that the viceroy was dying. He arrived too late. It only remained for him to meditate in silence over his friend's dead body. I'm told he wept."

What a pity! I should so much have liked to catch a glimpse of Monsieur de Lesseps. The founder and president of the Suez Canal Company was a celebrity. The boys at our school spoke of little else. He had aroused fierce controversy ever since Sa'id Pasha had authorized him to excavate the canal linking the two seas. Those of his opponents who were not afraid, as the British were, that the isthmus of Suez would become a French colony, dismissed the project as impracticable or ruinously expensive.

"Do you think Isma'il Pasha will challenge the concession granted to the Suez Canal Company?" my father asked Nassif Bey.

"We shall see. The late khedive himself debated that question on his deathbed."

Our trip to Alexandria was unconnected with the viceroy's terminal illness, even though Nassif Bey had taken advantage of it to recover his stethoscope. The fact was, my father had come to meet someone off a boat. A young Syrian refugee named Nada Sahel, she was a Greek Catholic like us, and her parents had been killed during the massacres at Damascus.

Papa decided to use the occasion to introduce me to Alexandria because I would be celebrating my thirteenth birthday that January. Nothing could have given me greater pleasure. I had never been out of Cairo before, nor had I ever gone travelling with my father or seen the sea.

We went down to the harbour in the middle of the morning. The ship from Beirut had arrived, sure enough, but without Nada. Unable to obtain a berth at the last minute, she had booked one on another vessel scheduled to arrive a week later. To my great delight, our stay in Alexandria would be longer than planned.

There was no question of moving to a hotel; Nassif Bey, who considered hospitality the fifth cardinal virtue, would have been offended. He had told us at the very outset that his home would be available to us for as long as we wished.

We lunched with him, and I made the acquaintance of his wife, an energetic little woman with her hair done up in a bun, who discreetly withdrew from the dining room as soon as she had satisfied herself that all was as it should be.

Nassif Bey impressed me. I found it hard to fathom the close relations between him and my father. A wealthy Coptic physician and frequenter of the viceregal court, Nassif was an Alexandrian dignitary, whereas Dr Boutros Touta, a man of Syrian stock, had only a local practice in Cairo.

In the afternoon, Papa took me to the Place des Consuls to pay my respects to my cousin Rizqallah. The famous square, 400 metres long and planted with trees, was adorned at each end by a gushing fountain. Its massive buildings housed banks, shipping companies, the city's principal hotels, and foreign consulates identifiable by their flags and semaphores.

Then twenty-two, Rizqallah had recently been appointed third dragoman of the French consulate-general at Alexandria, a modest position but one that would sooner or later earn him the coveted status of a "French dependant". The job suited him perfectly. One could well imagine the resourceful Rizqallah acting as an interpreter and general factotum, an intermediary between the Europeans and the native administrators.

We were greeted at the French consulate-general by a tall *kawass* in Turkish costume, with two big pistols stuck in his sash. He went to fetch my cousin, who appeared soon afterwards, whistling to himself. Rizqallah had become more self-assured since his appointment. He was less intimidated by my father, I noticed, and addressed him in a more familiar manner, almost as an equal.

Rizqallah bore us off to his regular haunt, a café behind the Imperial Ottoman Shipping Office. Having ordered some drinks in a loud voice, he spoke gravely of Isma'il's accession to power.

"Tomorrow the new viceroy is due to receive all the foreign consuls in audience at the Cairo Citadel – an unprecedented ceremony in the European style. There are to be speeches."

Rizqallah's tone seemed to suggest that he was personally organizing this diplomatic function. He confirmed that Ferdinand de Lesseps had gone to commune with Sa'id Pasha's mortal remains during the night. He also told us that the French greatly regretted the viceroy's death and very much hoped that the new sovereign would not vitiate Egypt's cordial relations with Napoleon III.

Less than ten minutes later the *kawass* came to inform Rizqallah that he was urgently wanted at the Grand Hôtel de France, where his services were required by a Parisian banker desirous of visiting the Arab quarter. Rather put out, my cousin took leave of us and went off to exercise his diplomatic skills in the souks.

In the days that followed, Papa showed me the handsome villas bordering the Mahmudiya Canal and took me on a donkeyback excursion into the countryside near Ramlah. He spent most of the time at the hospital with Nassif Bey, however, and left me to explore the centre of Alexandria by myself. At the age of thirteen I could not, of course, fully appreciate the remarkable character of this cosmopolitan city, with its abrupt transitions from Piraeus Street to Lombart Street or from the Midan Attarine to the Via Garibaldi.

I had discovered a little inlet near the Place des Consuls. There, seated on a rock in the balmy air, I would survey the sea for hours on end. Sailing ships and steamers passed in the distance, and a liner's siren could be heard from time to time.

2

A certain amount of tension had reigned in the city since Sa'id Pasha's death. My cousin Rizqallah found this worrying, but Papa smilingly reassured him.

"It's always like this. Whenever a viceroy dies and his successor is waiting for the firman from Constantinople that will sanction his official investiture, the masses get worked up and the Europeans are called to account. The atmosphere is a trifle more tense than usual, perhaps, but it has to be said that the late khedive granted the Europeans so many privileges . . ."

And then the Xavier-Saillard affair burst upon the scene, plunging the whole city into turmoil. Even Nassif Bey, usually so imperturbable, betrayed signs of uneasiness.

A French merchant, Adolphe Xavier-Saillard, was quietly going about his business in the harbour area when an Egyptian soldier struck his horse with a stick. The horse reared and fell on its back in the gutter. Infuriated, the Frenchman scrambled to his feet and threw a punch at his assailant, whereupon the latter summoned several of his comrades, who rushed at Monsieur Xavier-Saillard, tied his hands together, and put a noose around his neck. The merchant was dragged off to Zaptiya police station with a yelling mob at his heels. Children threw stones at him, women spat in his face.

The consulate had been alerted by some European witnesses of the incident. At once, the senior dragoman, assisted by Rizqallah and several armed men, hurried to the police station to secure the Frenchman's release.

"I've never seen the consul in such a state," my cousin told us. "He's sent the viceroy a telegram demanding that the guilty parties receive exemplary punishment."

"Thirty lashes on the sole of the foot, I suppose," said Papa. "That's the going rate."

"No, no, he insists that the soldiers be put in irons in the Place des Consuls, and that their commanding officer be publicly stripped of his rank. The ceremony must take place in the presence of a large military contingent and last at least an hour."

My father shook his head. "Isma'il Pasha can't possibly agree to that. Having only just come to power, he'd find it a genuine humiliation."

"The consul is threatening to land some French troops for the defence of our compatriots."

"Our compatriots . . ." Doubtless it wouldn't be long before Rizqallah's recent appointment made a French dependant of him, but all the same! Papa didn't react.

The next day, in an atmosphere of hectic excitement, the French consulate took evidence from the European witnesses. Several people had heard the crowd shout, "Death to the Christians! The pasha who protected the Christians is dead!" These witnesses confirmed that Monsieur Xavier-Saillard had been struck repeatedly on his way to Zaptiya.

Late that afternoon a young French engineer who had just arrived in Egypt to take up his duties with the Suez Canal Company presented himself at the consulate. He had been present throughout the incident and stated that the soldier's blow had missed Monsieur Xavier-Saillard and struck the horse instead.

"Having got to his feet," he added, "Monsieur Xavier-Saillard went for his assailant and horsewhipped him several times."

The consul requested him not to include "this superfluous detail" in his deposition.

The young Frenchman looked surprised. "But it's true!"

"Our compatriot had been brutally assaulted. Whether or not he horsewhipped his assailant is quite unimportant," replied the consul.

"If it's so unimportant, I don't see why —"

"Listen, *mon vieux*," the consul said curtly, "you've only been in Egypt five minutes — you don't know a thing about this country. One of our nationals was very nearly murdered yesterday, and the culprits were members of the forces of law and order. It's not just a question of punishing an undeniable crime, but of making a public example. The natives must be shown that France intends to be respected."

Very upset by this exchange, the young man decided not to give evidence at all. Rizqallah, ever on the alert, caught up with him outside the consulate and thought it might pay to escort him to his hotel.

"His name is Étienne Mancelle," he told us. "I'll introduce him to you."

The Place des Consuls had never witnessed such a crowd. All the Europeans in Alexandria seemed to have assembled there, but they were not the only ones to stroll round the fountains, where the grilled sweetcorn vendors had installed their little carts. The square was a sea of turbans and tarbooshes, caps and bowler hats, interspersed with the bonnets of numerous European ladies eager not to miss the show. The two jets of water lent a festive air to this punitive ceremony.

The French consul, who was ensconced on his balcony, had seated Monsieur Xavier-Saillard — white suit, haughty expression, glossy moustache — on his right. Surrounding them were various European dignitaries and several French naval officers whose ships lay at anchor in the harbour.

"I have received your telegram," Isma'il Pasha had wired the French consul. "I, too, am anxious to set an example and rectify the views of ill-intentioned people. I shall grant you more than you request of me. I myself am coming to Alexandria, and I shall prove to Europe and France that I have not ceased to merit your trust."

"At least he hasn't come to preside over the ceremony in person," Papa remarked in a low voice.

Heralded by a roll of drums, some soldiers marched into the square. They flanked half a dozen men chained together and followed by their lieutenant, a young man of twenty or so, who was weeping. Moved by the sight of the officer's tears, I wanted to get closer to him and contrived to steer my father in that direction.

After a long pause, a general strode up to the culprit and, with an abrupt movement, ripped off his badges of rank. Then he took the man's sword and handed it to a blue-uniformed *kawass* from the French consulate, who was standing beside him. Applause rang out, soon to be drowned by another roll of drums.

We had managed to get close to the young lieutenant. That was when my father spotted the scar on his ear.

"But I know the boy!" he muttered. "I remember him."

It was at Mendela, a village in Upper Egypt, seven or eight years earlier. While on a medical tour of inspection, Papa had come across a strange gathering: all the villagers were filing past the tax collector, a Turk, who was seated beneath a palm tree. It was that greasy official's job to count the number of adults in each family, but how to distinguish adults from children? The *nazir's* highly individual method involved the use of an iron ring wielded by one of his henchmen: any person whose head would go through the ring was exempt from paying tax, so every family had to make its children try on the iron crown — for the older ones, an extremely painful procedure. They wept, their faces twisted with pain and sometimes streaked with blood. The parents shouted and threatened them while the Turk calmly smoked his chibouk. That was how my father had come to treat a boy of twelve or thirteen whose ear had been torn by the ring — a keen-eyed boy who irresistibly reminded him of that weeping officer in the Place des Consuls.

"A strange spectacle, doctor, don't you think?"

I turned, startled by an unfamiliar voice speaking unaccented French. Limping towards us was a smartly dressed man leaning on a cane with a mother-of-pearl knob. He raised his hat and introduced himself in a rather theatrical tone.

"Albin Balanvin, journalist."

My father looked surprised. "Delighted to make your acquaintance," he said, "but how did you know I was a doctor?"

"Oh, I know a lot of things," the stranger replied. Then, with the same supercilious air, "Why have they only chained those soldiers, doctor? It's rather imprudent. They should have been crucified, don't you agree?"

I hadn't the heart to smile, but it was hard to resist the charm of this ageless, rather effeminate-looking man.

"Just look at my consul waving his little tricolour! Exquisitely tasteful of him, don't you think? By the way, I can see your nephew standing quite near him . . ."

Rizqallah was, in fact, chatting with several of those present on the balcony. All smiles, he circulated among them with an obsequious air that didn't appeal to me.

"So you know my nephew, too?" said Papa.

"I know everyone," the journalist replied mournfully, as if suffering from a professional disability. When my father questioned him about the consul's attitude, he sniggered.

"Come, doctor, you must be well aware that the French consul has been itching to bring your new viceroy to heel ever since he came to the throne. Forgive me, I said 'your' viceroy. You're Syrian, aren't you? An Egyptian Syrian . . . I get confused by all these different categories . . ."

On the contrary, Albin Balanvin seemed perfectly at home in our world. We learned that he had lived in Egypt for thirty years or more, and that he was helping to launch a weekly newspaper, *Le Sémaphore d'Alexandrie*, whose Cairo correspondent he would be.

The ceremony was drawing to a close. The young lieutenant was still weeping. My father vowed to go and see him early the next day.

Rizqallah was approaching us accompanied by a young man with a very gentle expression. Smiling indefatigably, he made the introductions.

"Monsieur Étienne Mancelle, who has just arrived in Egypt to take up his duties as an engineer with the Suez Canal Company. My uncle, Dr Touta."

In his turn, Papa introduced the journalist. Albin Balanvin bowed deeply, then surprised his young compatriot by inquiring if he was satisfied with his half-board arrangement at the Grand Hôtel de France.

That night, in gratitude to the viceroy for having ensured that justice was done, many buildings in the European quarter were brightly illuminated. Flags flew from all the consulates, the one exception being that of Great Britain.

"The British detest us," observed Rizqallah.

Always that "us" . . .

The next day, thanks to a letter of recommendation from Nassif Bey, my father was admitted to Alexandria's army barracks. He was ushered into a grimy room and offered a pipe and some coffee while Walid al-Ahlawi was being sent for.

The former lieutenant had dried his tears, but his expression was defiant and uncommunicative. It took my father a good fifteen minutes to convince him that he was neither a policeman nor a spy employed by the French consulate, and that he meant him no harm.

"I did nothing," the ex-officer kept saying in a dull voice. "I didn't even know my men had detained a European."

In the end he deigned to talk. Yes, he came from Upper Egypt, but he'd never heard of a village by the name of Mendela. When my father asked about the scar on his ear, the young man stared at him with renewed suspicion. He'd been injured by a comrade while training, he said, clearly wondering what kind of trap he was being lured into.

"Everyone here in the barracks knows how I hurt myself," he added.

My father's embarrassment must have reassured him, because he gradually lost his hunted look and started to eye him with a trace of insolence.

"Anything else you'd like to know about my scar?"

To change the subject, Papa asked what the future held for him.

"How should I know?" Walid al-Ahlawi said angrily. "I'm just a private soldier now. A private soldier fit only to take a stick and hit a wretched European — is that what you wanted to make me say? There, I've said it. Now I must be punished."

The interview achieved little. When saying goodbye to Walid al-Ahlawi, my father tried to slip a guinea into his hand. The young man declined it with a brusque gesture, glaring at him fiercely.

"If ever you should need anything," Papa said simply, "come and see me. I live in Cairo, in New Muski Street. Just ask for Dr Touta."

Walid al-Ahlawi turned on his heel without a word.

3

The approaches to Alexandria harbour were too dangerous to permit a steamer to enter it by night. Delayed by an accident en route from Beirut, the *Phénix* was compelled to wait until after sunrise to enter the roads, and since the harbour was not deep enough to enable her to tie up alongside, the passengers had to be ferried ashore in dinghies. They still hadn't emerged from customs by ten o'clock. My cousin Rizqallah, who had insisted on accompanying us, was showing increasing signs of impatience.

"They're bandits, those boatmen," he told us indignantly. "They take steamers by storm. They swarm aboard, shinning up ropes even before the gangway has been lowered, seize the luggage, and compel the passengers to follow them. Once in the middle of the harbour, they demand an exorbitant fee and threaten to throw the luggage overboard. The authorities are incapable of injecting some order into the system."

Rizqallah was, for the umpteenth time, vituperating against "the natives' congenital inefficiency" — a phrase he must have picked up at the French consulate — when we suddenly saw the porters make a concerted dash for the door of the customs shed and squabble over the passengers' bags.

Standing on tiptoe, we scanned the crowd for a sixteen-year-old girl we'd never seen before. A distant cousin, Nada Sahel was the only daughter of a Damascus silk merchant who had been killed, together with his wife, during the massacres of 1860. Since then she had been living with relations in Beirut. It was they who had written to my father and asked him to welcome her to Egypt, where numerous Christian refugees were arriving every week.

"That's her!" I cried, pointing to a tall, slender girl with very dark hair, who had lowered her shawl.

Papa didn't even have time to be surprised by my exclamation, because Nada instinctively turned towards us. I had been expecting to see a tearful orphan, still traumatized by her parents' tragic death, but the girl who looked at us inquiringly was smiling.

"Nada Sahel?" asked my father.

Her dark eyes answered for her. I had never seen a face that thrilled me more.

Not far away, Rizqallah was causing a commotion. Eager to draw attention to himself, no doubt, he was tongue-lashing the two porters who had grabbed Nada's trunk.

As for me, I was speechless. My heart was pounding. I'd taken only a few seconds to fall in love with Nada. I was blind to Alexandria from that moment on. Everything revolved around her. I could not stop thinking about her olive-skinned hands, her eyes, her laugh . . .

Papa had arranged for her to spend one night at a convent near the Place des Consuls. In Cairo she would become a boarder with the Dames du Bon Pasteur, who were better qualified than a doctor of fifty-two to assist a young orphan on her road through life.

Rizqallah was waiting for us on the platform next day, all smiles.

"I've managed to take a day off," he announced. "I'm coming to Cairo with you."

This was a surprise — a nasty surprise for me, who had been looking forward to several hours in the train in Nada's company. She even seemed unsurprised by my cousin's appearance. It was just another of the novelties she'd experienced since leaving Beirut.

At the booking office, passengers were arguing over the price of tickets, which had risen yet again overnight. The haggling went on interminably. My father, who had always had a horror of such negotiations, left them to Rizqallah. The latter hurried from counter to counter, talking volubly and playing the grand seigneur.

"Unless I'm much mistaken, doctor, we shall have the pleasure of travelling together," said a familiar voice in the background.

Albin Balanvin limped towards us, leaning on his cane with the mother-of-pearl knob and accompanied by young Étienne Mancelle. The journalist bowed deeply to Nada and kissed her hand.

"I hope, mademoiselle, that your voyage in the *Phénix* was not too unpleasant, and that Cairo will be to your taste."

She was too shy to answer. At this the young engineer stepped in and asked, in a gentle voice, if she found travelling by rail uncomfortable. Nada replied that she had never set foot in a train before.

Meanwhile, Rizqallah was waving his arms about in the middle of the platform. He had managed to obtain an entire compartment by slipping the stationmaster a modest bakshish. We joined him.

"Sit beside the window, mademoiselle," Balanvin said in his theatrical voice. "You too, Mancelle. Egypt will be gracious enough to unfold before your eyes. Do you realize that, as recently as ten years ago, we should have had to sail up the Nile in a *cangia*? The trip took six days and nights, not a mere six hours."

Half an hour later, when the locomotive had still not deigned to leave, my cousin went in search of information.

"They're waiting for Sherif Pasha, a big landowner, who said he would be taking the train."

Balanvin tapped the knob of his cane. "I told you the train was far quicker, didn't I, mademoiselle?"

Nada burst out laughing. She looked even lovelier when she laughed.

Twenty minutes later, several baggage-laden carts appeared on the platform. Walking slowly behind them in the shade of a parasol wielded by his secretary came Sherif Pasha. The stationmaster rang a bell. Instantly, a crowd of peasants swarmed aboard the third-class carriages, which were open to the sky. The bell sounded again, and the train moved off with a jerk that dislodged Balanvin's suitcase from the luggage rack and deposited it on Rizqallah's lap. Nada burst out laughing again, and good humour took command of the compartment.

On the outskirts of Alexandria, Lake Mariout resembled an immense pink carpet stretching away into infinity. Étienne Mancelle, who was peering out of the window, declared himself fascinated by the sight. Travelling at sixty kilometres an hour, the locomotive sped towards the verdant plains of the Delta. I hardly dared look at Nada, who was sitting on my side of the compartment.

"I've learned some interesting facts about poor Xavier-Saillard," Albin

Balanvin told my father a little later. "Just imagine, the day before his accident he'd made 30,000 francs on the cotton market."

"A tidy sum . . . "

"But nothing compared to all the millions he'd made previously."

My father nodded. Then, delighted to be able to tell the journalist something in return, he said, "By the way, I had an hour's talk with the lieutenant who was reduced to the ranks in the Place des Consuls."

"Walid al-Ahlawi? He's a regular hero in his barracks! I'm sure he confided details of the ovation his comrades gave him after the ceremony in the square — and of the new sword they've presented him with. Do tell, doctor, please!"

The man was beginning to irritate me. A violent jolt absolved Papa from having to reply. The train abruptly slowed as it approached Kafr-ad-Dawwar station, and we halted with a deafening screech of brakes.

The third-class carriages emptied, to be refilled at once by a throng of new passengers in *galabiyas*. Other peasants, squatting beside the track as though indifferent to what was going on, received the smoke from the locomotive full in their faces. Bales of cotton and sundry packages were tossed out on to the platform in total confusion.

A quarter of an hour later the train was once more speeding through the countryside, whose countless irrigation ditches made it resemble a gigantic net. Étienne Mancelle seemed enthralled by the muddy villages with their sparse clumps of vegetation. Now and then he would utter an exclamation at the sight of half-naked peasants bent double in their fields like motionless bronze statues.

Nada looked all at sea. I had noticed the day before that she knew nothing of Egypt, not even the name of its capital city. I longed to talk to her, but the presence of all these knowledgeable adults made me tongue-tied.

Rizqallah tried to strike up a conversation with her, but he was captured by Balanvin, who kept asking him seemingly futile questions about the organization of the French consulate-general at Alexandria.

"You mean to tell me, dear friend, that the consul never works in the afternoons? Perhaps he needs a long siesta . . . "

Fields of *barseem* and cotton stretched away into the distance. From time to time, voluminous sails could be seen gliding along a waterway hidden from view by a curtain of palm trees.

"Is that the Nile?" the young engineer asked excitedly.

The river finally appeared in all its splendour. The train slowed before traversing the twelve spans of the new iron bridge.

"Being an engineer, my dear Mancelle, you'll appreciate the quality of this structure," said Rizqallah. "Even the piers are made of iron. Did you know that if this bridge had existed five years ago, Isma'il Pasha would not be viceroy today?"

Étienne looked at him inquiringly. Proud of the reaction he'd elicited, my cousin was only too pleased to elaborate, though he had eyes only for Nada.

"Before the bridge was built, the train used to stop on the bank and the carriages were ferried across the Nile. While making a trip in 1858, the then crown prince, Ahmed Pasha, insisted on remaining in his carriage during the crossing. Many local peasants, attracted by the prospect of a substantial bakshish, pushed it down to the ferry. They pushed it at a run, assisted by the wind. The carriage went faster and faster. Under its own momentum, it overran the chocks and fell into the Nile. Some of the passengers managed to jump out of the doors, but the crown prince, being stout and less agile, drowned."

"And because of that accident —"

"— his cousin, Isma'il Pasha, is viceroy today."

Nada started to laugh. Étienne Mancelle, who had thought it incumbent on him to assume an air of solemnity, burst out laughing in his turn. Within seconds, the whole compartment was convulsed with mirth. I realized that day, for the very first time, that Nada's laugh was irresistible.

At Tanta station, where a longish stop was scheduled, Étienne Mancelle got out on the platform. He returned a quarter of an hour later, out of breath and smiling broadly.

"Believe it or not," he said, "a donkey-driver just offered to sell me 'Monsieur de Lesseps's donkey'!"

Our smiles surprised him.

"My dear Mancelle," Albin Balanvin said sadly, "you really do have a lot to learn about this country. We'll see to it, never fear. In the meantime, please ignore the 10,000 other Egyptian donkey-drivers, all of whom will offer to sell you the donkey on which dear Ferdinand is alleged to have deposited his backside."

Mancelle blushed. Sensing his embarrassment, but without having understood the story of the donkey, Nada asked him a question that had been troubling her since the start of the journey.

"What exactly *is* the Suez Canal?"

Étienne Mancelle's face brightened.

"The Suez Canal, mademoiselle," he said fervently, "is one of the most ambitious projects in human history – the dream of every great man who ever passed through Egypt: Alexander, Julius Caesar, Bonaparte . . . Thanks to the genius and determination of Monsieur de Lesseps, this historic scheme is now becoming a reality. We're going to link the Mediterranean with the Red Sea by driving a canal 160 kilometres through the desert. Imagine, it will cut the route to India in half. Ships outward bound from Europe or America will no longer need to sail round Africa . . ."

Although the young engineer had never yet set foot in the Suez desert, he seemed to know every little hummock and fold in the terrain. How many studies on the subject had he read? How many lectures had he attended?

"I ought to employ you as scientific correspondent of the *Sémaphore d'Alexandrie*," Balanvin said with a smile.

The name of this future newspaper struck me as peculiar. The semaphores I'd seen on the coast were there to send signals to ships at sea. What signals did Balanvin and his friends propose to send, and to what ships?

Nada was half asleep. I glanced at her furtively from time to time, my heart overflowing with love.

It must have been six o'clock that evening when Étienne Mancelle suddenly levelled his forefinger at the window: some conical shapes stood outlined against the horizon.

"The pyramids," he said

"What are the pyramids?" asked Nada.

4

The first issue of the *Sémaphore d'Alexandrie* appeared a few weeks after our return to Cairo. The editorial, couched in an oblique style quite hard for the boy I still was to comprehend, announced that the new weekly would "resolutely defend the progress of civilization in Egypt" and "European interests" while maintaining its independence of all foreign powers. The editor even indulged in an ironical pun on "the consuls' place" in the country.

Albin Balanvin's article attracted more notice than most. People with some knowledge of current politics, like my father or Nassif Bey, could read between the lines. As for me, I was obviously too young to grasp the innuendoes.

FROM OUR CAIRO CORRESPONDENT
To the Editor:

1 March 1863

I need hardly tell you, sir, that the new reign has opened under the most favourable auspices. Ever since his installation, Isma'il Pasha has embarked on his task with a zeal and enthusiasm that have earned him universal admiration. This austere monarch, who rises early and retires late, seems immoderate only in his hours of work.

At Constantinople, whither he went to pay his respects to the Sultan, he received the most cordial of welcomes. It is true, of course, that the new viceroy has been lavish with his largesse. Instead of offering His August Master 30,000 carbines, as some had advised, he chose to present him with his steam frigate, the Feizi-Jihad, *which was accepted in an exceedingly gracious manner.*

In Cairo the new viceroy has made a deep impression on all his visitors. Thirty-two years of age, he is a red-bearded man of medium height and robust constitution. His sphinx-like face conceals fierce emotions, and his eyes, which are often half closed, can flash like lightning.

Pleasant in manner and a brilliant conversationalist, Muhammad Ali's grandson is capable of discoursing on any topic. French, which he speaks to perfection, is his usual language. He learned it as a boy in Vienna, before going to study at Saint-Cyr.

Isma'il Pasha is reputed to be an excellent administrator, as he has shown in managing his personal finances. His income, which was some two million francs eight years ago, now amounts to five times as much. It is predicted that he will do the same for the public exchequer!

This enlightened prince is anxious that his country shall enjoy the benefits of civilization. Our compatriot Mariette Bey has learned from his own lips that a monumental museum is to be built at Ezbekiyah, and that he will be in charge of it. Another Frenchman, Bruguières Bey, has just been entrusted with the reorganization of Cairo's School of Medicine.

But you will doubtless be wondering, sir, about the future of the Suez Canal. You must be aware that the French consul-general was deeply affected by the first speech Isma'il Pasha delivered after his investiture. In the presence of the entire diplomatic corps, he spoke out against the forced labour system. This was tantamount to condemning the manner in which work was proceeding on the Canal. Ferdinand de Lesseps hastened to reply that forced labour was not in current use at the construction sites on the Isthmus. The thousands of peasants conscripted by the Egyptian government are paid a wage. Conscription, perhaps, but not forced labour . . .

The fact remains that digging continues. Contingents of fellahin turn up at regular intervals. In addition to the 20,000 men toiling in the Suez desert, 20,000 more are on the way to relieve them and another 20,000 on the way to their homes. That, you will say, deprives agriculture of 60,000 pairs of hands. But after all, sir, Egypt has at least five million inhabitants!

For some weeks now, Ferdinand de Lesseps has been plied with fulsome compliments. "No one is more of a Canalist than I," the viceroy told him in the course of conversation. His Highness is said to have added, in a somewhat cryptic fashion, "But I want the Canal to belong to Egypt, not Egypt to the Canal."

I am told that the Xavier-Saillard affair has left something of a bitter taste in Isma'il Pasha's mouth. I am not in a position, sir, to confirm the rumours that the viceroy requested the Emperor to recall the French consul-general, nor that the Emperor flatly refused. This may, after all, be merely malicious gossip. The consul-general's term of office will soon be up in any case. If his departure were brought forward by a few weeks, it would simply be to enable our distinguished compatriot to enjoy a well-earned rest.

Albin Balanvin

5

Aunt Angéline had already inflated our few days in Alexandria into a whole epoch. To her women friends she described the death of Sa'id Pasha, the attack on Monsieur Xavier-Saillard and the punitive ceremony in the Palace des Consuls in a wealth of impressive detail – and this although my father, knowing his younger sister's tendency to exaggerate the smallest fact, had been careful to tell her as little as possible.

Let us be fair. Although my aunt was forever distorting reality, she always did so in a positive manner, to augment or enhance it. Angéline multiplied figures, never divided them, and she cultivated the superlative as a matter of course. Her brother had always been "the finest physician" in Cairo and her husband "the biggest jeweller".

No one would have imagined that Angéline was my father's sister. They differed in every respect, and the age gap only accentuated their dissimilarity. The milky complexion and rounded contours of the one contrasted with the dark skin and lean, almost emaciated frame of the other. Papa spoke little, whereas his sister held forth continuously. He was always at pains to find the *mot juste* – influenced, no doubt, by his training as an interpreter and a physician – whereas she seemed to rummage in her vocabulary with both hands and toss words into the air at random.

In those days Aunt Angéline was already lying about her age. She swore she was only thirty-five but had already passed her fortieth birthday. Her 190 pounds, on the other hand, were impossible to disguise. My father was always urging her to lose a little weight so as to alleviate the hot flushes from which she suffered.

Angéline was in a constant state of ferment. She spoke, fidgeted and perspired, simultaneously spraying herself with essence of bergamot. I used to find the scent reassuring. In Aunt Angéline's proximity I sensed a maternal warmth of which my brother Alexandre and I had been deprived.

I can still see her at home in the early afternoon, slumped on a lilac ottoman with flesh overflowing her half-open bodice, fanning herself furiously and pleading for air, air.

"*Hawa, hawa!*"

Angéline Falaki complained of a heatwave at the first hint of spring, sometimes even in midwinter. I recall her turning to her son and whispering somewhat histrionically, in a deathbed voice, "Lolo, Maman's pet, bring me a drop of water. I'm dying, truly I am!"

Twenty-three-year-old Lucien, the big ninny, was watching the progress of a fly on the drawing-room window. He rose with an effort and poured her a glass of cold water from the earthenware jug, then resumed his inactivity. The only child in the house since his three sisters got married, my cousin wore grey spats all year round in the belief that they made him look like a French engineer at work on the Suez Canal.

On Sundays, when she came to lunch with us, Angéline would enter with a cry of "*Hawa, hawa!*"

Our maidservant, whom she terrorized, wrung her hands. "But all the windows are open, *ya sitt Angelina!*" she protested.

My brother and I had nicknamed Angéline "Aunt Hawa". Lolo, whose horizons were rather limited, told her, '*Ya mami*, you were born for a cold climate. You should have lived in Damascus or Constantinople."

Alfred Falaki's jewellery shop was in Muski Street, a seething anthill that gave off mingled aromas of dust, fried fish, and grilled mutton. All day long, heavily laden donkeys and camels threaded their way between pedestrians, beggars, stray dogs, and infants being suckled or smacked or having their heads shaved by the roadside.

While waiting for customers Uncle Alfred would stand outside the shop, a potbellied, resplendent figure. He was the real shop window, what with his gold fob watch, pink diamond tiepin, and enormous ring – never the same ones twice. Nothing that went on in the bustling Muski escaped him. In a loud voice he would hail passers-by, dispense advice, tell the owner of the coffee shop opposite to make him a *mazbout*, or comment on current affairs.

The "biggest jeweller's in Cairo" was no great shakes to look at. Lolo, who lethargically officiated there six days out of seven, was its only employee. He opened the steel shutters at ten o'clock in the morning and shut them for lunch and a siesta at one, but the shop remained open until late in the evening, every candle alight.

Though far from being the biggest jeweller in Cairo, Angéline's husband was regarded as an astute businessman and first-rate haggler. One of his favourite ploys, in the heat of an argument, was to pull off his ring or pluck out his tiepin and tell the client, "Here, you can have it as a gift! Keep it, don't buy a thing, I give up!"

Angéline always referred to her brother as "the Doctor", a title that lent her reflected glory. She made a meal of it in front of her women friends, interminably boasting of his putative exploits. If he caught her fantasizing, she would simply shrug and flutter her fan, telling herself that, if she were in Dr Touta's place, she would be on first-name terms with all the potentates on earth.

Angéline was still trying to remarry her brother at this stage. She thought it abnormal that a widower saddled with two young children should not set up house again. Papa, however, was perfectly content with things as they stood. He had decided, once and for all, to live alone, cherishing his wife's memory and running his home with the help of a maidservant.

But Angéline seized on any excuse to raise the subject. When she lunched with us on Sundays, she would pull a face and say, with her mouth full, "This tahina needs more lemon juice. In your poor wife's day . . . "

But if the sesame-seed sauce was made *in situ*, the main dish always came from Aunt Hawa's kitchen. She turned up at our house accompanied by her own maid, who carried a steaming dish on her head.

Angéline was forever making inquiries about potential wives for Papa, who found it infuriating.

"All right, all right," she would say, "I won't do anything more. Anyway, what *have* I done? *Ayyuh!* Next thing you know, I'll be blamed for talking to my friends! Is that a crime? Just tell me if it is!"

She had even been known to engineer meetings with young widows. On those occasions my father really lost his temper. Angéline would then pronounce herself offended, feign tears, and swear on the head of her husband, the precious Alfred Falaki, that she would never darken our doors again. On average, these estrangements lasted forty-eight hours. As one who idolized her elder brother and couldn't do without him, Angéline would very soon reappear on our doorstep, her arms laden with delicacies.

But did she really, in her heart of hearts, want "the Doctor" to remarry? Everyone remembered how jealous she had been of my mother, even though she praised her to the skies posthumously. Papa's first wife had robbed her of her brother, so to speak, and people doubted whether a second would be spared her resentment.

Aunt Angéline had personally accompanied Nada to the Dames du Bon Pasteur. These French nuns took in day girls, but also orphans, foundlings, and even young negresses from Darfour or the Sudan who had been bought out of slavery by missionaries. Their pupils were taught French and elementary mathematics, but, more especially, needlework, deportment, and religious knowledge.

Nada seldom left the convent for the first few months of 1863. The nuns deemed it necessary to keep an eye on her throughout the week.

On Sunday afternoons I would invent some excuse to go and prowl around the Maison du Bon Pasteur in Shubra. I never saw anything, of course. The boarding school was as hermetically sealed as a prison, but my pulses raced at the very thought that Nada was there behind those grey walls, only a few yards away.

Drawing on the little I knew about the layout of the interior, I constructed an entire universe. I saw Nada and her schoolmates walking in pairs along the gloomy cloister with the benches ranged along its walls. I saw her in the courtyard, leaning over the little niches planted with clematis and roses. I pictured her in one of the three grille-enclosed chapels that formed a Latin cross with the fourth reserved for the public. Yet I balked at picturing her in the boarders' dormitory, where every bed was surmounted by a black crucifix.

Abandoning my observation post, I would make a small detour via

Shubra Street, an avenue flanked by giant sycamores, where the finest carriages in Cairo paraded on Sunday evenings. The harem carriages were preceded by barefoot attendants who ran ahead to clear the way. Seated at the foot of a tree, I used to daydream, imagining myself a general, an admiral, a prince of the viceregal family. With Nada across the saddle bow of my white charger, I galloped off into the plain beyond the sycamores . . .

6

Not long after he arrived in the Suez desert, Étienne Mancelle wrote to my father giving us his news. He was well, he said, despite the rather primitive living conditions. His admiration for Ferdinand de Lesseps had steadily grown, and he gave a lyrical account of "the great civilizing venture" in which he was taking part. In a postscript the young engineer asked my father to present "his respects to Mademoiselle Nada". He also enclosed a big coloured map of the isthmus for him to give me.

Few gifts could have been looked at more often or put to better use. I pinned the map to the wall of my bedroom. It was not only a permanent geography lesson but provided immense scope for all my dreams.

Most of the map was occupied by desert, which was printed in burnt sienna. Areas already under cultivation appeared in green and the two seas in pale blue. A dotted red line indicated the course of the famous canal that was to link them. Another dotted line, this time in brown, represented the freshwater canal. I filled in these lines as work on the two canals progressed.

I can still see myself, ruler in hand, explaining "the great civilizing venture" to my young brother Alexandre for the umpteenth time.

"Up there is the Mediterranean, down there the Red Sea. The canal starts up there at Port Sa'id and will end at Suez. At the moment it's got as far as Lake Timsah, halfway there."

"And the brown line?"

"The brown line is the freshwater canal."

"I'd have thought one canal was enough."

"Certainly not, *ya fellah*! They serve two different purposes. The maritime canal will connect the two seas, the freshwater canal will supply the whole of this desert area with drinking water. You don't want them to have to go on transporting drinking water on camelback, do you?"

Alexandre didn't want anything at all. My lectures bored him.

At school, however, the Très Chers Frères never ceased to extol the merits of Ferdinand de Lesseps. He was not only a Frenchman like themselves, but a Christian into the bargain. The Suez Canal Company was a French project and enjoyed the blessing of Almighty God.

"The canal will be a great route for enlightenment, civilization and information," explained our headmaster, Frère Ildefonsus. "It is a great waterway that will transform two worlds into a single world and all nations into a single human race."

He said this in the tone of voice he used for the Creed, reminding us that Moses and his people had roamed the desert near Lake Timsah, and that the Holy Family, too, had called a halt there. To us, his listeners, all these events seemed to fit with perfect coherence into a visible and invisible universe. We had quite as much reason to believe in the Suez Canal Company as we did in One, Holy, Catholic and Apostolic Church.

The hagiography of Saint Ferdinand had begun in 1832, in the reign of Muhammad Ali.

"De Lesseps had been appointed French vice-consul at Alexandria," recounted Frère Ildefonsus. "When he landed in Egypt he was obliged, like his fellow travellers, to go into quarantine. He spent his time in the hospital reading. That was when he came across a paper written for Bonaparte by a French engineer and devoted to the possibility of linking the Mediterranean and the Red Sea. This idea would never leave him.

"During his stay in Egypt, de Lesseps made the acquaintance of Prince Sa'id, an overweight boy whom his father compelled to skip, go riding several times a day, and follow a draconian diet. The French vice-consul secretly fed him macaroni, and they became friends."

Frère Ildefonsus passed swiftly over the next reign, that of 'Abbaas, who had no love for the French. In any case, Ferdinand de Lesseps had left Egypt to take up diplomatic posts elsewhere.

"In 1854 'Abbaas was assassinated by two Mamelukes and Sa'id became viceroy. As soon as he heard the glad tidings, de Lesseps caught the first boat to Alexandria. He was eager to advocate the project that had matured in his mind over the years: the digging of a canal between the two seas. Sa'id gave him a friendly welcome. He presented him with a fine Arab horse and invited him to join him in the desert near Lake Mariout, where he was encamped with his army. De Lesseps, who was a first-class horseman, made an excellent impression on the viceroy.

"At sunset late one afternoon, when he had just jumped a stone wall, Sa'id Pasha took de Lesseps by the hand and sat him down on a divan at his side. The Frenchman judged that the time had come to explain his project. He discoursed at great length on the benefits of linking the two seas. Then he said, 'What a claim to fame it would be, Highness! The Egyptian monarchs who erected the Pyramids, those useless monuments to human pride, have lapsed into oblivion, whereas the name of the prince who opened the great maritime Suez Canal would be blessed for centuries and generations to come.'

"Fired with enthusiasm, Sa'id Pasha summoned his generals and invited them to sit on folding chairs outside his tent, then asked de Lesseps to outline his plan. The generals listened wide-eyed, but their views were not consulted. The Suez Canal would come into being. It would do so despite the uneasiness of Constantinople and the scepticism of those who pronounced it ruinous or impracticable . . .

"Five years later," Frère Ildefonsus concluded in a vibrant tone, "excavation commenced. And that was the start of the magnificent route along which, one day and for evermore, peace and justice, enlightenment and truth will traverse the Egyptian desert."

In order to get to Timsah, the growing town near which his construction site was situated, Étienne Mancelle had had to take the train to Benha, and from there another train to Zagazig. At Zagazig he boarded a *dahabiya* which, hauled along the bank by two mules, took twelve hours to travel as much of the freshwater canal as had already been dug.

Timsah's first living quarters were beginning to go up on a broad plain 300 yards from the lake. Mancelle was allotted a bungalow in the so-called "Bachelors' Quarter". His next-door neighbour, Félix Percheron, also belonged to the Highways Department. He was a member of the old brigade, one of the engineers who had gone ashore on the isthmus five years earlier, when Port Sa'id was still a deserted stretch of beach inaccessible to larger vessels. His face tanned by the desert sun, Percheron loved to play the old soldier.

"That twelve-hour trip of yours was a picnic, *mon cher*! You don't imagine we had a *dahabiya* to take us to Pelusium Bay, do you? We lived under canvas with rats gnawing our toes. We kept our guns handy, too, believe you me, because we never knew when the Bedouin were going to attack!"

To excavate the preliminary channel in Lake Manzalah, Percheron's Arab labourers had to delve in mud. They scooped it up in both hands, squeezed it against their chests to drain it, then plastered it to the backs of their neighbours, who carried it like a hod. This mud, which gave off an unbearable stench of hydrogen sulphide, was dumped on either side of the channel. When dried by the scorching sun it formed a kind of dyke, but one rainstorm was enough to wash it all away.

Percheron described how the earliest huts, built on piles, were carried away by wind, rain, and sandstorms. He also described the building of the lighthouse, the workshops, the forges, the careening basin. The marshy beach had become Port Sa'id, a genuine town of several thousand inhabitants, with cafés, barbers, tailors – even its own Seltzer plant.

"And we achieved all that despite the jeers of the British! No ship will ever dare land on such a dangerous coast, they said. I'm joking, yes, but it was a struggle, Mancelle. A real struggle."

He repeated the words, driving his fist into his palm.

Mancelle had been assigned to Construction Site No. 6. One morning less than three weeks after taking up his duties, he was immensely surprised to see the Almighty turn up in person: Ferdinand de Lesseps was making a tour of inspection in the desert. The president and founder of the Suez Canal Company drove around in a strange vehicle: a kind of charabanc fitted with wide cast-iron wheels and hauled by six dromedaries, each with an Arab driver on its back.

The engineers present went to welcome him. Mancelle approached the great man with a pounding heart. He saw a robust-looking sixty-year-old with a small moustache, his smiling face framed by an abundance of silky white hair. Ferdinand de Lesseps shook hands with each man in turn.

"Gentlemen," he said, "remember what nonsense the enemies of the isthmus talked! They began by telling us that the two seas were on different levels. Then they said that ships would refuse to put in at Port Sa'id, and that navigation in the Red Sea was too dangerous. There are still a few good souls who insist that the canal will become a ditch filled with stagnant water or be choked by wandering sands. I've even heard it said that we'll have to re-excavate it every year!"

Hearty laughter all round.

"You laugh, gentlemen, and rightly so," de Lesseps went on. "But spare a thought for our unfortunate shareholders in Paris, who are forever being harassed and urged to dispose of their shares. Our enemies spread false rumours, print false reports, sound false alarms. They hope to foster a belief that, even if the canal becomes a reality, ships will steer clear of it. All our studies demonstrate the contrary, of course. It is up to you, gentlemen, to complete this task. You are engaged in removing the only obstacle left by Providence on this great international trade route!"

Ten days later my father received an emotional letter from Étienne Mancelle:

Timsah, 6 March 1863
Dear Doctor,
At twilight every evening I go for a stroll along the lakeshore. At the sound of a rifle shot, an army of flamingos rises like a pink cloud traversed by the rays of the setting sun. This sublime spectacle restores Timsah to itself alone. But have I any right, these days, to speak of Timsah?

The day before yesterday, Monsieur de Lesseps called together all the employees present at the site. Our president and founder opened with some of the encouraging words his heart knows so well how to devise. "In me," he told us, "you will always have a friend and father, for to me you are all, without exception or distinction, members of one big family."

It was in the course of this affectionate address that he made the following solemn declaration: "At the entrance to the canal there is a town, Port Sa'id, dedicated to the memory of the late viceroy; another town is rapidly taking shape here. We began the canal under Sa'id; we shall complete it under Isma'il. From this day forward, let the name Timsah be replaced by that of Ismailia, and in the future may the uniting of the waters of the Mediterranean with those of the Red Sea also unite the names of Sa'id and Isma'il, both of which are dear to our hearts."

This announcement was greeted with a triple salvo of cheers. That is why I am not writing to you, and will no longer do so, from Timsah, but from Ismailia.

Yours very sincerely,
Étienne Mancelle

Étienne Mancelle rode to Construction Site No. 6 on horseback every morning. Before reaching it he would pause on the summit of a dune, fascinated by the spectacle before him. The canal, as yet waterless but scores of yards wide, was a trench running south. The young engineer couldn't tear his eyes away from that deep, man-made gash between Africa and Asia. Here, the map of the world was in process of transformation.

A mass of grey ants was milling around below him. Hundreds of labourers armed with picks and shovels were carving out the bed of the future canal. Hundreds more loaded the spoil into rush baskets and passed them up the embankment from hand to hand. There, other half-naked men hoisted the baskets on to their backs and emptied them a short distance away. Between them, the construction sites on the isthmus had removed seven million cubic metres of spoil in the space of four years.

Étienne bent a thoughtful gaze on those illiterate peasants whom the authorities had summoned, sometimes from the other end of Egypt, to take part in this "great civilizing venture".

"They're docile enough," Percheron had told him, "but you should have seen the first contingents! The fools thought they wouldn't be paid, so they tried to escape during the night. Our Bedouin horsemen had to round them up like sheepdogs."

"You must look at it from their point of view," Étienne said softly. "They've had to leave their fields and families to come and work here . . ."

"But I told you, Mancelle, they're being paid: strong men three piastres, men of average build two-and-a-half, and one piastre apiece for the under twelves. You won't find better wages anywhere in Egypt. As a rule, the only payment a peasant conscripted for public works can expect is a thrashing with a stick or the *kurbash*."

"What's that?"

"My dear fellow, you'll soon learn to recognize the *kurbash* by the delightful sound it makes. Crack, crack! There's nothing to beat a whip for pacifying the Arabs and showing them the error of their ways."

Étienne couldn't bring himself to smile.

"The fellah," Percheron went on, "is like the wife of Molière's Sganarelle: he asks to be beaten. Beaten by his peers, mind you, not by us. Besides, the thing we dislike most is having to be ruthless ourselves. The gangs of peasant labourers are escorted here by army officers and sheikhs. The responsibility for seeing that the work gets done, and thus for discipline, is theirs. I'll take you to the Arab village and show you a delightful oxhide spread out on the ground: it's the so-called bed of justice, and it's filled with the most persuasive arguments. You'll be able to see for yourself how willingly the guilty take their medicine."

In the Arab village a few days later Étienne actually witnessed the punishment of a young man who had stolen a crate of figs. He was spread-eagled face down on the ground with his feet strapped to a post. A sturdy brute, stark naked so as not to hamper his movements, took a whip and gave the thief nine lashes on the soles of his calloused feet. From the sound, he might have been beating metal.

Not daring to avert his head, Étienne merely lowered his eyes. He recalled the words of the president and founder:

"Treat the natives well. They're men like you."

The next day he reverted to the subject of forced labour. Percheron interrupted him angrily.

"My dear fellow, you still don't know a thing about Egypt. This country is just a desert traversed by a river — an invaluable but capricious river in need of constant supervision. Peasants have been mobilized to build dykes and dredge canals since the dawn of time. Do you think they'd do so of their own free will, without compulsion?"

"That's just it. Agriculture is disrupted by the absence of all these men we compel to work here."

"So? Won't the Suez Canal make Egypt prosperous?"

"The Company could have recruited labourers in other countries."

"You're joking! For one thing, it would be too expensive. For another, I would remind you that it's forbidden under the terms of the concession, which clearly stipulates that four-fifths of the labourers must be Egyptians. Do you know who insisted on that proviso? The British! Yes, my friend, the British, because they were afraid the isthmus of Suez would become a French colony. So please, Mancelle, give these girlish arguments a rest! The British, who now bombard us with their hypocritical philanthropy, didn't suffer from any such scruples when they built the railway line from Alexandria to Cairo. Their peasant labourers didn't benefit from the same medical assistance as ours, take it from me. Those rails, my friend, rest on hundreds of Egyptian corpses."

7

Nada was suffocating at the Dames du Bon Pasteur. Nothing could have been less congenial to her than that cramped little world where a girl had to keep her eyes permanently lowered. One could sense her eagerness to be released as soon as possible. My father had obtained permission for her to leave the convent once a month, or thereabouts, when it was our turn to give a family lunch. I dreamed of those occasions for weeks in advance.

Aunt Angéline, who thought Nada should be married, had but one idea in her mind:

"Lolo, Maman's pet, we're lunching at the Doctor's tomorrow. The orphan girl will be there. You must wear your white suit, you look so smart in it."

For the present, however, Papa wouldn't hear of Nada's getting married. He had been struck by the girl's lack of formal education, which was doubtless a product of the two-and-a-half years she had spent shuttling between Damascus and Beirut after her parents' tragic death.

"She's only sixteen," I heard him say to Aunt Angéline one day. "There's plenty of time."

Being only thirteen, I felt that the time couldn't pass quickly enough, although there was no folly I wouldn't have committed, in my dreams, in order to carry Nada off and marry her . . .

Lolo wasn't the only one to put on a white suit: Rizqallah had taken to coming from Alexandria every month, just to attend our Sunday lunches. It was clear to me from his manner alone that he came on Nada's account.

I recall how annoyed he was, on one occasion, to learn that the girl had been detained at the Bon Pasteur for an Adoration of the Blessed Sacrament.

My cousin always had plenty to say for himself, thanks to his job as dragoman of the French consulate-general. He was a good raconteur, too, and spoke with the authority of one who rubbed shoulders with the powerful. It rankled with me whenever Nada listened to him at table.

Rizqallah seemed nonetheless embarrassed by the presence of his father, Boctor Touta – and understandably so. Papa's half-brother couldn't open his mouth without swearing. He uttered insults in Arabic at the drop of a hat. Prefacing his imprecations with a raised hand and a curl of the lip, he delivered them in a thunderous voice that enunciated each syllable with almost sensual pleasure. Sometimes he would translate one or another of his favourite gibes into French, making them sound cock-eyed but even more obscene. The uncouth boor more than once gave my cheek a familiar pinch and boomed, "Well, you little pimp, I hear you're doing well in class!"

Rizqallah, the eldest of Boctor's thirteen children, had left home to go and work in Alexandria. Boctor himself spent part of his time in the provinces, where he engaged in all manner of obscure business transactions. He dealt in scrap metal, old wagons, obsolete equipment. He also bought plots of land from insolvent creditors, having first insulted them roundly. Boctor could often be seen pencilling figures on greasy scraps of paper which he rather bizarrely secreted in his shoes – sometimes, even, under his tarboosh.

Our maidservant, Om Mahmud, disliked Papa's half-brother and employed various superstitious techniques designed to ensure that he never crossed our doorstep again. After Boctor had left, she would smash an earthenware jug and vigorously sweep up the fragments as though obliterating his footprints.

No one was surprised by Boctor's vulgar remarks when he attended family functions – they were part of the scenery, so to speak – but the presence of an outsider, and a girl in particular, made them an embarrassment.

But Nada seemed deaf to them. She even forbore to smile when Boctor Touta, as a matter of course, called one of his offspring "son of a dog".

My older boy cousins always tried to sit opposite Nada at table. Personally, I preferred to slip into the place on her left or right, where I could sense her breathing beside me and, without even turning my head, see her hand resting on the table. I had no need to speak, I could listen to her laughter. Those were my month's most exhilarating moments.

I really knew next to nothing about Nada. All I had heard was that she had been away visiting some cousins when the Damascus blood bath of 1860 occurred, and that she had lived with them in Beirut for over two years after that, like other Christian refugees whose one dream was to settle in peaceful, prosperous Egypt.

Nada never spoke of her childhood, and I didn't dare question her about it. Once or twice, with his typical lack of tact, my brother Alexandre asked her about her home in Damascus. She gave him an evasive answer, and I hurriedly changed the subject.

Whenever Aunt Angéline referred to "the orphan girl", Papa would growl, "The girl's got a name."

Half an orphan myself, I preserved only the vaguest recollection of my mother, who had died when I was three. Om Mahmud, who always spoke of the unknown woman with tears in her eyes, had been not only her servant but her confidante and adviser during the early years of her marriage. My mother failed to conceive despite all that her husband's medical expertise could do. Om Mahmud, though completely illiterate, was familiar with some ancestral remedies for the barren state. Her name alone seemed to vouch for this: she was known as "Mother of Mahmud", even though no one had ever seen her mysterious son and she herself appeared to have forgotten him.

Unbeknown to her husband, my mother consulted a kind of marabout who, in return for ten piastres, made her drink some turtle's blood. She awaited the effects of this medicine for several months, but in vain, so Om Mahmud took her to see another specialist. This one made her walk on some smouldering incense, inflicting minor burns on the soles of her feet. All she had to do thereafter was circle the Great Pyramid seven times. That evening she returned home exhausted, running a high temperature, and firmly resolved never to take her maidservant's advice again.

"Two months later she was expecting a baby," Om Mahmud told me. "She was expecting you, the child of the Pyramid. It's her you get your bright eyes from."

The child of the Pyramid . . . Having long haunted my dreams, this story ended by making me smile. Today I look back on it with affection, telling myself that my mother twisted her ankles on the stony desert soil to give me life. I like to regard it as symbolic: by making seven circuits of the Great Pyramid, hadn't that young woman, born in the Lebanese highlands and married on the banks of the Nile, become a true Egyptian?

To Aunt Angéline, my mother's major defect was her membership of a Maronite family. She had married in a Greek Catholic church, to be sure, but how could that wholly efface the original stigma? Angéline used to call her "the Maronite" just as she later referred to Nada as "the orphan girl". I think she blamed them both for not having been born in Egypt.

Nada attracted me all the more because she came from elsewhere – a mysterious and disturbing "elsewhere", but one that in some way constituted our identity. The Toutas also hailed from Syria, after all. Even though 150 years had elapsed since our forebear's arrival in Egypt, weren't we still, in our own and everyone else's eyes, *Shawam*, or Syrians?

One Sunday in May, when lunch was nearly ready, Nada could not be found in the drawing room or the dining room. Rather puzzled, I was making for the rooms on the first floor when I caught sight of her sitting on the tall ashwood bench under the stairs, doubtless resting after the long walk from school. One of her legs was doubled up beneath her gown, the other gently swinging in the air. Not expecting to be seen by anyone, she had removed her shoe. She wasn't wearing stockings! Flustered by the sight, I couldn't tear my eyes away from that aching, enchanting little foot, which suddenly stopped swinging.

Nada had seen me. She could have tweaked her skirt down, but she didn't.

"Why are you pulling that funny face?" she said with her habitual, cheerful smile. "Have I shocked you?"

Because I was three years younger, Nada treated me rather like a child. This permitted us to indulge in certain familiarities denied to my older male cousins like Lolo or Rizqallah. Not really knowing whether to remain a child or to render myself more interesting by acting in a manly, self-assertive manner, I constantly wavered between the two.

"You've got lovely eyes, Maxime," she said, still smiling.

Ah, that shapely, swinging foot ... How I longed to take it in both hands and knead it gently. How I yearned to go down on my knees, bend over that olive-skinned foot and clasp it to my cheek ...

Deftly slipping her shoe on, she got up.

"Let's go and have some lunch," she said.

8

And so, without knowing it, Rizqallah had become my adversary, my rival. I hated that white suit of his.

One Sunday, Om Mahmud was ingenious enough to trip with the steaming dish of *molokhiya* in her hands and spill some sauce on the detested garment. Apart from the fact that my cousin nearly scalded himself, I was delighted to note that the green stain resisted the salt that our poor maidservant, on the verge of tears, went to fetch from the kitchen. Aunt Angéline advised Rizqallah to scrub the stained sleeve with a horsehair brush dipped in a mixture of soft soap, honey, and arrack, but the mark had not entirely gone the following month. Its outlines were still quite visible on the elbow.

My cousin couldn't have afforded a new white suit at this stage. It wasn't until two years later that he supplemented the meagre wage he earned at the French consulate by entering the employment of Monsieur Adolphe Xavier-Saillard. Papa heard this by chance from Albin Balanvin, whom he happened to meet in town.

"Well, doctor, it seems your nephew has come to the assistance of poor Xavier-Saillard . . . "

Rizqallah himself confirmed that he was doing "odd jobs" for the Frenchman, whom he had doubtless met on the occasion of the celebrated incident in January 1863. My cousin was one of the consular officials who had gone to release him from the police station. Ever adept at drawing attention to himself, he must have been busy in the days that followed. Rizqallah was like that: he observed people and listened to them, then beguiled them and never let go. We should never have made the acquaintance of Étienne Mancelle in Alexandria if my cousin hadn't escorted the young engineer to his hotel after his unfortunate interview with the French consul. I suspect that, once extricated from the clutches of a yelling mob, Adolphe Xavier-Saillard must have found himself overwhelmed with solicitude by the consulate's third dragoman.

I never knew exactly what Monsieur Xavier-Saillard employed Rizqallah to do during this period. Was he sent to verify the number of bales of cotton being loaded on the quayside at Alexandria? Did he check the crop to ensure that no dishonest overseer adulterated milk-white, luxury cotton with greyish cotton of the second grade? Or did he simply act as an intermediary between his employer and the local authorities, as he did at the French consulate?

Xavier-Saillard was already regarded as one of Alexandria's wealthiest businessmen. His mishap had awakened certain memories. Specifically, it was said that he had squeezed a vast sum of money out of the late viceroy, Sa'id Pasha.

"A million Egyptian guineas," Albin Balanvin told my father.

"A million!"

The journalist tapped the knob of his cane. "Monsieur Xavier-Saillard claimed that sum as an indemnity. He asserted that Sa'id Pasha's father had orally promised him, fifteen years earlier, the concession on one of the port transit services, and that he had never received it."

"An oral promise? Sa'id Pasha could have sent him off with a flea in his ear."

"But doctor, you know how the late viceroy hated to be pestered. My charming compatriot, who enjoyed the support of two or three European consuls, kept hammering on his door. He finally landed a very nice form of compensation: the toll receipts from the new lock on the Mahmudiya Canal."

"But that's outrageous!"

"Quite so, but that wasn't the end of it. Several envious members of the court reproached the viceroy for having granted the concession to a foreigner. Sa'id Pasha was so annoyed, yet again, that he ended by taking his lock back and compensating Xavier-Saillard to the tune of 250,000 francs. And that's all of a million Egyptian guineas, isn't it?"

* * *

At the time when Rizqallah began to do "odd jobs" for him, the Frenchman was becoming even wealthier thanks to the cotton boom. All imports from the United States had ceased because of the Civil War, sending prices soaring. Being a producer as well as a merchant, Adolphe Xavier-Saillard profited twice over. Egypt's long-fibre cotton was in great demand throughout the world. At Liverpool the white gold trebled in price in an atmosphere of frantic speculation.

"Some lots are sold and resold as many as forty or fifty times without ever leaving the warehouse," Rizqallah told us, his eyes shining.

All Egypt was gripped by the craze. Throughout the valley of the Nile, everyone from the humblest peasant to the biggest landowner planted nothing but cotton. The viceroy himself bought one parcel of land after another, and anyone disloyal enough to reject the khedive's offers had his irrigation ditches blocked or his labourers spirited away overnight. Grain, in which everyone had lost interest, began to run short. The price of foodstuffs rose in consequence, but wages failed to keep pace.

"I must make up my books for the month," Rizqallah would say, avidly pursing his lips.

His father was admiring.

"He's going places, the son of a dog!"

9

One Friday in February 1864, when we were finishing our supper, there was a knock at the door. My father picked up the lantern and went to answer it, expecting an emergency.

Outside, looking embarrassed, stood a lean, swarthy young man.

"I'm Walid al-Ahlawi," he said in Arabic.

The name meant nothing to my father. Mechanically, he raised the lamp higher. That was when he saw the man's scarred ear.

"You said if I ever needed anything . . . "

The young officer no longer looked as haughty and rather insolent as he had at Alexandria barracks a year before. My father remembered having given him our address. Walid al-Ahlawi was clearly in need of something.

"How much do you want?" Papa asked without more ado.

The young man slowly shook his head. Then, in a diffident, almost inaudible voice, he said, "I want to learn to read."

Taken aback, my father invited him to sit down. The storm lantern, which he had put down rather too quickly, almost went out. Its wavering flame licked the glass before casting big shadows on the wall.

The man whom I had seen weeping in the Place des Consuls, and of whom I had often thought since then, was there before my eyes in our dining room. The whole situation seemed unreal.

Walid al-Ahlawi had acquitted himself well in Upper Egypt, whither he had been transferred after the Xavier-Saillard incident. This had quickly earned him reinstatement to his lieutenant's rank, as if the Egyptian military authorities, having been humiliated by the French consul, were eager to annul his punishment. The young man had just been posted to the barracks at 'Abbassiya, on the outskirts of Cairo, but he realized that his illiteracy would debar him from further promotion.

"I'm well aware," he told my father, "that senior posts in the army will always be reserved for officers of Turkish origin, but learning to read and write Arabic would at least enable me to attain the rank of *yusbashi* some day."

"I'm a doctor," said Papa. "Why don't you consult a sheikh. He, at least, would teach you to read passages from the Qur'an."

"I don't know any sheikhs," Walid replied simply.

He declined to share our meal and rose to leave despite his obvious hunger. Egyptian soldiers were always so poorly fed. They didn't appear to wash much, either, because the young officer stank of sweat.

From the following week onwards, Walid came to our house every Friday evening. My father began with the alphabet, getting him to chant *'alif, ba, ta, tha* like a child. After three or four sessions he taught him to hold a pencil, and the young man proceeded to scrawl his first clumsy characters.

When lessons ended, my brother Alexandre and I would sneak into the room on the pretext of bringing Walid some tea or coffee. We heard him describe how, when he was thirteen, some soldiers had taken him away by force, together with all the men and most of the women in his village, to dredge the Mahmudiya Canal.

"I ran away once, but they caught me. I ran away a second time. They caught me again and gave me a dozen strokes of the *kurbash* on the soles of my feet. There wasn't a third time, but more than once I thought I'd die from carrying baskets of earth in the blazing sun. On the towpaths you could still see the bones of fellahin who had died while digging the canal in the time of Muhammad Ali."

"Twenty-nine thousand of them," said my father, and he made his pupil write a two, a nine, and three little dots.

Walid al-Ahlawi had a small cross tattooed on his wrist.

"But you don't have a Christian name," Alexandre pointed out one day.

"Why should I have a Christian name?" the young officer retorted angrily.

Walid was very much a Muslim. He told us that the tattoo was intended to help him escape military service because his parents needed him in the fields and obviously couldn't afford to buy him out. Young men were conscripted into the army for an indefinite period, so one never knew when they would be back. Some families cut off their sons' forefingers, extracted their teeth, or blinded them in one eye by applying rat poison.

"My parents preferred to pass me off as a Copt. Why should I blame them?"

But the law had been changed, unfortunately. Coptic peasants were drafted just like Muslims, so Walid's tattoo no longer served any purpose. Early one morning he and the other youngsters from his village were marched to the Nile, where a boat was waiting for them. Chained together, they sailed off despite the tears and entreaties of their mothers, who pleaded with the soldiers, slapping themselves on the cheeks and covering their faces with dust.

Although very harshly treated at first, Walid chose to remain in the army. He became a sergeant at forty piastres a month, then managed to rise to the rank of lieutenant. The French consul had broken his heart by getting him reduced to the ranks at Alexandria. He would never forget that humiliation, but he now dreamed of becoming a *yusbashi*, or captain, at five Egyptian guineas a month.

One Friday evening, when Nada was there for once, she joined us just as the lesson was ending. The young officer was amused by the way she spoke Arabic, Syrian fashion.

"Why do you say *jim* and not *gim*, the way everyone does?" he asked.

He wrote the letter *gim* on the sheet of paper in front of him and then, proudly displaying his new-found knowledge, converted it into *jim* by adding two dots. Nada bent over his handiwork with knitted brow – the Dames du Bon Pasteur taught nothing but French – and the lesson ended on a note of general hilarity.

IO

Excavated with pick and shovel, the Suez Canal ploughed its way slowly across the desert. I followed its progress step by step on my wall map of the isthmus, sticking in little red flags made of pins and paper. The freshwater canal was also progressing – indeed, one of its branches had actually reached the Red Sea. This brought us a heartfelt letter from Étienne Mancelle, who enthusiastically described how the inhabitants of the desert had hurried to the spot and lain down on their bellies, sniffing the water with delight. "'The Nile, the Nile!' they cried as the last dam was demolished and the canal mingled its waters with those of the startled sea . . . "

Our friend was so bedazzled by the desert, he seemed oblivious of the diplomatic battle raging over the Suez Canal. At Constantinople the Sultan was uneasy. The canal boded no good as far as he was concerned, and the British artfully played on his fears. Why should such a trench be dug in the heart of his empire? Why permit the French to establish a colony between the Mediterranean and the Red Sea? Presented with a *fait accompli*, the Sultan declined to approve the agreement concluded between his vassal, the viceroy of Egypt, and Ferdinand de Lesseps. He now made some very specific demands: the Suez Canal Company must return its territorial concessions on the isthmus and cease to employ forced labour.

"I never knew the Sultan was so concerned about the fate of Egypt's peasants," my father said drily.

"Or the viceroy," said Nassif Bey. "When I think how it was forced labour that made Isma'il the wealthiest landowner in the country . . . "

The viceroy wanted to withdraw the Company's licence to mobilize thousands of peasant labourers, but Ferdinand de Lesseps firmly opposed any modification of the agreements made in the reign of Sa'id Pasha.

"Isma'il has proposed submitting the matter to arbitration," said Nassif Bey, who was always well-informed. "He has requested Napoleon III to mediate in the dispute between Egypt and the Company."

"Napoleon?" My father was dumbfounded. "You mean France is going to settle the Franco-Egyptian dispute?"

"Yes, in a manner of speaking. But the emperor will have to play a very shrewd game if he wants to avoid pushing Egypt into the arms of London or Constantinople."

It was all far too complicated for me.

Napoleon III's judgement filled several pages in the *Sémaphore d'Alexandrie*. It was a model of diplomatic compromise. The emperor ruled that forced labour be abolished and that 60,000 hectares of land in the isthmus of Suez be returned to Egypt. In return, the Egyptian government must assume responsibility for completing the canal and pay the Company large sums in compensation.

Étienne Mancelle was sad to see his peasant labourers depart. In his heart of hearts, however, he was relieved, never having approved of the principle of forced labour. He had discovered that these peasants, who hailed from distant villages, were obliged to spend a large proportion of their wages on the cost of the return journey. What was more, he couldn't stand the brutality of some of the site overseers. He kicked up such a fuss when one of his men had his wrist broken by a blow from a *kurbash* that his colleague Félix Percheron rebuked him for being ridiculous.

"You're crazy, Mancelle! Perhaps you'd like to organize their recreational activities as well? It wasn't your methods that got the Pyramids built, take it from me!"

To replace its contingents of fellahin the Company launched a huge campaign to recruit volunteers from all around the Mediterranean. Étienne found himself in charge of an international gang consisting of many Greeks and Piedmontese. New earth-moving machines designed especially for the Suez Canal were transported to the site. Étienne felt at home with them. A new and even more exciting stage in his career beckoned under the auspices of Progress and Industry.

The Egyptian government paid the sum of money demanded of it but decided not to carry out the work at its own expense. Ferdinand de Lesseps had to lodge several complaints before the viceroy finally arranged for the remaining stretch of the freshwater canal to be excavated. He did so in the good old way, by raising an army of peasant labourers with the aid of the *kurbash*. Forced labour had been abolished by the Company, but not – as Albin Balanvin pointed out – by Egypt.

FROM OUR CAIRO CORRESPONDENT
To the Editor:

10 February, 1865

You will doubtless recall, sir, that the Emperor's ruling assigned the Egyptian government responsibility for completing the freshwater canal. Well, after a slight delay probably necessitated by technical preparations for the said task, I can assure you that work is under way. Having taken the matter in hand himself, His Highness is supervising the venture with his usual vigilance and solicitude.

Over 100,000 fellahin have been mobilized in the area bounded by Cairo and Al-Wadi. Wrested away from their fields but dominated by a single desire, to serve their country, these men have performed a miraculous feat that defies all criticism. I have just toured thirty-five kilometres of canal dug in less than three weeks, almost without technical aids. You should have seen, sir, the good will and enthusiasm that reigns on the site. Picture 100,000 men toiling away to the strains of the fife without even pausing to eat, each striving to complete his task more quickly than the rest. The approach of Ramadan has redoubled the enthusiasm of these worthy peasants, whose state of mind would seem incredible to anyone who has not seen them at work with his own eyes.

The Company may rest assured that the viceroy's efforts in this matter surpass all those exerted by his predecessors, and one can only commend the alacrity with which he is keeping his promises.

Albin Balanvin

II

Aunt Angéline owed her reputation as a matchmaker to an extremely rare feat: during the winter of 1862 she had contrived to marry off all three of her daughters – Rose, Marguerite, and Violette – to the three Dabbour brothers.

"Angéline pulled off a treble," her women friends used to say with admiration and respect.

Her success was the product of several years' work. Once on the track of the Dabbour brothers, all of whom were civil servants, "Aunt Hawa" never relaxed her grip. Alfred Falaki, too, did his bit by hinting at the prospect of substantial dowries: to hear him talk, each of his daughters would leave home with a mountain of jewels. Although he didn't say this in so many words, the Dabbour brothers took the bait. They discovered, rather belatedly, that Alfred's hints committed him to nothing. Their wives would inherit sooner or later; in the meantime, however, they would have to rely on their civil service salaries.

Aunt Angéline claimed that her daughters had married for love. She rhapsodized about each of the young couples and irritated my father by referring to them as turtledoves.

The Dabbour family, which was very well known in our Greek Catholic community, bore such a long familiar name that it never occurred to anyone that *dabbur* meant "hornet" in Arabic. Never, that is to say, until a few days before the wedding ceremony, when some wag made the connection between the "hornets" and Rose, Marguerite, and Violette. Thereafter, everyone revelled in the pun, and the notion of the hornets sipping nectar from the three Falaki blossoms passed into family folklore.

The first fruits of those unions were quick to manifest themselves, but at the worst possible juncture. My memory has a tendency to confuse the various misfortunes that descended on the country at this period, but they succeeded one another almost without a break, as if heaven were hell-bent on punishing Egypt for her excessive prosperity.

In the early summer of 1863 a strange epidemic broke out in the villages of the Delta. Animals were overcome with languor, then suddenly collapsed as if poleaxed. Not an ox or *gamousa* seemed exempt from this hecatomb, to which my father gave the barbarous term "epizootia". I thought I also caught the expression "lesser otites", which kept running through my head.

Having ravaged all the cattle in Lower Egypt, the plague proceeded to move up the Nile. Deprived of animals, the peasants could no longer keep their waterwheels turning, and the cotton crop was jeopardized. The viceroy decided to import large numbers of cattle from Syria, Greece, Anatolia, and Italy, but the shipments never reached their destination. It was said that the animals died as soon as they landed in Egypt, or that they were cornered en route by the inhabitants of Alexandria, who consumed them as butcher's meat.

In Cairo we were short of everything. The Sunday *molokhiya* was served without mutton or chicken – a real aberration. Epizootia and its unappetizing concomitants became the staple topic of conversation at table. Alfred Falaki excelled at this type of anecdote, as if his shop window afforded a panoramic view of the countryside.

"Dead animals are being thrown into the Nile. You can see them drifting along with the current. Sometimes they get washed up on the banks or choke the canals. I leave you to imagine the stench!"

I quailed whenever he uttered the latter phrase, one of his favourites, because it seemed to send suspicious odours wafting through the dining room.

"There's one spot," my jeweller uncle went on, "where hundreds of corpses have accumulated. They've formed a dam and obstructed the flow of the Nile. The army is having to disperse them with cannon fire, that's the gospel truth!"

The "lesser otites" disappeared as mysteriously as they had come, only to be succeeded by another disaster that concerned us just as much: the Nile rose in an abnormal manner.

We followed the progress of the flood, as we did every summer, thanks to the *munadi* or town crier of our district. The old man never presumed to begin by announcing the number of cubits the river had risen. In a hoarse voice, he first paid homage to the Prophet. Then, addressing himself to Almighty Allah, he requested his protection for each of the generous inhabitants of the house outside which he happened to be.

"Almighty Allah, protect Dr Boutros! Almighty Allah, protect his son Maximos!"

At each of his litanies, the one-eyed child who accompanied him cried *"Insha' Allah!"* in a shrill voice and held out his hand to catch the half-piastre someone might, or might not, throw him.

This year, the *munadi* spread alarm wherever he went. The rise of the silty waters, laden with the red soil of Nubia, was at first thought to herald a plentiful flood and give promise of abundant crops. As the days went by, however, the danger became more apparent. In a single week the river rose another two cubits. At Rodah Island it eventually passed the twenty-third *pik* on the nilometer, an unprecedented occurrence.

My cousin Rizqallah, looking grave, informed us at lunch that Sunday that the cotton harvest was in jeopardy. He promptly left for Alexandria. Two days later the Nile exceeded the maximum height allowed for by Stephenson, the engineer who had built the Alexandria–Cairo railway, and flooded the track.

While returning from Assiut in a steam yacht belonging to a prince of the viceregal house, Nassif Bey had seen whole villages submerged. The inhabitants, crowded on to hillocks or dykes, called to the crew to rescue them. My father's colleague felt uncomfortable.

"We ought to do something," he said to the prince, who stood on deck beside him.

The pasha merely shrugged. "What, for instance?" he retorted.

And the yacht continued on its way.

It was after this famous flood that the viceroy devised an original system for keeping watch on the waters of the Nile. Thousands of peasants were conscripted every season and stationed all along the river with heaps of stones beside them, their task being to repair any breach at once if a dyke began to give way. At night, torches were lit. To prevent anyone from falling asleep, a cry was uttered and taken up by each watcher in turn. It travelled the length of Egypt in one direction, then in the other, then back again, and so on. I was fascinated by this device, which I pictured as a huge, noisy, torchlit snake.

I was fifteen when cholera made its appearance at Alexandria. This was in June 1865, after the pilgrims had returned from Mecca. Only a few isolated cases were reported at first, so no one was genuinely alarmed. Then, in the middle of the month, the number of deaths abruptly began to rise. The epidemic reached Tanta, then Cairo.

Isma'il Pasha was at Ras at-Tin Palace in Alexandria. One afternoon it was rumoured that he was about to leave Egypt to escape the cholera. Extremely alarmed, a number of local Europeans hurried to the palace, where the viceroy received them looking very ill-at-ease. He toured the audience chamber, uttering a friendly word to each, then said "Good evening, gentlemen!" and disappeared into his private apartments. Not long afterwards the persons present, crowding round the windows, saw him board the viceregal barge and make for his yacht, which put out to sea. Before long the *Mahrousa* was just a speck on the horizon: Isma'il Pasha was out of reach of the cholera.

Panic ensued. All the steamers bound for Marseille, Beirut or Constantinople were taken by storm. People even fought to get on board sailing ships. Accompanied by his family, Adolphe Xavier-Saillard quit Alexandria without managing to give instructions to any of his closest associates: they had all taken flight. He hurried to the French consulate, where my cousin Rizqallah was arguing with a number of vociferous people demanding berths on a ship. Xavier-Saillard drew him aside.

"My dear friend . . . "

He had never addressed him as that before.

"My dear friend, I'm leaving, as I do every year, to take the waters at ·Carlsbad. I know I can count on you . . . "

Rizqallah, who had been tempted to flee himself, decided to remain in Alexandria. He would manage the chaos at the French consulate, and, on the other side of the square, guard Monsieur Xavier-Saillard's coffers.

* * *

My father shook his head when he heard the viceroy had fled. "His grand-father, Muhammad Ali, did the same to us in 1831 . . . "

Nassif Bey, the Coptic physician, was less of a fatalist. Egyptian to the marrow, he railed against these imported sovereigns who were incapable of sharing the misfortunes of their adoptive subjects. "That's what comes of having a Turkish dynasty!" he kept saying.

Marguerite, the Falakis' second blossom, gave birth to a little Dabbour under difficult conditions, the local midwife being averse to leaving her house at any price. Aunt Angéline refused even to cross the street. She had barricaded herself into her apartment and wouldn't open a single window. This was doubly surprising on her part, given that the public health department recommended ventilation as a means of preventing the disease. It must be said, however, that doctors themselves were engaged in a grand debate on the subject. Was cholera contagious or not? How was it spread?

"By direct contact with undergarments, faeces, et cetera," declared Nassif Bey, who advocated, among other things, dipping coins in vinegar before touching them.

My father espoused another theory. "There's a kind of choleric aura," he explained. "Its harmful influence affects those within its radius unless they have taken the requisite prophylactic measures. One should avoid overeating and overexertion, which debilitate our organs and render them susceptible to invasion by cholera. Above all, one should guard against depression. Persons troubled by fear of the disease are the first to succumb to it."

Fortified by this belief, my father went among the sick just as his mentor, Clot Bey, had done thirty-four years earlier. He divided his time between the temporary hospital installed on the esplanade of the Ezbekiyah Gardens and the one set up near my school by the Frères des Écoles Chrétiennes.

People used to hammer on our door every night. My father would pick up his medical bag, don his tarboosh, and hurry off to tend some patient in the vicinity.

Early one morning, while he was out, I heard someone urgently knocking on our door. A highly agitated man asked me, on behalf of Dr Touta, to give him some ammonium acetate. I knew I must never give anyone any of the flasks locked up in the cabinet on the ground floor. After a moment's hesitation, I decided to put on some clothes and deliver the medication to the relevant address in person.

"Be quick," the man shouted, "she's dying!"

The small, dim, evil-smelling room we entered ten minutes later was almost entirely taken up by a high bed big enough for three. A pale-faced woman of about forty was lying back against the pillows. My father was taking her pulse with a preoccupied air while ten or twelve frightened children cowered in a corner.

Convulsed by stomach cramps, the patient vomited every quarter of an hour. Her diarrhoea, which was impossible to stem, had soiled the bedclothes. My father kept making her drink infusions of camomile or tea. Having diluted the ammonium acetate with water, he proceeded to chafe her hands. Then he lifted the bedclothes at the foot of the bed and instructed the oldest child to massage her feet.

I was just leaving when he told me to go and buy some leeches.

"Leeches?" I repeated stupidly.

"Hurry up, Maxime!" he snapped, sounding quite unlike himself. I had to get some leeches, and quickly.

I walked the length of New Muski Street, knocking on the door of every shop or house. The only response I got was a volley of oaths. One or two kind souls sent me on wild-goose chases. They directed me to a retired midwife, a Greek grocer, a renter of camels ... An hour later, worried and ashamed, I returned empty-handed, but no one took any notice of me. The sick woman had stopped vomiting and her cheeks had taken on a little colour. She was over the worst.

At night, whenever someone knocked at our door, my thoughts turned to Nada. I dreamed that cholera was stalking her and heard Nassif Bey's self-opinionated voice in my head:

"The disease follows an arbitrary course. Sometimes it seems to hesitate as though selecting its victims and calculating how many hapless souls it means to lay low. Then, having gathered its strength, it swoops on its prey at lightning speed ... "

I would wake up in a lather of agitation. The convent's thick walls reassured me, though. She's safe there, I told myself, and I began to appreciate the care with which the Dames du Bon Pasteur sequestered their boarders from the outside world.

Albin Balanvin had been summoned to France at the end of May to settle an inheritance. He doubtless regretted being so far from the epidemic and unable to comment with relish on the cowardice of certain authorities and the lack of organization displayed by others. What a lot of splendid copy he missed! It's true, however, that the *Sémaphore d'Alexandrie* had suspended publication . . .

Étienne Mancelle remained at Ismailia, which had become his new home. He wouldn't have dreamed of joining the deserters who were leaving Suez and making their way by stages to the Mediterranean, leaving sick and dead behind at every stop en route. At the end of June he exchanged a cordial handshake with Ferdinand de Lesseps, who had been conscientious enough to return to Egypt to assume personal control of relief operations on the isthmus.

All the beds in the European hospital at Ismailia were occupied. Work on the construction sites had ceased, and the carpenters who remained in the workshops were making nothing but coffins.

Not having seen his colleague Félix Percheron for a couple of days, Étienne went and knocked on his door. There was no answer. He hammered on it with just as little success, so he decided to force the lock.

Percheron was lying in bed, delirious. His incoherent mutterings harked back to the early days of engineering work on the canal, Pelusium Bay lashed by gales, rats attacking the tents, marauding Bedouin . . . Étienne ran to the hospital to fetch help. An hour later he returned with a company doctor.

"Another one," said the latter, who never saw anything but cholera cases.

Étienne was disconsolate. At nightfall he went home, profoundly dejected, remembering his many arguments with Percheron. Only two days earlier his colleague had subjected him to a long tirade on the subject of the Egyptian mentality:

"Some day, my dear fellow, you'll realize that the fellah kisses the hand that strikes him . . ."

And, a little later:

"Stop digging, my dear fellow, stop digging – you'll turn up something unpleasant. In this country it pays to live on the surface."

The next day Étienne was awakened by yelling in the street. He opened his window, heart pounding, to see Percheron outside, dressed and freshly shaved. Having recovered from what was no more than a bad fever, he was fulminating against the swine who had broken down his door.

In August, when the *Mahrousa* finally returned to Alexandria, Isma'il Pasha was welcomed by a party of officers in full-dress uniform. He was informed, with all due discretion, that the epidemic had carried off 60,000 of his subjects. The viceroy distributed some rewards. Oddly enough, the name Boutros Touta did not appear on the lists of deserving persons. My father said nothing. It wasn't in his nature to complain.

Napoleon III remedied this omission the following year. Dr Touta received an official communication from Paris informing him that his meritorious conduct had been reported to the emperor, who was graciously awarding him a silver medal. The Frères des Écoles Chrétiennes jointly received a similar letter. Other recipients of medals included the Dames du Bon Pasteur, three of whom had died while tending the sick. Reckless creatures! I shivered in retrospect.

12

The cholera helped me to discover my father. I'm not referring to his heroic attitude at the time, but to what followed. Hitherto so secretive, he began to tell us about himself. It was as if the epidemic had dislodged some inner block that reconciled him to his past.

Although my brother Alexandre and I were no strangers to the name Clot Bey, of course, we had no idea what an important part the French doctor had played. We learned to our surprise that our father had originally been employed as an interpreter – as had Nassif Bey, incidentally – and that he had become a doctor only by chance.

Boutros Touta first met Dr Clot one afternoon in September 1827, when he had just turned sixteen. We Syrians still wore blue or black turbans in those days, white being reserved for Muslims.

"It's hot today, you may remove your headgear," began the Marseillais physician, who was still imperfectly acquainted with local customs.

My father stammered his thanks but made no move to comply. He was thoroughly intimidated by this ebullient man, who possessed, in his eyes, the immense asset of being French. Physician-in-chief to Muhammad Ali, André-Barthélémy Clot had personally drawn up the plans for the medical school at 'Abu Zaabal, which was still a huge construction site on the edge of the desert. To get there, young Boutros had left Cairo two hours before, astride the little grey donkey that was laden with his modest wardrobe.

Dr Clot received him in an unfurnished, unfinished room. Books and various other objects were stacked along the walls, including all the treasures the Marseillais had procured in France before leaving for

Egypt: the sixty volumes of the great medical dictionary, surgical instruments, anatomical diagrams. Boutros got a start when he caught sight of a skeleton seated on the floor in a corner. He later learned that this marvel had been specially prepared by convicts attached to the naval hospital at Toulon.

Dr Clot asked him two or three questions, leaving him little time to reply.

"Good," he said in his Marseille accent, "you have a pretty fair knowledge of French. An ulama will assess your Arabic, but I warn you: I insist that my interpreters, too, study medicine. Are you prepared to learn anatomy? Are you capable of learning pathology and surgery?"

Taken aback, my father uttered a few halting words that must have been construed as an affirmative. Finally, the doctor asked his name.

"My name is Boutros Touta."

"Boutros is your first name?"

"Yes, it means Pierre in Arabic."

"I shall call you Pierre, it's simpler."

Then, striding up and down the room, he launched into a fierce tirade: "The Arab world has relapsed into barbarism since Avicenna's day. Egyptian medicine is a disgrace. But can one even call it medicine? In this country, the art of healing is practised by ignorant barbers who exploit the direst superstitions. Poor Bonaparte had no time to change much, alas! Fortunately, your viceroy, Muhammad Ali, is a great man who plans to lead Egypt back to civilization. He has commissioned me to reorganize your public health service, and reorganize it I will, take it from me!"

The Qur'anic schools had selected 500 Muslim pupils to study medicine. They spoke nothing but Arabic, however, whereas all the teachers were French or Italian. This was why Dr Clot had hit on the idea of recruiting eight young Christians to act as interpreters and translators. Most were Greek Catholic or Maronite, *Shawam* like Papa, but they also included two Copts (one of whom was Nassif, the future bey) and a lone Armenian.

"Pierre" Touta's colleagues, all older than himself, were not due to arrive until the next day. He spent a solitary, sleepless night in the interpreters' dormitory. Standing at a still unglazed window overlooking the plain, he wondered what he was doing in this frightening place. He was afraid of Dr Clot and the ulamas, afraid of medicine and the seated skeleton.

And his fear, on that moonless night, was intensified by the cries of hyenas unearthing corpses in the graveyard nearby. "Reorganize it I will, take it from me!" Dr Clot had said in a menacing tone, as if Pierre were personally responsible for the chaotic state of the health service in a country that didn't even acknowledge him as one of its own.

Those first few weeks at medical school were a terrible ordeal. Close to despair, Pierre Touta more than once came within an ace of throwing in his hand and running away. The young interpreters began by memorizing a lesson; then they recited it to the teacher, who checked to see if they had fully understood it, which wasn't always the case. Next, my father and his colleagues translated the lesson for an ulama, who attached far less importance to content than to linguistic purity. The interpreters had to start from scratch again and again until, in the end, they didn't even know what they were saying.

Pierre Touta derived little consolation from his comrades in misfortune. In this atmosphere of constant tension, each interpreter thought only of himself and poked fun at his neighbours' mistakes. What most depressed my father, however, was his inability to find a niche. He felt he had no language of his own and belonged nowhere. His French left something to be desired, and so did his Arabic. He was treated like a student by the teachers and thoroughly despised by the students. He occupied a limbo between two languages, two cultures, two nationalities – a feeling which I myself was to experience in due course.

He owed his salvation, if I may put it that way, to a monk belonging to our Melkite Church. A first-class linguist, Don Raphael translated two basic works of reference into Arabic for Dr Clot: a physiological treatise in 1827 and a treatise on pathological anatomy the following year. The eight young Christians were forever consulting these treasures. Gradually, by dint of seeking the right word and dealing with precise concepts, they became passable interpreters while waiting to become excellent medical students – certainly among the best at 'Abu Zaabal.

"I warn you," Dr Clot had said that first day, "I insist that my interpreters, too, study medicine."

My father had been too excited at the time to worry about a minor detail like that. He, who couldn't stand the sight of blood, was going to have his fill of it!

One morning a soldier was carried into the big amphitheatre. He was in agony, having fractured his shoulder three months earlier, and had been carted around from one barracks to another before finally landing up at 'Abu Zaabal. My father would never forget how the man screamed as he was held down by force while attendants bared the area to be treated.

But it was Dr Clot's wish that his interpreters should do more than merely attend all his demonstrations. More than once during the winter of 1828 he put a scalpel in Pierre's hand and invited him to repeat the movement he had just demonstrated. The young man complied, trembling uncontrollably. This infuriated the doctor.

"What are you trying to do," he thundered, "enlarge the wound?"

The students had no need of an interpreter to bombard Pierre Touta with derisive laughter.

The following year 'Abu Zaabal medical school became the scene of an awkward controversy. Dr Clot wanted to teach dissection, but the ulamas fiercely opposed this in the name of Islam. The French doctor was disgusted by their obscurantism.

"They think it's normal to castrate unfortunate infants and turn them into eunuchs," he protested, "but they're averse to making corpses suffer!"

One of my father's colleagues – Nassif, I believe – suggested a possible answer. Why not send for some cadavers belonging to black soldiers? Islam would be safe because dissection would be carried out on idolaters who were inferior even to Jews. It seemed a shrewd idea, and the ulamas were happy to wink at it. For all that, the first dissections took place in secret, with the amphitheatre double-locked and guarded by attendants ignorant of what was going on inside. A separate door gave access to the room where the dead were laid out and washed in accordance with Islamic custom.

It was during one of these sessions that a gloomy-looking student named Ashmouni walked up to Dr Clot. On reaching his side, he produced a folding scalpel from under his *galabiya* and slashed him several times. The blade sprang shut, as luck would have it, but the physician-in-chief was cut on the head and arm.

The minister of war came to 'Abu Zaabal medical school in person to try the case, but refused to hear Dr Clot's evidence because he was a Christian. Although he sentenced the assailant to the galleys at Alexandria, no one ever knew if the penalty was really enforced.

From day that on, Pierre Touta felt closer to Dr Clot, who had befriended him. The incident seemed to have affected the French physician's spirits, but he remained as resolute as ever. When Egypt went to war with Syria not long afterwards, he didn't hesitate to sabre and shoot cadavers in the amphitheatre so as to teach his pupils how to reduce certain fractures. Noticing that Pierre's hand continued to shake, he finally told him, "Stop thinking about your own little self, Pierre. Think of the people whose pain you're going to relieve."

That, I believe, was the day my father became a doctor.

13

Aunt Angéline was obviously fantasizing when she asserted that, on leaving medical school, young Dr Touta gave lessons in Arabic to one of the leading sheikhs at al-Azhar University. It is nonetheless true that my father knew the language perfectly. In knocking at his door, Walid al-Ahlawi hadn't made a bad choice.

The young officer's Friday night lessons were suspended during the cholera epidemic. They ceased for good a few months later, when he was sent off to fight in Crete.

I wasn't sorry to see him go, I must admit. I was alarmed by the intimacy that had grown up between Walid and Nada, even though they had met on only two or three occasions. A liaison between a Muslim of peasant stock and a Christian girl boarding with the Dames du Bon Pasteur was quite inconceivable, of course, not that this prevented me from having some frightful nightmares. I dreamt that Nada implored me to give Walid a billet-doux written, curiously enough, in Turkish; that she met him in an alleyway behind the convent; even that she was pregnant by him, and that, to avoid scandal, my father had sent for a discreet midwife after marrying Nada to Rizqallah in short order . . .

Walid al-Ahlawi waged a strange kind of war in Crete. It was at the Sultan's urgent request that Egyptian soldiers had been sent to fight the Greek rebels on the island. Since neither France nor Britain looked kindly on this operation, Isma'il Pasha prevaricated. His generals were instructed to win the Cretans over, bribe them if necessary, and engage in hostilities only in the last resort and with a wealth of precautions.

Walid's battalion was encamped near Apocorona, an unhealthy area rife with pernicious fevers. By a cruel quirk of fate, the insurgents launched their first attacks on the Egyptians, not on the Turkish troops. Surrounded, short of food, and weakened by disease, they were subjected to enemy fire for several days without making any real response. Walid feverishly questioned his immediate superiors, but they seemed as puzzled as he was. The commanding general's tactics did not appear in any military manual. This non-battle, which ended in a shameful retreat, left a bitter taste in the young officer's mouth.

Having become suspicious of Egyptian soldiers, the imperial Ottoman commissioner decided to incorporate them in Turkish units. Thus, it was side by side with bashi-bazouks that Walid's regiment stormed the fortified monastery of Arcadi some weeks later. Occupied by 500 Cretans, this stronghold was protected by a tower crammed with ammunition. Eight Egyptian companies were ordered to advance on this tower and set it ablaze while the imperial forces attacked from the other side. The fierce battle that ensued inflicted many casualties on both sides.

The flag of the 7th Egyptian Infantry Regiment was the first to fly from the walls of the devastated monastery. The next day Walid al-Ahlawi was promoted to the rank of *yusbashi*. He proudly announced this to my father in the first letter he ever wrote. Papa found fourteen errors in it and vowed to inform his pupil of them the next time they met.

Having entered the war reluctantly, the viceroy was compelled, as the weeks went by, to commit more and more forces rather than submit the Egyptian army to humiliation. His own yacht, the *Mahrousa*, transported 2,000 reinforcements to the field of battle. Isma'il Pasha now planned to take advantage of events in Crete to prod the Sultan into new concessions that would render Egypt a trifle more independent.

Nassif Bey, well-informed as ever, told my father that the viceroy had resolved to provide himself with a genuine army. "He aims to equip it with needle guns and line the coasts with American cannon. We're even to get a navy."

"He'll have to pay for all those things."

"Yes indeed! He'll have to pay for the weapons and pay the Sultan to authorize us to buy them. I presume a new tax will be levied on the peasants.

My dear Boutros, to those who govern us the fellah is like a sack of flour: there's always something left even when it's empty. You have only to beat it."

But Isma'il Pasha was preparing to introduce some other novelties with more expenditure in view. I was sixteen when, in May 1866, we heard that a firman had granted him succession in direct line of descent. The Egyptian throne would pass, not to the eldest member of the viceregal family, but to the eldest of his own children. This announcement caused a stir in Cairo and figured prominently in our family discussions.

"It's a sensible measure," said my father. "Succession in direct line of descent will eliminate any jockeying for position by potential heirs."

Rizqallah shed a diplomatic light on the matter. "Sultan 'Abdal 'Aziz has granted Isma'il succession in direct line of descent because he'd like to apply the formula to his own family. It suits him that Egypt should try the experiment first and pave the way for him."

"How much is the Sultan going to make out of it?" asked Alfred Falaki, who only understood numerical explanations.

"Seventy thousand purses a year, so they say."

"Very pretty!"

My jeweller uncle always said "Very pretty!" in such cases, like a connoisseur of painting confronted by a masterpiece.

Less than a year later, Isma'il was granted the title "khedive". This news caused still more of a stir in Cairo, even though no one was too sure what the word meant. Some favoured "he who succeeds", others simply "lord", but everyone agreed that "khedive" had a fine ring to it and accorded the viceroy a special status in the Ottoman Empire. Ten other appellations had been suggested to Sultan 'Abdal 'Aziz, who had rejected them all.

"Isma'il himself would have preferred the title 'aziz'," said Rizqallah. "But that was impossible."

"I don't see why," said Lolo, who never saw anything.

"Think. The Sultan styles himself 'Abdal 'Aziz."

"So what?"

"'Abdal 'Aziz means 'servant of the powerful'!"

"Well?"

"Well, you idiot, how could the Commander of the Faithful possibly be the servant of his vassal, the viceroy of Egypt?"

"How much did it cost, the title of khedive?" asked Alfred Falaki from the other end of the table.

"That's still uncertain, but Isma'il has just advanced the Sublime Porte 365,000 pounds sterling."

"Very pretty!"

14

The medal awarded to my father by Napoleon III had remedied the scandalous neglect to which he had been subjected by the Egyptian authorities. It was a trifle too late for them to atone by granting him the title of bey, for example. An appointment made more than a year after the cholera epidemic would only have underlined their original sin of omission.

In the spring of 1867, Nassif Bey discreetly suggested that the palace award him a consolation prize. Why not include Dr Boutros Touta among the dignitaries who were to accompany the viceroy to Paris for the World Exhibition? This suggestion was duly noted by the grand chamberlain, and one morning in June my father received instructions via a mounted courier to pack his things and prepare to embark at Alexandria in a week's time.

He was very excited, not by the honour that was being done him – Boutros Touta had no time for honours – but at the prospect of travelling to Europe for the first time in his fifty-six years.

Accompanied by Ferdinand de Lesseps and several pashas, Khedive Isma'il sailed from Alexandria aboard the *Mahrousa*. My father, together with sundry other less exalted persons, left in another boat, the *Masr*, commanded by the aptly named Poisson Bey. The interior doors of this floating palace were made of lemonwood, the locks and hinges of silver. On deck, when the sea was calm, my father had some interesting conversations with the distinguished astronomer Mahmud Bey, director of the cadastral service, several of whose works were to be exhibited in Paris. He complained bitterly of the lack of standard units of measurement in Egypt.

"Do you consider it acceptable, doctor, for us to have five different kinds of *pik* for linear measurement, all differing in accordance with their particular use? Why not measure cloth using the same unit for silk and wool? Why does every town have its own unit of measurement? The Tanta *pik* isn't the same as the Alexandrian, which differs in turn from the Cairene. A civilized country can't go on this way! I shall raise the matter with His Highness."

The viceregal frigate's arrival in the roads of Toulon was saluted by ships of the French fleet, bedecked with flags, and the shore batteries kept up a continuous fire. Isma'il Pasha, escorted by Ferdinand de Lesseps and other members of his retinue, boarded the imperial train that had been placed at his disposal. At Marseille, where a hundred-strong guard of honour awaited him, drummers sounded the general salute. The khedive dined at the station restaurant to the strains of the band of the 38th Regiment. A small crowd gathered behind the windows of the mezzanine, gazing with curiosity at the sovereign of Egypt and the promoter of the Suez Canal in turn.

On alighting from the train in Paris, Isma'il was welcomed by Baron Haussmann, prefect of the Seine. Escorted by lancers of the imperial guard, five state carriages in full livery conveyed him to the Palais des Tuileries with all the honours due to a crowned head. The Sultan's ambassador almost choked when he heard a chamberlain announce Isma'il, in a stentorian voice, as "His Majesty the King of Egypt!" It was a slip of the tongue, nothing more . . .

Napoleon III, who was suffering from an attack of rheumatism, did not show his face, but the empress was awaiting Isma'il in the Salon du Premier Consul. The khedive was enchanted by Eugénie, never suspecting that his august master, Sultan 'Abdal 'Aziz, would fall in love with her some time later. He was escorted back to the foot of the grand staircase, which was flanked by two rows of troopers from the household cavalry, with the same ceremony that had greeted his arrival. State carriages then conveyed him and his retinue to the Pavillon de Marsan, where suites of rooms had been reserved for them.

Paris filled my father with wonderment. The city's wealth and splendour surpassed all his imaginings. He was driven from the Tuileries to the Hôtel de Ville, from the Hôtel de Ville to the Opéra, from the Opéra to the

Châtelet ... It was a whirlwind succession of dinners, concerts, and multifarious tours on foot, as well as visits to the various pavilions of the World Exhibition on the Champ-de-Mars.

Isma'il Pasha, who had studied in Paris in the time of Louis-Philippe, seemed greatly impressed by the transformations wrought by Baron Haussmann. Accompanied by Nubar Pasha, his Armenian minister of foreign affairs, he inspected the great boulevards, the Rue de Rivoli, the Avenue de l'Opéra, the new bridges over the Seine, the Jardin du Luxembourg, the Parc Monceau.

Before reaching the Egyptian pavilion, visitors could see a *dahabiya* moored on the Seine. This sumptuously decorated boat with a triangular sail had been towed from Alexandria to Marseille, whence it had been transported to Paris by canal and river. Princess Mathilde was ceremoniously welcomed aboard one afternoon and rowed down the Seine to Saint-Cloud by a dozen Nubians in full-dress uniform.

The Egyptian pavilion was proving a great attraction. Under the supervision of Mariette Bey, the famous Egyptologist, a pharaonic temple had been carefully reconstructed complete with painted plaster statues and numerous precious objects on loan from Cairo Museum. A 2,000-year-old mummy was unwrapped in the presence of the emperor and empress. Eugénie held her nose, but the prince imperial took a keen interest in it, and even bore off some of the bandages as a memento.

An Arab bazaar had been set up a little further on, with a covered gallery pierced by close-meshed *mashrabiyas*. There, seated on the ground and surrounded by the tools of their trade, craftsmen imported from Cairo busied themselves for the benefit of visitors. Silversmiths, woodworkers and chibouquiers plied their customers with Turkish coffee.

Isma'il had also commissioned a sumptuous *salamlek* in which to welcome distinguished Parisians. This building, which boasted a monumental doorway and was flanked by a cupola and small columns of white marble, was covered with arabesques. Seated on a red satin divan and smoking a hookah, the khedive seemed in excellent spirits. This was where my father saw him at close quarters and was even able to have two brief conversations with him.

Isma'il always wore a tarboosh at the exhibition – besides, that was his identifying feature. In town, whenever he wanted to pass unnoticed, he would remove it, produce a collapsible opera hat from his overcoat, punch it open, and elegantly put it on his head.

"One morning," Papa told us, "we saw him get to the Egyptian pavilion an hour late. He had just been to a famous tailor's, where he ordered fourteen dozen pairs of trousers, eight dozen waistcoats, and as many overcoats!"

In the khedive's honour Baron Haussmann gave a gala dinner at the Hôtel de Ville attended by all the emperor's ministers, the presidents of the Grands Corps de l'État, and the marshals of France. The throne room was decorated with tricolours and red flags bearing the gold crescent and star. The dinner was followed by a concert for 500 people in the Salon des Arcades, in the course of which Mademoiselle Rose sang *Plaisir d'amour*.

The khedive was tireless. One day he would receive the board of the Suez Company, dine with Baron de Rothschild, and follow a debate in the Palais Législatif; the next, he would attend the steeplechases at Vincennes and visit the imperial mint or the emperor's stables. He found almost nightly opportunities to manifest his love of the theatre. He could be seen at the Opéra, the Châtelet, the Français, and – of course – at the Variétés, where he listened again and again to the gorgeous Mademoiselle Schneider, his mistress of the moment, though he was not alone in being so honoured. The celebrated actress's dressing room had been christened *"le passage des princes"*.

To my father, however, one of the most memorable features of his stay in Paris was the audience the khedive granted to the opponents of slavery. He was present with the astronomer Mahmud Bey when those French and British gentlemen asked Isma'il what steps he intended to take to put an end to the scandal.

"I thoroughly approve of your initiative," the viceroy replied, "being firmly opposed to slavery myself. But you see, this practice has been current in Egypt for twelve centuries. It cannot be abolished overnight. The only way of ending it is to attack the evil at its root: the slave trade must be suppressed. I am curbing it as much as I can, but the Egyptian government can only penalize its own subjects. It is Europeans, protected by their national flags, who, on the pretext of looking for ivory in the Sudan, are carrying off men, women and children for sale as slaves. If the trade persists, as it does, the blame should be laid at Europe's door."

The abolitionists politely took their leave of the khedive without having been genuinely convinced by his arguments.

Mahmud Bey smiled. "When I think," he murmured, "that Isma'il has four legitimate wives, that each of them has six white slave women and dozens of black slaves, and that his harem is guarded by eunuchs . . . "

My father forbore to reply; it wasn't for a Christian to comment on matters that didn't concern him. He was quite ready, on the other hand, to enter into another discussion of the problems that genuinely preoccupied the astronomer: for example, the existence in Egypt of five different calendars.

"It's absurd," said Mahmud Bey. "Everyone gets mixed up. Do you consider it reasonable, doctor, that landowners should adopt the Arab calendar because it gains them ten or twelve days a year? A civilized country can't go on this way. I shall raise the matter with His Highness."

They returned to Egypt after making a detour via Constantinople. The *Masr*, still commanded by Poisson Bey, was carrying vast quantities of objects purchased from Parisian shops by the khedive. As for the *Mahrousa*, it had a number of extra passengers aboard: the French chefs and servants whom Isma'il Pasha had recruited in Paris to lend his reign new lustre.

15

In Cairo, the effects of the khedive's European trip were very soon apparent. Isma'il Pasha's carriage was no longer preceded by barefoot *saïs* but by mounted grooms wearing red tunics like the postilions of the French emperor's postal services. Visitors to 'Abdin Palace encountered footmen in powdered perukes and knee breeches and ushers attired in black with chains on their chests.

Some Cairenes may have sniggered at this. Personally, I was fascinated by this monarch who used to tell his entourage, "My country is in Africa no longer. We're part of Europe."

Not having been lucky enough to go to Paris like my father, I made Paris come to me. On Sunday evenings I liked to station myself on the promenade and watch the viceroy ride in state along Shubra Street. Sometimes, instead of Isma'il, it was his wives or daughters who were driven past in closed carriages by English or French coachmen wearing cockaded hats.

The khedive had been bowled over by the sight of Baron Haussmann's public works in Paris. Now he was eager, in his turn, to carve out boulevards, create public squares, and align the fronts of buildings in order to make his capital a modern city that would impress foreign visitors during the inauguration of the Suez Canal.

"Cairo is going to become a regular Paris," was Alfred Falaki's comment on the khedive's projects.

Dozens of hectares had been cleared and levelled between Ezbekiyah Square and the palaces on the banks of the Nile. Isma'il granted plots of land free of charge to anyone who undertook to erect a building costing at least 2,000 pounds in a short space of time. My jeweller uncle was one of the first to put his name down.

To the Editor:

25 November 1867

I am writing to you, sir, amid dust and noise. Nothing can be heard here save the pounding of hammers. The centre of Cairo has become one vast construction site. Buildings are being frantically razed, knocked down and destroyed in strict accordance with the recipes of Baron Haussmann. Once full of charm, this city has been enjoined to look like Paris with the minimum of delay. All must be in readiness for the inauguration of the Suez Canal, the date of which has yet to be fixed.

You are familiar with the Ezbekiyah, that vast esplanade in the centre of the city, with its sycamore, eucalyptus, carob and lemon trees. Forget it, sir. I have the honour, if not the pleasure, to inform you that the Ezbekiyah is to be replaced by a vulgar version of the Bois de Boulogne.

This oasis has been reduced by half to release land for speculation. It is presently being enclosed by tall railings like the Parc Monceau. It will be traversed by four wide thoroughfares flanked by pavements and adorned at their inter- section by a gigantic ornamental pond. Erected around it, so we are told, will be an opera house, a theatre, and a circus. Yes, sir, your eyes did not deceive you: a circus, which will be entrusted to the care of Monsieur Raincy.

Running from the Ezbekiyah is a boulevard designed to lead to the Citadel at any cost. According to my calculations, this fantastic excision will have to eliminate or truncate some 700 buildings or public monuments. Any recalcitrant edifices will be destroyed by gunfire. Some of the inhabitants have been expro- priated, others left with half a home and invited to build a new façade aligned with its neighbours.

Let us be honest, sir: not all of Cairo's rather dilapidated mosques have been beheaded. Many have simply been repainted. Ochre and pink are giving way to vivid splashes of white and blood red. The effect is extremely pretty, as you can imagine.

The owners of more than one palatial residence have not confined themselves to replacing their mashrabiyas *with shutters and employing Italian neo-Gothic* materials of the most pretentious kind. They are tearing down old ceilings with painted beams and ancient tiles of Persian faience. All that remain are white and gilt drawing rooms with blue ceilings and mahogany furniture upholstered in imitation leather.

In the streets, trees are giving way to cast-iron street lamps. Gas lighting is being introduced. Long live progress, sir! The Cairo of the Fatimids and the 'Abbassids, the Cairo of the Umayyads, is in the process of adopting a casinoesque style.

Albin Balanvin

16

Until 1867, the year I turned seventeen, I don't think any Frenchman had ever crossed the threshold of our home. We lived in different worlds, it must be said. The Europeans regarded us more or less as natives. In the few places where we did rub shoulders with them, they were always our superiors: superior to my father in the old days, when he worked at the hospital under the orders of Dr Clot; superior to me at school, under the tutelage of the Très Chers Frères; superior to Rizqallah at the French consulate . . . In an Egypt fascinated by Europe, Europeans felt they were in conquered territory. We enjoyed neither the same prestige nor the same privileges.

After the World Exhibition, however, my father's attitude changed. He seemed far more at ease with the French, as if the simple fact of having seen their country, with its marvels and its shortcomings, entitled him to mingle with them. He benefited, in a way, from the warm welcome accorded the khedive in Paris. He had seen Egypt admired and respected on the banks of the Seine, and it may have been because he now felt a little more Egyptian that he was better able to consort with them.

Hence the wholly matter-of-fact tone in which he informed us that Étienne Mancelle was passing through Cairo, and that he had invited him and Albin Balanvin to our next Sunday lunch. Two Frenchmen at once! I was secretly apprehensive of their encounter with the family. How would Aunt Angéline behave? Wouldn't Lolo make a fool of himself in his spats? And what about Uncle Boctor? My God, Uncle Boctor!

It was Balanvin's reaction that perturbed me most of all, because everyone at our lunches talked at once. No one could resist telling a story, however false or apocryphal, and there were always five or six family members ready to contest the speaker's assertions with noisy claims of their own that were just as far-fetched and uttered with the same conviction. As a journalist, and thus careful to check the veracity of statements on principle, how would he react? Balanvin's caustic tongue threatened to create an incident.

The nearer Sunday came, the more of a fuss I made about the forthcoming meal. My father, by contrast, seemed quite happy to offer his guests a *kubayba*, and was surprised when I suggested a less oriental menu. My brother Alexandre was no help to me in this ordeal; in his usual, carefree way, he proposed to ask Albin Balanvin for an autographed copy of the *Sémaphore d'Alexandrie*. As for Lolo, who had heard that a French engineer from the Suez Canal was coming, he couldn't contain his excitement.

Utter turmoil reigned at home that Sunday morning. It had occurred to us at the last moment that the Frenchmen might prefer wine to arrack, so some bottles had to be bought in a hurry. Our maidservant, Om Mahmud, lost her head to the extent of smashing a jug *before* the dread guests' arrival, as if that could prevent them from coming.

Nada had been there since mid-morning to help with the preparations, but not even her peals of laughter were enough to dispel my dire forebodings.

Étienne Mancelle knocked on our front door at one o'clock precisely. He seemed delighted to see us again and shook my hand warmly. As thin as ever, he bore the marks of the desert on his face, and his tan lent him a more manly appearance. He was promptly offered some wine but said he would prefer arrack.

We had only just begun to ask him about his trip when I was horrified to hear Aunt Angéline's voice:

"*Hawa, hawa!*"

"But all the windows are open, *ya sitt Angelina!*" Om Mahmud whimpered from the doorway.

The heavy watch chain draped across Alfred Falaki's black *stambouline* made the jeweller look like a palace usher, and the emerald ring on his finger was in the worst possible taste. Lolo — wearing spats, of course — followed him in, and their maidservant brought up the rear with a huge dish of *kubayba* on her head, its aroma mingling with Aunt Angéline's essence of bergamot.

One by one, with much commotion and vociferation, other members of the family arrived. Rose, Marguerite and Violette, accompanied by their civil servant husbands, the three Dabbour brothers, gave news of their respective offspring. One or another of my cousins always had a child on the way. It was their only *raison d'être* and principal topic of conversation.

I almost failed to see Albin Balanvin come limping in on his cane with the mother-of-pearl knob, but my father had already greeted him and was making the introductions. The journalist's keen gaze seemed to transfix me.

"Sometime, monsieur, could you autograph a copy of the *Sémaphore d'Alexandrie* for me?" asked my brother, although I had forbidden him to pester our guest.

"Why sometime?" Balanvin replied with the faint smile that never left his lips. "Bring me a pen."

By degrees, I relaxed. Rizqallah, looking elegant and very much at ease, formed a perfect link between the two guests and the members of the family. I had forgotten that, at Alexandria, my cousin mingled with French people all day long.

Albin Balanvin, with a glass of arrack in his hand, seemed interested in what Alfred Falaki was telling him about fluctuations in the price of diamonds. In Lolo, Étienne Mancelle had found an attentive listener who hung on his every word and – God be praised! – said nothing himself. My father was happily chatting with Nada in a corner. I began to feel better.

"Lunch is served! The *kubayba* won't wait!" cried Aunt Angéline, who had acted as mistress of the house since my mother's death.

My father seated his sister opposite him with the two Frenchmen on either side of her. Uncle Boctor was banished to the far end of the table, flanked by Rose and Violette, whose shrill complaints were intended to drown his oaths. As for me, I had managed to insinuate myself into the place on Nada's left.

The meal very soon reached cruising speed, its exclamations, laughter, and countless intermingled conversations silenced from time to time by the voice of a talented orator who had managed to hold the table's attention with a set piece of some kind.

Angéline flapped her fan and glared at one of the maids, who was offering a guest the dish from the wrong side.

"I suppose you're familiar with *kubayba*, my dear Monsieur Mancelle," said my father.

"Oh," the engineer replied, "it's not very often served on the isthmus, but that makes it all the more tempting."

"You shouldn't have put any tahina on the meat," said Aunt Angéline. "It spoils the flavour."

At once, there followed a noisy and confused debate about the best way of preparing *kubayba*. Alfred Falaki firmly insisted that the flavour of sesame was essential, and that, on the contrary, the meat should be positively smothered in tahina. Several of the ladies promptly disputed this dangerous theory.

"You don't know a thing about *kubayba*, take it from me!" cried the jeweller.

His sons-in-law entered the fray, and even Uncle Boctor loudly voiced his opinion from the end of the table. My father thought it advisable to put a temporary stop to this everlasting argument.

"Tell us, Monsieur Mancelle, how is work on the Suez Canal progressing?"

"We have no more fellahin on site, doctor, as you know."

"They've all been transferred to the viceroy's estates," observed Balanvin.

A roar of approval greeted this remark. The engineer waited for it to subside.

"The Company has been obliged to employ volunteers at great expense," he went on. "These days our labourers are Arabs, but our seamen are Greeks. Piedmontese miners handle the explosives, and we also employ Dalmatians and Montenegrins. There are plenty of hotheads and desperadoes among them, but on the whole our army of workers is waging a valiant fight for progress."

"The British thought they would doom the Canal by getting peasant conscripts banned," my father put in.

"Their plan has failed, my dear doctor, thanks to the machine. The mechanical excavators designed by Couvreux and the endless-chain dredgers of Messrs Borel and Lavalley are working wonders. Machinery and steam have never been employed more intelligently and energetically anywhere else in the world, I can assure you. The maritime canal is being tackled throughout its length, depth and breadth from Port Sa'id to Suez."

"But who's doing the digging?" asked Lolo, who hadn't understood.

"The machines, monsieur, the machines! Some of them can extract up to 3,000 cubic metres a day. In power and size, the Suez Canal's dredgers exceed anything of their kind that has ever been built. Picture those colossal machines in the middle of the desert, belching their dark plumes of smoke into the blue sky . . . Chains of buckets revolving under steam power – they're what excavate the soil. But it's not enough simply to excavate. The spoil must be removed as well."

"I don't see – "

"Normally, a timber chute is sufficient. But when the dredgers pull back to excavate the centre of the canal, several dozen metres from the bank, this won't work any more. A chute can be lengthened, but there's no gradient. What's to be done?"

"Yes," said Lolo, sounding perturbed, "what indeed?"

"Never fear. Monsieur Lavalley, who's a genius, has designed some very large dredgers equipped with conveyor belts as much as seventy metres long. They empty torrents of soil and water on to the banks all day long, and even at night, by artificial light."

"And how much does each of these machines cost?" asked Alfred Falaki, twisting his ring so that the emerald flashed.

"In the region of 6,000 francs per dredger per day."

"Very pretty . . . "

By the time the *kubayba* came round again, Étienne Mancelle had launched into another technological dissertation. Carried away by his own enthusiasm, he spared us no detail:

"Towing those gigantic dredgers requires the utmost care. Picture two lines of men, one on each bank, hauling on the tow ropes. They advance very slowly so as not to propel the machine along too fast. Four more teams hold mooring ropes while the captain directs operations on deck. Then there are two foremen on each bank to relay his orders . . ."

Nada, on my right, was listening abstractedly. She must have been bored by all this talk of dredgers and excavators, spillways and barges. Either that, or her mind was on other things. Opposite us, Aunt Angéline was fanning herself. Being quite uninterested in the conversation, she remarked casually, for something to say, "But I thought all your labourers had died of cholera?"

Étienne Mancelle was momentarily taken aback. "Some did, it's true," he went on politely. "The epidemic took an especially heavy toll of our medical staff, a sad fact but a tribute to their devotion to duty." Étienne turned to my father. "I'm aware that other doctors, here in Cairo, also showed remarkable dedication . . ."

Approving cries rang out as everyone acknowledged this well-turned compliment. Albin Balanvin raised his glass of arrack and proposed a toast to my father. He greatly amused the table with a little extempore speech.

"You, at least, Dr Touta, devote yourself to your art. You don't share the pretensions of my compatriot, Dr Rigaudier, who has discovered himself to be an Egyptologist. The worthy doctor keeps digging up stones in the desert behind the Pyramids. His patients are getting worried. They say he buries the living and unearths the dead."

Étienne Mancelle assured us that Ismailia was the healthiest town in the world. It already had 4,000 inhabitants and was looking more and more like a luxuriant oasis.

"The palm trees and acacias in the Place Champollion are beginning to attain a reasonable height, and there are flowers in all the gardens of the European quarter. The other day I even saw some vines."

"But Ismailia can't have much to offer in the way of entertainment," said Rizqallah.

"Don't you believe it! People give little parties. Ladies sing, gentlemen play the violin or the accordion. And that's not counting the horse races in the desert and the hunting parties on Lake Timsah. On 15 August they even held a regatta on the lake to celebrate the emperor's birthday."

Rizqallah smiled. "I still prefer Alexandria," he said.

"But Ismailia will be the new Alexandria! When the Canal is finished it will be *the* great port on the route to India – a seaport in the middle of the desert!"

Everyone raised their glasses again, this time to the completion of work on the Canal.

"We'll do it," Étienne said eagerly. "Our sails are filled with the wind of the modern age!"

* * *

It was five in the afternoon, and the light was beginning to fade. The last of our guests had just departed, and we were lighting the oil lamps.

"Nada's getting married," my father told me, quite casually.

I gave a start and nearly burnt myself.

"Is she?" I said in a blank voice.

"Aren't you going to ask me her fiancé's name, Maxime?"

Mechanically, I put the lamp down on the table.

"Well," I said, "who is it?"

"Étienne Mancelle. An excellent match, don't you think?"

"Oh, yes," I mumbled, then pleaded a call of nature and disappeared upstairs.

My legs would hardly carry me. When I got to my room I didn't even have the strength to take hold of Étienne's gift, the coloured map of the Suez isthmus, and tear it off the wall. I threw myself on the bed face down and wept as I'd never wept before.

An infinity of time passed. They must have knocked on my door at supper-time. Perhaps I said I was tired and wanted to sleep. Whatever the truth, I didn't awake until daybreak. Instantly, a thought crossed my mind, transfixing me like a dagger: Nada was getting married. I felt feverish and shivery.

My father looked in on me that morning. He barely examined me, diagnosed a stomach upset, prescribed a day off school and a starvation diet. As if I could have moved, let alone swallowed anything!

Nada was getting married. She was going to marry Étienne Mancelle, the Suez Canal engineer. I remembered something: on arrival yesterday he had handed her a little bunch of roses and said, "Flowers from the gardens in our desert."

Our desert . . . Their desert . . . Nada was getting married. I would never hold her bare foot in my hands, never clasp it to my cheek.

17

I tried in vain to think of other things during the days and weeks that followed, but everything reminded me of that wedding. I woke up several times a night, abruptly overcome with sadness.

I should have liked to be angry with Nada. She was leaving me, yes, but had we ever really been together? She could have had no idea how madly in love with her I was.

I should have liked to cry treachery. Nada was marrying a Frenchman, but how could I accuse her of defecting to the enemy? She was joining forces with the object of our deepest admiration: France.

I naturally thought of hanging myself, of starving myself to death, of cutting my wrists or throwing myself into the Nile clutching a cannon ball.

I did none of those things, naturally. I just lost interest in everything. At school the Très Chers Frères noticed this and conveyed their surprise to my father.

Did he suspect my feelings for Nada? He didn't broach the subject, either then or in the future. Our relations were always characterized by extreme reticence.

I spent more and more time daydreaming at the foot of a tree in Shubra Street, on the lookout for some closed carriage containing a lady of the harem. I imagined her to be a lovesick princess who wanted to marry me – imagined that Nada, mad with jealousy, was pining away in her desert home.

I took to feeling sorry for myself. "The child of the Pyramid" remembered that he was an orphan and wept for the mother he scarcely remembered.

"It's her you get your bright eyes from," Aunt Angéline would say. "She died before her time, poor thing. *Maskina!*" To which Lolo, nodding his head, would add gloomily, "It was Alexandre who killed her."

This imputation of murder was a reference to my brother's birth. To understand it, however, one had to go back much further, to the early 1830s, when Dr Clot tried to set up a medical school for women.

Venereal diseases were ravaging the Egyptian army at that time, so it was imperative to tackle the seat of the infection, in other words, women. However, no male physician was entitled to treat them. How could Muslim women undergo medical training without coming into contact with men, and Europeans to boot? Dr Clot had the idea of recruiting some black and Ethiopian slave women. Muhammad Ali, who took a close interest in the health of his soldiers, approved this plan. One morning, therefore, my father, Nassif and the other Christian interpreters accompanied Dr Clot to the slave market to choose ten young women of robust constitution. Housed in an annexe of the medical school under the supervision of two eunuchs, they were taught the rudiments of medicine.

The results of their training exceeded the French doctor's hopes, so he resolved to defy the ulamas' prohibition and recruit some young Arab women. A dozen of them entered the hospital as patients and were trained in secret. I happen to know that the young interpreters did more than translate their lessons: one particularly amenable girl named Zannouba offered her body to the more sexually adept in a little room behind the dispensary. Her name cropped up in the family years later, on the occasion of my birth. My mother would normally have employed one of the two Greek Catholic *dayas* who served our whole community, but my father had confidence only in Zannouba, who had since become senior midwife at Cairo's school of midwifery.

"School" was, perhaps, an unduly ambitious word to apply to that modest institution, whose young inmates were closeted like those of a harem. In addition to delivering women in a birthing chair, they were taught how to bleed, cauterize, and vesicate. An elderly sheikh came to teach them to read and write, and it was one of Zennouba's jobs to check, once a month, that they were still virgins. They were married off on leaving the school.

My father turned up there one morning in December 1849 and asked for the midwife-in-chief. The old porter was unimpressed by the visitor's medical title, but he promptly reconsidered his attitude in return for a few piastres. Dr Touta then entered the classroom, where Zannouba was demonstrating some obstetrical procedure to her pupils with the aid of a dummy. The young women rose and modestly covered one eye in token of greeting.

"Have you come looking for an *aroussa* to marry?" Zannouba asked my father.

"No, it's you I need."

Her startled expression told him that he'd been clumsy. It was all so long ago . . .

I was born without difficulty, thanks to Zannouba's expert hands, as if it had been preordained that "the child of the Pyramid" could only be welcomed into the world by a true daughter of the Nile.

Two years later, when my mother was pregnant with Alexandre, the midwife-in-chief had ceased to practice and retired to her native village, so one of our community's two *dayas* was summoned instead. I don't think the *daya* was directly responsible for my mother's death. My father certainly never blamed her for it, even if he may secretly have told himself that Zannouba would have prevented such a disaster.

"Your poor mother never had a chance," Aunt Angéline used to say.

"*Maskina!*" Lolo chimed in. "It was Alexandre who killed her."

18

The preparations for Nada's wedding were breaking my heart. I fled from the house as soon as I heard her departure or her trousseau mentioned. The least allusion to the town of Ismailia gave me nervous tremors.

In spite of his modest income, my father was determined to see Nada married in style. He insisted on giving her away in person and invited Alexandre and me to accompany him to Ismailia for the ceremony.

The bad attack of tonsillitis that confined me to bed on the eve of their departure was not a sham, but, as my father used to say, "Bad blood always ends by provoking bad fevers." So they went off without me, leaving Om Mahmud to nurse me, or rather, to comfort me like a baby — me, a baby of seventeen.

The old woman came waddling into my bedroom from time to time. She would sit on the edge of the bed and lay her hand on my forehead, muttering to herself. I seem to think she called me Mahmud.

The little church at Ismailia was full to overflowing. Weddings in "the Venice of the desert" weren't an everyday occurrence, and none of the French colony's ladies would have missed such a ceremony for the world. Ill at ease in her wedding dress, Nada was introduced to countless strangers and subjected to countless glances, countless real or imaginary murmurs. Étienne Mancelle, beaming all over his face, shook one hand after another, convinced that his young bride was feeling just as euphoric.

He had just left the "Bachelors' Quarter" and moved into a five-roomed house, complete with veranda and garden, near the Place Champollion. His neighbour Félix Percheron had helped him to move his meagre furniture, which he had supplemented with various purchases made at *La Belle Jardinière*, Ismailia's department store.

"I wouldn't buy anything at all if I were you," Percheron had told him. "I'd wait and see. Those Levantines have different ways from us."

He uttered the word "Levantines" with pursed lips, clearly mystified by his colleague's choice. He was slightly less mystified when he saw Nada's beautiful face under her bridal veil.

Étienne was eager to show his wife everything right away: the European quarter where they were to live, but also the bustling Greek quarter and even the Arab town with its cafés and its wooden mosque. Nada was dazed by it all. She felt oppressed by the desert that hemmed in the town on every side. Head spinning, she joined her new husband in a big brass bed draped in a mosquito net. She was still awake hours later, her eyes red with weeping. Lying beside a blissfully snoring stranger, she spent most of the night yearning for Cairo and her convent.

Alexandre, who had never been away from Cairo before, bombarded me for weeks with descriptions of the isthmus. I brusquely cut short his accounts of the Suez Canal by saying that it no longer interested me in the least. I had no wish to know the colour of the church at Ismailia or the dimensions of the Place Champollion. The banks of Lake Timsah left me cold, and I couldn't care less about Messrs Borel and Lavalley's patent dredgers. But Alexandre persisted, delighted to be able to show off his knowledge and comment on his impressions.

A month later, when my father passed me the couple's first letter, I took it with a trembling hand. I was firmly resolved not to read it, but some masochistic impulse got the better of me.

> The director-general [wrote Étienne] gave a big ball at carnival time. A piano and two cornets provided the music. The polkas and sung quadrilles went on until suppertime. We were still dancing at five in the morning . . .

Nada had added a few polite words in a round, rather slanting hand – the same as the one on the envelope. It was the first time I had seen her handwriting. From then on, any messenger turning up at our door made me quake with excitement.

Ismailia was not without its charms. Nada gradually got used to her new life. She spent most of the day at home. From the veranda she could see the young palm trees growing in the Place Champollion and, in the distance, the Jebel Ataqa, which vaguely reminded her of her native Syria. All day long, barges laden with stone, timber or barrels seemed to glide across the sand as they sailed down the freshwater canal on their way to Suez.

In the afternoon Nada sometimes went shopping at *La Belle Jardinière*. She was invited to tea on Wednesdays by the wife of the director of dredging, a rather snobbish Lyonnaise who treated her with condescension. The ladies present exchanged recipes and titbits of local gossip.

Étienne came home at nightfall, steeped in sunshine and covered with dust. Now and then he would take his wife for a stroll through the ill-lit souk in the Arab quarter. The Café Soliman – four bare brick walls roofed with rush matting – was the liveliest place in Ismailia. Shrill music issued from the establishment until late at night. A handful of third-rate dancing girls came to perform there and display their charms, but Étienne and Nada never went inside. It was no fit place for a young wife educated by the Dames du Bon Pasteur.

The members of the French colony held modest dinner parties two or three times a month. They took it in turns to entertain, chatting together and making music. There was always a piano or a violin on hand to accompany a soprano voice. A young mining engineer who worked at the same site as Étienne amused the company by claiming to be able to read people's fortunes in coffee dregs. The ladies tricked him and provoked roars of laughter by surreptitiously swapping cups. Nada sometimes took part in such amusements, but she found it hard to relax in a circle that accepted her only because she was married to a French engineer.

On rare occasions the small community's existence was enlivened by Company-sponsored events. Étienne, in his habitually lyrical way, would describe a totally uninteresting hunting party or a water carnival on Lake Timsah:

The regatta began at two p.m., after a religious ceremony conducted by Mgr the Archbishop of Alexandria. Suez and Port Sa'id were competing for the prizes. The sailors of the Occident and the Orient had met to engage in this peaceful contest halfway along the future Canal of the Two Seas, foreshadowing the rendezvous that will, in a few years' time, be kept on the same spot by the commerce of the entire world . . .

For her part, Nada wrote of the vine cuttings that grew in her garden. Her letters filled me with longing. I pictured her on her veranda at the day's end, watching barges glide silently past laden with stone, timber or barrels, as the sun went down behind the distant pink crests of the Jebel Ataqa.

19

Ismailia was never far from my thoughts. From now on, it was I who questioned Alexandre and marvelled at his lack of precision. How were the houses around the Place Champollion laid out? Did the verandas face each other? Were the palm trees interspersed with rose bushes? My brother's vague replies annoyed me.

"But you didn't see a thing!" I told him irritably.

He stared at me in surprise.

It was Isma'il Pasha who succeeded in diverting my attention, if only slightly, from Ismailia. That summer of 1868, everyone was wondering why the khedive had gone to Constantinople and, more especially, why he didn't return to Egypt. He was said to be suffering from laryngitis and desirous of following a grape diet on the Bosphorus. Reports of his health sounded excellent, but still he stayed on without fixing a date for his return.

"I don't understand," said my father. "Isma'il wanted direct succession, and he got it. He wanted the title of khedive, and he bought that too. What more does he want? Each of the Sultan's favours costs us a fortune."

In July it was announced with a great flourish that Tewfiq, the khedive's eldest son, had obtained the title of vizier. The *Masr*, under Poisson Bey's command, left Constantinople at once, her mission being to collect the prince and return with him as quickly as possible. "The fellahin had better brace themselves for a new tax," growled my father. "I knew that grape diet boded no good . . . "

The khedive had spent a great deal of money on financing the military expedition to Crete and undertaking major projects such as the completion of the railway line between Alexandria and Suez. The national debt was growing, and the government had had to sell the sugar harvest to the Anglo-Egyptian Bank in advance, but a new loan of eight million pounds sterling obtained from the Oppenheim Bank had just given the public exchequer a new whiff of oxygen.

At long last, it was announced that the khedive would return on 22 September. He was to be accorded a special welcome at Alexandria.

"Nassif Bey has invited me to attend," my father told me. "If you'd like to come too . . . "

How could I have resisted such a suggestion? It was almost five years since I'd last seen the sea and the little inlet near the Place des Consuls. But the sight of those steamers . . . My first trip to Alexandria had introduced me to Nada; my second would only underline her absence. I realized that as soon as the train, enveloped in a pall of black smoke, pulled out of Cairo station with a horrible screech of metal on metal.

The scent of seaweed, which smote me in the face on arrival, exhilarated me. It was September, not January like the last time. Nassif's house still backed on to the sea, but I was happy to be given the same room at the rear.

I awoke the next morning with a positive itch to go swimming. Bathing wasn't a conventional activity as yet – the famous Palloni Baths had only just opened – but, to my great surprise, my father offered to accompany me out of town to a beach near Ramlah.

We took a little train and got off at the last stop. From there it was a fair walk through the dunes before we saw the sea.

My father undressed completely. Never having seen him naked before, I hardly dared look. He had already walked down to the sea and dived in, however, so my only recourse was to follow suit. I had never felt closer to him. By the time we finally emerged, sated with water and salt, it never even occurred to me that the two of us were naked. We dried off in the sun, lying side by side on the warm sand.

"We ought to build a villa here," I heard him murmur.

That may sound a commonplace idea today, but at the time only a few eccentrics would have considered spending their summer holidays beside the sea. Although the khedive had just built himself a palace at Ramlah, bathing had yet to become fashionable. Alexandria prided itself on being a city of gardens, not beaches. To compete with Cairo it relied on its banks, its businesses, its fine shops, its café concerts and its two famous theatres: the Zizinia, owned by Count Zizinia, the Belgian consul-general; and the Debbane, belonging to Count Debbane, consul-general of Brazil.

At six a.m. on 22 September I was roused from my slumbers by an impressive cannonade: the *Mahrousa* was entering the roads. It was reported that the dowager khediva had ventured out beyond the fairway to welcome Isma'il home.

Nassif Bey got dressed in a hurry and told his coachman to harness up. He wanted to be one of the first Alexandrian dignitaries to get to Ras at-Tin Palace, where the constituent bodies would be filing past all morning. When receiving the consuls in solemn audience at midday, the khedive put their minds to rest about his state of health.

"He looks as fit as a fiddle," Nassif Bey assured us on his return.

"There's nothing to beat a grape diet," my father remarked with a smile.

Nassif had managed to get himself on to the list of the khedive's personal physicians, a position he had held during the previous reign. This impressed me. I felt very insignificant in the presence of this handsome, prematurely white-haired man whom Aunt Angéline commended for being rich and condemned for being a Copt.

My father and he were linked by a wealth of memories. Despite their many differences, their years at medical school had engendered a profound intimacy between them. Indeed, I sometimes felt it was their disparity that had preserved their friendship. Nassif Bey, who had started from higher up the ladder, was amassing all the trumps. Boutros Touta considered Nassif far more brilliant than himself without regarding this as a natural injustice. It was simply so, and that was that. Their good relations stemmed partly from my father's fatalistic attitude in this respect. Not being on the same level, they could never collide. Nassif Bey was too ambitious and too concerned to dominate those around him to have tolerated a rival so close to him. Appointed bey at the age of forty-two, numbering several princes among his patients, and regularly summoned to the bedside of the patriarch of the Coptic Church, he practised medicine with enthusiasm and elegance in equal measure.

As for my father, he had always been conscious of the relativity of things and the fragility of his vocation. One day, when Aunt Angéline had alluded yet again to "my brother the Doctor", I heard him mutter, "Am I really a doctor? Did I choose to be one? My teacher, Dr Clot, chose for me . . ."

Although Nassif Bey's wife seldom showed her face, she actively supervised the domestic staff in their big house, where coffee was forever being served to a stream of male visitors. My father's colleague, who was always entertaining, enjoyed a reputation for being the best-informed man in Alexandria apart from the governor.

When I asked him a question about the Place des Consuls, he told me sternly, "The Place des Consuls no longer exists."

I was dismayed by this abolition of my principal landmark, but all Nassif Bey meant was that the square had been rechristened with the name of the Egyptian dynasty's founder: it was now called the Place Muhammad Ali. Happily, I soon realized that it was nothing of the sort. The inhabitants of Alexandria still called the heart of their city the Place des Consuls and would long continue to do so.

Rizqallah had arranged to meet us in the square at five that afternoon. When we got there a small, cheerful, jostling crowd was already watching the final preparations from around the fountains. Workmen were completing the installation of countless gas jets and iron *fanous* with multicoloured paper shades, which were intended to provide exceptionally bright lighting.

We found Rizqallah in the company of a European in breeches, riding crop in hand, whom I didn't at first recognize. My cousin made the introductions in his court chamberlain's voice:

"Dr Pierre Touta, Monsieur Adolphe Xavier-Saillard . . . "

The latter barely glanced at us. He was supervising some workmen who, perched on a ladder, were putting the finishing touches to the decoration of the imposing ochre and pink façade of his business premises.

"Tell those idiots not to climb that ladder four at a time," the Frenchman told Rizqallah angrily. "They'll end by breaking it."

And he stalked off on his bandy legs without greeting us.

"He's very preoccupied with those decorations," Rizqallah explained. "He doesn't want to be outdone by the Suez Canal Company."

What I most remember about that first night of celebrations, which was followed by two more, is an orgy of lights. All the leading banks and business houses strove to surpass each other in daring. Cicolani's big stores, all of whose chandeliers were alight, glittered like a thousand jewels. The hundreds of Chinese lanterns on the Xavier-Saillard building echoed those of the Suez Canal Company. As for the Oppenheim Bank, which had just lent the khedive millions at an exorbitant rate of interest, it had seen fit to sheath its façade in a massive triumphal arch on which four backlit transparencies represented the Nile, the desert, the Red Sea, and the Mediterranean.

Carrying us along with it, the crowd surged towards the house of Monsieur Antoniadis, which was decorated *à la* Pompadour, and its superb illuminated garden. The murmur of the fountains slightly muffled the voice of Sekkina, the celebrated chanteuse who was singing in one of the reception rooms – a rather husky voice, but capable of soaring far into the upper register and electrifying any audience. All Egypt went into raptures at the sound of it.

Applause rang out, together with shouts and cheers, Sekkina appeared at a window and gave us a little wave of acknowledgement. She was all of fifty years old – not as young and pretty as I had imagined.

"She used to tote baskets of mud on building sites," my father told me when we walked on. "That little diamond-studded tarboosh was a gift from Sa'id Pasha, who was crazy about her. They say she lends it free of charge to wealthy families for their brides to wear."

"She can afford to, take it from me!" said Rizqallah. "Sekkina is immensely wealthy, and not all her income derives from her singing tours. Her husband, who's considerably younger, never lets her out of his sight. He functions as her pimp – her servant, too, perhaps. The other day, when Sekkina was out riding on the banks of the Mahmudiya Canal, he trotted along in front of her donkey –"

Our conversation was cut short by the whistle of the first rockets. The whole sky became threaded with multicoloured streaks of light, and one explosion followed another in a wild tattoo. It was doubtful if Alexandria had ever witnessed such a pandemonium.

"What exactly are we celebrating?" my father mused softly.

It was not until ten or twelve days after our return to Cairo that the astonishing news became public: on that first night of celebrations in

Alexandria, the khedive had escaped an attempt on his life. He was driving past the old Stock Exchange in his open carriage when two heavy metal balls, bristling with razor-sharp blades, fell from the second floor. One of them hit the ground a few feet from the carriage, the other struck the dashboard before bouncing off into the road.

"But *we* were outside the old Stock Exchange that night!" my father exclaimed. "We were there when the cortège went past, and we didn't see a thing."

No one had seen anything at all, if the truth be told. What made the circumstances surrounding this assassination attempt seem all the more peculiar was that the second floor of the old Stock Exchange had been unoccupied for several months, and that it was not searched after the event.

Isma'il Pasha received countless messages of sympathy from all over Egypt, in fact the Armenian community went so far as to hold a service of thanksgiving for his deliverance.

"So who armed the criminals?" Alfred Falaki kept asking.

Suspicion fell on two princes who coveted the throne despite the new rule of direct succession: Mustafa, the viceroy's brother, and his uncle Halim. But had there really been an assassination attempt? Sceptics claimed in private that it had been crudely staged to get rid of Prince Halim, or simply to buttress the khedive's position.

My father's comment: "Isn't the regicide the measure of a true king?"

The Alexandria incident had already been forgotten when the Cairo Theatre affair took place. Albin Balanvin revelled in it.

FROM OUR CAIRO CORRESPONDENT
To the Editor:

9 April 1869

It is my painful and perplexing duty, sir, to inform you of an event which has just occasioned the greatest agitation here.

On the evening of 2 April, regular visitors to Cairo Theatre noticed with some surprise that the viceregal box was unoccupied. Various rumours circulated behind the scenes, but it was not until the next morning that the director of the theatre, Monsieur Séraphin Manasse, caused a sensation by revealing that he had foiled an attempt on His Highness's life. Thus, for the second time in only a few months, some wretch had attempted regicide!

Monsieur Manasse asserted that one of the wooden columns beneath the sovereign's box had been drilled throughout its length and a miner's fuse inserted. His statements were promptly confirmed by an examination of the said column. The fuse, which was connected to a gas jet in the corridor, led to a bronze mortar loaded with bullets and powder and situated under the khedive's armchair itself.

You will readily imagine, sir, the indignation provoked by these facts, which quickly went the rounds. It was with a keen and inexpressible feeling of gratitude that all concerned gave thanks to Providence for having averted a terrible disaster.

Now that the initial wave of indignation has subsided, however, people have begun to question the feasibility of such an act. Since His Highness can have no enemies, the question remains unanswered. Besides, the circumstances surrounding this odious venture seem odd. How did some criminal manage to drill through a column from top to bottom, insert a fuse, and install an incendiary mortar, when the theatre is open for rehearsals all day long, crowded with people every evening, and guarded by janitors at night?

The government, to its credit, has contributed to the discovery of the truth by appointing a committee of inquiry consisting of the consuls at Cairo of France, Britain, Greece, and Italy. The committee's first step has been to order the arrest of Monsieur Manasse and several of the theatre's artists and staff.

I can disclose that a reconstruction has just been arranged, not at the theatre, but at the 'Abbassiya. The authors of this experiment carried realism to the lengths of loading the armchair on which His Highness was to sit with an appropriate weight. Well, the charge, when detonated, was powerful enough to propel the armchair less than eighteen inches into the air and set the carpet on fire, nothing more.

Certain individuals are wondering if this was not just a sham assassination attempt engineered by some plotter intent on posing as a saviour, making a show of his loyalty, and persuading the khedive to reward him for (putative) services rendered.

At all events, I note that the intervention of Providence has been considered less exalted in this case than in that of the failed attempt at Alexandria. One or two deputations have presented addresses and a cantata was sung by a select few, but the consular corps has made no collective move to congratulate the sovereign on his fortunate escape.

The theatre has reopened despite the absence of Monsieur Manasse, and His Highness has had the good taste to continue to patronize it so as not to detract from the public's enjoyment by staying away. He has thus demonstrated, yet again, the strength of character with which he is endowed.

Let us, sir, forget this regrettable episode. And, while we are speaking of the theatre, permit me to confirm that work has commenced on the new opera house at the Ezbekiyah. It is being conducted with vigour at His Highness's request. The auditorium must be ready for the opening of the Suez Canal in a few months' time, but I shall doubtless have an opportunity to revert to that subject in detail in a future dispatch.

Albin Balanvin

20

The assassination attempt at Alexandria supplied the fuel for many a heated family argument, punctuated by oaths from Uncle Boctor. I took an active part in them, having been a witness of that invisible drama, if it may be so described. The Cairo Theatre affair rekindled the controversy, even though Albin Balanvin's article reduced it to a charade.

Balanvin intrigued me. I envied him for knowing everything ahead of everyone else. Who exactly was this enigmatic man? Where did he come from? How did he know Egypt so well? Many tales were told of him. Aunt Angéline claimed that his name was the only French thing about him, that he was the natural son of a pasha and had been brought up in Constantinople. She came out with various facts concerning the journalist's childhood, gleaned from heaven alone knew where, and modified them in the course of her successive accounts.

Nassif Bey, who was better informed, believed that Balanvin was a former Saint-Simonian, and Balanvin himself confirmed this at the end of a lunch during which the arrack had flowed rather more freely than usual.

His real name was Victor Dussolier. Born of lower middle-class parents in Versailles, he had severed relations with his family at an early age and moved to the Ménilmontant district of Paris. The printing house where he worked as an assistant typographer was situated less than a hundred metres from the building in which Prosper Enfantin, supreme head of the Saint-Simonian religion, had installed some forty of his disciples. It was a print order that first brought Victor into contact with the sect. It became a surrogate family sufficiently utopian and eccentric to captivate a youth of seventeen.

Bearded and long-haired, the Saint-Simonians got themselves up in a strange costume that made them look like Renaissance knights. They dreamed a great deal of Turkey and Egypt while awaiting a female Messiah whose appearance in the East was said to be imminent.

Young Victor, who was fascinated by "Père" Enfantin, chose a pseudo-nym of the same resonance: Balanvin. His adoptive first name was almost mandatory: pronounced *à la française*, Albin Balanvin seemed to crack like a flag in the wind. The new disciple spent some time at the house in Ménilmontant before being assigned to the first party to leave for Egypt in March 1833.

The Saint-Simonians caused a great stir in the port of Marseille. Chanting hymns, they wore the costume of the Mission to the East: white trousers (the colour of love), red waistcoats and berets (the colour of work), violet tunics (the colour of faith), jackets with puff sleeves, and flowing scarves. Each had his name embroidered on his chest in big letters. The dockers wanted to throw Enfantin's disciples into the harbour, but they embarked in the *Clorinde* to the cheers of the crowd.

They reached Constantinople after twenty-four days' sailing, only to be detained and deported as soon as they showed their faces. Although the Mission to the East had got off to a bad start, young Albin thoroughly enjoyed these vicissitudes. The Saint-Simonians headed for Salonica and then for Alexandria, where another party had already disembarked.

In Egypt, Père Enfantin's disciples were cordially welcomed by the French vice-consul, who was none other than Ferdinand de Lesseps. They managed to obtain an audience with Muhammad Ali and acquaint him with their grand design. This was to transform the East by means of industrial techniques and wed it to the West. The pasha gave them a rather sceptical hearing.

Père Enfantin, who had graduated from the École Polytechnique, dreamed of constructing a canal that would link the Mediterranean and the Red Sea. Albin was a member of the party that accompanied him into the Suez desert to inspect the area. The expedition was somewhat bizarre, like every venture undertaken by the head of the new universal religion. And that, because Muhammad Ali had other priorities, was as far as it went.

Albin never witnessed the advent of a female Messiah, but he did discover the opposite sex by way of Cécile Fournel, Suzanne Voilquin, and several other militant Saint-Simoniennes of very loose morals. Being the baby of the party, he became the pet of these boundlessly inquisitive ladies, who didn't hesitate to involve him in their escapades. They loudly applauded him when he acted on the stage of the little *Teatro del Cairo* of the period. There is no doubt, however, that Albin was more susceptible to the charms of Arab youths of his own age.

The Saint-Simonians played a very active role during the cholera epidemic of 1835. Like Dr Clot Bey after them, they did not believe that the disease was infectious and tackled it bare-handed. Eager to fathom the mystery of "the yellow sickness", which the natives ascribed to an evil spirit, they carried out a number of autopsies. Cairo lost 35,000 inhabitants that year, or one-third of its population, and Albin saw several of his companions die.

The following year, Père Enfantin's followers toasted his birthday in champagne. They held a riotous all-night party enlivened by dancing and hashish, but their hearts weren't in it any more. The expedition to Egypt was subsiding into a slough of disillusionment.

Enfantin returned to France a few months later. Albin had ceased to be impressed by the grandiloquent, nebulous ideas of the pope of Saint-Simonism, so he decided to remain in Cairo, where he now felt at home. Having got to know a number of French expatriates, he found employment in a variety of minor capacities. Accompanied by a young guide, he travelled the length and breadth of Egypt and journeyed up the Nile as far as the Third Cataract. His accounts of these excursions, which were very colourful, began to appear in Parisian newspapers.

In Paris meanwhile, Père Enfantin was raising the dust. His "International Society for the Study of the Suez Canal" had made a crucial discovery: contrary to long-standing belief, the Mediterranean and the Red Sea were on the same level. This favoured the construction of a direct canal as advocated by Ferdinand de Lesseps. Curiously enough, however, Enfantin drew a different conclusion: no gradient, no current; no current, no deep canal. Accordingly, he argued in favour of an indirect route via Alexandria and Cairo, incorporating a kilometre-long viaduct suspended twenty metres above the Nile.

Albin Balanvin, by now an accredited correspondent of *Le Gaulois*, poured scorn on this far-fetched scheme and earned himself a congratulatory letter from Ferdinand de Lesseps. Being jealous of his independence, however, the journalist hastened to criticize the way in which de Lesseps had usurped the canal idea.

Sa'id's reign provided Balanvin with plenty to write about and laugh at. In veiled language, his caustic pen disclosed the extravagances of a viceroy who enjoyed playing soldiers and never moved from one town to another unless surrounded by his generals and followed by his army. Ferdinand de Lesseps distrusted this unclassifiable journalist who clearly favoured the Suez Canal but insisted on remaining his own man. They were alienated for years by an article that caused a stir in 1860.

"What else could I say?" Balanvin protested. "Ferdinand de Lesseps wasn't very scrupulous when it came to floating the Suez Canal Company. In January 1860 he was left with a lot of shares on his hands. Not knowing what to do with them, he subscribed for them on the viceroy's behalf without consulting him. The sum involved was eighty-eight million francs, representing a 176,000 shares."

"Eighty-eight million!" exclaimed my father.

"Very pretty!" said Alfred Falaki.

Sa'id Pasha received a communication which he handed to his secretary without even reading it. Some days later de Lesseps asked him for the first payment on his subscription.

The viceroy was staggered. "What payment?"

"But I wrote to Your Highness!" retorted the founder of the Suez Canal Company. "Your Highness's silence confirmed the subscription . . . "

Sa'id disliked complications. Rather wrily, in the soldierly language he favoured, he told the French consul, "That de Lesseps of yours has buried me in it muzzle-deep."

21

Had the angels in heaven conspired to make me forget Nada? My first job, at the age of nineteen, should have been the most delightful in the world: to act as a guide and interpreter to some young French ballerinas who had come to Egypt for the opening of the Suez Canal.

I had just finished my schooling with the Très Chers Frères. In Cairo, the inauguration of the Canal was the only topic on everyone's lips, and excitement steadily mounted as the event drew closer. While awaiting the arrival of Empress Eugénie and the khedive's thousand other guests, the city's inhabitants circulated the wildest rumours. Some claimed that the Sultan would oppose the festivities by force, others that the Emperor of Austria had declined to attend, and that his defection would be followed by that of the majority of the crowned heads of Europe. As for Alfred Falaki, he assured the customers of his jeweller's shop that an enormous rock had been discovered in the bed of the Canal between Port Sa'id and Ismailia – a rock so huge that no dredger could dislodge it.

Nassif Bey had informed us that the palace was seeking some young people with an adequate command of the French language. They were to be placed at the service of the khedive's guests during their stay, and some would even accompany them to Upper Egypt. Thanks to Nassif's recommendation, I was engaged without difficulty and assigned to the Cairo Opera.

Built in a mere six months, the opera house on Ezbekiyah Square was inaugurated in Isma'il's presence on 1 November 1869. The princesses, smothered in jewels, watched the proceedings through the grilles over their boxes. When the curtain went up, eight artistes launched into a cantata composed by Prince Poniatowski in honour of the khedive, a bust of whom had been erected centre stage. This drew an immense ovation, followed by a performance of *Rigoletto*. Fifteen other works were featured in the programme for this exceptional season, for which some great Italian opera singers and forty-odd young Parisian ballerinas had been recruited. Selected for their beauty as well as their talent, these young ladies had been conveyed to Cairo under close escort and accommodated, for additional safety's sake, in Ezbekiyah's disused police station.

Like that of another of the Frères' ex-pupils, my very humble role was limited to escorting the party to rehearsals twice a day. We could barely exchange a word with the ballerinas, some of whom were chaperoned by their mothers. We were not even at liberty to enter the auditorium and watch them rehearse, but the few words I did exchange with a delightful redhead, accompanied by sidelong glances and surreptitious smiles, were enough to put me into a state verging on ecstasy. Hitherto, my only experience of sex had been some purchasable embraces – in a hovel off Ezbekiyah Square, to be precise.

The 5,000 French inhabitants of Alexandria had been preparing for the arrival of Empress Eugénie for several weeks. They had formed an organizing committee, one of its vice-chairmen being Monsieur Xavier-Saillard.

The entire French colony was afoot when *L'Aigle* entered the harbour at dawn on 23 October. Little girls rehearsed their curtseys and the organizing committee remained in permanent session at the consulate-general while awaiting instructions from the consul, who had left aboard a small steamer, with Ferdinand de Lesseps, to receive Her Majesty's instructions.

Hours went by. Then, just before midday, the organizing committee was informed that the imperial visitor had gone straight on to Cairo, and that she regretted not having been able to receive the colony. The French were immensely disappointed, but consoled themselves that night – after a fashion – by festively illuminating the consulate and most of their homes.

It was during her stay in Cairo that Eugénie expressed a wish to attend an Arab wedding.

"What a fortunate coincidence!" said the khedive, who did all he could to please her. "There's going to be a wedding at the palace today."

Having taken leave of the empress, he promptly summoned one of his officials and told him, "You're getting married tonight."

The flabbergasted young courtier was given no time to query this statement. Within the hour he was found a bride whom the viceroy was gracious enough to provide with an adequate dowry.

Eugénie, who was enchanted by the ceremony, wished the young couple much happiness and many children.

I don't think it's an exaggeration to say that the *Sémaphore d'Alexandrie* devoted a total of thirty pages to the opening of the Suez Canal. The editor of that increasingly influential weekly was shrewd enough to employ his best writer, Albin Balanvin, to cover the whole of the festivities. The result was a firework display in print. The former Saint-Simonian's articles were in stark contrast to those of all the European journalists in Egypt at Isma'il's invitation. Even on the most moving occasions, he preserved his own, singularly ironical approach — one that was beginning, people said, to prove a serious thorn in the khedive's side.

FROM OUR OWN CORRESPONDENT
To the Editor:

Port Sa'id, 16 November 1869

L'Aigle left Alexandria and entered the roads of Port Sa'id just before seven this morning, saluted by some sixty vessels dressed overall in the colours of every nation. During the next few hours the sovereigns and princes present exchanged visits from ship to ship, each visit being accompanied by salvoes of gunfire. I was informed, sir, that the Dutch ship alone discharged her cannon some 600 times. Whether or not this music charmed the empress, her radiant smile never faltered.

The Emperor of Austria was the first to present himself on board L'Aigle and greet Eugénie. He had arrived here yesterday from Palestine, after a very stormy passage. A positive tempest was raging, and everyone tried to dissuade him from leaving Jaffa, but Franz-Joseph insisted on keeping his promise. He was rowed out to his yacht in the thick of the storm. In order to gain the deck he had to be roped and hoisted aboard. Two native seamen fell into the sea in the course of this valiant expedition.

This afternoon, a religious ceremony without precedent in the East took place on the beach in front of the Quai Eugénie. Two platforms had been erected, one for the Muslim religion, the other for the Catholic. I regret having been unable to obtain a translation of the address delivered by the Grand Sheikh of Cairo. I can, however, assure you that the eloquence of Monsignor Bauer, almoner of the Tuileries, had crossed the sea with him. The quality of his voice and the beauty of his gestures were remarked on by everyone present. "The hour that has just struck," declared the eminent churchman, "is not only one of the most solemn of this nineteenth century, but one of the greatest and most decisive ever witnessed by mankind since the beginning of its history here below."

Tonight, Port Sa'id is lit by countless rockets. The town and the roads are on fire. Permit me, sir, to enjoy a night's repose — deservedly, I feel — before embarking on the historic crossing of the Canal, which is set for tomorrow.

Balanvin slept little that night. At one in the morning, on leaving a dinner party, he noticed a lively commotion in progress outside the governor's residence: it had just been reported that a ship was blocking the Canal. Panic reigned in official quarters. The telegraph wire was already humming with announcements that the crossing had been cancelled.

Ismailia, 17 November 1869

Last night there occurred an unfortunate incident — one on which I do not care to dwell. Believe it or not, sir, the Latif, an Egyptian frigate, ran aground at kilometre 28 between Port Sa'id and al-Qantarah in consequence of an ill-judged manoeuvre. All efforts to dislodge her proved in vain. The Canal was blocked!

At three in the morning, accompanied by a thousand sailors, the khedive betook himself to the place in person. "If need be," he declared, "I shall have the Latif blown up." On hearing those courageous words, Monsieur de Lesseps embraced him . . . His Highness spurred the workers on, directing operations in person, and his sagacity enabled the frigate to be refloated.

This morning the hour of the decisive test struck at last. At half past eight, L'Aigle, flying the imperial standard, entered the Canal followed at a distance by the vessels of the Emperor of Austria, the Crown Prince of Prussia, the Prince of the Netherlands, the ambassadors of Russia and Great Britain, and several dozen warships or merchantmen that had applied to undertake the crossing from one sea to the other.

The empress, her face tense with excitement, was standing on L'Aigle's poop deck with Monsieur de Lesseps in attendance. The ship progressed at a prudent speed of no more than two-and-a-half knots, but after a few kilometres she increased speed to six, then seven knots. The encampments along the route, which were decorated, saluted the flotilla as it passed. The Latif did at least serve some purpose: when the leading vessel drew level with her, she broke out all her flags and fired all her guns. The sovereigns, who had no knowledge of last night's incident, thought this a charming gesture on the khedive's part.

By the afternoon a huge crowd had assembled on the dunes of Site No. 6, near Lake Timsah. Having no news of the flotilla, and being ignorant of whether the empress had halted en route or was continuing her journey in L'Aigle, thousands of anxious spectators trained their binoculars on the Canal. The horsemen who kept on arriving from al-Qantarah were impatiently questioned, but they knew nothing.

All at once, shouts were heard. An immense hubbub ran the length of the dunes: the tops of the imperial yacht's masts had come into view. Before long, the dark bulk of the ship that was carrying Her Majesty — and, with her, Monsieur de Lesseps' fortunes — rounded the bend and emerged from behind a hillock of sand. Every member of L'Aigle's crew was drawn up in the bow. On the poop deck, surrounded by her entire retinue, the empress waved her handkerchief as she gazed at the splendid scene that was unfolding before her eyes. The first cannon shot rang out. Then the spectators gave vent to their enthusiasm, weeping and hugging each other. Hats flew into the air. With tears in their eyes, the Company's engineers shook hands in silence.

The Austrian ship, which had been following at a distance of 500 metres, was treated to more salvoes and more cheers. Emperor Franz-Joseph, standing on the capstan barrel in travelling costume with a chiffon scarf over his hat, waved graciously to the crowd.

Half the Suez Canal had been covered in eight-and-a-half hours. L'Aigle dropped anchor in Lake Timsah, and the vessels of the sovereigns and ambassadors who had followed her for seventy-eight kilometres took up their stations around her.

The khedive came aboard and, after presenting his respects to the empress, threw himself into the arms of Monsieur de Lesseps. It was their second embrace in less than twenty-four hours. We would never have believed His Highness capable of such a display of emotion. It proves that he has entirely forgotten the minor differences of opinion that existed between his government and the Suez Canal

Company, of which Monsieur de Lesseps has always been the most complete expression.

Dinner was marked by a touching incident. The empress had only just sat down at table when, overcome by emotions held in check for too long, she had briefly to retire to her suite to give free rein to her tears. Need I tell you, sir, that they were tears of joy?

Albin Balanvin was welcomed at Ismailia by Étienne Mancelle, who was highly elated but also rather bemused by the invasion to which his town had been subjected. Since the previous day, the streets of "the Venice of the desert" had been thronged with many thousands of noisy people of every race and provenance. Members of the Jockey Club rubbed shoulders with whirling dervishes and Circassians in pelisses. In order to accommodate this influx of guests and European tourists, the authorities had been obliged to erect numerous tents along the freshwater canal and equip them with beds or simple mattresses. The local Bedouin, for their part, had pitched their own tents, which were decorated with fabrics of many colours.

The next morning, Eugénie caused a sensation by riding on horseback to the edge of al-Gisr, escorted by a squadron of pretty Amazons. She wore a broad-brimmed straw hat adorned with a green veil and had a palm-leaf fly-whisk at her waist. Elegantly mounted on a dromedary for the return trip, the empress rode back to Monsieur de Lesseps' chalet to receive the ladies of the isthmus in audience. Nada would have liked nothing better than to join that primped and perfumed party, but the doctor had strictly forbidden her to do so.

Ismailia, 19 November 1869

Will you permit me, sir, to draw a veil over the so-called "ball" held at the viceroy's new palace last night? The number of guests was disproportionate to the size of premises, spacious though they were. People trampled on each other's feet. I fled as soon as they stormed the buffets, thereby sparing myself a sight of the appalling crush that ensued. Allow me simply to enumerate the various dishes on the menu, all of them most welcome in the midst of the desert: game pâté à la Dorsay, *ox tongue* à l'anglaise, *various aspics* de Nérac, *quail galantine* en belle-vue, *filets* à l'impériale . . .

I rather hesitate to tell you about a small party, organized in the greatest of secrecy, which had as its setting a luxurious dahabiya *moored on the freshwater canal. The host had invited no journalists, but those devilish chroniclers poke their noses into everything. In default of firm information, they simply guess.*

On board the dahabiya *were several famous chanteuses and some exceedingly attractive dancing girls. The guests turned up discreetly, one after another. We did not, of course, recognize any of the very exalted figures present. Once they were all aboard, the* dahabiya *cast off and cruised for two hours on Lake Timsah.*

That is as far as our information goes. Having promised not to name the guests, we fear that we shall offend the owner of the dahabiya *by revealing that it was His Excellency Isma'il Saddiq Pasha, His Highness the Viceroy's minister of finance.*

Albin Balanvin

At eleven-thirty on the morning of 20 November, *L'Aigle* made her triumphal entrance into the Red Sea. The conquest of the desert had rendered every map in the world obsolete. The khedive flung himself at Ferdinand de Lesseps and embraced him for the third time.

Étienne Mancelle, who witnessed this incident, would gladly have done the same. A fascinated spectator on the bank of the Canal, he was observing the fairy-tale scene and the fifty-odd vessels that had left Port Sa'id a few days earlier. A shout jolted him out of his reverie.

"Mancelle! Mancelle!"

His colleague Félix Percheron was waving a telegram.

"Hard luck, *mon vieux*, it's a girl . . . "

Étienne almost fainted with joy. A child! He had a child! His daughter, who shared a birthday with the Suez Canal, would – of course – be christened Eugénie.

PART TWO

Roses in the Desert

I

Why should I have become a doctor? I was too well aware of the mistrust, and sometimes the contempt, in which my father and his local colleagues were held. Europeans did not regard them as authentic practitioners. As for the natives, they reserved their trust for bonesetters. Only our *Shawam* families cherished a genuine respect for Dr Boutros Touta, especially since he had been awarded the medal by Napoleon III. But that respect was not enough for me.

My father made no attempt to persuade Alexandre and me to follow in his footsteps. Not having chosen to become a doctor himself, he may not have wished to force our hand. I never sensed that this modest man was openly in love with his profession and guided by one of those heart-stirring passions that wins disciples.

In any case, I had no wish to tend the sick and dress wounds. Dr Touta's natural generosity had not transmitted itself to his sons. I felt more inclined to shine and seek the limelight, if only to attract Nada's attention.

Albin Balanvin's example fascinated me. From the age of fifteen or sixteen onwards, I devoured his pieces in the *Sémaphore d'Alexandrie*, secretly nursing a wish to be able, some day, to put my own name to such articles.

The first time I told my father of my plans, he stared at me in astonishment.

"A journalist? You want to be a journalist?"

In his eyes journalism wasn't a profession — or not, at all events, a profession for me. He frowned, and I could guess what he was thinking.

The few newspapers that did exist in Egypt were all edited by Europeans. I would be refused employment on the grounds that I had been educated by the Très Chers Frères.

"There's an under-cashier's job going at the Imperial Ottoman Bank, so I'm told," he said rather hesitantly. "It's a respectable concern. You might like to apply . . . "

That night, taking my courage in both hands, I knocked at Albin Balanvin's door.

The servant who opened it looked me up and down with a suspicious air before going to tell his master. The latter appeared in a green satin dressing gown and gold-embroidered Turkish slippers.

"Come in, my young friend, come in!"

He took my hand in his and held it a trifle too long.

"To what do I owe the pleasure?"

The mischievous man had instantly divined the object of my visit, I suspect, and was deliberately spinning out the preliminaries.

"I trust you bring me no bad news of the Doctor?"

Albin Balanvin never called my father "the Doctor" in a sarcastic tone of voice. I had been struck, ever since our first meeting in the Place des Consuls, by his natural liking for Papa — and no two men could have been more different, God knows.

We made our way into a spacious drawing room lit by several candelabra and pervaded by a scent of incense. The walls were covered with pictures, the windows shrouded in heavy crimson curtains, and the room was cluttered with portières, plump cushions and succulent plants. Presiding at its centre, reflected in an enormous wall mirror, was a statue of a handsome Greek youth in white marble.

"Sit down beside me," said Balanvin, subsiding on to a sofa with mahogany arms. "Hassanein will bring us some coffee. How do you take it? Very sweet? Ah, *mazbout*. You're absolutely right . . . "

Embarrassed and ill at ease, I explained the purpose of my visit. He let me talk, let me trip over my words. He himself said nothing, just puffed at the mouthpiece of his hookah.

"You're right to prefer your coffee *mazbout*," he said finally. "Coffee should indeed be drunk like that: neither too bitter nor too sweet."

I stared at him with my mouth open.

"Yes, yes, I'm quite insistent on that point: coffee should fall midway between the two. The same goes for its temperature. You don't drink it boiling hot, I trust?"

I could feel my hair prickle and the blood rise to my cheeks.

His tone changed abruptly.

"But journalism, you see, is the opposite of coffee: when you write, you must be crystal clear – you must choose which side you're on. Lukewarm won't do for a journalist!"

I gave him a look of blank inquiry.

"Why do you want to be a journalist?" he asked brusquely.

"To tell people things," I stammered. "To tell them what's going on."

"They won't give a fig for your reports, my young friend!" He was almost shouting now. "As for your ideas, you know where you can put them!"

I buried my nose in my coffee cup, incapable of uttering a word. Balanvin was still incensed.

"Being a journalist means interpreting the world. In-ter-pre-ting it, you follow me?"

I nodded without really knowing what he meant.

"You must seek, search, try to find out all there is to know and understand it. But afterwards you must turn it into a work of art. A work of art, you hear?"

"I won't take up any more of your time," I said in a subdued voice.

Balanvin's expression changed as abruptly as if he had removed one mask and donned another.

"You speak Arabic, don't you? You may be able to help me. I need to know how forced labour is being organized at the khedive's sugar refinery in the Tanta district. Would you be willing to go there and conduct some inquiries for me?"

After experiencing such a variety of emotions, I didn't know what to say. I was torn between delight at being entrusted with a journalistic mission and disappointment at being reduced to playing the commercial traveller in the provinces – I, who already dreamed of penetrating the corridors of power.

I was in as much of an emotional turmoil when I said goodbye to Albin

Balanvin an hour later as I had been on arrival. Countless ideas were milling around in my head.

When I think back on that expedition to the Tanta district, I'm amazed at my own naivety and lack of common sense. Fancy setting off blindly like that, without having devised some unobtrusive method of gleaning the information Balanvin wanted! But I was young — a mere youth of twenty.

My father grumbled but let me go. He seemed unconvinced, either of the usefulness of my mission or of my ability to carry it out. At least he was satisfied that I'd been taken on trial by the Ottoman Bank, where a humble post would be awaiting me on my return a week later.

I had no difficulty in finding the viceroy's properties, which occupied the entire district. As soon as I emerged from the station I saw detachments of peasants marching off to work under military escort. There could be no question of accosting them. In any case, which of those fellahin could have told me how forced labour was organized? At a loss, I watched them trudge past without the least idea of how to fulfil my assignment.

Near the station I found a disreputable inn that went by the high-flown name of the Locanda Khédiviale. In return for a few piastres I was offered a urine-scented cell equipped with a straw mattress. I spent the evening by candlelight, chasing the fat black cockroaches that crept in under my door and ran around on the ceiling. My dreams were populated by visions of the horrible creatures scuttling up and down the slender white body of the Greek youth in Balanvin's drawing room.

I awoke with a start at dawn, roused by the muezzin's nasal tones. It was cold and damp. This entirely Arab town, of which I knew nothing, felt as if it were at the end of the world. I was very far from producing the "work of art" of which Balanvin had spoken. A feeling of utter despair crept over me.

That morning, not knowing what else to do, I sat down at a café table. A crazy idea occurred to me. Why not try forced labour for myself? After all, I had only to buy a *galabiya*, take off my shoes, and insinuate myself into a working party of peasant conscripts. But how would I manage to escape afterwards?

Two men at a nearby table were heatedly arguing over a pot of honey.

They shouted and stormed at each other in an absurd and irritating way. I was about to get up and go when I heard them mention the sugar refinery. The khedive's sugar refinery . . . I strained my ears, and it wasn't long before I gathered that they were employed there as overseers.

After that, I lapped up every word of their conversation. They eventually noticed this, and one of them enlisted me as a witness in his defence. I drew up my chair and offered to buy them a coffee. They wanted it *mazbout*, so I expatiated on the subject. Coffee, I said, should be neither too bitter nor too heavily sugared . . .

"Don't talk about sugar," said one of them, "we get enough of that at work!" And he roared with laughter.

We spoke of their hours of work, then of forced labour. The fellahin were marched to the refinery in parties of 100 or 200. Were they paid? I asked.

"Oh yes, their fares are paid both ways."

"No, I meant remunerated."

"They get a pot of honey a month."

Further discussion was devoted to hours of work, rations, and floggings with the *kurbash*. I bought the pair another round of coffees. They talked inexhaustibly, delighted to tell a stranger about the sugar refinery where they worked for low wages plus one or two perquisites. Pots of honey, for instance.

Having extracted all I could from them, I left the men at the hour of the midday prayer and hurried back to my cell in the Locanda Khédiviale to note down – in a fever of excitement – everything they had told me. I no longer needed to disguise myself as a fellah. I knew all there was to know.

The day after I returned to Cairo I presented Albin Balanvin with a dozen sheets of paper bearing a well-polished account of what I had gleaned on the spot. He scanned them quickly, asked me a few questions, and gave me a small sum of money on behalf of the *Sémaphore d'Alexandrie*. I was in seventh heaven.

His article was due to appear two weeks later. I awaited its publication with mounting impatience.

The first few lines surprised me: they contained a series of reflections on aspects of the forced labour system that were completely new to me. The rest of the piece left me stunned. Although it dealt with the khedive's sugar refinery – indeed, with nothing but – it embodied none of the ideas I'd expressed so eloquently in my report. Balanvin's article concluded with the pot of honey, and that was all. Why had he bothered to send me so far afield? I was not only furious but terribly hurt.

This article was destined to cause a rumpus in the corridors of power. The newspaper *L'Égypte*, which was financed by the palace, published an editorial that referred indignantly to "persons who spread gross slanders". It was said that one of the khedive's leading associates had gone to the *Sémaphore*'s offices in Alexandria and uttered some less than veiled threats: another such broadside, and the weekly would be closed down at once.

Albin Balanvin was congratulated on his temerity by Sa'id's enemies, and also by certain Europeans, but he aroused the hostility of some wealthy landowners. One of them was Adolphe Xavier-Saillard, who fired off a volley of insults in the presence of my cousin Rizqallah.

"That lousy *Sémaphore*! I hope the governor of Gharbiyah doesn't make a habit of wiping his backside on that rotten rag. He may read it – *if* he knows how to read – and decide to deprive me of the two batches of conscripts he gives me every year to sow my fields and harvest my cotton!"

The pot of honey touched a chord with Balanvin's readers. I now understood why, being an excellent journalist, he had ended his article on that detail – a detail of which I myself was the source, after all. I began to feel proud of having collaborated on such a piece. By degrees, the article became my own. I pictured my signature on it, read it with Nada's marvelling eyes . . .

My colleagues at the Ottoman Bank had no idea that the new under-cashier was a person of importance, a journalist who had just revealed the secrets of the khedive's sugar refinery. Although elementary prudence prompted me to remain silent, I itched to flaunt my real identity. I already pictured myself bidding those pen-pushers farewell. "Goodbye, gentlemen," I would tell them with a flourish, "I'm off to become a journalist!"

While waiting, I learned to count wads of banknotes with a moistened fingertip. I navigated between Egyptian guineas, Ethiopian talaris, English shillings, Turkish paras and sequins, Indian rupees, French napoleons . . . During their trip to Paris for the World Exhibition, the astronomer Mahmud Bey had remarked to my father, "Do you think it acceptable, doctor, that we should use six or seven different currencies? I shall raise the matter with His Highness . . ."

But His Highness only paid in pots of honey.

2

Ever since her move to the new quarter of Cairo bounded by the Ezbekiyah Gardens and the palaces beside the Nile, Aunt Angéline had cherished great ambitions for Lolo. The wife she was seeking for him must be well-off, good-looking, gentle but spirited, titled if possible, and – needless to say – of the Greek Catholic faith. Very few girls combined all these attributes, even though the prospective mother-in-law extended her research to Damietta, al-Mansoura and Alexandria, but she was uncompromising.

"A Maronite? Never! What has my son done to deserve to marry a Maronite?"

Lolo himself made no demands. Comfortably housed, well-fed, gas-lit, and warmed by the family atmosphere, "Maman's pet" revelled in his bachelor existence. Even his more impetuous requirements were fulfilled at home – by the Falakis' maidservant, who was a thorough slut.

The aforementioned Fawzia flustered all the young men of the family. When you knocked on the Falakis' door she had a way of opening it only a crack as if the house were a brothel, and her ripe lips murmured words of welcome. Her plunging neckline held your gaze, and when she bent forward – as she often did – you could see her nipples.

Fawzia regularly raised the price of her nocturnal services. Lolo protested at this, but she would advance on him, lift her arm, and envelop him in an odour of armpit that sent him into raptures. At midnight, when his parents had gone to bed, he would join her in the candlelit pantry, tear off her gown, seize her swarthy flesh in both hands, and make the sleeping house resound with his braying.

* * *

The Falakis were on to a good thing. Having undertaken to build a house costing in excess of 2,000 pounds, they had paid nothing for its site in this new, airy, well-laid-out quarter, which had become the most exclusive residential district in Cairo. My jeweller uncle congratulated himself daily on having jumped at the khedive's offer, and liked nothing better than to survey his home from the Citadel. He often went up there, never omitting to take a customer with him.

"There!" he would say eagerly, aiming a forefinger at the forest of minarets spread out below them. "You see my house?"

And the customer would go into transports of admiration, possibly telling himself that this crook of a jeweller might offer him a discount.

Other members of the family also profited from the viceroy's unexpected initiatives, for instance Boctor Touta, Rizqallah's father, when the so-called *muqabala* law was promulgated. He never tired of the subject.

"What has the khedive dreamed up this time?" my father asked wearily.

"It's a fabulous idea!" Boctor exclaimed. "It'll suit everyone. The state will be able to pay off all its debts and the landowners will make money. Listen closely: those who pay six annual instalments of land taxes right away will have their tax liability permanently reduced by half. That means that, by the time I die, I shall have paid half as much tax as I would have done in the normal way!"

"It sounds a rather complicated formula."

"Complicated my mother's fanny! Six years' land taxes amount to thirty million pounds sterling, or precisely the extent of the national debt. No more national debt – just like that! As for the landowners, they'll make the equivalent of an investment yielding eight per cent in perpetuity. An indirect investment that doesn't violate the Islamic ban on interest-bearing loans."

"I don't follow," said Lolo.

"Use your brains, you nancy-boy! By paying only half as much tax for evermore, the landowners will pocket a return of eight per cent on their capital."

"So?"

"So, *ya tiz*, it's the same as if they were lending at eight per cent!"

Lolo scratched his head and frowned.

Rizqallah, Boctor's son, also knew how to tread the road to riches, but in his own way. Monsieur Xavier-Saillard was now employing him full-time. Having become the wealthy businessman's briefcase-carrier, my cousin had quit the French consulate, where no job — not even that of senior dragoman — measured up to his true ambitions. He wanted to make money, lots of money. In Monsieur Xavier-Saillard's employ he did at least juggle with figures all day long.

I can still hear him say, jokingly, "We make eighty per cent: we buy at twenty and sell at a hundred." But I ended by wondering if it really was a joke. Anything was possible in the frantic climate of speculation prevailing at this period.

Rizqallah's time at the French consulate had enabled him, as foreseen, to become a French "dependant". This status exempted him from coming under local jurisdiction and paying taxes. His manservant benefited too: being employed by a "dependant", the scrawny youngster escaped conscription into the army. In other words, it was in his interests to behave well and thank heaven for the three daily helpings of beans he received in lieu of wages.

"He's the dependant of a dependant," my father said drily.

3

It occurs to me that I know very little of Walid al-Ahlawi's doings at this period. Had he volunteered for service in the Sudan so as to earn double pay and a possibility of promotion? Or had he been forced to go there, as he subsequently claimed, perhaps in support of his theories about khedivial imposture and British rapacity?

I don't even know exactly when he left, but he must have reached the outskirts of Khartoum early in 1872, when Sir Samuel Baker, then in the khedive's service, was requesting reinforcements to fight insurgent tribesmen. The expedition entrusted to the famous explorer was not unambitious, its purpose being to enable Egypt to control the entire length of the Nile from its sources to the Mediterranean.

"Isma'il dreams of a great African empire which will make him wealthier, more powerful, and even more independent of Constantinople," Nassif Bey explained.

Walid al-Ahlawi very soon realized that he was not taking part in a military picnic. This war was a hundred times more arduous than the Cretan campaign in which he had won his promotion to *yusbashi*. After several months in the Sudan, the young officer still couldn't get used to the sweltering heat, the humidity, and the appalling conditions in which he was living. The clashes with the natives who resisted "pacification" were incredibly violent. Walid was ill for three days after finding the mutilated body of one of his comrades, who had been horribly tortured. He asked to be sent home, but his request was denied. Baker Pasha, who addressed him in person through an interpreter, underlined the need to continue this civilizing mission:

"We're not here simply to establish trading posts, nor to open up great lakes to navigation. Our primary role is to wrest men, women and children from slavery . . ."

Walid thought of the "eunuch factory" his battalion had come across on the outskirts of a village near Gondokoro: boys of six or seven, destined for distant harems, had been emasculated with a razor. Their wounds having been treated with boiling oil and powdered henna, they were buried waist-deep for twenty-four hours to assist the healing process. Walid would never forget the dull-eyed gaze of one child in particular. He resigned himself to remaining in the Sudan – he had no choice in any case – but he felt a fierce loathing for Baker, as if he reproached the man for having cheated him with a false argument. That loathing he extended by degrees to the British in general. He could not endure their arrogance and contempt. Even their courage and efficiency rendered them hateful to him.

Walid al-Ahlawi had begun by hating the French for having him unjustly reduced to the ranks in the Place des Consuls. He now, for less evident reasons, hated the British. He also hated the khedive, who was ultimately responsible for everything. Wasn't it Isma'il Pasha who had suffered him to be demoted in public, and wasn't it he who, ten years later, had sent him off to this bloodbath in Black Africa?

In Cairo we were very ill-informed about the colonial expedition. The newspapers usually confined themselves to reprinting the khedive's victorious communiqués without being able to verify them. This obviously applied to L'Égypte, which was subsidized by the palace and never failed to arouse Albin Balanvin's scorn.

"In that rag," he used to say, "only the date is correct."

Where the conquest of the Sudan was concerned, the Sémaphore's correspondent was reduced to posing sarcastic questions. He made up for it by tackling other, more accessible subjects such as domestic politics or the theatre.

When I told him about a fit of panic to which the counters of the Ottoman Bank had succumbed because of a false rumour concerning Treasury bonds, he urged me to put the story down on paper by way of practice. I eagerly complied, doing my utmost to polish the style of my article, which I brought him the next day.

Balanvin skimmed through it. "Not bad," he grunted.

My cheeks burned with delight.

"Let's look at it in greater detail," he went on, picking up a red pencil. "Come and sit down beside me."

He drew a thick red line through the first paragraph.

"Useless."

He did the same to the second.

"Why not come straight to the point?"

I was dismayed. In the next few minutes my article – the culmination of twelve or fifteen drafts, every word of which had been carefully weighed – started to bleed all over the place. I gritted my teeth, trembling with anger and disappointment.

"It's not bad," Balanvin repeated, laying the piece aside on a low table. "We'll try to find a little space for it in the *Sémaphore*. In future, though, please stop trying to be conventional. Produce a work of art, my young friend. A work of art!"

I nearly kissed him.

The article appeared the following week, unsigned and completely revised. A detailed account of the incident at the Ottoman Bank concluded with a veiled message from Balanvin, who paid exaggerated homage to the tireless activities of the ministry of finance:

> *The Treasury bonds churned out there day and night are doubtless destined to have an extremely productive effect on the national economy. Before long, however, conventional methods will be insufficient, and there is talk of ordering a more powerful printing press capable of meeting all the government's needs . . .*

Balanvin was fundamentally uninterested in the Ottoman Bank episode. It was just a "news item", to use his disdainful description. As he saw it, the story's sole purpose was to serve as a pretext for an impudent comment.

I was beginning to fathom the journalistic difference between us: the *Sémaphore's* correspondent had literary pretensions; my primary aim was to tell a story.

4

One Sunday in March, as I rose to leave, Albin Balanvin handed me a pamphlet. Published in Paris, it was signed with a pseudonym and entitled: "The death throes of the Suez Canal, the futility of its achievements to date, and its imminent demise."

"They say this piece is causing quite a hullabaloo in Company circles. It might be interesting to go to Ismailia and take a closer look. I don't care to, myself. Would you like to go?"

Sheer excitement made me resume my seat uninvited. I was naturally bowled over by Balanvin's proposal, by all the faith in me it implied, but still more by the prospect of visiting Nada's town.

Of course I would go, I said, without even thinking of the excuse I would have to give the Ottoman Bank. Balanvin offered to write to two senior members of the Suez Canal Company's board and apprise them of my forthcoming visit.

"And don't forget to go and see Étienne Mancelle and his charming wife," he added.

Superfluous advice, to say the least.

Informed of my visit to Ismailia, where I was to spend five days, Étienne replied by return that a room was awaiting me at his home, and that I would be much more comfortable there than at a hotel. Nada had endorsed this invitation by scribbling a few words in the rounded, rather slanting hand of an ex-pupil of the Bon Pasteur.

"You can't go there empty-handed," my father told me. "You must take them a present for the house."

I had plenty of choice, the Suez desert not being overly well-provided, but I was unused to shopping for such things. After spending an entire morning in the shops in Muski Street, I gave up and went to Falaki's to buy a small clock.

"I've got just what you need!" Uncle Alfred assured me.

He always had just what any customer needed. On his advice I bought a table cuckoo clock in a silver-plated case.

"I'm letting you have it very cheap," he told me.

"It's a gift at that price," Lolo chimed in. It was like a choirboy's mechanical response to the officiating priest.

He wrapped up the clock in a page from the *Moniteur égyptien*, *L'Égypte*'s new title – a rather questionable choice from every point of view – and secured it with innumerable knots, almost as if the cuckoo might fly away.

I was captivated by Ismailia's little station, which was situated in the middle of the desert. A kind of balcony ran the length of the timber building, its flimsy arches supported by small columns. Bedouin and vendors of figs were seated placidly on the track. They moved only two or three times a day, when a locomotive's distant whistle heralded the arrival of a train.

Étienne Mancelle, in riding boots and a khaki shirt, greeted a female acquaintance who had alighted from the train ahead of me, somewhat hampered by her crinoline. He had filled out a little. We exchanged a cordial handshake before boarding his tilbury. The horse went trotting along a sandy road flanked by spindly trees and came out in the Place Champollion.

"We're there," Étienne said cheerfully, aiming his whip at a house with lilac shutters.

I had a lump in my throat. It was five years since Nada's marriage – five long years since I had seen her.

The door opened to reveal a little girl, who came running towards the tilbury but stopped short when she saw me.

"Well, Eugénie, how about a *bonjour* for Maxime?" said her father, who clearly doted on her.

But I only had eyes for Nada, who had appeared in the doorway and was standing there with her arms folded, smiling at me. I gave her a little wave to hide the turmoil inside me.

Eugénie caused a diversion by running back to her mother. Nada picked her up and came to give me a welcoming kiss. I rediscovered the scent of her skin, which I had stolen a hundred times during our family lunches, when I bent towards her to retrieve the napkin that so often slipped off my lap.

"This is our guest room," she told me as we climbed the stairs. "It overlooks the square. Eugénie and Lucien sleep in the room across the passage. I hope they won't wake you."

Lucien was two years old. Étienne had mentioned, when announcing his arrival, that the birth had been a difficult one. Thereafter I had pictured Nada's figure bloated and ruined by her pregnancies, but the young woman at my side had never looked more enchanting.

My cuckoo clock was warmly received. I was nonetheless surprised, on entering the drawing room, to see a host of similar knick-knacks including a pendulum clock, a carriage clock, and a fat-bellied marine watch on a mahogany stand. From the look of it, Ismailia's shops were even better stocked than those of Cairo or Alexandria.

We lunched on the shady veranda, a delightful spot furnished with wicker-work chairs and shielded from the sun by a luxuriant vine. Nada addressed the maidservant in Arabic with a lingering Syrian intonation.

I was asked for news of all the family. We spoke in detail of every member, starting with my father, for whom they both cherished a genuine affection. Then I told Étienne the exact purpose of my trip.

"You'll put the wind up the Company's bigwigs," he said pensively. "The *Sémaphore d'Alexandrie*'s comments are held in dread here. Still, I congratulate you on landing a job with such an influential newspaper."

I explained that I was an associate of Albin Balanvin's, not a member of the weekly's editorial staff.

"Ah, dear Balanvin," Étienne said with a smile. "His reports of the inauguration were eagerly read and fiercely debated here, I can tell you. No other journalist was bold enough to be so outspoken about certain matters. It might be wise not to mention his name too loudly ... However, I'm sure you'll do your best. In any case, I'm at your service."

It wasn't the ticklish nature of my assignment or the proximity of Eugénie and Lucien that prevented me from getting off to sleep before three that morning; it was the mere fact of being there in Ismailia, only a few steps from Nada's bedroom. I had never felt so attracted to her, but the acquisition of a husband and two children made her seem more inaccessible than ever before. Étienne called her "my little dove", which struck me as absurd and embarrassing.

My first appointment with a senior official was set for ten in the morning. I made my way to the Company's headquarters, an imposingly palatial and luxurious office building overlooking Lake Timsah.

"I'd assumed you were French," the official said stiffly. "I should have known. That name of yours, Touta . . . "

Taken aback by his reaction, I forgot my first question. His air of disdain intensified as he watched me clumsily riffling through my notebook. I wasn't a European, wasn't really on the staff of the *Sémaphore d'Alexandrie*, and, what was more, I didn't know my job. All at once, the chief engineer's condescending expression infuriated me. I decide to hit back by peppering him with questions.

"Can you explain," I asked, "why your first two years' operations have been a disaster?"

The Frenchman frowned. "The word disaster does not seem to me to – "

"In 1870, according to Monsieur Bauche's figures, only 486 vessels made the passage from one sea to the other. You expected many more, did you not?"

"That figure is completely out of date."

"I know. The tally in 1871 was 765."

"Allow me to point out that over a thousand ships passed through last year."

"Yes, 1,082. In terms of tonnage, however, even that figure fell far short of your expectations."

He looked disconcerted. Then, adopting a different tone, he showed me into an armchair at the other end of the room and invited me to join him in a cup of coffee.

"You see that propeller-driven ship over there?" he said thoughtfully. "That's where our true business lies. There still aren't enough steamships in the world, unfortunately, and the Franco-Prussian War has delayed the process of modernization."

"Is it true," I asked, "that nearly one vessel in three ran aground in the Canal during the first year?"

"It is, but accidents are becoming fewer every quarter. Some of our pilots have yet to master the manoeuvres necessary to cope with the current and the bends. They only have a single propeller, and their rudder-blade is too small."

An hour later the chief engineer accompanied me to the door of the office building and invited me to call on him again if necessary. I walked back to the Place Champollion filled with pride and satisfaction.

If anyone failed to be impressed by my journalistic status, it was Nada. The *Sémaphore d'Alexandrie* meant nothing to her. I was nonplussed at first, then delighted to realize that my presence in Ismailia pleased her for other reasons. With me there, she almost felt back in the bosom of the family, as witness her occasional tendency to address me in Arabic, a language she no longer spoke except with servants or street vendors.

"In this place, *mon cher*, you're in France!" I was told by Félix Percheron, Étienne's colleague, during a dinner party given by the director of dredging.

Étienne was busy all day. The rhythm of my own days was governed by my appointments, which left me time to chat with Nada. She showed me around the town, and it thrilled me to walk at her side. People doubtless mistook me for her brother, but I imagined myself her beau. We paid two visits to *La Belle Jardinière*, where I helped her to choose a Chinese tunic in silk and an English frock for little Eugénie.

Ismailia possessed a bathing establishment beside Lake Timsah open to ladies in the mornings and gentlemen in the afternoons. Nada invited me to join her there at lunchtime. I turned up a little earlier than foreseen, my interview with the hospital's chief medical officer having been curtailed, and caught a distant glimpse of her emerging from the water with two other young women. They were laughing and uttering childish little shrieks, their wet bathing dresses clinging to their bodies. Then, very quickly, they disappeared from my field of view.

Nada's hair was still damp when she left the baths half-an-hour later. Her face was glowing and her full lips, devoid of rouge, merged with her olive skin in a way that set my pulses racing.

[132]

We returned to the house, where the manservant brought us a light lunch on the terrace. It was hot, and Nada, who had automatically slipped off her shoes, idly rubbed her foot against the leg of her wickerwork chair. Nada's bare foot . . . She yawned, eyelids drooping. Swimming had tired her. I smiled at her, feeling slightly dizzy and capable of any mad impulse.

"Heavens, I've some sewing to do!" she said abruptly, getting up. "My gown will never be ready for tonight . . . "

The party given by the director of dredging, to which we had been invited, enabled me to observe Ismailia's French community at my leisure. Everyone knew each other and assembled under similar circumstances several times a month. I heard numerous allusive little jokes whose meaning escaped me. Nada, looking radiant in a pink satin gown that left her shoulders bare, seemed very much at ease among these Europeans. The shy Syrian girl of old had become a self-assured young woman whose effect on men was plain to see. I didn't care for the way in which several of them kissed her hand on arrival.

A small group of men had gathered in the smoking room. I was welcomed there by our host, who introduced me as a journalist from the *Sémaphore d'Alexandrie*. This drew one or two exclamations of surprise, then conversation resumed and I was forgotten.

Everyone's attention was focused on a person of far greater interest: a member of the Company's main board who had arrived from Paris the day before. The news wasn't good, he said. The shareholders, who had not received a dividend since the Canal opened, were up in arms – indeed, some of them were demanding that the Company go into liquidation.

"The loan raised only five million francs," said the director. "We ought to increase our transit charges."

"So let's increase them!" Félix Percheron called out. "Our customers are taxed on their net tonnage, which is a swindle."

"You're quite right," the Parisian replied. "We tried to charge the shipping lines a rate based on gross tonnage, and the courts upheld us, but the British, Italian and Austrian shipowners have demanded that the matter be submitted to international arbitration."

"Oh no, not international arbitration! It was our beloved Napoleon III who ruled against the use of forced labour, don't forget."

The discussion was cut short by applause and a babble of women's voices. Everyone was summoned to the drawing room to listen to an Offenbach duet with piano accompaniment.

"Not again!" growled Percheron, who was clearly tiring of the limited repertoire, and he went off to smoke a cigar on the terrace.

After this little recital, which was much applauded, the ladies begged the new inspector of telegraphs, a lively young man, to tell their fortunes. Excitedly, they peeled off their gloves in turn. When Nada surrendered her pretty palm to the pomaded Parisian, he explored every line of it, and then, in a portentous voice, announced, "Mademoiselle, I foresee a wedding within the year."

All the ladies burst out laughing, and the sheepish fortune-teller was loudly informed that Madame Mancelle was a mother twice over.

On the eve of my departure Étienne suggested a walk after dinner. He usually went for a half-hour stroll along the freshwater canal at dusk. "Those twilight excursions are his only form of self-indulgence," Nada had told me with a smile.

It was a delightful evening, the sky moonless but liberally sprinkled with stars. Several couples were promenading among the rose bushes in the Place Champollion.

"Do you know of a single town in the world that tends its plants as well as our Venice of the desert?" Étienne asked me.

My knowledge of the world's towns was very limited. Here, a waterer daily toured the streets in charge of a small cart fitted with a spigot and drawn by a camel. This strange vehicle was by way of being emblematic of Ismailia. I promised myself that I would mention it in my article. I would also mention the undelivered letters displayed under glass outside the post office. Their addressees had left for India or Europe. Perhaps they would read them some day, already faded, when putting in once more at this seaport in the middle of the desert . . .

We walked as far as the freshwater canal. The banks, on which two rows of trees had been planted, were unlit. Étienne, in high spirits, extolled the merits of Ismailia's desert air. He strode on ahead of us, stretching his arms like a gymnast and doing breathing exercises.

Nada paused to watch a lantern-lit boat pass by. The crew hailed us in broken French. We replied in fluent Arabic, which delighted them. One of them broke into a love song. It faded as the boat glided off, heading for Suez.

"Ya layli, ya 'ayni . . ."

Nada turned to me. There were tears in her eyes. Without thinking, I leant towards her and kissed her moist eyelids. I felt her breath on my cheek, inhaled the scent of her skin, brushed her parted lips with the back of my hand, and felt her tremble. But she released herself and we walked on in silence. Étienne, far ahead of us by now, was still at his breathing exercises.

5

Need I say that the Suez Canal took second place in my thoughts on the train back to Cairo? I thought only of Nada.

We parted without making the slightest reference to the previous night's cataclysm: a few banal words of gratitude on my part, a most insistent invitation on hers to pay Ismailia another visit, and all in front of her smiling husband, who was holding the reins of his tilbury . . .

"You're looking odd," Alexandre remarked when I came home.

I shrugged, torn between the fear of giving myself away and an almost overpowering desire to talk about Nada. But my clumsy oaf of a brother was the last person to confide in. Confide what, anyway? I was wholly ignorant of Nada's feelings. Hadn't she simply yielded to a momentary impulse, a sudden, potent surge of emotion? But I could recall other features of my stay: her mealtime exclamations in Arabic, unintelligible to Étienne and underlined by the humorous twinkle in her eye, or the way in which she'd whispered "I'm so happy!" in my ear at *La Belle Jardinière*, a remark that had no obvious bearing on the length of poplin in her hand. What *could* I have told Alexandre?

I was the centre of attention at our family lunches for two Sundays in succession. Questions rang out from all directions.

"Did you go near the Canal?" asked Aunt Angéline, spraying herself with essence of bergamot. "I hear the sunlight's so strong, you can see the water steaming."

"What nonsense!" exclaimed Uncle Alfred. "If the water were steaming, it would have evaporated. On the contrary, I've been told that the water from the two seas combines to chill the Canal. One of my customers has even seen blocks of ice floating on the surface, and that's a fact!"

My cousin Rizqallah listened abstractedly to this climatic debate. All that interested him was the Canal's financial temperature. His employer must have had some interest in the business, either as a shareholder or as a user.

"Is it true," he asked me, "that the Company is proposing to base its transit charges on gross tonnage instead of net tonnage?"

He looked put out when I replied in the affirmative, or perhaps it was only a pretence to make himself seem important. Lolo, sitting opposite us, was scratching his head with a puzzled expression.

I had handed Albin Balanvin a long article crammed with detailed information and almost devoid of comment. Having read and reread it, he finally muttered, with a look of disgust, "This is just reportage."

I'd been afraid of a remark like that, but how could I have written the piece any differently? I had neither the ability nor the desire to "do a Balanvin". It was indeed reportage. I had looked and listened, learned things and taken pleasure in setting them down on paper. Was that a crime?

Balanvin was nonetheless forced to concede that, despite one or two platitudes, my article formed a coherent whole. Everything was adequately strung together: descriptions, statistics, quotations, explanations. While making no attempt to embellish the current situation, I concluded that the figures were moving in the right direction, and that the Canal would sooner or later meet its targets.

The *Sémaphore*'s correspondent deleted a few sentences here and there, altered a word or two, and then said, "This article merits a signature. What pseudonym do you want to adopt?"

I chose the ultra-French name Armand de Maubuisson, which made him smile.

A pseudonym was doubly essential, in fact, because I wasn't an accredited journalist and had the misfortune to bear an oriental name. Maxime might have been acceptable, but not Touta.

I owed my first name to our patriarch, the great Maximos. My father, who much admired him, had made his acquaintance in 1849, some months before I was born.

The circumstances of their meeting were exceptional. My father and some other Greek Catholics from Egypt had travelled to Aleppo, in Syria, to pay their respects to the patriarch. The latter had returned from Constantinople in triumph, having finally, after more than a century, obtained the Sultan's civil recognition of our Church. Thanks to that historic decree, we would no longer be dependent on the Greek Orthodox patriarchate and subjected to the snubs and persecution of a clergy that had made us pay dearly for our allegiance to the Pope. In Syria our priests could at last exercise their ministry without being obliged to do so in secret. We would have our own courts and our own taxes, because Maximos III Mazloum had been officially designated head of "the Romeo-Catholic nation".

Aleppo, the native city in which he had been forbidden to set foot for forty years, gave him a triumphal reception. The cathedral, illuminated by countless candelabra and wreathed in clouds of incense, was packed with weeping Greek Catholics.

The leading inhabitants of the Salibiya district gave a number of parties in the next few days. This was where my father made the acquaintance of a young silk merchant from Damascus. A handsome man with a ready smile, Georges Sahel spoke admiringly of his only daughter, Nada, then aged two. One of the priests present misunderstood the thrust of his remarks.

"Monsieur Sahel," he broke in, "doubtless the good Lord meant to punish you for some sin or other. Rest assured, though, His mercy is great. Next time he'll give you a boy."

The merchant from Damascus exchanged a look of amusement with the doctor from Egypt. They discovered in the course of conversation that they were distant cousins. This sowed the seeds of a friendship that Georges Sahel sustained by paying two or three business trips to Cairo in the years that followed.

There was nothing worldly about the patriarch. He spoke little at the parties held in his honour, scarcely touched the food, and avoided looking at the lady of the house. Maximos was very distant towards women in general, and would only grant them an audience from behind a grille. An austere man, Maximos slept on the floor and always wore an iron chain next his skin by way of penitence. My father thought he looked very tired.

It should be added that the patriarch had been struggling all his life, initially in the bosom of his own Church, where some suspected him of heretical tendencies, and then against the Greek Orthodox patriarchate, which aimed to bring the Greek Catholics to heel. He settled in Constantinople with a view to approaching the Sultan. He was prevented from doing so for years, but his iron determination, his diplomatic finesse, and his knowledge of Turkish, Arabic, French and Italian enabled him to obtain the celebrated firman at last.

Some months after my father returned to Egypt the atmosphere at Aleppo rapidly deteriorated. One night, several Christian houses on the outskirts were looted and their occupants beaten up. It was feared that the Salibiya district, where the various bishoprics were situated, would be attacked in its turn. Our patriarch had to take refuge with a Greek Catholic dignitary, but not before he had gone to the cathedral and consumed the Eucharistic bread and wine to preserve them from desecration.

The sun had just risen when gangs of Muslims appeared outside Salibiya. They broke down the gates, looted the churches and set them on fire. Maximos managed to get away, but only by disguising himself as a Muslim woman. I often think how bizarre it must have looked: an austere churchman with a veil over his head, perhaps with a necklace and bangles as well . . .

The governor of Aleppo was determined to ensure the safety of a patriarch who had just been acknowledged by the Sultan. He procured him an escort of five carriages for his escape from the city, but this time Maximos was obliged to disguise himself as a European general. Our patriarch reached Antioch in this get-up. Then he boarded a ship bound for Beirut, where he arrived exhausted after encountering a violent storm.

My father saw him again in Egypt some years later, on the occasion of the opening of the Alexandria–Cairo railway. Maximos took the first train accompanied by sundry distinguished figures including Ferdinand de Lesseps, but he was very weak and permanently afflicted with a severe pain in the leg.

"You should rest, Beatitude," my father told him, "and give up horseriding."

His advice was ignored. Sensing that he was near death, Maximos redoubled his efforts to build churches, fend off the Greek Orthodox, combat the Latinizing proselytism of European missionaries, and thwart the intrigues of such of his own bishops as aspired to succeed him. He died at Alexandria in terrible pain, after a urinary occlusion lasting several days. This was in the high summer of August 1855. His body was conveyed to Cairo by train. I was too young to attend his funeral at the church of Darb al-Geneinah. The heat was stifling, apparently, and the choristers were mopping their brows with silk handkerchiefs. As for Aunt Angéline, she moaned incessantly and threatened to expire.

"But for Maximos Mazloum," my father often said, "we would still be pariahs."

I sometimes think of my celebrated namesake with a touch of affection.

6

My article appeared the following month. It earned me another success in the family circle, immediately followed by a tirade on my choice of pseudonym. Was Armand de Maubuisson sufficiently French? There were two conflicting schools of thought on the subject, just as there were on the way *kubayba* should be served.

Although one or two paragraphs had been cut at Alexandria, the article overjoyed me. I read and reread it with infinite satisfaction.

Étienne Mancelle, whose reaction I had been dreading, wrote soon afterwards to congratulate me and let me know that the piece had been generally well received at Ismailia. I delightedly passed this news on to Albin Balanvin.

"Compliments aren't always a good sign," he growled.

The *Sémaphore* subsequently received two or three letters fiercely condemning my total ignorance of the Suez Canal's operating procedures and accusing me of a wish to blight the Company's reputation. Balanvin was greatly amused by the distress they caused me.

"Believe me, my young friend, you'll get far worse than that before you're done. In our trade, one has to learn to take some hard knocks."

He never spoke a truer word.

In the next few months the *Sémaphore d'Alexandrie* received two temporary bans on publication because of vitriolic articles written by its Cairo correspondent. But Balanvin, who enjoyed the backing of his editorial board, was undeterred. Not only did readers clamour for his articles, but advertisers were insistent that their publicity material should henceforth appear on the same page.

Balanvin took a very keen interest in Egypt's finances. One of his pieces, which attracted great attention, denounced the khedive's policy of public indebtedness and almost openly accused him of leading the country into bankruptcy. Our friend had never gone so far before. To my astonishment, the *Sémaphore* escaped suspension.

It was eleven o'clock the following Monday night when someone knocked on our door. I was surprised to find the journalist's black servant standing there with a storm lantern in his hand.

"What does your master want at this hour?" I asked him.

"It's the doctor I've come for," he said in a tremulous voice.

He had initially run to fetch Dr Rigaudier, but the amateur Egyptologist – the one who was said to bury the living and disinter the dead – had not yet returned from a scientific expedition to Wadi Natroun. The terrified man had then thought of summoning my father.

We reached Albin's side fifteen minutes later. He was sprawled, unconscious, on his big brass bed. A bloodstained sheet was draped over the window ledge. On the floor, broken into several pieces, was his cane with the mother-of-pearl knob.

"They escaped through the window when they heard me come home," the servant told us. "There were two of them."

I was outraged and wanted to summon the police, but my father, having sent for hot water, clean cloths and a bottle of arrack, asked me to help him instead. We carefully divested Albin of his jacket and shirt. His skin, white as alabaster, was criss-crossed with big, dark welts.

He recovered consciousness by degrees, thanks to the arrack. "What splendid copy for a piece in the *Sémaphore*," he muttered feebly, but he couldn't muster a smile.

The incident caused a big sensation in Cairo as well as in Alexandria. The *Sémaphore* published an indignant editorial, and the French consul expressed his outrage to the Egyptian authorities. The khedive personally ordered an investigation, but it came to nothing.

My father had been correct in diagnosing two cracked ribs and a fractured leg. Balanvin's assailants had also gone to work on his wrists as if meaning to deprive him of the use of a pen. Our friend would be immobilized and confined to the house for several weeks. Not being the type to practise journalism in his bedroom, he would normally have had to discontinue his articles. But how could he remain silent after such an attempt to intimidate him?

One afternoon, when I was paying him a visit, he asked if I would help him out. My response went without saying. It never even occurred to me that I would be running a risk by collaborating with the *Sémaphore*'s correspondent.

"Of course," he said, "you won't be able to attend all the parties I'm invited to by people hoping to buy me. Influential figures don't know you, so they won't confide in you, but at least you'll be able to keep your eyes and ears open and bring me a few whiffs of the air beyond these walls."

In accordance with Balanvin's instructions, I promptly went hunting. Every two or three days I brought him the results of my research, which were not invariably conclusive. My work at the bank suffered, needless to say — in fact journalism almost earned me instant dismissal when, having claimed to be very ill, I was one day spotted in Ezbekiyah Square by the deputy chief cashier. He was a corrupt individual, fortunately, so I purchased his silence for the price of half a month's salary.

It was fascinating to work with Balanvin and see how he transformed the information I'd gleaned here and there by supplementing it with his visitors' anecdotes, or simply with his own knowledge and intuition. One seemingly anodyne fact, when brought into conjunction with two or three others, would suddenly take on its full significance. It was like assembling the pieces of a jigsaw puzzle and fitting them together.

I discovered the joy of ferreting things out and getting to the bottom of them. Balanvin was an unrivalled, ever observant investigator. Nothing escaped him. He seemed to know everything about everyone at any given moment. I felt constantly subjected to his merciless gaze, which could be terribly scathing. Always a trifle on my guard, I weighed my words a dozen times before uttering them.

It seemed natural to me, having gathered some facts, to marshal them and then to set them out in an article as clearly as possible. Balanvin, for his part, turned facts into a "work of art". The material metamorphosed under his pen. It almost changed its nature, becoming impudent and provocative. I guessed that I would never be able to write like that, but at least my contact with such a brilliant writer was teaching me to love words and shun platitudes. Clarity was not the same as insipidity.

There came a day when the *Sémaphore*'s Cairo correspondent strode into his drawing room armed with a new cane with a mother-of-pearl knob. "Journalists are more than mere pen-pushers," he told me sharply, "they're witnesses." Then, running his hand gently over the marble youth's chest, he went on, "We're witnesses, advocates, prosecutors. Sometimes, too, we're tried, convicted, and punished."

7

FROM OUR CAIRO CORRESPONDENT
To the Editor:

20 August 1873

We have just emerged, sir, from three days of spectacular festivities held in celebration of the firman which His Majesty the Sultan deigned to grant His Highness the Khedive. There were triumphal arches and illuminations everywhere. The government is estimated to have spent one million francs on this occasion.

The firman establishes Egyptian sovereignty. From now on, Isma'il Pasha is free to raise loans, maintain armed forces of unlimited size, pass laws, and conclude treaties with foreign powers. Egypt remains an integral part of the Ottoman Empire, to be sure, but no other province enjoys such a measure of independence.

No one ever got something for nothing, you will say, and you are right. In order to gain such privileges the viceroy has had to make considerable efforts and substantial concessions. His subjects will doubtless be grateful to him.

One man has played an essential part in all these negotiations. I refer to Abraham Bey, the khedive's representative in Constantinople, who never ceased, throughout the years, to plead his master's case in the most persuasive manner. That astute Armenian, a brother-in-law of Nubar Pasha, the minister of foreign affairs, succeeded in winning over numerous Ottoman officials and several newspapers. At the same time, he fulfilled the wishes of His Imperial Majesty with the greatest discretion.

Everyone knows that Sultan 'Abdal 'Aziz is a lover of animals in general and birds in particular — an enthusiasm that does him credit. Well, sir, I can assure you that Abraham Bey did everything humanly possible to present His Majesty with the finest, healthiest and rarest specimens obtainable.

Although Abraham Bey's knowledge of ornithology was on the meagre side, he was fortunate enough to come across an excellent catalogue, illustrated by a Parisian artist, which he purchased and presented to His Majesty. The latter's eye was drawn to three remarkable species of birds: the barnacle goose, the crowned goura, and the radiant lolophore. The khedive's representative promptly ordered a certain number of them despite their high price. The Sultan was gracious enough to accept them as a gift, but he soon noticed that his aviaries were in poor condition and broached the subject to Abraham Bey. The latter wired the khedive suggesting that some new aviaries be ordered from Paris. Isma'il Pasha instructed him to proceed, knowing that the bill would be some 100,000 francs.

In the months that followed the Sultan extended his solicitude to other varieties of birds, so Abraham Bey bought some Amherst pheasants and bronze crows in Europe. Later, he moved heaven and earth to obtain some live couroucous — without success, alas. His Majesty, who was tactful enough not to insist, contented himself with some tricoloured budgerigars, some collared doves, and a score of arguses specially imported from India.

I would not like you to think, sir, that Sultan 'Abdal 'Aziz restricts his interest to birds alone. On more than one occasion the khedive's representative was prevailed on to obtain him some race horses or dogs of a very rare breed to be found only in London. His Majesty also expressed a wish to be presented with some livestock. When apprised of this request, the khedive assembled 400 sheep of various colours, 50 rams from Fayoum, and numerous cows from Menoufiya Province, and chartered a special ship, the al-Mansoura, to lay these gifts at His August Master's feet.

In readiness for his sojourn in Constantinople, Isma'il Pasha commissioned some major improvements to his estate at Emirghian. A special pavilion was built for the Sultan, who had promised to visit him there. The most costly materials were assembled for that purpose, and the embellishments that had been planned for the other buildings were cut back so as not to outshine His Imperial Majesty's quarters. For the estate as a whole, 30,000 electric globes and as many Chinese lanterns were ordered from Paris.

Isma'il Pasha arrived in Constantinople on 21st May, preceded by his reputation for generosity. All the city's senior officials hurried to Emirghian to welcome him. It was a veritable procession. The khedive expertly thanked each of those present in his own special way.

Received by the Sultan with conspicuous tact and benevolence, Isma'il Pasha reassured him of his filial sentiments and intimated that he was not unaware of the Sublime Porte's financial problems. Dare I suggest, sir, that the gift of 680,000 Turkish pounds he made on this occasion will accelerate the Sultan's endorsement of the celebrated firman?

Albin Balanvin

8

Isma'il the Magnificent balked at no financial sacrifice. That year he decided to marry off four of his children at once – Crown Prince Tewfiq included – and decreed that the festivities should continue for a full month.

I shall never forget those four weeks of splendour and extravagance. The presents destined for each of the young couples filled whole carriages protected by nets made of iron mesh. Escorted by soldiers in full-dress uniform, these carriages progressed through the streets of Cairo at a walking pace to enable us to marvel at the solid gold plate, the diamond-studded chibouks, and countless other precious objects.

Every evening, singers, dancers, jugglers, acrobats and clowns performed in front of the pink and green palace of Qasr al-'Aali, the queen mother's residence, where the four fiancées were temporarily accommodated. On the esplanade, refreshments were served free of charge to "all respectable persons", while hundreds of sheep, lambs, chickens and turkeys were distributed in working-class districts.

Nassif Bey, who was privileged to attend one of the four weddings with his wife, gave us a remarkable account of the proceedings. The queen mother, smothered in jewels, descended an immense staircase with crystal banisters, accompanied by slaves wielding outsize ostrich-feather fans. Next, the bride made her entrance between two rows of eunuchs, each bearing a lighted candelabrum. The guests jostled for the best places, the doors were closed. Then ladies of the court dipped into some big sacks filled with fine gold coins and threw handfuls of them in the direction of the persons present.

"They rained down on us, those golden suns, with a sound like leaves rustling in the wind," said Nassif Bey. His wife, who picked up fifteen of the coins, proposed to have them made into a necklace.

But the nuptials of the khedive's four sons were to be outdone by another wedding – one that was not only far more important in our eyes but infinitely more alarming: that of Rizqallah. My cousin informed his dumb-founded family by letter that he had become engaged to a Mademoiselle Aghion.

A Jewess! Aunt Angéline almost fainted and had to be revived with a large dose of arrack.

"A Jewess!" she kept repeating. "He's going to marry a Jewess!"

Lolo, looking appalled, debated the steps to be taken. Would Rizqallah still be socially acceptable? Should they ask our priest to say a special Mass, or even invite the bishop to come and renew his blessing on our houses?

Alfred Falaki, hand on heart, declared, "I've only one quarrel with the Jews: the way they carry off little children with a view to slaughtering them and drinking their blood."

My father cast his eyes up to heaven. Where this subject was concerned, he knew that a refutation from God himself would be futile.

So Rizqallah was going to marry a Jewess . . . His father, Boctor, was reputed to have a weak heart, so the family dreaded his reaction. They were quickly reassured: the old rogue knew that the Aghions were one of the wealthiest families in Alexandria. Having uttered a few oaths for form's sake, he readily reconciled himself to the misfortune that had overtaken the eldest of his thirteen offspring. It was no longer a question of whether Boctor Touta would accept the Aghions, but whether the Aghions, who were bound to be persons of refinement and distinction, would fall over backwards on meeting Boctor Touta.

Rizqallah's audacity impressed me. Without going so far as to suppose that he was marrying for love – my cousin never based his decisions on such flimsy considerations – I couldn't exclude the possibility that emotion had played its part. Perhaps the geographical context should be taken into account. Alexandrian society differed from that of Cairo. What smote us like an earthquake might be no more, in Alexandria, than a fleeting scandal. In that highly cosmopolitan city the relations between the various communities obeyed a very complex chemistry. Unexpected links could be forged between people of the same social standing, and, since Rizqallah had the knack of rising in the world . . . He was already one of those Alexandrians who, when boarding a train to Cairo, said grandly, "I'm going to Egypt."

The fact remains that his marriage enriched Aunt Angéline's vocabulary. There had been "the Maronite" in the person of my mother and "the orphan" in that of Nada. Now we had "the Jewess", who would keep tongues wagging for years to come. Not only because she was Jewish, but, above all, because she was wealthy.

How relieved I would have been, six or seven years earlier, to learn that Rizqallah was getting married! He could have married anyone he liked – a Maronite, a Copt, a Jewess, even a negress from Darfour – as long as Nada escaped the lure of his white suit.

Now, I couldn't have cared less about his marriage plans. The woman I loved belonged to someone else. She lived a long way off, in a desert where roses grew. It would be too dangerous to go and see her, or even to write to her. She had let me kiss her moist eyelids for the space of a sob. I clung to that moment. Perhaps she loved me . . . Better to nurse that illusion than risk being rejected by her for ever.

9

Alfred Falaki had been engaged in legal proceedings for five long years. He was suing the entire world, or almost, because the four villains who had burgled his shop during the celebrations held to mark the opening of the Suez Canal were of four different nationalities: Egyptian, French, Italian, and Greek. Their arrest – a pure stroke of luck – had led to the recovery of the bulk of the stolen objects from a stable in Shubra. Still missing, however, were a score of watches and clocks whose return my uncle was vehemently demanding, together with compensation for damage inflicted during the break-in. Justice was taking its course.

The Egyptian appeared before a native court presided over by a former storeman at the arsenal. The latter, who was practically illiterate, had a reputation for integrity. It was rumoured that at a previous trial, having received a substantial *bakshish* from the plaintiff and an even more substantial *bakshish* from the defendant, he had acquitted the latter but returned the other's money down to the last piastre. Uncle Alfred, who had heard this story, slipped a few banknotes into his hand and won the case.

The remaining three burglars were another matter. The native courts had no jurisdiction over them, so each had to be tried by his consular court.

The Italian promptly disappeared, and it was thought that he had left Egypt. His consul, who was genuinely apologetic, offered Alfred Falaki a *mazbout* coffee and launched into a long, moving account of the difficulties of his work. My uncle emerged with tears in his eyes, feeling that he had made a friend – even, perhaps, a customer.

The Frenchman was tried fairly quickly, thanks to some string-pulling by Rizqallah. He was sentenced to reimburse Uncle Alfred for half the missing items, but he lodged an appeal. The case was duly referred to a court of higher instance in France, and Alfred was still waiting for news of it five years later.

As for the Greek, he was a notorious rogue already charged with several other crimes. Although only too willing to punish him, the Greek consul adroitly intimated to my uncle that his wife adored jewellery. The next time Alfred came to see him, he handed him a little box containing a pair of silver earrings. The consul hummed and hawed, then pocketed them. Just then, Uncle Alfred caught sight of a carriage clock on the desk that bore a remarkable resemblance to one of the pieces stolen from his shop. Instinctively, he put out his hand to examine it.

"No, no, don't touch it!" cried the consul. "I never sell family heirlooms. I don't even want to hear your offer. Say no more, I beg you, it would distress me too much. And now, please go . . . "

And, seizing my uncle's hand, he promised to look into his case and showed him out.

Some weeks later it transpired that the Greek crook had changed his nationality: he was now a Spaniard. Legal proceedings would have to be reinstituted from scratch. Weary of the whole affair, Alfred Falaki decided to kiss his clocks goodbye.

If the judicial reform of 1875 had been introduced a few years earlier, Uncle Alfred would have been able to obtain satisfaction. It was Khedive Isma'il's great achievement – his sole success, when all is said and done. I'm not sorry the *Sémaphore d'Alexandrie* championed it. I'm even less sorry that the battle enabled me to take an additional step into journalism. The "Falaki trial", as we called it in the family, had sensitized me to judicial matters. I even venture to say that it was I who convinced Albin Balanvin of the absurdity of the prevailing legal system.

"I'm bored to death by the subject," he had told me in 1874, during the months that followed his convalescence. "If it amuses you, write me some short pieces about it. Personally, I won't do a thing."

I think he rather regretted it later on. Having opted out and left me free to acquire some competence in the field, he found himself wrong-footed when judicial reform became the burning issue between Egypt, the European powers, and the Sublime Porte.

In Alexandria, the *Sémaphore* cobbled together some rather pedantic editorials in favour of reform. As for Armand de Maubuisson, he occasionally managed to slip in some short articles couched in the simplest and clearest language possible. My arguments were subtly presented with a view to reassuring the numerous European readers who were alarmed by the prospective changes.

"Try to charm them, and you'll rub them up the wrong way," growled Balanvin. "Journalists always try to please their readers. You must learn to *displease* them, my young friend."

I listened to him, rather at a loss, but I couldn't manage to argue aggressively in favour of what I found self-evident. It was absurd that foreigners should escape the jurisdiction of local courts and be subject to that of seventeen or eighteen different consulates.

"Absurd? Why absurd?" protested Cousin Rizqallah. "From the racial and religious aspect, Egypt is too diverse a country to have a single legal system, don't you see that? Besides, a semi-civilized country can't lay claim to a modern legal system."

The "French dependant" cited an additional argument – one that must have been whispered in his ear by Monsieur Xavier-Saillard:

"Enterprising and generous Europeans have settled in Egypt and invested substantial sums there. They did so on the strength of long-established treaties and conventions. You don't change the rules in the middle of a game. In any case," added Rizqallah, "you must stop writing about the subject. It's ridiculous."

I modestly confined myself to citing individual cases and underlining the system's lack of coherence. I only once ventured a comment, part of which was published.

> Is it acceptable that a crime committed jointly by persons of several different nationalities should give rise to separate verdicts, and thus to different penalties? It can be in no one's interest to allow such a system to continue. Possibly valid for the protection of a handful of Europeans in the time of Muhammad Ali, it is no longer justified today, when scores of thousands of them have settled in this country. Being far more numerous now, foreigners have far more opportunities to commit crimes and go to law with Egyptians or each other. Their privileges are redounding to their disadvantage. Egyptians refuse to do business with such

favoured individuals, and commercial relations are restricted in consequence.
Foreigners have provided themselves with a defensive legal system, a breastplate.
But, like all breastplates, this one restricts their movements . . .

Two weeks later, with an air of disdain, Balanvin handed me a note from Nubar Pasha inviting me to call on him. The minister of foreign affairs, a long-standing advocate of judicial reform, had been impressed by Armand de Maubuisson's article and wished to congratulate him on it. I stared at the engraved card unable to believe my eyes, flushed with excitement. Balanvin shrugged his shoulders.

"Beware of that Armenian. Nubar has served four viceroys in succession. He's a chameleon, and artful as a wagonload of monkeys."

I made my way to the minister's residence brimming with pride. I was kept waiting for a very long time in an ante-room adorned with a big statue of the Virgin Mary. Nubar Pasha finally received me and shook hands. He realized I wasn't French from my accent. Although this must have annoyed him, he was too good a diplomat to show it and invited me to join him on the sofa.

"Sit on my right," he said informally. "I'm a little hard of hearing in the other ear. I've smoked too heavily for years."

This preamble made me feel a trifle more at ease. "Ah, he pulled the deaf trick on you!" was Balanvin's comment when I described the interview.

Deaf or not, the old diplomat knew how to make himself heard. I realized later that he hadn't summoned me there simply for the pleasure of congratulating me. If he revealed an unpublished detail of his plan for mixed courts, it was obviously with a view to my mentioning it in a future article. Nubar had the knack of sending signals to European powers and awaiting their reactions, only to deny it all later.

This was exactly what happened here.

The minister of foreign affairs restated his plan in broad outline. It was that all civil and commercial cases involving persons of different nationalities should be heard by special tribunals to be known as mixed courts. But he added a new proviso: although European magistrates would be in the majority in such courts, they would become Egyptian civil servants from the date of their appointment onwards.

I quickly made an article of this, and Nubar just as quickly issued a denial. I was not only staggered but doubly humiliated because the editor of the *Sémaphore* wired Balanvin demanding to know the identity of the idiot who signed himself Maubuisson.

The Egyptian government's official scheme was made public a few weeks later. It embodied what I had written, word for word. The *Sémaphore*'s editor devoted a leader to it but omitted to congratulate the idiot in Cairo. As far as that gentleman was concerned, I didn't exist.

IO

I can still picture myself opening the front door, in response to several vigorous knocks, and being confronted by an army officer in full-dress uniform. What with his tarboosh, his frogged, steel-grey tunic, and the sword at his side, Walid al-Ahlawi was unrecognizable. No one would have associated him with the young officer who had come to ask my father to teach him to read eleven years earlier, still less with the weeping lieutenant who had been publicly reduced to the ranks in the Place des Consuls.

Walid had spent three years in the Sudan and Darfour – three hellish years which he found it impossible to describe, not knowing where to begin. The colonization of those wild regions under the command of British officers engaged at great expense by the khedive had at least earned him the rank of *bimbashi*, as his epaulettes proudly proclaimed.

Spontaneously, we sat down around the same table where he had begun to decipher the alphabet. My father eyed his former pupil with a trace of affection.

"When I was young," he said, "we knew nothing about Black Africa. At medical school the map pinned up in the lecture hall showed it as a big, blank space. Each of us populated it with the products of our imagination. I put in tigers, lions . . . "

"It was better that way," Walid said gloomily.

The campaign against the slave trade had been a complete failure. Walid had realized this on the way back to Khartoum when his boat passed three *dahabiyas* filled with slaves bound for Sennar. To him, Black Africa was an evil memory – one he was striving to forget.

Walid didn't really relax until he saw Om Mahmud bring in the coffee.

He addressed her in familiar terms, but our maidservant was struck dumb by the sight of this major in uniform. She told us later that he reminded her of Mahmud, the mysterious son whom no one had ever seen. She didn't sweep the room for three days after Walid's visit — her way of bringing about the return of a person she liked.

I myself was not unaware of Walid al-Ahlawi's appeal. A dark-skinned man of thirty-three, he gave off a disturbing aura of strength. One felt that he had been moulded by all the ordeals he had undergone since childhood, and that behind his sphinx-like expression lurked the seeds of rebellion.

"You should have taught me Turkish, doctor," he told my father. "Every other branch of government has been made to use Arabic in recent years. Why should the army be excluded from this universal rule? We're commanded by Ottomans who compel us to speak their language and utterly despise us."

Walid's words reminded me of a remark of the khedive's, voiced in private and reported by Balanvin. Someone had asked him why he didn't simply break with Constantinople and proclaim Egyptian independence.

"It would be suicide," the khedive replied. "We're just a sprinkling of Ottomans in a sea of Arabs."

I refrained from informing Walid of this remark. It wasn't for us Christians to meddle in a dispute between Muslims. However, I did mention in the course of conversation that I was working for a French-language weekly based in Alexandria. The *Sémaphore* meant nothing to him. He merely growled, "Alexandria is a city where Europeans make the law."

I pointed out that the law had just been reformed, at least in part. Walid simply shrugged. He didn't appear to cherish any high hopes of the mixed courts whose establishment had preoccupied us so greatly. I realized that a gulf separated him from the readers of the *Sémaphore*. I myself was midway between them. I was a kind of intermediary, but an intermediary incapable of serving as a link.

"I couldn't have taught you Turkish," my father said with a smile. "Not many of us *Shawam* know the language."

And he went on to tell Walid how his grandfather, Antoun Touta, born at Aleppo in Syria, had settled in Egypt in 1740 or thereabouts. Walid politely asked a few questions, but I'm not sure the subject interested him much. In any case, how could we have told him everything and explained it all to him?

Antoun was one of a generation of Christian immigrants who had found peace, and in many cases prosperity, on the banks of the Nile. They succeeded in adapting to a country wrapped in medieval slumber for centuries and governed in an utterly chaotic manner by rival Mamelukes. Having become a highly successful businessman, Antoun landed the coveted post of customs inspector of the town of Rosetta.

The Toutas of the second generation were less fortunate, or less politically astute. In the belief that it behoved them to greet Bonaparte's soldiers as liberators, their carried their enthusiasm too far. My grandfather became General Menou's interpreter, but one of his brothers, 'Aziz Touta, enrolled in a small army of Christian volunteers in the service of the occupying power. Rather than be lynched, 'Aziz was compelled to leave Egypt with the French when they withdrew in 1801. He became one of the Emperor's Mamelukes and followed him to Waterloo. My grandfather, who was less pro-French, chose to remain in Egypt. His house was burnt down, but he survived.

The third generation grew up in the shadow of Muhammad Ali, grateful to the founder of the Egyptian dynasty for having done away with the Mamelukes and protected minorities. My father's youth was coloured by this process of relaxation and modernization, which was assisted by the country's former enemies. It was the French who reorganized the army, the public health service, and the irrigation system, and it was people like us who acted as intermediaries thanks to our command of languages and our skill at dealing with people.

Three generations: the immigrant, the renegade, the citizen . . . Not that this prevented us Toutas of the fourth generation from remaining *Shawam*, jealous of our origins and our traditions.

II

In the weeks following his visit to our house, Walid al-Ahlawi found another reason to inveigh against the khedive.

"Today he's selling the Canal, tomorrow he'll sell his palaces. The next thing you know, he'll be selling us . . ."

FROM OUR CAIRO CORRESPONDENT
To the Editor:

26 November 1875

As you can imagine, sir, people here talk of nothing but the incredible news that was made public yesterday. Incredible news but true: the British government has indeed purchased, for 100 million francs, the 177,642 shares in the Suez Canal held by the khedive. At the time of writing, the seven strongboxes containing those share certificates are no longer at the British consulate in Cairo. They have already been loaded aboard a steamship from India and will be in the vaults of the Bank of England by early next month.

The transaction was conducted in secret, with unprecedented speed and daring. Within a few days, the house of Rothschild in London placed four million pounds at Isma'il Pasha's disposal. The French government and its bankers could do nothing but fume and weep into their handkerchiefs. At another time, sir, Great Britain might have acted less unscrupulously and ridden roughshod over our susceptibilities in a less brutal manner. But France, having only just recovered from her setback in the Sudan, is still very sick.

So Britain now owns almost half the capital of the Suez Canal Company. Today, she can control the canal that was created without her and against her wishes. This is in the nature of things: having become the main users of that waterway, the British have every reason to want to determine the rules of transit themselves. In addition to this commercial consideration, there is the question of political security, since the Company holds the key to the door that leads straight to India. Hitherto, thanks to the cannon of Gibraltar, the British fleet had a guaranteed access to the Mediterranean. From now on it will have unrestricted access to the Red Sea.

"I want the Canal to belong to Egypt, not Egypt to the Canal," the khedive declared at the beginning of his reign. Today, sir, the Canal is half in British ownership. Who will own Egypt tomorrow?

While on the subject of quotations, allow me to recall the words of the late Lord Palmerston in 1859: "We have no need of Egypt. We want it no more than a sensible man who, having an estate in the north of England and a residence in the south, desires to own the inns on the way. His sole requirement is that the inns be well kept and permanently open, and that, when he comes their way, they will provide him with mutton cutlets and post horses."

But that was in 1859, sir. The Suez Canal did not yet exist; the British pronounced it impracticable. Today, it is open. And Lord Palmerston, God rest his soul, is dead!

Albin Balanvin

12

"Someone ought to go to Ismailia and record the reactions of the people on the isthmus," Balanvin told me. "Could you manage to get away for two or three days?"

I hurried off to inform the chief cashier of the Ottoman Bank that a beloved uncle of mine had died in Alexandria. Then, too pressed for time even to send anyone a telegram, I caught the very next train. With a little luck I would reach Ismailia that evening.

I had travelled there the first time, two years earlier, in a state of trepidation. I was justifiably nervous of the reception reserved for an amateur newspaperman, and my emotional turmoil at the prospect of seeing Nada for the first time since her marriage didn't help. This time the journalist alighted on the platform armed with far more self-assurance and a little notebook full of addresses. As for the lover . . . The unforeseen nature of this trip had absolved me from dwelling on that aspect of it.

The train was late, of course, and I didn't get to Ismailia until ten o'clock at night. The dimly lit station seemed even smaller than it had the first time. It was rather too late to turn up at the Mancelles. After depositing my bag at the Hôtel des Voyageurs, however, I couldn't resist walking to the Place Champollion. Light was seeping through the lilac shutters. I knocked. After a moment or two an upstairs window creaked open and Nada's head appeared. Her startled expression gave way to a smile.

"This *is* a surprise!" she said, kissing me on both cheeks. And, on learning the reason for my trip, "Étienne will be disappointed. He's away in Port Sa'id for the whole of this week."

"What a shame, I was counting on him to tell me what people here are thinking."

She sent the maidservant to bed and, without more ado, showed me into the kitchen, where she put a kettle on the stove.

"You want to know what the locals are thinking?" she said casually. "There are two schools of thought, I'd say. Some people, like Étienne's colleague Félix Percheron, are outraged by the sale of the khedive's shares. Less outraged at the British, incidentally, than at France's ineptitude. Then there are others, like my husband, who look on the bright side. They tell themselves it's better to have the British inside the Company than against it."

I was dumbfounded. In a couple of sentences, Nada had just summarized the gist of my future article. It had never occurred to me that she might be interested in such matters.

"I was looking through the latest issue of the *Sémaphore* yesterday," she said a little later, in the same casual tone. "It makes no mention of the negotiations between Isma'il and the British. Strange that no one, not even Balanvin, caught wind of what was afoot . . ."

So Nada now read the *Sémaphore*! I was touched but rather perturbed by the exacting way in which she seemed to scrutinize our articles. Then, pouring me some tea, she brought the conversation round to more conventional topics and asked after every member of the family. I couldn't help but tell her about the scene Alfred Falaki made on discovering a silver bangle from his shop adorning the ankle of Fawzia, the maidservant, and on hearing her pert explanation: "I was given it by *Khawaga* Lolo."

Nada laughed uproariously at my evocation of Lolo's nocturnal escapades. This broke the ice between us. She was once more the mischievous young girl who, at table long ago, had helped us torment my cousin in spats by spiriting away his fork.

She opened a tin box and offered me a sesame biscuit. I nibbled it slowly, like a child, relishing every grain. No meal had ever given me such pleasure.

We talked a little of her and Ismailia. She referred to her native Syria from time to time, but without labouring the subject. We also reminisced about Aunt Angéline, Rizqallah, Om Mahmud, Lolo, and Uncle Boctor and his oaths . . . It was after eleven-thirty. Propriety forbade me to stay any longer.

"I'll walk you back to the hotel," she said.

"But you can't make the return trip alone at this hour!"

"Why not? Étienne always says that Ismailia is the safest town in the world."

"The healthiest, the safest, the most practical, the most elegant . . . "

She started laughing again. Nada's laughter was irresistible.

We strolled across the Place Champollion, which was lit by new gas lamps. I discovered how warm a November night in Ismailia could be. "The warmest nights in the world," as Étienne would doubtless have said.

We walked slowly. I savoured every step, every moment, with a feeling of intense happiness. Nada was at my side, a mute but palpable presence. The hem of her gown brushed my leg occasionally.

The Hôtel des Voyageurs loomed up ahead — far too soon, it seemed.

"I'll walk you back," I said on impulse.

She smiled but raised no objection.

On the way back we passed some couples in the distance, evidently returning home from a dinner party. Several of the houses in which lights had been burning the first time we passed them were now in darkness.

"Tomorrow is Sunday, don't forget," Nada said. "All the Company's offices will be shut. You'll be able to meet some people after Mass. Oh, by the way, I'm invited to lunch at Félix Percheron's. Come with me, he'll be delighted to see you. Yes, yes, of course you must!"

A little crack in the roadway almost made her lose her balance. She caught hold of my arm, and we walked on like that.

The clock of the Roman Catholic church struck twelve. The palm trees quivered in a faint breeze.

"Let's walk a little further," she said.

I hadn't dared to suggest it. It was darker in the little streets around the square, where the verandas of the houses formed a sort of covered way. All at once, I took her hand and pressed it lingeringly to my lips. She closed her eyes.

"Nada," I murmured.

She gently released herself.

"It's late, I must go home. Shall we see each other at eleven o'clock Mass?"

On the doorstep she blew me a kiss and, without a backward glance, disappeared into the house with the lilac shutters.

* * *

At the entrance to the church, two Red Sea shells had been cemented into the wall to serve as stoups for holy water. I crossed myself, scanning the congregation for Nada as I did so. She wasn't there. I sat down in a pew on the right of the aisle, behind some gentlemen in dark suits. I sighted the director of dredging surrounded by his family. He eyed me without a sign of recognition.

Just as the organ struck up, Nada entered the church looking very elegant, her face half hidden by a little lace veil. She gave me a faint smile. Félix Percheron, who followed her in, caught sight of me and nodded several times to convey that he was expecting me for lunch without fail. His big black moustache lent him a piratical air. Nada was accompanied by someone else, quite a young man with pomaded hair, whom I recognized as the fortune-telling inspector of telegraphs. He wore a sly expression I didn't care for.

I spent the whole service gazing at Nada, who was seated on the left of the aisle only a few feet away. I had never before had a chance to look at her like that, free from all constraint. I found her erect, slender form intensely arousing. With her olive complexion set off by the white of her gown, she put all her fair-haired neighbours in the shade. I brimmed with love, anxiety, jealousy . . .

The first few sentences of the sermon escaped me, but I pricked up my ears when I heard the priest ramble on about "good and evil *actions*". One or two nods from the gentlemen present and a fleeting smile from Nada confirmed that this pun on the secondary meaning of the French word, "shares", was the priest's way of adapting his sermon to circumstances. Everyone knew what he meant when he spoke of "*actions* that prove expensive and *actions* one regrets", "*actions* that help an enterprise to grow and those that devalue it". In Ismailia, France was deriding Britain. Between the Kyrie and the Confiteor, the Church's eldest daughter was summoning God to bear witness against perfidious Albion . . .

Outside on the parvis, the gentlemen's shoes and the ladies' bootees were white with desert sand. I was able to renew my acquaintance with the director of dredging and several other Company officials, two of whom agreed to see me that afternoon. I also had to keep my lunch appointment at Félix Percheron's, because I was due to leave early the next morning.

*

Percheron still lived in the Bachelors' Quarter, although he more or less cohabited with two Sudanese girls whom he had bought at a clandestine slave market not long before the Canal opened. His "little harem", as he called them after a drink or two, had not exactly endeared him to Ismailia's polite society, but he was such a veteran of the isthmus that no one dared to criticize him openly.

Étienne Mancelle and he could not have been more different, but chance had thrown them together, and Nada's husband was too easy-going a man to fall out with anyone. Always inclined to see the good side of people and things, Étienne told himself that Percheron had saved the Sudanese girls from slavery, and that they enjoyed better treatment than many legitimate wives.

Nada, for her part, had found Percheron among her wedding presents: he was part of the furniture, so to speak. The society of certain Company wives had been a great deal more burdensome to her than the braggadocio of this Auvergnat with the soul of a colonist. She had curtly stopped Percheron in his tracks when he ventured to make a pass at her. Since then he had desisted, in awe of this attractive young woman who did not accord with his mental picture of "the Levantines".

Drinks were served by a black manservant in an immaculate white *galabiya*.

"Ladies first, Ahmed!" growled Percheron, who never addressed him in anything but a series of short, sharp barks.

I had no need to steer the conversation: the sale of the khedive's shares was on everyone's lips.

Nada was being addressed by the deputy director of warehousing. "My dear lady," he said, "I'm not like your husband, who sees good in everything. This British incursion into the Company is very worrying."

"Worrying?" Percheron burst out. "Outrageous and alarming, you mean! Our government has been monstrously short-sighted yet again. We shall now have to set our clocks by the British, then it'll be teatime for everyone. Ahmed, tea!"

The manservant cocked an ear, looking uneasy.

"No, you fool, no tea. No whisky either. Wine — good wine from home, while there's still time — before the British inflict their rules on us. Ah, the British! I can still hear them pouring scorn on our project when Port Sa'id was just a deserted beach inaccessible from the sea. We lived under canvas with rats gnawing at our toes. We kept our guns handy, too, believe you me, because we never knew whether the Bedouin were going to attack at any moment. Meantime, back in London, the British were scoffing and sniggering. We ignored them – we built the Canal. Their ships proceeded to take advantage of it, and now they've snaffled it themselves. The French government? Pah!"

There followed a long discussion on the British entry into the Company's board of directors. We were still at it over coffee.

Some appointments awaited me. I offered to escort Nada home on the way, but she told me not to worry. She was sure the inspector of telegraphs would be glad to offer her his arm. Percheron accompanied me to the door and vigorously pumped my hand.

"Ahmed!" I heard him bark as I walked off. "Cognac!"

My interviews dragged on. One of the engineers absolutely insisted on taking me on a tour of Lake Timsah by steam launch. On our return we met one of the transit officials, a genial, talkative man who took me for a genuine journalist from the *Sémaphore* and detained me at his home until dinnertime.

Somewhat embarrassed, I knocked on the lilac door at nine o'clock that night. There was no answer. Feeling terribly disappointed and rather anxious, I was about to go when Nada appeared.

"Forgive me," she said. "The nursemaid has gone home to the Arab village for the night – I had to put the children to bed myself. No, no, you're not disturbing me . . ."

Eugénie, whose birth had coincided with that of the Suez Canal, was six years old. She now had a second little brother, born since my first visit to Ismailia.

"Would you like to see them?" Nada asked. "They're asleep."

We went upstairs and tiptoed into Eugénie's bedroom – she was cuddling two dolls and whimpering in her sleep – then visited the boys' room.

"They're beautiful, all three of them," I said softly.

The room I'd slept in the first time was set back a little and approached by a few more stairs. The door was ajar.

"It was blue the last time you saw it," Nada told me. "Now it's pale pink."

"Pale pink?"

"Yes, my favourite colour. Pink goes very well with the ashwood furniture. If you'd care to see it . . . "

While climbing the last few stairs, Nada missed her footing and caught hold of the banister. She grimaced with pain, then leant on my arm. I helped her into the pink room, which was lit by an oil lamp, and sat her down on the bed.

"Would you like me to unlace your shoe?" I asked.

Very carefully, I removed the cloth bootee with the patent leather toe. Her foot was in my hands. I massaged it gently. She winced. I put my lips to that pretty little, painful little foot, and the world gave a sudden lurch . . .

We were lying against each other. When I brushed her lips with my fingertips she almost bit me. I cupped her face in my hands and kissed her passionately.

"This is madness," she moaned.

She kissed me back, full on the lips, and gripped my shoulders, crushing her breasts against me.

Clumsily, I tried to remove her gown. She helped me, almost tearing off her skirt in the process. The next minute we were glued together, one on top of the other, panting, filled with mingled tenderness and violence.

I don't know how long we lay there afterwards, side by side in the dancing light of the oil lamp, entangled in the bedclothes, sated and motionless.

I was roused from a half-sleep by a child's cries.

"My God, Eugénie!" said Nada, swiftly getting out of bed.

She pulled on her clothes, hurried to her daughter's bedside, and soothed away her nightmare with the promise of some orange-blossom tea. Then she returned. She kissed me, telling me again that I was mad, that we were both mad, and that I must go at once.

It was a balmy night. The Place Champollion smelt of desert and roses.

13

My train departed very early in the morning. I had no chance to say goodbye to Nada, having left her like a thief the night before, but I took away the memory of her moans, the taste of her lips, the scent of her skin.

The stationmaster, wearing his official tarboosh with its brass plate, sang out, *"Mesdames et messieurs les voyageurs, en voiture!"*

Ismailia was undoubtedly the only town in Egypt where railway employees had to make their announcements in the language of Molière.

"In this place, my friend, you're in France," Félix Percheron had told me the day before. "And it'll never be England, believe me. Queen Victoria may have bought half the Canal from that nitwit of a khedive, but if she wants the Venice of the desert she'll have to march over our dead bodies!"

What did I care about Victoria? My queen's name was Nada. She had given herself to me, I had given myself to her. I was mad, as she said — mad with joy. And, to tell the truth, a trifle uneasy.

We had deceived her husband, a man of integrity. That he most certainly was. At the time of the Xavier-Saillard affair in 1863 he had braved the French consul's displeasure by refusing to suppress part of his evidence. He had also, for three or four years, refrained from paying court to Nada out of respect for my father's wish that she should complete her education.

"Étienne is an irreproachable husband and a perfect father," Nada had told me the first night, while making the tea.

Étienne Mancelle's superiors must also have appreciated his merits, as witness his successive promotions. Originally in charge of the Lake

Timsah section, he had just been appointed deputy head of the transit division, whereas his colleague Percheron, although older and his senior in terms of length of service, had been stagnating for years in the materials division.

A strange mixture of emotions overcame me as the locomotive, spewing clouds of black smoke, gained speed and launched itself into the desert. I condemned myself for deceiving Étienne Mancelle, but hadn't he robbed me of the woman I loved? Hadn't he started with the immense asset of being French? I had just made love to the mother of his children, the woman who legally belonged to him. That lent Nada an added attraction: her marriage to a Frenchman rendered her even more desirable. Not only was I taking her from Étienne; I was, in a sense, taking advantage of his passport. Through Nada I was drawing a little closer to a country that fascinated me: the France whose snow-laden pine forests and red tiled roofs I had drawn pictures of as a schoolboy without ever having set eyes on it.

I was in a blind alley, I realized as the days went by. I couldn't send Nada a letter without involving her in a considerable risk, so I waited for a sign of life from her, which never came. But could she, for her part, risk writing to me? Did she even want to do so, after what might have been no more than a chance occurrence? This uncertainty tormented me.

I flirted with some crazy notions of getting a note to her by way of some messenger or other. Why shouldn't I go to Ismailia myself? Because Nada's feelings for me seemed far from sure, and I feared a negative, even violent reaction on her part. Perhaps she felt that ours was an act of folly which had to be consigned to oblivion for ever. In that respect, at least, I lived in ignorance. Her silence was preferable to a rejection that would have cut me to the quick.

I lost my appetite after returning from Ismailia. My father, who noticed this, asked me two or three times if I was feeling all right. He didn't press me, however, but preserved the characteristic discretion which, at bottom, formed a great barrier between us. There were many times in the course of my life when I would have welcomed being interrogated or even bullied by this father who was overly respectful of other people's privacy or too diffident to invade it.

There were times when I preferred Aunt Angéline's attitude. She wore her heart on her sleeve, he concealed it; she embroidered, he minimized. By dint of extolling the merits of "my brother the Doctor", she eventually became better known than him. A rather scatterbrained friend of hers was one day heard to refer to my father as "the brother of the Doctor's sister".

14

In Alexandria, Monsieur Xavier-Saillard's businesses were booming. The French entrepreneur had enlarged his premises: the celebrated initials "X-S" were now carved on a second palatial building in the Place des Consuls.

Rizqallah's mysterious trips to Cairo were becoming more frequent. There came a day when he triumphantly informed the family circle, "We're creditors to the khedive."

Aunt Angéline claimed that my cousin came from Alexandria every fortnight with two suitcases stuffed with pounds sterling, and that he delivered them to the palace in person. The suitcases were so heavy, she added, that a brace of guards had to help him up the grand staircase. However, her story was robbed of all plausibility by certain other details of her own devising, for instance that one of the suitcases had accidentally burst open on the platform at Bab al-Hadid station.

So Monsieur Xavier-Saillard had become a creditor of Isma'il Pasha's. The latter now borrowed money wherever he could and at any rate of interest demanded of him. At the beginning of his reign, European capital had been placed at his disposal with remarkable alacrity. A new public loan was floated every two years or so. The "Villages" loan was followed by the "Railways" loan, which was followed by the *Dayrah*, the *muqabala*, and several others. But the big credit houses refused to go any further. Compelled to meet his financial obligations, the khedive was descending an ever more slippery slope. He now borrowed money from small bankers or even from straightforward businessmen like Monsieur Xavier-Saillard.

"Egypt's creditors in London and Paris are getting worried," Nassif Bey explained. "They're urging their governments to step in."

In May 1876 the khedive was forced to set up a National Debt Fund managed by European commissioners. Some months later the Franco-British condominium was promulgated by decree: henceforth, the public finances were now to be supervised by two comptrollers-general, an Englishman and a Frenchman.

"Two official receivers," said my father.

"A better name for them," said Nassif Bey, "would be the new government of Egypt."

Condominium . . . It was a new addition to our vocabulary, a magical word to be used in any and every context.

"I hope the condominium will look into the lighting in our street," said Alfred Falaki. "Those gas lamps are no good, they're always going out."

No one dreamed that the first consequence of the Franco-British takeover would be a grim assassination committed in the corridors of power. Hardly had the comptrollers-general been appointed when it was announced that Egypt's redoubtable minister of finance, Isma'il Saddiq Pasha, the most powerful man in the country apart from the khedive, had disappeared. Albin Balanvin had crossed his path on two or three occasions. It was the party aboard Saddiq's yacht that had featured in his report on the opening of the Suez Canal.

Popularly known as "Mufattish", Isma'il Saddiq Pasha was the terror of the peasants. It was he who regularly decreed the raising of new taxes, setting a certain sum for each province and leaving it to the local authorities to extract it with the aid of God and the *kurbash*. The authorities helped themselves on the way, but woe betide those who failed to come up with the stipulated sum!

A foster-brother of the khedive's, Mufattish had filled his own pockets during each of these operations. His agricultural estates covered vast areas and his harem comprised over 300 women including the loveliest dancers in Cairo.

But the provinces, bled dry for years, were at the end of their tether. There was little left to be extracted from them. Once the account books had been opened to foreign comptrollers, the minister of finance became not only redundant but dangerous.

Commenting on the sinister rumours that were circulating in Cairo,

Nassif Bey explained that the khedive had had two alternatives. "He could either make Mufattish a scapegoat or eliminate him. So, he decided to make him scapegoat and then eliminate him."

It was said that the minister of finance, officially banished to the Sudan, had been taken up the Nile by boat and strangled on board. He had put up a fierce fight, apparently. The senior official charged with recovering his seal, which was required for the certification of public documents, was badly bitten and lost the use of a finger. From then on, he always appeared in public wearing a glove . . . In the next few weeks, all Mufattish's property was appropriated by the khedive, whose agricultural estates increased to the tune of 30,000 feddan.

FROM OUR CAIRO CORRESPONDENT
To the Editor:

14 December 1876

The disappearance of His Excellency Isma'il Saddiq Pasha continues to give rise to the strangest rumours. Some go so far as to claim that the minister of finance has been assassinated! They are mischief-makers, however, and I decline to give them credence.

You cannot imagine, sir, how much I should have liked to give you some accurate information about this sad affair. Unfortunately, too many contradictory rumours are circulating in Cairo. In such cases, it is always better to be guided by official sources.

It appears that His Highness had for some time suspected Mufattish of perpetrating criminal acts. His fears were reinforced when the comptrollers-general discovered a deficit of 1,500,000 pounds in the National Debt Fund. Mufattish is also said to have incited the provincial sheikhs against the condominium and accused the viceroy of "surrendering our finances to the infidel". Saddened, the khedive deemed it sensible to obtain his associate's resignation and remove him from Cairo to prevent him from persisting in his dishonest activities.

It seems, sir, that advantage was taken of one of the numerous drinking bouts in which Mufattish was weak-minded enough to indulge to get him to sign his letter of resignation. The viceroy, who took a deep personal interest in this affair, is said to have accompanied his foster-brother to the palace at Gezira, where a boat was waiting with steam up. After bidding him farewell — a heart-rending occasion, one assumes — *the khedive entrusted the ministry of finance to his son Hussein and convened the cabinet to approve Mufattish's banishment to the Sudan. Outraged by the documents shown them, which proved their colleague's guilt, the ministers voted unanimously in favour of exile.*

Over a period of several days, reports confirmed that the boat, with blinds down, had completed each stage in its journey to the Upper Nile. I do not know why Mufattish failed to reach his destination alive, but I am told that heat, brandy, and — no doubt — excessive emotion had proved too much for the robust forty-six-year-old's constitution. Such is the information I have received from official sources, sir, and it would be highly improper of me to appear to question it.

Albin Balanvin

15

"We should never have let her go by herself," my brother Alexandre kept saying in a tearful voice.

I was just as distressed in spite of my silence, and I shared his opinion: we should never have let Om Mahmud go back to her village near Damietta, which she hadn't revisited for an eternity, on her own. The circumcision of a grand-nephew, whose parents she didn't even know, was insufficient reason for such a trip. Although terrified of the smoking, steaming machine, she had insisted on taking the train alone. It was as if she had been overcome by an irrepressible urge to see her family once more.

"The ceremony had only just begun," her sister told us, "when we saw her fall to the ground. 'Mahmud, Mahmud,' she muttered, 'where are you, *ya Mahmud*?' Then she died. Poor Khadiga!"

Khadiga? It was the first time we had heard our maidservant's first name – she had always been known by that of her mysterious son – but we were too upset to interrupt the woman in black.

"We buried her on the evening of the circumcision."

"In which cemetery?" Alexandre asked quickly, as if doubting the death of the woman who had been a second mother to us.

"No, no cemetery," Om Mahmud's sister replied. "She didn't want that."

"What on earth do you mean?" cried Alexandre, who was losing his temper.

"She didn't want that, I tell you. The men who were carrying her corpse stopped halfway to the cemetery. She was too heavy – she refused to go

any further. It happens sometimes. The people in the funeral procession —
there were a good two dozen of us — formed a circle round her. We said,
'It's getting late, Khadiga, the sun will be setting soon. Come on, *habibi*,
make a little effort.' But she wouldn't hear of it."

"And then?" I said impatiently.

"Then we buried her, right there beside the road."

Alexandre could restrain his tears no longer. He dashed out of the
room, leaving me alone with this unknown woman to whom I had nothing
more to say.

She asked me for a little money, pretending to weep and tear her hair.
I gave her fifty piastres. She redoubled her groans and beat her breast as
I pushed her towards the door. A sudden question occurred to me.

"Why did Khadiga call herself Om Mahmud? Where is this son of
hers?"

The sister stopped groaning. "She was a fraud," she said coldly. "She
had no son — she wasn't even married."

I hustled her out, beginning to wonder if she really was Khadiga's sister.
One thing seemed certain, alas: our poor old maidservant was dead. To us,
she would always be Om Mahmud.

My father merely nodded on learning that he had lost his housekeeper of
twenty-five years' standing, but we sensed that he was shaken by her death.

"The Doctor looks as if he'd been widowed a second time," Aunt
Angéline told her women friends.

In the next few weeks my father began to talk of building a seaside
villa at Ramlah, the beach where we had bathed together in 1868. The land
belonged to some Bedouin and would not cost much. As for the house, it
could be built thanks to his share of a legacy from an elderly uncle in
Beirut.

He was promptly accused of folly by most members of the family.
Marooned amid sand dunes and fields of wild figs, several kilometres
from Alexandria? What was he going to do there? Boctor Touta was
more astonished than most.

"If you want a house," he said, "move out into the countryside like a
civilized person. I'll find you an *'ezba* ten times as nice as that whorehouse
of a villa you plan to build."

"Take care," warned Alfred Falaki, "you'll be building on sand in more senses than one. Firm foundations are essential. Look at the way my house has appreciated in value. Me, I took advantage of the khedive's offer. You have to snap up a bargain when you see one."

Papa's only response was a vague smile. His mind was made up. He proposed to spend ten days at Nassif Bey's in Alexandria, purchasing the land and finding a builder. The plans were already drawn up in his head. In addition to the main house, which would have eight bedrooms, there was to be a small servants' annexe.

"Om Mahmud could have lived there," he murmured.

Alexandre was twenty-five and I was twenty-seven. We were no longer of an age to have a maidservant living on the premises. In any case, no woman could have fulfilled Om Mahmud's various functions, which were as much emotional as domestic. It was decided instead to engage a manservant, and that was how Hosni entered our home.

The youngest of my Dabbour cousins' children promptly became confused and called him Mahmud. Whether in mimicry, for fun, or for some more obscure reason, we took to calling him Mahmud ourselves. This amused him, and before long Hosni became Mahmud to the entire family.

16

The counters in the Imperial Ottoman Bank were faced with slabs of marble, but not simply to impress our clients: we rang coins on them to distinguish the genuine from the counterfeit. That sound was to grate on my ears for years on end.

I performed my cashier's duties conscientiously but without enthusiasm. My thoughts were elsewhere. I even managed, during lulls when no customer presented himself at my window, to fish out my notebook and surreptitiously jot down some minor detail, some idea, or even some simple turn of phrase that could sometime prove of use in an article.

My work for the *Sémaphore d'Alexandrie* remained unknown for quite a while, but I couldn't resist mentioning it to a colleague at the time of the great legal reform controversy. The following week, all the cashiers knew of my sideline. The name Armand de Maubuisson meant nothing to them. It must be said that very few of the bank's employees read the *Sémaphore*, and that my pseudonym seldom appeared in it. Besides, I have noticed over the years how few readers take the time to memorize a signature. This did not prevent the other cashiers from nicknaming me "the Journalist" and then "The Sémaphore". They ended by saying it quite mechanically, without even smiling.

"*Ya Sémaphore*, give me change for twenty . . . *Ya Sémaphore*, where did you put that ledger?"

The word meant nothing when they used it, whereas for me it evoked the art of writing, the outside world, freedom . . .

Late one Thursday morning in March 1877, the sound of coins ringing on marble never ceased. Three or four customers were queuing at my window, and I was serving an insufferable Armenian shopkeeper who insisted – as usual – on withdrawing a substantial sum in ten-para coins. My eye was suddenly caught by the figure of a woman half hidden by the queue. Instinctively, I rose to my feet and peered through the grille. It was Nada!

She gave me a faint smile. Heart pounding, I asked my immediate neighbour to stand in for me. Then, without waiting for him to reply, I made for the exit, abandoning the Armenian and his ten-para coins.

Nada! It was Nada!

"What are you doing here?" I asked when we were outside in the arcade, brushing her gloved hands with my lips.

She pretended to be put out. "Is that how you greet people in Cairo?"

People! As if Nada could ever be "people"!

"I came to say hello," she added with a mischievous look in her eye.

I would have kissed her if we hadn't been in the street.

"How long are you staying?" I asked feverishly.

"About five hours. My train leaves late this afternoon."

Amused by my stupefied expression, Nada pretended to admire the arcade. Then she explained that Étienne had gone to Port Sa'id on business for two days. She had left the children with their nursemaid, making her swear to say nothing to anyone, and boarded the early morning train with a veil over her face, praying to heaven not to be spotted by anyone she knew.

My heart was on fire.

"Come on," I said, grabbing her little suitcase. "I'll take you to the Ezbekiyah."

The gardens had been created for the Suez Canal celebrations, so she couldn't know them, never having been back to Cairo since her wedding. Étienne was so in love with Ismailia that he refused to leave the place except on business trips to Port Sa'id. He had taken her to France only once, to introduce her to his family. We had received a letter from Normandy – a letter that had made me feel ill for days.

To conceal the turmoil inside me, I launched into a knowledgeable account of the Ezbekiyah's history.

"It used to be a huge basin – it became a lake when the Nile was in flood. They held regattas there by torchlight. The water receded in winter, to be replaced by a sea of greenery, but Muhammad Ali drained the area, which became a forest in the middle of the city. Then the khedive cleared it and turned it into a gigantic park in the French style."

"How are you?" asked Nada, who hadn't made the trip to attend a lecture on Cairo's urban topography.

I smiled in answer. "And you?"

"I get rather lonely down there. I was hoping for a line from you. You've never written to me."

I felt my cheeks burn, unable to get a word out. How could I explain that I hadn't dared to write for fear of embarrassing her terribly, or of breaking a link that struck me as tenuous in the extreme. But I could tell from her expression that she had guessed it all.

We walked on, side by side, to the western entrance of the Ezbekiyah. I could hardly breathe for joy.

Nada was impressed by the tall railings. It cost half a piastre to pass the turnstile, which surprised her.

"The gardens were laid out by French engineers. They cost a fortune — it takes an army of gardeners to maintain them, too — but I think the half-piastre serves mainly to keep out the poor and the beggars."

We set off along the path leading to the belvedere. On our right, the photographic pavilion displayed various scenes mounted on pasteboard. I told Nada that Lolo had had himself immortalized there in an Ottoman field marshal's uniform, mounted on half a wooden horse. She laughed so heartily that one or two promenading couples turned to look.

We paused briefly in front of the artificial grotto to watch the leaping cascade.

"Mind the spray," I said, "you'll get wet."

But Nada stood there motionless, eyes half closed.

"It's Cairo water," she said in a low voice. "I've never forgotten the smell."

We ascended the belvedere by way of a narrow path paved with palm-tree trunks. The view was superb. Part of the new quarter lay spread out below us. I pointed out the Falakis' district, with its handsome houses and surrounding gardens.

"Uncle Alfred got an excellent bargain," I said, laughing, "— not for the first time. Lolo stands to inherit a lot of money. You could have married him."

She stared at me in surprise.

"Why did you say that?"

"No reason — silly of me. Forgive me." Then, in a low voice, without looking at her. "It broke my heart when I heard you were going to marry Étienne. I've never got over it."

She paused and turned to me. Her expression was filled with tenderness.

"Nada . . . "

Her fingers brushed my lips, silencing me. "You promised to give me lunch," she said.

I took her arm, and we made our way down a shady path to a quiet little café restaurant provided with arbours where customers could eat in seclusion. It was a delightful spot, kept cool by the climbing plants that covered its trellis-work.

"It's wonderful, this café of yours."

"At least one can breathe here, as Aunt Angéline would say."

"*Hawa, hawa!*"

We spent the whole meal laughing and gazing into each other's eyes.

"You must be tired," I said over coffee.

Nada didn't reply.

"Shepheard's is only a stone's throw from here," I went on in a murmur.

She gave a little shrug, like someone devoid of ideas and open to suggestions. I called the waiter at once.

Shepheard's struck me as more anonymous than the New Hotel, which was much patronized by the French. We got there a few minutes later. Nada lowered her veil as we crossed the famous terrace with its two little sphinxes. A uniformed page hurried up and relieved me of her overnight case, then led the way to the reception desk.

"I'm sorry, sir," said the receptionist, "we don't have a room left."

"Not even for one night?" said Nada from behind me, half lifting her veil and favouring the man with an irresistible smile.

The room overlooked the hotel's magnificent grounds. The young page, anxious to earn his bakshish, told us that gazelles frisked around among the bushes and appeared below the windows from time to time.

Nada came over to me as soon as the door had closed behind him. We kissed slowly, lingeringly, as if we had been waiting for each other since time immemorial. Filtering through the shutters over the french windows came shafts of sunlight and the sound of gardeners watering the flower beds.

"Nada, Nada . . . " I murmured, incapable of saying anything else.

Her gown was fastened down the back. I undid the little black cloth buttons, one by one, with a calm deliberation that surprised me, but the sight of her bare shoulders drove me wild. I put my lips to them, intoxicated by the scent of the olive skin I had dreamed of so often. She gently shook her head, and her dark hair, loose now, brushed my cheek.

My hands caressed her breasts, gently rediscovering the shape of them, enveloping them, clasping them. I don't know which of us led the other towards the big brass bed . . .

All I remember of my state of mind when I accompanied Nada to the station two hours later is a feeling of euphoria. We belonged to each other, we shared a secret, and nothing would ever be the same.

"Don't wait on the platform," she told me. "I hate goodbyes."

I had just opened my mouth to reply when she quickly lowered her veil.

"Don't move," she said softly. "I can see the deputy director of dredging behind you."

Nada had concocted a story for use in the event of some untimely encounter. She would say that she had gone to Cairo for a family reason, the death of an elderly aunt. If the trip should come to her husband's ears, she had devised a rather convoluted yarn about a female relation from Beirut who was visiting Cairo, and of whom I had informed her via a colleague passing through Ismailia. As luck would have it, the deputy director of dredging had seen nothing.

Nada gave me a little wave from the window of her compartment. Having promised not to linger on the platform, I blew her a kiss and disappeared into the crowd.

17

"No, no, don't write to me," she had said. "It would be too dangerous. And besides, I'd find it too distressing."

I could have kicked myself for not querying that remark. Why "too distressing"? It was impossible for me to find out now, because another meeting seemed unlikely. I couldn't see myself arriving in Ismailia, checking into the Hôtel des Voyageurs, and waiting for Nada to join me in a disguise of some kind. As for her, she would find it very difficult to repeat her Cairo escapade, always assuming that she truly wanted to do so. I sensed that we had just lived through a unique experience. Our few hours together in the Ezbekiyah and then at Shepheard's – didn't their magic derive from their impromptu nature?

Such were the questions that preoccupied me while coins rang on the marble counters of the Imperial Ottoman Bank. At least I knew that Nada loved me. Simultaneously tormenting and intoxicating, her absence helped me to devote myself enthusiastically to the observation of political developments, which now occurred in quick succession.

Several times in the next few months, I caught sight of Walid al-Ahlawi in the region of Opera Square. The spruce *bimbashi* of old was almost unrecognizable in his grubby uniform and worn-out boots. He was one of the 2,500 officers whom the high command, which was composed of Turks, had placed on half-pay and contrived to select from among those of Egyptian stock. Very poorly paid to begin with and heavily in debt, these officers were in dire straits, especially if, like Walid, they had wives and children to support.

I hardly dared say hello to the man for fear of embarrassing him, but one afternoon we bumped into each other outside the Ottoman Bank. He declined the coffee I suggested, pleading an urgent engagement. Our conversation, which lasted only a minute or two, was chilly in tone. I could sense that Walid was seething with fury. He railed against the Turks, but also against the "European government" headed by Nubar Pasha, the Armenian. We were no longer ruled by comptrollers-general, in fact, but by duly appointed ministers of foreign nationality: Rivers Wilson, an Englishman, was minister of finance, and de Blinières, a Frenchman, minister of public works.

I never discovered exactly what part Walid al-Ahlawi played in the notorious demonstration of 18 February 1879, but I'm sure he was one of the army officers who manhandled Nubar and Wilson before locking them up in an office. The Armenian was shoved up against a wall and the Englishman had a hair or two plucked from his beard.

It was later rumoured that the khedive had personally incited these native officers against the "European government" in order to rid himself of it. The fact that Nubar was dismissed immediately after undergoing this assault on his person makes it seem likely.

"Isma'il has a strange way of defending his ministers," my father said drily.

Prince Tewfiq, the khedive's eldest son, was put in charge of the new government but given no time to distinguish himself: he, too, was dismissed after a month in office. Invoking "public pressure", the khedive appointed another prime minister and set up "a truly Egyptian government" without a single European in it.

I thought Walid al-Ahlawi would cry victory, the more so because steps were taken to improve the lot of native officers, as his new boots bore witness, but no. When we ran into each other by chance in Muski Street, his only comment was, "Those ministers are Turks to a man. There isn't a genuine Egyptian among them."

His remark made me feel uneasy. I myself could never be a genuine Egyptian in Walid's eyes. Although resident on the banks of the Nile for a century or more, my family were *Shawam*, and the *Shawam* were hated in the countryside, where some of them, like Uncle Boctor, lent money at exorbitant rates of interest. True, I was the son of Dr Touta, whom Walid greatly respected, and who had taught him to read and write his own language. I doubtless read and wrote Arabic better than Walid himself, but being employed by the Ottoman Bank, a Franco-British establishment, and working for a French-language newspaper under French direction, I certainly didn't impress him as a "genuine Egyptian". I was a *khawaga*, a gentleman from elsewhere.

Khedive Isma'il had gone too far. A few months later, having abandoned their attempts to make him see reason, London and Paris decided that he was no longer fit to be viceroy of Egypt and managed to convince the Sultan of this fact.

On 29 June a telegram from Constantinople addressed to "ex-khedive Isma'il" put an end to a reign lasting sixteen years. Tewfiq's accession was immediately saluted by the cannon of the Citadel. Next morning, the deposed viceroy took the train to Alexandria. Father and son exchanged a moving farewell embrace, and the ladies of the harem, dressed all in black, wept noisily in their closed carriages outside Bab al-Hadid station.

On arrival in Alexandria, Isma'il went aboard his yacht, the *Mahrousa*, accompanied by his wives, his children, and some of his concubines, bound for Naples, where the king of Italy had put the Palazzo della Favorita at his disposal. Numerous local dignitaries and European residents came aboard to pay their respects, among them Dr Nassif Bey and Monsieur Adolphe Xavier-Saillard.

The sun had not yet set when the *Mahrousa* cast off. Standing on deck, the deposed khedive slowly waved farewell to the soil of Egypt on which his grandfather Muhammad Ali had landed seventy-eight years before.

Nassif Bey shed a tear despite himself. He had been one of the physicians accredited to this magnificent gambler and inventor of the title khedive, yet Isma'il had never once summoned him to his bedside in sixteen years on the throne.

"I don't even know if he has any hair on his chest!" my father's colleague said sadly.

Two weeks later we read in the *Sémaphore* that Nassif Bey had been appointed one of the new khedive's personal physicians.

"He's on his third viceroy," commented my father, who asked me to wire him our congratulations.

* * *

Tewfiq was quite unlike his father. Isma'il the Magnificent's successor was a colourless young man, thrifty, monogamous, and far from regal in demeanour.

"The youngster does have certain qualities," said Nassif Bey, "but they're those of a private individual."

Balanvin's more malicious comment: "Louis XVI has succeeded Louis XIV."

Tewfiq was not the ex-khedive's favourite son, as everyone knew. The ladies of the harem acknowledged his princely title, but only with reluctance. His mother was a former slave who had caught Isma'il Pasha's eye while making a bed in the palace one evening. This had placed her rump in an inviting position, so the story ran, and Isma'il had been unable to resist it. He honoured her with a brief fling that left her pregnant. In accordance with custom, she moved into Qasr al-'Aali Palace, nicknamed "the nursery", for her confinement. And that was how a slave woman became the viceroy's fourth wife and how Tewfiq, the eldest of his father's surviving sons, succeeded him on the throne.

The new khedive found himself at the head of a bankrupt country run by Europeans. He had to contend, not only with discontentment among native army officers, but also with the machinations of his father, who was clearly not resigned to exile.

FROM OUR CAIRO CORRESPONDENT
To the Editor:

18 July 1880

The new khedive's courtesy and good manners are winning everyone's heart. Reservations about him are gradually disappearing. The well-intentioned have been reassured and the ill-intentioned disconcerted.

His Highness appears in Shubra Street in a very unpretentious carriage from which he waves to those whom he meets and acknowledges their tributes with his habitual benevolence.

Tewfiq Pasha cannot, however, be ignorant of the machinations of persons in the entourage of certain pretenders to the throne. I refer to the supporters of Prince Halim, which will not surprise you unduly, but also to those of the ex-khedive.

They are undoubtedly acting on their own initiative, for I can hardly believe, sir, that Isma'il Pasha would personally seek to hamper the actions of his beloved son.

The new khedive is being compelled to take some painful decisions aimed at restoring the country's finances. For example, he has just announced the abolition of the muqabala. *In 1871, as you know, this ingenious law enabled landowners who paid six years' taxes in advance to be permanently exempted from half their fiscal liabilities. Well, it's no longer so: from now on, they will have to pay their taxes in full.*

It was the European comptrollers of the national debt who requested that the muqabala *be annulled. The khedive was reluctant to comply. True to habit, he went to seek inspiration from the British and French consuls, who provided him with excellent grounds for reassurance: they pointed out that all those who had subscribed to the* muqabala *were Egyptians. Wouldn't they some day benefit from the restoration of their country's finances?*

I would wager, sir, that the landowners' public spirit will triumph over the resentment occasioned by this painful but doubtless essential measure.

You may object that the government has broken its promise of 1871. But in politics, sir, promises are binding only on their recipients.

Albin Balanvin

The abolition of the *muqabala* earned us a memorable performance by Boctor Touta. Rizqallah's father could not find words harsh enough to describe this breach of contract.

"I paid that goddamned *muqabala* in return for lifelong exemption from paying half my taxes. I did the state a service, and what's my reward? Ah, poor me!"

Vulgar as ever, Boctor was unrestrained in his vituperations against the new khedive. "That swine Tewfiq! He's got us by the balls — by the balls, I tell you!"

Aunt Angéline shut the windows, tried to stem the flow, brought him a soothing draught of orange-blossom tea.

"I'm worried about Boctor," Papa told me the next day, looking anxious. "He's always had a weak heart."

We decided to pay him a visit at his apartment in the Muski. The windows were open, and his oaths could be heard outside in the street. Seated on a stool with his feet in a bowl of soapy water, Boctor was fiercely haranguing half a dozen neighbours on the subject of the *muqabala*. At one point, carried away by the depth of his emotions, he punctuated the tirade with a resounding fart.

"His constitution is stronger than I thought," my father muttered as we left.

Rizqallah entirely reassured us during a trip to Cairo the following month. In lieu of the *muqabala*, his father had merely paid off some arrears of taxes. He had also taken advantage of the law to regularize some shaky title deeds, the fiscal authorities having received instructions to encourage landowners to accept the khedive's offer by showing them some latitude. All in all, Boctor had done well out of the *muqabala*.

18

That summer, Alfred Falaki took me aside and confided a secret: he was going to open a second jeweller's shop — "a branch", as he grandly termed it — in Alexandria. Lolo would have managed it in the normal course of events, but my uncle had no wish to commit financial suicide: he knew that his dolt of a son was just capable of opening and closing the steel shutters. He had engaged a manager, therefore, but was keen to publicize the new establishment. Being aware of the *Sémaphore*'s influence, he wanted to insert an advertisement and was counting on me to obtain him a favourable price.

Highly embarrassed, I pointed out that I wasn't directly employed by the weekly and that, in any case, journalists didn't handle that sort of thing.

"I understand," he said. "What's your percentage?"

My embarrassed smile was misinterpreted.

"Ah, I see you know your business!" he grumbled, rubbing his signet ring on the back of his sleeve to make it shine.

I didn't know how to extricate myself. After vaguely promising to put in a word for him at the *Sémaphore*'s offices, I managed to change the subject.

Uncle Alfred resumed his attack several times in the next few weeks. Luckily for me, he still hadn't settled on the wording of his advertisement. Not wanting to waste good money, he consulted me.

"I want something along these lines: 'Alfred Falaki, Jeweller, best prices offered. Muski Street, Cairo. Rue des Sœurs, Alexandria.' Or do you think I should put Alexandria first?"

I played on his doubts by replying in a very hesitant manner. I pointed out that he certainly ought to start with Cairo, where his main shop was situated, but that the Alexandrians would be offended if their city took second place . . .

This question kept us going for months. Meantime, the shop in Alexandria was doing good business. Uncle Alfred drew the appropriate conclusion:

"To hell with the advertisement! Journalists are thieves – be damned if I'll ever give them a piastre of my money!"

Aunt Angéline was also pursuing me at that period, but for another reason: she had decided to find me a wife. The expert matchmaker not only had the Falaki-Dabbour "treble" to her credit; she had also scored some other notable successes, such as the remarriage of an extremely ugly and tic-afflicted widow to a handsome young cousin of the Dabbours. It was true, admittedly, that the widow lived in a mansion over Damietta way, and that her poor state of health was an auspicious sign . . .

However, "Aunt Hawa" had sustained two undeniable defeats: for all her efforts, neither Lolo nor my father had emerged from the celibate state.

It was clear that her brother, now seventy, would never marry again. He would live – and die – "cherishing the memory of the Maronite", as Angéline put it between flaps of her fan.

As for Lolo, she was at last reconciled to having him under her wing. One sensed that "Maman's pet" enjoyed life to the full. He had settled into snug bachelorhood, spicing it up with his scullery amours. Fawzia, the Falakis' maidservant, as alluring as ever, continued to render her nocturnal services at intervals and prices determined by herself. Every month, their beneficiary had to present her with a ring, a bracelet, or sometimes a necklace.

"Fawzia will soon be opening her own jeweller's shop," my brother Alexandre used to say with a smile. I suspected him, too, of enjoying her ebony body from time to time.

Now forty, Lolo Falaki no longer tried to look like a French engineer on the staff of the Suez Canal Company. The clerks of the mixed courts were his new role models. At the shop he was never to be seen without a tarboosh, a dark suit with lustrine sleeves, and a pencil stuck behind his ear. That, at least, was how he pictured the employees of those honourable institutions.

So Aunt Angéline had taken up the hunt again. Having lost her brother and decided to hang on to her son, she had set her sights on me. I struck her as an easy prospect.

"You, with those bright eyes of yours . . . "

With Angéline and her women friends, marriageable girls were the principle topic of conversation.

"I've found you an absolute pearl," she whispered in my ear, enveloping me in essence of bergamot. "A genuine sweetheart. Her father owns a hundred feddan in the Fayoum."

Uncle Alfred, who was listening with half an ear, said mechanically, "A hundred feddan? Very pretty!"

But I had no desire to get married. Nada was the only woman who interested me, and she lived far away in a desert where roses grew. Three times she had sneaked back to Cairo, and three times we had taken the same room at Shepheard's. On the last occasion, however, Étienne had returned from Port Sa'id a day earlier than planned. Finding his wife gone and being unable to get any sense out of the incoherent nursemaid, he became alarmed. Then Nada turned up with her overnight bag. She had to trot out her prearranged story: the relative from Beirut passing through Cairo, my message to that effect via a colleague . . . Étienne, who took it at face value, anxiously inquired if the trip hadn't been too tiring. All at once she felt immensely guilty, lying to such a trusting and loyal husband. Whatever happened, she couldn't do so again. Shepheard's was over.

Sometimes, when the memory of her fragrant skin and firm breasts tormented me too cruelly, I brought myself to pick up some woman of easy virtue in the Ezbekiyah Gardens. Like me, my colleagues at the bank were familiar with those overly made-up, overly strident Greeks or Jewesses who took us off to some seedy room in the neighbourhood. They were reputed to be very skilful, but none of them ever made me forget Nada, not even for an instant.

To please Aunt Angéline I sometimes accepted her invitations to tea, feigning ignorance of the fact that I would be confronted by some virgin with downcast eyes, meekly seated beside her mother. I found those girls of good family dull and boring. One little laugh from Nada would have put them all in the shade. In case of necessity, I preferred my humiliating encounters in the Ezbekiyah Gardens.

Fawzia, the Falakis' maidservant, brought round pastries on a silver tray. Her gaping bodice lent a little piquancy, if I may put it that way, to those insipid tea parties. Whenever Lolo extended a hesitant hand towards the tray, I always wondered if it would close on an almond pastry or something else!

I would listen vaguely to the ladies' chatter without enriching the conversation with what they expected of a journalist ("My nephew edits the *Sémaphore d'Alexandrie*," Aunt Angéline used to say), still less of a cashier at the Imperial Ottoman Bank ("My nephew is a banker"). I had no wish to shine in such company.

"*Hawa, hawa!*" my aunt would groan whenever conversation flagged, prompting me with a conspiratorial glance from behind her fan.

19

I doubt if Walid al-Ahlawi needed a matchmaker some years earlier, when he married the sister of a comrade in the 4th Infantry Regiment. He had already fathered five or six children by early 1881.

I have never really known what made him join the regiment commanded by Colonel 'Arabi. Chance, perhaps, or "the hand of God", as he would have said. Alternatively, he may have contrived to obtain a transfer to the regiment because he was enthralled by the future revolutionary leader's brilliant rhetoric.

Mounting agitation reigned in the barracks. Native Egyptian officers blamed the minister of war for yet another batch of Turkish promotions and demanded his replacement. Three colonels, one of whom was 'Arabi, called on the prime minister and delivered a petition to this effect.

Some days later the signatories were summoned to the ministry of war "to receive instructions". Hardly had they got there when they were deprived of their swords and brought before a military court presided over by the chief of staff, Stone Pasha, an American in the khedive's service.

"Our leaders had taken precautions, of course," Walid told me. "For some days, there had been sinister rumours of a boat with three steel chests aboard: their occupants were to be taken to the Upper Nile and drowned like Mufattish. The court had only just convened when several units of the 1st and 4th Infantry Regiments burst into the ministry courtyard. We had no difficulty in releasing our colonels. Then the whole of the 1st Guards Regiment, with band playing and colours flying, marched from Qasr al-Nil to 'Abdin Palace to request the khedive to study the petition. Tewfiq immediately dismissed the minister of war and reinstated the three colonels."

"That's what you call a *pronunciamento*," Albin Balanvin told me, tapping the knob of his cane.

Emboldened by their success, the officers submitted another petition. This time there was no summons to the ministry of war and no military tribunal. The government agreed to modify the promotion system, grant more appropriate rates of pay, and substitute real butter for the loathsome mixture of suet used in army cookhouses. Going even further, Tewfiq Pasha promised to bring the army up to a strength of 18,000 men.

Euphoria reigned. During a grand banquet held at the ministry of war, 'Arabi called for three cheers for the khedive.

Not long afterwards I passed Walid al-Ahlawi outside the Imperial Ottoman Bank. He was wearing a smart new uniform and proudly sporting the extra stripe that marked him as a lieutenant-colonel, a *qa'imaqam* earning thirty Egyptian guineas a month.

"Relations between the officers and the palace are set fair," I remarked to Balanvin.

"That's not what I hear about town," he replied.

I realized some weeks later, after a brief conversation with Walid at a café in the Ezbekiyah, that he was right. When I stressed the difference between Khedive Tewfiq and his father, the new *qa'imaqam* almost spat back, "A viper can only give birth to a viper!"

In reality, each side remained on its guard, convinced that the other was up to some skulduggery. The colonels suspected the palace of bribing some of their subordinates at great expense. They trusted only one man, the new minister of war, who had warned them, "If you hear I've been dismissed, beware: it means trouble."

Consequently, the minister's dismissal in the middle of August caused great concern in military circles. When the officers heard that the 3rd Regiment had been summoned to Alexandria, panic was complete. Walid al-Ahlawi, whom Balanvin had asked me to pump for information, was very worried.

"We know perfectly well why the 3rd has been summoned to Alexandria: those bastards plan to cause an accident at Kafr al-Zayat bridge and send the train plunging into the Nile. Our boys won't make the mistake of going to Alexandria by train. They'll march there if necessary!"

They went neither by train nor on foot. Instead, several regiments chose to mutiny. On 9 September the bank's counters were buzzing with the rumour that troops had taken up their positions outside 'Abdin Palace. I entrusted my window to a colleague and hurried off to the palace. Approximately 4,000 men were drawn up in a square, bayonets fixed. They had also brought some cannon with them.

I had no difficulty in locating Colonel 'Arabi. A thickset, round-shouldered man, he was on horseback with his sabre drawn. Walid al-Ahlawi was standing a few feet away, very erect, a steely look in his eye. Involuntarily, I remembered the scene in the Place des Consuls. Eighteen years had gone by since then. How different Walid looked from the tearful young lieutenant who had submitted to his public degradation with bowed head!

The balconies of the buildings nearby were already crowded when Khedive Tewfiq turned up in his carriage, accompanied by his ministers, Auckland Colvin, the British comptroller-general, and several other dignitaries. He was very pale. We were unaware that, having been warned that troops were on the march, he had driven all the way from Turah to the Citadel and from there to 'Abbassiya, hoping to gain the support of loyalist regiments, but to no avail.

In my haste I had brought neither notebook nor pencil with me. Everything I saw that afternoon etched itself into my memory, however, and I found it easy to give Balanvin a detailed description of the scene later on.

Tewfiq Pasha seemed panic-stricken. He kept turning to the members of his entourage as if seeking their instructions. Colvin's whispered advice was to stand firm.

At length the khedive ordered 'Arabi to sheathe his sabre and dismount. The rebel colonel obeyed and marched up to Tewfiq to present his grievances. The viceroy would doubtless have caved in at once if Colvin hadn't whispered something else in his ear. He then withdrew, leaving the Europeans present to negotiate with the mutineers.

I was watching the scene, but naturally I couldn't hear what was said. I learned later that the insurgents had demanded the prime minister's dismissal. They were informed that the khedive had sent Constantinople a telegram on the subject, and that it would be proper to await the Sultan's reply.

"We shall await his reply," said 'Arabi. "If it turns out to be unfavourable, we shall expect him to send an envoy to settle this dispute."

Not long afterwards the Austrian consul came hurrying out of the palace to inform 'Arabi that the khedive had agreed to appoint a new prime minister. Suspecting a ruse, the rebel leader demanded to see a written declaration to that effect, which was duly brought him. He retired to the centre of the square to read it. I could hear little from where I was, but the cheers of the officers in the front ranks were eloquent enough.

The leaders of the mutiny then requested the honour of kissing the khedive's hand. They were invited into the palace but went in one by one for safety's sake. It was as if memories of the Mamelukes whom Muhammad Ali had exterminated in the Citadel seventy years earlier were still green.

As soon as the regiments had returned to their barracks I hurried to Balanvin to report on this latest pronunciamiento.

"No, no," he told me, "I don't propose to describe a scene I never witnessed. Sit down at my desk, pick up a pen, and write."

For once, he deemed it necessary to submit a "news item", as he disdainfully termed it. The *Sémaphore d'Alexandrie* printed my detailed article on the military revolt of 9 September 1881 over the signature of Armand de Maubuisson, but it didn't earn me any congratulations from the weekly's editorial board. To those gentlemen, who paid me by the line via Albin Balanvin, I still didn't exist.

20

Could it have been the mutineers' audacity that prompted me, too, to do something rash? The idea suddenly occurred to me when I was asked by my father to go and inspect the progress of work on the villa at Ramlah. Three days' leave from the bank would also enable me to call at the *Sémaphore*'s offices, where I had never yet had a chance to introduce myself. So far, so reasonable.

A colleague was leaving for Ismailia the following week. I gave him a letter – a crazy letter – to be discreetly delivered to Nada. Couldn't she find some means of getting away for forty-eight hours and joining me in Alexandria? "I'll be waiting for you," I wrote, at Sidi Gaber station on Tuesday, 20 September . . . "

My colleague returned to Cairo with his mission half accomplished: he had safely delivered the letter to its addressee but failed to bring back the expected reply. No message had been left at his hotel the next day. This was understandable enough, after all. Nada hadn't had time to make such a decision and devise a plausible reason for absenting herself. I was hopeful nonetheless. On the eve of the appointed day I took the train to Alexandria, convinced that she would join me there.

The offices of the *Sémaphore* were in Sherif Street, quite close to the Place des Consuls. I went there feeling rather apprehensive because I knew that Balanvin had been reproached for employing the services of a non-European. Although only occasional and camouflaged by the name Armand de Maubuisson, my work seemed to tarnish the weekly's reputation.

"Showing your face there would be pointless," Balanvin had told me more than once. "You'd be likely to get a poor reception."

The receptionist, to whom I'd given my pen name, returned from the offices upstairs with the information that no one could see me. Then he ostentatiously turned to another visitor. Infuriated, I hurried up the stairs.

Four shirt-sleeved journalists were playing cards in a big room on the first floor. Two or three others were laughing uproariously. It wasn't exactly the scene I'd been expecting.

"Would you kindly direct me to the editor's office?" I asked one of the card players.

"What's your business?" he said sternly, without even looking up.

I was about to reply when a door opened along the corridor. The three jokers fell silent at the approach of a big man of about fifty with a sheaf of paper in his hand.

"Monsieur Bartillat?" I said, going up to him.

His sole response was to adjust his pince-nez.

"I'm Maxime Touta."

"Never heard of you."

"I'm Armand de — "

"Make up your mind, monsieur, I've no time for joking."

"Armand de Maubuisson, who has sent you articles from Cairo . . . "

He readjusted his pince-nez, manifestly annoyed.

"I see. Well?"

I hesitated for a moment, not knowing whether to pursue the matter calmly or start shouting. Just then someone called out, "The theatre page is already set, Monsieur Bartillat."

"Already set?" the editor exclaimed. "But that flop isn't worth writing about. Hold it!"

And he went off to talk to his staff, abandoning me in the corridor.

I left the offices of the *Sémaphore* seething with rage and shaken by the fiercest emotions. I pictured myself seizing that odious individual by the scruff of the neck, whipping off his pince-nez and hurling it to the floor. I could almost hear the glass crunch underfoot.

The scent of seaweed soothed me. A warm breeze was blowing through the palm trees beside the sea. Alexandria in September was an exhilarating place to be. I thought of Nada, telling myself that she would be arriving tomorrow, and her image instantly banished that of the man with the pince-nez.

I planned to take her to a hotel, but the first night I would camp at the villa on my own – an amusing experiment. All I needed were two blankets, a pillow, a little portable stove, and a saucepan, and those I had brought with me from Cairo.

When I came to hire a conveyance, the rivals for my custom tugged at my sleeve and shouted. I eventually settled on a cabriolet with a rather shabby leather hood but a frisky-looking horse. I took hold of the reins with pleasure and made for Rosetta Gate. Before leaving the city I did a little shopping: bread, cheese, tea, candles . . . Then I trotted off along the road to Ramlah.

I fell instantly in love with that ribbon of fine white sand flanked by bushy pepper plants. The Catholic cemetery slumbered peacefully near the handsome convent of the Dames de Sion. The road was almost deserted at this early hour of the afternoon. From time to time I passed farm carts laden with black-veiled peasant women squatting in rows, or garishly painted villas enclosed by tall palm trees swaying in the sea breeze.

I reached little Bulkeley station in less than an hour. All I had to do now was find the track that led to our house. This was easier said than done. I had to turn around three times, having guessed that the sea lay beyond the dunes without being able to see it. The directions I was kindly given by the few people I encountered in the fig fields proved to be utterly fanciful. At long last I was shown the way by a beaming Bedouin, one of those who camped among the existing properties in winter and guarded them for their owners.

And that was when I saw the blue and green expanse of the sea. The sight took my breath away. How could anyone dare to criticize my father for building himself a house there?

The Bedouin, who was soon joined by two other members of his family, escorted me to the villa. I assured them that I didn't need anything and handed over the modest sum my father had agreed to pay them. Even so, they returned an hour later to present me with some dates and Barbary figs.

The house was as my father had wanted it: plain and sturdy. Inside, the walls still gave off a strong smell of plaster. The workmen had gone, their work done, leaving a fine old mess behind: planks, broken tiles, broken glass, sawdust. A mound of rubble occupied the site of the future annexe, whose construction had been postponed until the following year.

I spent several hours clearing up. Then, after making myself a frugal supper by the light of two candles, I wearily climbed the stairs to the best room in the house, one of those that overlooked the sea. I slept on the floor, on the blankets I'd brought from Cairo.

There were only two trains Nada could have taken from Ismailia, one that got to Alexandria at eleven in the morning and another at five in the afternoon. I felt almost certain she would be on board the first of them.

I tethered my horse in front of Sidi Gaber station at ten o'clock. It was ridiculous: no train had ever arrived early – or even on time – in the history of the Egyptian railways, but impatience proved too much for me. I kept glancing at the big clock and peering along the track.

My legs were like jelly when the train pulled into the station thirty-five minutes late. I scanned the platform, leaning against a column, and my heart leapt whenever a young woman appeared at a window. A dozen times I thought I had spotted Nada in the crush of porters. A dozen times I almost darted forward. The platform slowly emptied, the last of the beggars dispersed. Before long there was no one left but some railway employees engaged in a noisy altercation.

Before leaving the station I made renewed inquiries about the next train, asking the same question at every window to be on the safe side. No doubt about it: the train was due in at five that afternoon, as it was every day. There was nothing to do but wait.

I should really have gone to say hello to Cousin Rizqallah or paid my respects to Nassif Bey, but I was afraid one of them might ask me to dine with him. In any case, Nada was the only person I wanted to see. Rather than roam the streets, I decided to go for a drive along the Mahmudiya Canal. That would take me past Palace No. 3, where I had seen Sa'id Pasha on his deathbed during my first visit to Alexandria in January 1863. My first meeting with Nada . . .

Palace No. 3 had been superseded by Ras at-Tin and was now just a khedivial harem. In front of the heavy wrought-iron railings I saw two old eunuchs seated on a bench, knitting with skeins of wool around their necks. I remembered how we had entered the palace that night: the sputtering torches, the viceroy's pavilion, the nurses bustling to and fro, and Nassif Bey anxiously asking my father, "Have you brought my stethoscope?"

No, there was nothing to be seen. I made instead for the Antoniadis Gardens nearby, which were said to be tended by forty gardeners of every nationality. I spent a long time in that earthly paradise, strolling amid aloes, lemon and mandarin trees.

The five o'clock train got in just before six, fifty-five minutes late. Nada wasn't on that one either. I was shattered. How could I have imagined that she would manage to come to Alexandria so easily, or even that she would want to do so, simply because I had asked her to? How could I have arranged all this and convinced myself that it would work?

I got back into the trap with my head throbbing, took the reins and whipped up the horse. I drove to the outskirts of town without even knowing what I was doing, and it was in the same semi-conscious state that I reached the villa an hour-and-a-half later. The light was fading. I threw myself down on the blankets, sick at heart.

I was awakened by a booming, sepulchral voice. Someone was hammering on the door downstairs. Although momentarily alarmed, I was somewhat reassured by the calmly persistent way in which the man kept calling *"Ya khawaga!"*

"Who is it?" I asked without opening the door.

"This is the Touta house, isn't it?" said the voice.

"Yes. Why?"

"Because there's a lady waiting in my cab."

That galvanized me. No cabby was ever welcomed so lovingly, but it wasn't him I longed to kiss. Nada had already alighted from the cab. Her weary face broke into a smile.

"We've been driving around for three hours," said the turbaned cabby. "All the lady knew was that you lived near Fleming Beach."

I tipped him royally, and he set off into the darkness.

Nada fell into my arms. We kissed with a kind of joyful frenzy, but she could hardly stand, she was so tired.

"Would you like something to eat?" I asked. "There's some, er . . . bread and cheese."

She smiled. "How extravagant of you!"

I covered her face with kisses.

"To be honest," she went on, "I'm dog-tired."

"I hardly dare show you the bedroom . . . "

Laughing, she stretched out on my blankets fully dressed — "as an experiment" — but a moment or two later her eyelids drooped and she fell asleep. The candlelight danced over her face. I gazed at her entranced. I had often seen Nada laugh, I had more than once seen her face transfigured with pleasure, but I had never yet seen her asleep. It was an immense joy. I continued to watch over her until far into the night. Then I, too, drifted off.

The sun had risen by the time I opened my eyes. Nada was no longer beside me. The shutters were half open and she was leaning on the window sill, gazing out at the sea — a sea as smooth as glass, as calm as a lake. Looking at them both, I almost choked with happiness.

The rustle of the blankets made her turn round. She had removed her travelling outfit and put on a sort of white chemise resembling a nightgown.

"What about a swim?" she whispered.

I didn't even have time to kiss her. Like a child, she ran across the deserted beach towards the vast, turquoise plain that merged with the sky. She paused just long enough to remove her gown, then slowly waded into the water. I also got undressed and followed her.

I wonder occasionally if some young Bedouin stationed behind the dunes may have been captivated, like me, by that dark, flowing hair, that slender waist, and those opulent thighs as they disappeared, little by little, below the surface of the warm sea . . .

Nada swam sidestroke — like all the young women at the Ismailia Baths, I supposed. Now and again she turned over on her back, breasts to the sky, and the sight of her dark fleece aroused me. I stretched out beside her, dazzled by the sun, lulled by the faint lapping of the wavelets.

We swam slowly, side by side, in the motionless water. From time to time our bodies brushed against each other before resuming their leisurely progress, then converged again, touched, and became entwined . . .

Two hours later, dry and more or less dressed, we were seated on the blankets on the veranda, eating bread and cheese. In fits of laughter, Nada explained why she had been obliged to travel via Cairo and catch a later train. On reaching Alexandria in the evening, she had taken a cab and instructed the coachman to do his utmost to find "a new villa at Fleming". "*Ya madame*," the poor man kept saying after two fruitless hours, "we don't have the address."

"It's not the address we're looking for it's the house!" she told him firmly. "Let's try this track to the right."

"You're mad," I said with my mouth full. "Fancy setting off like that, at night, with a stranger!"

"What else could I do? No one was waiting for me at the station."

I swore that I had got there at ten o'clock that morning. She pretended not to believe me, then reproached me for promenading in the Antoniadis Gardens "with God knows who". I devoured her with kisses.

"We'll come back here another time," I said, "when the house is in better shape."

She didn't reply at once. Then, looking more serious, she said in a low voice, "Happy times are best left unrepeated. Some of them come only once."

I was afraid to press her to say more on the subject.

Nada did not look back when the horse hauled us up and over the little sand dune, but I sensed that she was charmed by the fields of fig trees, the white road to Ramlah, and all that had escaped her the night before.

Her train was leaving at three that afternoon, mine a little later. I had suggested lunching on the terrace of the Café de France in the Place des Consuls. We chose a secluded, well-shaded table.

We had barely sat down when I saw the man with the pince-nez arrive with two other people. He snapped his fingers, and a waiter hurriedly conducted him to the other end of the terrace, where a table had been reserved for him.

"That's Bartillat," I told Nada, "the editor of the *Sémaphore*. I haven't told you about my visit to the newspaper's offices yesterday."

She shrugged her shoulders when I described what had happened.

"I was also looked down on at Ismailia – not by Étienne, of course, but by the other French people. Then I realized that, if you don't want to be looked down on, you mustn't belittle yourself."

"What do you mean?"

"I mean that, in the company of Europeans, we tend to apologize for what we are. I don't see why. Why should we feel inferior because we possess two cultures instead of one?"

This impressed me. "You're the one who should be a journalist," I told her admiringly.

We spoke awhile of journalism, which I found so tempting. I could almost certainly have landed a job with one of the Arabic-language publications recently founded by *Shawam* like ourselves. These new types of newspaper were steadily gaining popularity with the Egyptians because their straightforward style represented a break with the high-flown verbiage of the past. My own command of Arabic would have enabled me, with a little effort, to work for a newspaper like *al-Ahram*, founded by the Takla brothers, but for some reason I couldn't explain, I was insistent on writing in the language of Balanvin, Étienne, and the Très Chers Frères.

When the disdainful-looking French maître d'hôtel came up to take our order, I kept him waiting on purpose. Nada glanced at me mischievously, then asked him, "Don't you have any fuul?"

"Pardon, madame?"

"Fuul, beans."

The maître d'hôtel almost choked. "No, madame, we don't serve them."

"Even though we're in Egypt?" said Nada, looking annoyed. Then, abruptly, with the self-assured air of a Frenchwoman from Ismailia:

"Is your Muscadet well chilled? I hope it has plenty of body. What about the Beaujolais? Not too young, I trust? And the grape? What? You don't know the variety?"

The maître d'hôtel stammered a few incomprehensible words and almost clicked his heels before withdrawing. We giggled together like children.

Nada said, "I could also have asked him for some *taameya*."

"Pardon, madame?"

"Some *taaa* –"

"No, madame, we don't serve it."

We wept with laughter.

Nada had referred to the unique nature of our meetings. I savoured every moment we spent together, telling myself that it was unrepeatable. There was no guarantee that she would even consent to see me again. Had she been trying, during our conversation on the beach, to accustom me to the idea that this was the end?

I postponed the question until I was kissing her goodbye on the platform.

"You'll come to the villa again, won't you?"

The locomotive was noisily belching steam. Nada's rather sad little smile smote my heart.

21

I gave Balanvin only a very vague account of my visit to the *Sémaphore*. I had turned up at a bad moment, I said, just as the paper was being put to bed. He asked no questions, and there the matter rested.

The situation in Cairo was changing week by week. The officers' revolt had developed, imperceptibly, into a political insurrection. 'Arabi represented the army and the army represented the people, so he requested the khedive to set up a genuine, elected parliament.

"A parliament!" scoffed Balanvin, throwing up his hands. "We'll be getting another bunch of sheikhs and sycophants. The last khedive devised a so-called Chamber of Delegates to make himself look good in the eyes of the European powers. During the first session, when it was explained to those worthy provincial dignitaries that every parliament had benches on the left for the opposition, there was a frightful stampede: everyone wanted to sit on the right!"

Having secured the elections he had demanded, 'Arabi agreed to transfer his regiment to Tel al-Kebir as a conciliatory gesture. Instead of going straight to the station, however, the 4th Infantry Regiment entered Cairo by way of Bab al-Nasr Gate, marched through the Muski, across Ezbekiyah Square, and along Clot Bey Street, and called a halt at the Husayn Mosque. It was a triumphal progress. A big Cairo confectioner distributed sweets to the troops for the journey. 'Arabi and his officers were cheered by ecstatic crowds at every station the train passed on its route.

Some months later, thanks to information gleaned by Balanvin, the *Sémaphore d'Alexandrie* announced that a new government was to be formed with 'Arabi as minister of war. The Europeans were stunned by this news prior to its official confirmation.

Promoted to the rank of general and pasha, the rebel leader received a congratulatory telegram from Constantinople.

"They're rather ironical, these electric congratulations," Balanvin told me. "Turkey is currently backing a man who has always denounced Turkish domination. It's a touchingly realistic policy, but I don't know where it'll end."

The appointment of the new minister of war was followed by the wholesale promotion of 'Arabist officers: twenty-three lieutenant-colonels, Walid al-Ahlawi among them, obtained the rank of colonel. Our old friend was now an *amiralai* with a monthly income of forty Egyptian guineas. This second increment in less than two years would enable him to finish paying off his debts and rear his seven children in somewhat greater comfort. I was happy for him.

My father deputed me to go and congratulate his former pupil. Access to 'Abbassiya Barracks was barred to civilians, but an understanding corporal let me pass in return for the piastre he pocketed. Walid al-Ahlawi granted me only a brief interview, looking very preoccupied: he had just learned of his appointment to command the 5th Regiment based at Alexandria.

Was it pure chance that was taking him back to the city where he had been so profoundly humiliated? I'm inclined to think that he had been contemplating this move for a long time, and that he had spared no effort to obtain it. His absolute loyalty to 'Arabi – when other officers had been bought by the palace – would undoubtedly have entitled him to ask a favour. Besides, it was very much in the interests of the new minister of war to station a completely trustworthy man in an area of such strategic importance.

We experienced several weeks of great tranquillity, if not euphoria. Everyone seemed content: the officers – of course – and the people who followed them, but also the dignitaries well represented in the new Chamber of Delegates and even the Europeans, who were reassured by the changed atmosphere prevailing in Cairo. Khedive Tewfiq, agreeing with the native officers in this respect, seemed to fear only one thing: the ex-khedive's manoeuvres with a view to regaining the throne. Although in exile, Isma'il Pasha gave the impression of waiting in the wings.

There was great agitation on this score when word came that one of his wives, accompanied by her retinue, had sailed for Alexandria to undergo medical treatment in Egypt. Orders were promptly given to surround the ship with small craft and prevent her from landing.

In view of his age and respectability, Dr Nassif Bey was sent aboard to examine the princess. She indignantly refused. No physician would be permitted to enter her cabin, even if he complied with all the rules of propriety essential in such circumstances: dim lighting, the presence of eunuchs, a protective veil . . . Nassif Bey wired news of this setback to Cairo, adding that the princess had threatened to put an end to herself unless she was allowed to go ashore.

Tewfiq Pasha was on the point of giving way, as he usually did, when General 'Arabi personally ordered the ship to leave Egyptian waters. His initiative earned him the cordial thanks of the viceregal family.

But Balanvin was undeceived by this flurry of mutual affection. We had already entered a phase when accounts were to be settled and plots hatched.

FROM OUR CAIRO CORRESPONDENT
To the Editor:

2 June 1882

To tell you that calm prevails here would be a distortion of the truth. All manner of rumours, some of the wildest nature, are circulating in Cairo. I distrust such harem tittle-tattle, however, and prefer to stick to the facts. Permit me, sir, to recapitulate the series of events which have occurred in the last few months, and which have just come to a conclusion — albeit only temporary, no doubt.

At the beginning of April, news of a Turco-Circassian plot against nationalist officers caused a great stir in Cairo. One of the generals in 'Arabi's entourage claimed to have found some arsenic in the bowl of milk prepared for him nightly by his maidservant. 'Arabi himself and several of his associates were said to have escaped the assassin's blade by a hair's-breadth.

In the next few days it became necessary to arrest some fifty Turkish officers. How surprised we were to learn that they included General Osman Rifki, the former minister of war and bête noire *of the authors of last year's pronunci-amento! Taken into custody and handed over to expert gaolers, the general and* his friends were quick to confess their putative crimes. They were sentenced to degradation and exiled to the Sudan, but the khedive refused to ratify the sentence on the grounds that Osman Rifki was a pasha, and that the matter must be referred to the Sultan.

The atmosphere worsened from day to day. The cabinet ended by convening the Chamber and requesting it to proclaim the khedive's deposition. One officer publicly declared, "Tewfiq has only to take his suitcase and move into Shepheard's Hotel like the good foreigner he is."

The arrival at Alexandria of a Franco-British squadron on 20 May only exacerbated the nationalist officers' feelings. I am assured that several of them rallied to 'Arabi at 'Abdin Barracks and swore on a Qur'an and a sword to fight to the bitter end.

The joint Franco-British note of 25 May, which called for 'Arabi's dismissal and banishment, did nothing to settle matters. In the eyes of many Egyptians, the rebel leader, having become a political leader, was now a religious leader destined to drive out "the infidel".

On 26 May the government rejected the Franco-British ultimatum and resigned. Great confusion reigned in Cairo thereafter. The Italian, Austrian, German and Russian consuls saw fit to go to 'Arabi's residence and request his protection for European nationals. The general reminded them that he was no longer a minister. The consuls, who may have overlooked this minor detail, nonetheless appealed to his benevolent solicitude.

For their part, some local dignitaries went to the palace to request the khedive to recall 'Arabi. The head of the delegation, not content with kissing the hem of the khedivial stambouline, seized His Highness's hand and ran his lips over the back and palm of that merciful appendage. The following day saw the formation of a new government with 'Arabi as minister of war.

And there matters stand, sir. I would not venture to assert that the summer will end on the latter development. Everyone here is awaiting the arrival of the emissary dispatched by the Sultan to pour oil on troubled waters. Latest reports state that the pasha's vessel has left Constantinople and is on its way to Alexandria.

Albin Balanvin

22

The Sultan's special envoy, Dervish Pasha, reached Alexandria aboard the imperial yacht *Izzédine* on 7 June 1882. The khedive had wanted to be the first to welcome him, but 'Arabi ordered the commanders of the 5th and 6th Regiments to go to the boat at once. Thus the august visitor boarded the special train that was to take him to Cairo escorted by Walid al-Ahlawi and another colonel.

The nationalist officers had arranged things well. Dervish Pasha was cheered all the way to Gezira Palace by crowds who coupled the name of the Sultan, the Commander of the Faithful, with that of 'Arabi. Little urchins beat a tattoo on their bootblacks' boxes, crying "Long live Islam!"

Gratified by this welcome, Dervish Pasha received the 'Arabists at Gezira. He distributed nearly 200 decorations – including the Order of the Mejidiya for their leader – and assured them that the Sultan would be happy to entertain them in Constantinople. Echoes of these kindnesses reached the ears of the khedive, who was outraged.

Within forty-eight hours, however, the head of the Ottoman mission had entirely changed his tune. 'Arabi and his friends found themselves confronted by a brusque, unsympathetic man. When one of Walid al-Ahlawi's brother officers condemned the khedive's attitude, the Turk responded with a barely veiled threat: he went to the window and pointed to the Citadel, where Muhammad Ali had slaughtered the recalcitrant Mamelukes.

Word of this volte-face on the part of the Sultan's special envoy began to spread. When I expressed surprise at this, Balanvin merely chuckled. "My young friend," he said, "men of his type can always be made to see reason with the aid of very simple arguments. The khedive has been showering Dervish Pasha with gifts for several days. 'Bakshish Pasha' – that's what everyone calls him now."

A week later, alarmed by the tension prevailing in Cairo, the directors of the Imperial Ottoman Bank decided to transfer some of its securities and financial records to Alexandria, where the Franco-British naval squadron was lying at anchor. I and two other employees were instructed to accompany these documents and file them at the other end.

This trip was far from unwelcome. It would enable me to put the finishing touches to the villa, which my father wanted ready by July, and savour a little of Nada's lingering presence there. I might also have a chance to spend a little more time with Walid al-Ahlawi than I had on the last few occasions in Cairo.

The head office of the Ottoman Bank was in the Place des Consuls, not far from the equestrian statue of Muhammad Ali erected there some years earlier. Five metres high and cast in Paris after a model by Jacquemart, this bronze reposed on a white marble plinth. Hand on hip, the turbaned founder of the Egyptian dynasty proudly dominated the famous square that bore his name, though everyone continued to call it the Place des Consuls. I had a good view of his charger's massive bronze hindquarters from the bank's records department.

My cousin Rizqallah lived in a very opulent apartment on the sea front. He delightedly showed me his servants, his Louis XIII furniture, and his new carriage and pair, "one of the best-sprung conveyances in town". He also introduced me to his wife, the Jewess who still provoked so many whispers in the family.

Bella, née Aghion, belied her forename. She had a rather unattractive face and a pointed nose – "a Jewish nose", to quote that numskull Lolo – but a very sophisticated way with words. I was impressed by her direct gaze and by a lack of pretension surprising in a wealthy Alexandrian heiress. Her reasons for marrying a parvenu like Rizqallah would always remain a mystery to me.

We discussed the political situation. My cousin told me that the gunsmiths of Alexandria had never done brisker business. Many Europeans, fearing the worst, had been buying rifles and revolvers in the last few days. It was rumoured in town that some British and Greek officers had submitted a defensive plan to the consulates in case of disturbances. This envisaged moving foreign residents into the buildings around the Place des Consuls and erecting barricades, guarded by armed men, in all the adjoining streets. The consuls-general had turned this scheme down, however, because they felt such preparations would only heighten the prevailing tension.

The Egyptian army's 5th Regiment was stationed near Ras at-Tin Palace. With some trepidation, I went there and asked to see the colonel. After being kept waiting for a good half-hour, I concluded that Walid al-Ahlawi did not propose to waste his time on me. However, he eventually appeared in person and invited me to stay to dinner. I accepted with pleasure.

It was a frugal meal eaten without knives or forks: we all dipped our bread into the steaming dish of fuul in the middle of the table. The soldiers who served us were highly deferential toward their commander, not that he forbore to reprimand them harshly. Walid's new appointment had changed him. He spoke curtly, heedless of whether he sounded abrupt or even coarse.

I found him impressive, this man of forty in the prime of life. In spite of all that separated us, his effect on me was rather like that of an elder brother. Watching his dark, shapely, well-manicured hands as they vigorously dismembered his bread, I reflected that, had I been a woman, I would have found it hard to resist them. God alone knew why, but I had a sudden vision of Nada with Walid al-Ahlawi during one of his lessons at my home. I told myself what a handsome couple they would have made. I pictured them naked, face to face – pictured a pair of swarthy hands on Nada's buttocks . . .

Walid spoke at considerable length of the plans to modernize Alexandria's fifteen forts. Apart from the one at 'Agami, which was a long way from the city, all were dilapidated and ill-equipped. Most of them dated from Muhammad Ali's day, and some had even been built under Bonaparte. I was unaware, as he may also have been at that stage, that the renovation of these forts would be the crux of the conflict with the British in weeks to come.

After supper Walid took me on a tour of the barracks and the environs of Ras at-Tin Palace. We spoke of the khedive as a matter of course. Walid thought he was finished. For him, Egypt had only one leader, 'Arabi, and the Sultan would sooner or later accept this despite the baneful, mercenary role played by Bakshish Pasha.

That night, back in my little hotel room, I jotted down all that Walid al-Ahlawi had told me. Those notes, together with my own impressions, filled a dozen-odd pages in my notebook. I resolved to go and see him again the following week, as he had suggested.

On 11 June, a Sunday, I was one of a score of guests invited to lunch at Rizqallah's. My cousin presided at the head of his immense dining table flanked by the wife of the Greek vice-consul and the accredited mistress of the managing director of Ciccolani, the big department store. Also among the guests was the eldest son of Monsieur Xavier-Saillard, the spitting image of his father, who was bombarding Bella with social chitchat.

Just as the lobster was being served we heard an explosion in the street. No one seemed alarmed. Xavier-Saillard Jr, who had the bit between his teeth, told how, at a Cairo banquet in the reign of Isma'il, a huge silver dish had been brought before the khedive: curled up on it was a delightful Nubian slave girl, naked as Eve before the Fall, her appetizing flesh as black as if it had been roasted in the sun. This anecdote titillated all present while their crystal glasses were being filled with a delicious Alsatian wine.

Outside, the explosions were becoming more frequent. A servant came to inform Rizqallah that rioting had broken out in town. Lunch was temporarily suspended because one of the ladies had an attack of nerves. She was deposited on a divan in the drawing room and given smelling salts. We all gathered round. Her plunging neckline revealed a pair of delightful breasts . . .

My cousin instructed a manservant to ensure that the front door was securely bolted. Another was dispatched to close all the shutters. The Greek vice-consul wanted to go to his office but was persuaded to wait awhile. We went on with our lunch in the gloom.

At the coffee stage I slipped away, leaving Rizqallah to smoke a cigar with his important guests. Bella accompanied me to the door, counselling prudence. I'm sure she would not have let me go, being the thoughtful and sensible woman she was, had she known that the centre of Alexandria had become a battlefield, and that the streets were already strewn with dozens of corpses.

On reaching the Place des Consuls I was startled by a fusillade. I sheltered in a doorway, then sprinted to my hotel. The streets were deserted, and there was nothing much to be seen.

The proprietor of the hotel, eyes wide with terror, told me as much as he knew in a tremulous voice. At about two that afternoon, when the restaurants and cafés were packed, a scuffle had broken out in Rue des Sœurs, not very far from Alfred Falaki's shop. A Maltese drew his knife and wounded an Arab, then dived into a house nearby. The neighbourhood was up in arms in no time. Europeans fired shots from their windows, and furious locals, brandishing *nabouts*, smashed the skulls of any foreigners they met.

During the next few hours the British consul, Mr Cookson, sustained a serious head injury and several of his colleagues were badly manhandled. In the harbour, insurgents attacked a boatload of Europeans returning from a tour of the warships and drowned them.

"But where are the forces of law and order?" the hotel proprietor kept asking.

The 5th Infantry Regiment did not step in until late that afternoon. By nightfall, hundreds of soldiers had occupied the intersections and were searching passers-by for weapons.

It emerged later that the prefect of police was indisposed and had, perforce, been taking purgatives. The next day, when many people would have liked to call him to account, he was unavailable, deprived by a stroke of the use of one arm.

Walid al-Ahlawi assured me that he had done his best once the military commander of Alexandria ordered him to intervene. I have never understood why the order came so late. No one produced a satisfactory explanation in the course of the subsequent trial.

I sent my father a telegram reassuring him of my safety and informing him that I intended to prolong my trip to Alexandria. As for his own sojourn beside the sea, this might well be jeopardized by current developments.

I had written to the Mancelles only once, ten years earlier, and that was to thank them for their hospitality. It came hard to write to them both when I was interested in only one of them and yearned to convey my innermost feelings to her. However, I was prompted to do so by the exceptional nature of recent events and the repercussions they were bound to have had on the French colony at Ismailia. I wrote a fairly impersonal account of those events on the hotel's letterhead – my way of informing Nada that I was on the coast and thinking of her. At least one sentence in the letter, which alluded to the villa, was meant for her alone . . .

23

Bakshish Pasha had become very attached to the khedive. He made a point of accompanying him to Alexandria on 13 June and installing himself in Ras at-Tin Palace with the viceregal family. Their arrival caused a certain amount of agitation on account of the ceremonial gunfire that greeted it. Unwilling to wait any longer, a number of European families packed their bags and made tracks for the harbour.

There had already been many departures since the massacre two days earlier. Several banks had transferred their offices to ships anchored offshore. Ours being one of them, I worked down at the waterfront. From now on, our main task was to close the accounts of customers who were leaving Egypt.

Rizqallah was beside himself. "Five hundred dead, and the Franco-British squadron merely looked on through binoculars! In the old days, one blast on the consul's whistle would have been enough to bring our sailors ashore."

"Our" sailors . . . I regularly forgot that my cousin enjoyed the status of a French dependant. His remark reminded me that, in 1863, the French consul had threatened the Egyptian authorities with military intervention if Monsieur Xavier-Saillard's assailants were not punished as he himself prescribed. At a distance of nineteen years, the comparison between the two events seemed almost comically unreal.

Ras at-Tin palace was too vulnerable to the risk of bombardment. A few days later the khedive, accompanied by his family and Bakshish Pasha, left it and took refuge at Ramlah Palace, the immense pink edifice his father had built outside town.

"It makes little difference whether he's here or there," Walid al-Ahlawi told me sarcastically.

He had sent a note to my hotel inviting me to dinner again. This second visit to the barracks was even more interesting than the first. I met several officers there, and was able to gauge the extent to which they were hostile to Europeans and dreamed of a different Egypt. Knowing no languages but Arabic and a little Turkish, they felt thoroughly foreign in cosmopolitan Alexandria, where important business was transacted in French, English, or Italian, and where café waiters were named Socrate, Périclès, or Aristote.

The officers' contempt for the khedive was exacerbated by rumours reaching them from Ramlah Palace. It was said that, to his ministers, Tewfiq was displaying exaggerated zeal, declaring that if war broke out he would take a rifle and march at the head of the Egyptian army.

"We must find him a little rifle," a lieutenant-colonel of the 5th Regiment remarked in my presence, " – a nice, harmless one."

His comrades guffawed at this.

A letter was waiting for me when I got back to the hotel that night. The rounded, slightly slanting handwriting on the envelope made me feel faint with happiness. It contained a single sheet of pink notepaper.

Thank you for your letter, Maxime. I cannot say that it gave us pleasure. The events which you describe in such detail, and of which we had received very incomplete reports here, are both distressing and alarming. Once blood starts to flow, men never know how to staunch it . . .

I am writing these few lines in haste to give to some friends who are leaving for Alexandria in less than an hour's time, hoping to find berths on a ship bound for Europe. Ismailia hasn't known such a mood of panic since the cholera epidemic. Étienne spends half his time trying to dissuade staff from leaving.

What do the coming days and weeks hold in store for us? Being a journalist, you have a seat in the stalls, as it were. Keep your eyes open and take care!

It's a mistake to look back, Maxime. You have your whole life ahead of you. You'll do great things, and – like me – you'll have a family some day.

　　Much love,

　　Nada

I reread that letter innumerable times. Before long I knew it by heart and could recite it mechanically, pondering the significance of each and every line.

　　The straightforward, unadorned style was typical of Nada. Not an empty word nor a word too much. How many things were expressed or intimated in the paragraphs bounded by "Thank you" and "Much love", by that expression of genuine gratitude and the love whose manifestations I could picture in a thousand forms. Some phrases – "Being a journalist" – thrilled me. She, at least, believed it and believed in me: "You'll do great things . . . " But the final paragraph effaced all the others: "You have your whole life ahead of you . . . " Nada was drawing a line under the past and inviting me to do the same. "You'll have a family . . . " Was she endorsing Aunt Angéline's efforts to find me a wife? "Like me, you'll have a family . . . " That was clear enough. From now on she meant to devote herself entirely to her husband and children; she would cleave to her roses in the desert and forbid herself any more moments of folly with me.

　　As I read and reread those lines, my joy at receiving her letter evaporated. While she was about it, Nada might have enclosed a dried flower – a few petals from a wilted rose . . .

　　In the Place des Consuls, the mournful bells of the English church chimed three in the morning.

24

The British admiral, Sir Seymour Beauchamp, had received reinforcements. He was now in command of over 5,000 men aboard eight battleships and seven other vessels. On 10 July, on the grounds that the Egyptians were continuing to reinforce their coastal batteries, he demanded that all Alexandria's forts be disarmed.

The cabinet convened at once under the khedive's chairmanship. It replied, very firmly, that a few urgent repairs had been undertaken, nothing more, and that, after all, the forts were on Egyptian soil. Being the custodian of her rights and her honour, Egypt could not surrender a single fort or gun unless compelled to do so by force of arms.

Walid al-Ahlawi, who passed me outside Ras at-Tin barracks mounted on his charger, was in a fever of excitement. "If the British and French open fire," he called, "every treaty and agreement will be revoked. Egypt will be released from all her debts at a stroke. It'll unleash a holy war throughout the Muslim world. We shall have a genuine caliph at last!"

The previous day, European consuls had been invited to embark their nationals. *Kawasses* went from door to door in the middle of the night, rousing the laggards.

Adolphe Xavier-Saillard had quit Alexandria in mid-June. He remembered the cholera epidemic of 1865 and had no wish to be the last to escape, but his far more belligerent eldest son, whom I had met at Rizqallah's, wouldn't hear of leaving. Together with some other Europeans armed to the teeth, he planned, if the worst happened, to take refuge in a building in the Place des Consuls. "We shall never knuckle under to that riffraff!" he kept saying.

The Greek vice-consul had offered to shelter Rizqallah and his family aboard a Greek warship, the *Hellas*.

"Like to come with us?" my cousin asked half-heartedly.

He looked very relieved when I declined.

"In that case," he said, "you can have my apartment. You're at home there, so make yourself comfortable. I'll tell the servants."

And he hurried off to have a word with them.

On board the *Hellas* some hours later, Rizqallah saw the French squadron sail off in the direction of Port Sa'id. It would take no part in the fighting.

"The cowards!" cried a Greek businessman.

"I forbid you to speak like that!" my cousin said loftily.

"But the gentleman's right!" exclaimed a Marseille restaurateur, who was standing near them on deck. "They're cowards, our government. Those British sailors are ready to fight to defend 3,000 of their compatriots living in Alexandria. There are over 8,000 of us French, and they're leaving us in the lurch. Gambetta's got balls — he was ready to intervene, but that pansy Clemenceau managed to persuade our deputies to vote against it."

That 10 July, all the civilian steamers or sailing ships in port departed one by one. Bakshish Pasha's imperial yacht was conveyed to a place of safety, and the khedive's *Mahrousa* was towed to the Arsenal. Alexandria resembled a city of the dead.

I had authorized Rizqallah's servants, who usually slept on the terrace near their hen-coop, to come and sleep inside the apartment. Not venturing to occupy the bedrooms, they laid out their straw mattresses in a passage.

I spent the early part of the evening filling my notebook with all the little details I'd observed since the day before. "Being a journalist," Nada had written, "you have a seat in the stalls, as it were."

At about ten o'clock I went out on to the balcony and leant on the stone parapet. It was a glorious night. From time to time, one of the British battleships would scan the Egyptian dispositions by sweeping the coastline with her searchlights.

"Alexandria," Walid al-Ahlawi had explained, showing me a wall map, "resembles a boot with the sole facing Europe. It's very difficult to defend. We might, at a pinch, prevent a landing, but not a bombardment."

Seen on that peaceful night, there was something magical about the bluish beams of light from the British battleships. I thought of the *Phénix*, the ship that had brought Nada to Egypt one January night in 1863. Unlit at that period, the approaches to Alexandria were too dangerous to permit a boat to negotiate them by night. Crammed with Syrian refugees, the *Phénix* had been compelled to wait until daybreak before entering the roads.

At dawn, feeling rather bemused, I fell asleep on a Louis XIII bed facing the sea. "Keep your eyes open," Nada had written.

25

I awoke with a start, roused by the first detonation. It was just after seven in the morning. Several more bangs made the windows shake in an alarming manner, and then came pandemonium: all the Egyptian forts replied at once. Terrified, Rizqallah's two servants ran from room to room, asking for instructions. I told them to close the shutters. It was all we could do.

After a quarter of an hour I cautiously ventured out onto one of the balconies. There was little to be seen. The British ships seemed blinded by the sun and their own gun smoke, which the wind was blowing back at them. They took some time to adjust their aim. I knew from a reliable source that the Egyptian artillerymen had only a few poorly mounted Armstrong breech-loaders. Their other guns had little prospect of piercing the British ships' armour-plate. Facing them was *Inflexible*, a floating monster whose sixteen-inch shells threatened to hit the Egyptian's ill-protected powder magazines at any moment.

We got used to the roar of the guns as the hours went by. Rizqallah's servants did not stay put. One of them came out on the balcony, the other went to see if his hen-coop was still on the terrace. Towards noon, I made a cautious foray into the street.

Chaos reigned in the neighbourhood of the European hospital. Men were running in all directions, women screaming. I learned that a shell had passed through the main ward, killing some patients and injuring others.

That was not the only mistake Sir Seymour's gunners made. As I turned a corner, I was almost knocked down by a uniformed employee of the Egyptian Postal Service, who was carrying a bloodstained child in his arms.

"He's dying!" he shouted. "It's my son. I'm looking for a doctor."

The little boy's leg was bleeding profusely from the calf. I had seen my father treat a similar case.

"Put him down," I told the man, but he went on shouting.

I took the child from his arms and laid him down on the road myself. Not having anything to hand that could serve as a tourniquet, I tore off my shirt and knotted it firmly round the boy's leg above the knee. Meantime, alerted by his father's cries, several people had emerged from the houses nearby.

"It's my son!" he kept saying. "Is there a doctor somewhere?"

The wound had almost stopped bleeding, but I explained that the tourniquet must not be left on too long. Someone brought a plank on which the boy was borne away, God alone knew where to.

I continued on my way stripped to the waist. The streets down by the harbour were deserted save for a few dogs, which were howling mournfully. A sudden, violent cannonade compelled me to take refuge in the doorway of a small building. All the windows caved in with a deafening crash, and a shard of glass gashed my arm. Dabbing the cut with my handkerchief, I abandoned my excursion and made a long detour via the Arab quarter before returning to Rizqallah's apartment for a new shirt.

The bombardment continued until five that afternoon. One of the servants went in search of news and came back smiling triumphantly.

"Four British battleships have been sunk," he announced. "They may even have sunk a fifth. Admiral Beauchamp has been captured."

I went back outside at once. In the street, several men had gathered around a fountain. They were clapping their hands and uttering exultant cries.

"The admiral was taken to the station in handcuffs. He's already on his way to Cairo . . . "

Nassif Bey's house was only a short distance away, I rang the bell beside the garden gate, which was opened by a very dignified, mournful-looking manservant.

My father's colleague had aged a good deal, but he still had all his wits about him. Thanks to his numerous contacts, he also remained extremely well-informed about what went on in the city. He had just received word that all the Egyptian forts except that of 'Agami had been destroyed. Even as we spoke, he said, Sir Seymour Beauchamp must be quaffing champagne with his officers on board the *Inflexible*.

Nassif Bey's wife offered to put me up — not, of course, in the little room overlooking the sea, for fear of a renewed bombardment, but in the one my father had occupied at the front of the house. I thanked her, but explained that I must return at once to my cousin's apartment, which he had left in my charge. Then I hurried off to the barracks of the 5th Regiment.

A huge white flag was flying from the top of the fort, part of which had been demolished. Soldiers armed with buckets were putting out the last of a fire that had fortunately spared the magazine. An extremely nervous corporal informed me that the commanding officer was away. When I persisted, he cocked his rifle and levelled it at me.

An oath rang out from an upstairs window: it was one of the lieutenant-colonels I'd dined with three weeks earlier. The corporal promptly sprang to attention and let me pass.

Walid al-Ahlawi was indeed absent. Together with some other senior officers, he had joined 'Arabi at Ramlah Palace to present the khedive with a report on the situation. I awaited his return at the barracks for two hours, chatting with various officers and listening carefully to all that was said. Meantime, dozens of badly wounded men were being evacuated.

As soon as he returned, Walid was surrounded by his officers and pressed for the latest news. The *amiralai* was trembling with rage. I had never seen him in such a state.

It seemed that the khedive had angrily requested his army chiefs to defend Fort 'Agami against the British if they landed. His reasoning was impeccable: he had no right to cede any national territory without the Sultan's authorization. Bakshish Pasha, who was at his side, nodded approvingly.

"I don't know who we're dealing with," Walid told his subordinates, "hypocrites or madmen."

Then, catching sight of me, he added rather belligerently, "The press will decide which."

* * *

It was a sinister night. Alexandria was in total darkness except when probed from time to time by the electrical beams from the sea. Nada had urged me to be careful. If I hadn't been entirely so, it was because of her — because she had hinted that our own imprudences were a thing of the past.

All that could be heard in the morning was the rumble of carts laden with mutilated bodies and the wails of the women in black who followed in their wake.

As to what happened after that, I am still a trifle unclear to this day. The evidence was contradictory, and the trial failed to produce convincing results. All I know for sure is what I saw with my own eyes.

Accompanied by the sound of drums and bugles, Colonel Soliman Sami of the 6th Regiment went to the Place des Consuls, where he delivered a speech. He told the assembled crowd that Alexandria was going to be occupied by the British, and that they must evacuate the city after first rendering it useless to the invader.

The looting began soon afterwards. I saw soldiers smash shop windows followed by a yelling mob of people who helped themselves to the contents. They had already ransacked part of the Ciccolani department store when some uniformed cavalrymen appeared. Walid al-Ahlawi, who was among them, ordered the frenzied soldiers to desist, but they ignored him. Other officers intervened with just as little success. The looters had now been joined by some Bedouin who had ridden into town and were galloping wildly round the square.

Later, someone in the crowd sighted several Europeans at a window of the Grand Hôtel de France. Cries rang out and stones were hurled at the building. Someone fired a shot, sowing the seeds of panic. That was when the soldiers broke down the door of the hotel and charged upstairs.

It appears that the bodies of three Europeans, one of them that of Xavier-Saillard's son, were dragged out into the street. I did not see this myself; I can only state that Walid al-Ahlawi had left the square by then: knowing himself powerless to intervene and doubtless summoned to perform other urgent duties, he had already returned to Ras at-Tin barracks.

The first fires broke out late that afternoon. Several buildings in Sherif

Pasha Street were ablaze, and the Place des Consuls went up in flames at roughly the same time.

Horsemen galloped through the city to warn the inhabitants. A wholesale stampede ensued. Everyone made a mad dash for the railway station, trampling women, children and old men underfoot.

Several companies of the 6th Regiment had surrounded Ramlah Palace and were preventing anyone from entering or leaving. The khedive was a prisoner. Shouting to make himself heard above the wails of the little princes and their nursemaids, he called for some boots and a rifle. Old Bakshish Pasha, on the verge of tears, swore that he would die at his side. 'Arabi was requested to explain himself. After some palaver, he agreed to recall most of the troops. Those who remained were wooed all night long by the khedive and the head of the Ottoman mission, who distributed numerous decorations. When morning came, the viceregal family was surrounded, not by gaolers, but by fanatical defenders.

'Arabi had decided to regroup his army at Kafr ad-Dawwar, half-an-hour's march from Alexandria. A village separated from the city by Lake Mariut, it could only be approached via a narrow causeway built to carry the railway line, which rendered the place impregnable.

On its retreat, Walid al-Ahlawi's regiment bivouacked under the walls of Palace No. 3, on the banks of the Mahmudiya Canal. I spent several hours there with his officers, remembering Sa'id Pasha's death throes and Dr Nassif's anxiety about his stethoscope. The mood was tense. Now and then a dog could be heard barking as it roamed around inside the deserted building.

The regiment set off at nightfall. I, too, set off into the darkness, making for the centre of the abandoned city.

It was not until twenty-four hours after the Egyptian withdrawal that the British decided to land, and then with extreme caution.

'Arabi had summoned a special train to Alexandria to pick up the khedive and convey him back to Cairo. But Tewfiq had no wish to return to the capital, which was entirely in nationalist hands. Escorted by sixty cavalrymen, he pretended to make for the station but changed direction en route and went instead to Ras at-Tin Palace, where Sir Seymour Beauchamp was awaiting him.

The numerous Europeans who had taken refuge on shipboard were quick to come ashore. They were stunned by the sight that confronted them. The Place des Consuls was just a mound of rubble, the building that housed the mixed courts being one of the very few to have escaped the flames and devastation.

Rizqallah, having left the *Hellas*, toured the square three times, sadly shaking his head. The ruins of the French consulate, where he had embarked on his career, were still smoking. Xavier-Saillard's two office buildings had been gutted. Blocks of stone bearing the celebrated initials "X-S" had rolled to the foot of Muhammad Ali's equestrian statue, which was still intact. The founder of the Egyptian dynasty seemed to be contemplating the aftermath of the massacre with distaste.

My cousin inspected the ruins rather like a bailiff assessing a bankrupt's goods for distraint. He would go up to a gutted building, turn over a few scattered objects with the point of his shoe, then step back for a better look. He was keen to know if the owners had left, if they had returned, how much they had lost. There was a strange gleam in his sharp eyes.

The British put up notices informing the population that looters would be tried by court martial and arsonists caught in the act summarily executed. British officers seated at a table in the Place des Consuls — outside the mixed courts, as if to lend the proceedings greater legality — listened impatiently to their interpreters' rambling dissertations. I could hardly tear myself away from this spectacle except now and then, when I withdrew to jot down details in my notebook.

Once sentenced, the condemned men were summarily tied to a tree, shot, and buried. A few shovelfuls of sand were not enough, when night fell, to prevent stray dogs from disinterring their corpses.

Bakshish Pasha, who deemed his mission to be at an end, sailed for Constantinople aboard the *Ezzedin* amid a flurry of embraces. It now behoved him to explain to the Sultan why and how a foreign invasion force had landed in one of his provinces.

The khedive, for his part, issued a ringing proclamation to the effect that 'Arabi had been dismissed. British troops, he indignantly stressed, had seized Alexandria without a shot being fired. "This fact would dishonour the Egyptian army if the ineradicable disgrace did not fall entirely on the minister of war."

'Arabi was quick to repay the khedive in his own coin. Some days later a National Council, convened in Cairo with the participation of several princes, the Grand Mufti, the Coptic patriarch, the Grand Rabbi, and a hundred dignitaries, proclaimed that Tewfiq Pasha, currently guarded by the British army, had contravened the country's religious and political laws, and that, in consequence, his authority was null and void.

So we now had two governments and two authorities — not counting the British.

The *Sémaphore*'s journalists had all fled by sea on the eve of the bombardment. They returned to find the editorial offices devastated but the printing works untouched. They also found someone who had lived through those dramatic days on the spot, had conducted several long conversations, both before and after the bombardment, with the officers of the 5th Regiment, and who brought them an article that recounted the whole of the events in question. My piece did not seek to impress with purple passages; it was a meticulously detailed account of every development, however disturbing.

Bartillat, the editor of the *Sémaphore*, closeted himself with the article in what was left of his office. After an hour he hurried to the printing works.

"You're hired," he told me as he went. "How do you want to sign yourself?"

I replied, without a moment's hesitation, that my name was Maxime Touta, and that that would be my pen-name from now on. Bartillat removed his pince-nez and frowned, but raised no objection.

My article caused a sensation, as everyone knows, and had to be reprinted four times. Never since its first appearance in the spring of 1863 had the *Sémaphore* achieved such a circulation.

I often ponder on the circumstances of this episode, which had such a decisive influence on the course of my life. The article was very critical of all concerned, especially the British, and I believe that it was published only because of the terror that gripped so many Europeans on returning to their adoptive city: they blamed the occupation force for having bombarded it too heavily and, thereafter, for having delayed landing for forty-eight hours and spent another day getting into position. Excessive caution or machiavellianism? This debate was already raging when the *Sémaphore* hit the streets, and the four editions were sold out by the time the issue was banned by the British.

26

I was greeted on my return to Cairo by a letter of congratulations from Étienne Mancelle. "Everyone here is talking about you," he wrote. "We're very proud of you," Nada had added in her slanting hand.

I didn't care for the "we", but perhaps it was just a stock phrase. All that mattered was Nada's pride in me. After all, hadn't my primary motive in choosing to become a journalist been a desire to shine in her eyes? "You'll do great things," she had written.

I had been waiting for years to tell the other cashiers at the Ottoman Bank, "No, gentlemen, I won't be coming in tomorrow – nor the day after that. I'm going to be a journalist!"

But it didn't happen like that. The day I returned, the senior cashier – a Syrian who detested me – came over and held out his hand.

"Congratulations, *habibi*! Heartiest congratulations!"

He even contrived, when I told him I was leaving, to shed a tear.

My father greeted my sudden notoriety with a pensive air. He himself was not the type to court attention. Nothing irked him more than his sister Angéline's attempts to beat the drum on his behalf. A conscientious physician who had built his reputation on decades of unobtrusive toil, he was now confronted by an elder son whose name was better known than his own, at least in certain circles. This puzzled him somewhat. The practitioner in him found it hard to understand the observer I had become. He ministered to people and felt responsible for their condition. I put my finger on wounds – those I chose to point out – but did not bear any real responsibility for them. If the worst came to the worst, an inaccurate article could be corrected by another written with the same lucidity and self-assurance.

The only thing we had in common, perhaps, was our vocabulary. Having worked as an interpreter before becoming a physician, my father handled language with competence and respect.

"I knew my words before learning my diseases," he once told me with a smile.

Albin Balanvin had not waited until I returned to Cairo to congratulate me. His telegram comprised only two words: "Bravo, artist!" Coming from the man who had introduced me to journalism, this was worth all the smiles of my fellow employees at the Imperial Ottoman Bank. The *Sémaphore*'s correspondent never used words haphazardly. By "artist" he meant that even "reportage" could be a work of art.

Hardly any Europeans had been left in Cairo by the time Alexandria was bombarded. Balanvin was one of the few Frenchmen who had refused to leave.

"If I'm killed," he wrily informed the chief of police, an acquaintance of his, "I shall never forgive you."

The police chief, a dynamic individual, had not only guaranteed the Europeans' safety but seen to it with alacrity. He could not, however, prevent the townsfolk from expressing their anger. From time to time, a yelling mob progressed along our street leading two dogs in fancy dress: one, with a cross on its back, represented Admiral Sir Seymour Beauchamp; the other was the khedive. Every day, when the military band was playing outside Ezbekiyah Gardens, the "Englishmen's dog" was denounced by orators mounted on chairs.

Those members of our families who held "dependant" status had not forgone the chance to leave the country, taking advantage of the special trains chartered by their respective consulates. Alfred Falaki, who had mysteriously purchased Spanish-protected status, lowered the steel shutters of his shop, but not before he had emptied it of all the articles of value within. Some he buried in his garden, others he entrusted to a strongbox at the Ottoman Bank, and the rest he decided to carry on his person.

At the station, so Aunt Angéline told us, the jingle of necklaces and bracelets as they walked along the platform almost drowned the sound of the locomotive.

It had taken several compartments to transport their three daughters, Rose, Marguerite and Violette, their civil servant spouses, the Dabbour brothers, and their numerous offspring. The three intermingled families, all of whose children resembled one another, were an eternal source of confusion. All the boys wore sailor suits and all the girls wore plaits. Whenever you bumped into one of the latter at some family reunion, it was always the same old question: "Are you a rose, a daisy, or a violet?"

My brother Alexandre, who had recently married, was not "protected" by any foreign power. He nonetheless obtained some seats aboard a train bound for Palestine – at vast expense – and disappeared with his wife and two infants. "A second honeymoon seems highly advisable," he said with a rather sickly smile.

If the truth be told, more than one young man of our acquaintance would have volunteered to go travelling with the lovely Alice for the rest of his life. A timber merchant's daughter, she had plenty of refinement and the money to go with it, which was no disadvantage.

As for my father, he stubbornly refused to leave Egypt. "It's my country," he said darkly. I think the French occupation had scarred him for life. Throughout his childhood he had heard tell of the disastrous consequences of Bonaparte's sojourn in Egypt. His father and his uncles had been branded traitors, even though only one of them – the emperor's future Mameluke – had fought shoulder to shoulder with the French. My father was afraid that the *Shawam* of Egypt would once more be regarded as allies of the European invader.

"We've been cheated ever since the Crusades," he used to say, " – compelled to choose between the Christian occupiers and our Muslim neighbours. Sooner or later the occupiers will leave. Then we'll have to settle the problem of demarcation."

At the French consul's insistence, the nuns of the Bon Pasteur resigned themselves to leaving Cairo. On the night of 14 July, having said vespers for the last time, they departed with their orphan girls, leaving the convent at Shubra in the care of the holy Virgin. For safety's sake, they had adorned every door and window with a scapular of the Sacred Heart. It was not until the following night, after an exciting journey, that the travellers reached Ismailia, where they were housed on the first floor of the courthouse.

The next day, accompanied by her husband and children, Nada went to greet her former teachers on board a French sloop at anchor in the Suez Canal. "They were just as I had left them fourteen years ago," she wrote to my father. A Mass was celebrated on deck. At the Elevation, three blasts on a trumpet rang out and the captain addressed his crew in a stentorian voice: "Down on your knees!"

Étienne Mancelle, with tears in his eyes, leant towards his wife and whispered, "Religion is always beautiful, but how impressive it is on board ship, far from home!"

I cannot tell what Nada felt at that moment, but I picture her very erect and radiant in a white tussore gown with a curving bustle, a big parasol in her hand. I often think of that summery scene: Madame Mancelle in the splendour of her thirty-five years; Madame Mancelle with her family; Madame Mancelle staring straight ahead and trying to forget her past follies. She was Nada of Ismailia – Nada the inaccessible.

Ferdinand de Lesseps had been fighting to preserve the neutrality of the Suez Canal ever since the start of hostilities. He had obtained 'Arabi's assurance that Egyptian troops would not land on the isthmus. Now he had to convince the British, which was another matter.

On 26 July a British warship, the *Orion*, entered the canal and proceeded to Lake Timsah, where she dropped anchor. Infuriated by this, de Lesseps donned his ceremonial frock coat, complete with all his numerous orders and decorations, and went on board to protest. The ship's captain received him politely and assured him of his best intentions. The next day, however, the British press inveighed against the head of the Suez Canal Company. Vengeful articles proposed the creation of a second canal, parallel to the first, which would steal all the latter's custom.

Étienne Mancelle was dismayed. Félix Percheron, white with rage, proclaimed himself ready to place a stick of dynamite under the *Orion*. But that was not the ultimate extent of his indignation.

On 19 August a ball was held at the residence of one of the directors. The Mancelles had only just got home at about three in the morning when firing broke out in the Place Champollion. The children woke up and started crying.

British sailors were pursuing some invisible 'Arabist scouts. They inflicted several casualties before attacking the Arab village, whose terrified inhabitants fled into the desert. Meanwhile, the *Orion* and another vessel shelled the small neighbouring town of Nafishah.

Two days later Lake Timsah was crammed with British warships and thousands of redcoats were swarming through the streets of Ismailia. That afternoon, as he did every day, Félix Percheron went to smoke a few cigarettes and enjoy his usual brandy and soda in a café near *La Belle Jardinière*. On emerging from the establishment, he drove his fist into the face of one of General Wolseley's aides-de-camp. Several people intervened, and the incident had no repercussions.

27

A major confrontation was brewing between 'Arabi's army and the British expeditionary force. The *Sémaphore*'s editor had instructed me to go to the Egyptian headquarters at Tel al-Kebir because I was the only one of the weekly's staff who spoke Arabic. Besides, past experience suggested that Walid al-Ahlawi would make me welcome.

Every strategist knew that 'Arabi would concentrate his forces at Tel al-Kebir. Old Nassif Bey explained this to his friends a few days before being carried off by an embolism:

"For centuries now, that position has been considered the best one from which to repel an invasion from the east. The attackers are exhausted after crossing the desert, whereas the defenders, with their backs to the Delta, have plenty of food and water."

But the British generals did not see things in that light. On the contrary, they had massed their forces in the east, on the isthmus of Suez, because they judged it to be the ideal place in which to defeat the Egyptian army. The open countryside would permit them to engage in some bold manoeuvres without running the risk of a long defensive campaign. They had therefore done their best to encourage 'Arabi to remain true to tradition.

On arriving at headquarters, I made desperate attempts to find the commanding officer of the 5th Regiment. Everyone I asked claimed to have seen him very recently and sent me off on a wild-goose chase. The Egyptian troops were in chaos, but I eventually ran Walid to earth behind an immense stack of rifles. He embraced me for the first time ever, clearly pleased that I had made the trip.

"We're getting volunteers, grain and money from all over the country," he told me. "Several thousand Tripolitanian infantrymen have joined us, but they're very poorly armed. I had to send a train to Cairo to fetch some Remington rifles to replace their flintlocks."

Thanks to Walid, I managed to obtain an interview with 'Arabi during the days that followed. The nationalist leader, who received me in his tent, displayed complete confidence in the outcome of the battle and promised Britain a historic defeat. "Queen Victoria," he declared, "still has time to re-embark her expeditionary force. If not, a worldwide battle will be joined from Egypt to India, setting the whole of Africa and the whole of Asia ablaze . . . "

There were various skirmishes at the end of August. I could hear distant gunfire. At night in the officers' mess, Walid told me how Egyptian troops had thwarted the probing attacks of the British, who were numerically far inferior and exhausted by the heat.

On 26 August, however, a squadron of British dragoons succeeded in capturing the lock at Kassassin. From now on, the invaders would not run short of water. Almost at the same time, Egyptian officers were stunned to hear that their chief of staff, Mahmud Fahmi Pasha, had fallen into the hands of the British almost by chance, while touring the area in civilian clothes, wearing an overcoat and a tarboosh.

I was fast asleep on the night of 11 September, when the whole of the British army massed at Kassassin surreptitiously struck camp and got into line of march, regiment by regiment. Under cover of darkness, thousands of ghostly figures made their way across the fields of cotton and maize. They were all there: Highlanders, Bengal Lancers, members of the Brigade of Guards . . . Approaching to within a few score metres, they suddenly deluged the Egyptian lines with rifle fire. To the defenders of Tel al-Kebir, sheltering in their trenches, this was an unforeseen scenario. They had been expecting, when the time came, to exchange fire with enemies exposed to view on the open plain, whereas the red devils, with bayonets fixed, had attacked at point-blank range in the middle of the night.

'Arabi was one of the first to quit the field, followed by his officers and men. I went with them as a matter of course. We were already on board a train bound for Cairo when the cheers of the Highlanders and the Coldstreams announced that the battle was ending.

Walid al-Ahlawi's body was recovered the next day, riddled with bullets. His sabre was lying nearby, beside the carcass of his horse.

Three envelopes were found in the colonel's bloodstained tunic. One was addressed to 'Arabi, and I never discovered what it said. In the second letter, Walid enjoined his children to study hard, "because the Egyptians, if they cannot read and write, will never throw off the oppressor's yoke."

The third letter was addressed to "Dr Boutros Touta, New Muski Street" and contained some rather faded sheets of paper. They were the draft of a letter written by Walid to my father in 1866, after the Cretan campaign, to tell him of his promotion to the rank of *yusbashi*. This draft contained almost as many spelling mistakes as the original but included an additional passage that had been cut:

> When you came to see me at the barracks in Alexandria, doctor, the day after the public humiliation to which I had been subjected, you asked if I came from the village of Mendela. I said no, being at that time unaware of your intentions. Today I want to tell you that I do indeed hail from Mendela. I was the one you treated after that dog of a Turk, who had come to the village to collect our taxes, compelled us to put our heads through an iron ring . . .

My father had just learned of the death of his colleague Nassif Bey, which saddened him greatly. I didn't want to add to his distress, but he immediately guessed, on seeing my dejected expression when I came home, that something had happened.

Although Walid's letter moved him deeply, it did not surprise him as much as I had thought it would. "I knew," he said in a low voice. "I always knew it was him."

Aunt Angéline naturally concocted a romance out of this story, which didn't concern her. Mixing up its chronology and protagonists, she told how the colonel of the 5th, invoking the ties of affection that had existed between them since his childhood, had asked the Doctor to use his influence to persuade the khedive to make peace with 'Arabi.

Walid had taken part in all the skirmishes at Tel al-Kebir. He was always to be seen in the front line. His comrades had been impressed by his courage, his fighting spirit, and the inordinate risks he ran, some of which appeared suicidal. Personally, I had sensed that he was very disappointed by the turn of events. A few months earlier he had still believed in a genuine national revolution and hoped that 'Arabi, with the people's support, would become khedive in Tewfiq's place.

Had he been so fascinated by the leader of the nationalist movement that he failed to discern his shortcomings and illogicalities? I'm inclined to think that Walid's eyes were opened by the bombardment of Alexandria and the violence that followed it. Although he had been happy to intercede on my behalf and obtain me an interview with 'Arabi, I sensed a lack of enthusiasm on his part. He must have felt that the battle was already lost; he must have guessed that, as soon as the British attacked, several Egyptian generals including their leader would hastily board a train for Cairo in the hope of saving their skins.

Walid knew that I was at Tel al-Kebir. He also knew that, if he was killed, I would learn of the letter in the pocket of his tunic and forward it to my father. But why did he keep that draft? Why keep a secret that was, fundamentally, quite a minor one? Did he do so out of pride?

By asking myself those questions, I have come to the conclusion that, to Walid, the letter may have mattered more than its contents. It was the first he had written to anyone. In the same pocket was a wonderful letter, devoid of any spelling mistakes, addressed to his children.

It remains Walid's secret to the end. He took it with him to the grave — or rather, to a hole in the middle of the plain near Tel al-Kebir, dug by a weeping Egyptian soldier.

28

FROM OUR CAIRO CORRESPONDENT
To the Editor:

26 September 1882

The khedive's return to the good city of Cairo yesterday was a solemn and moving occasion. The numerous dignitaries waiting on the platform — ministers, ex-deputies, ulamas, beys, pashas, property-owners of all kinds — were afire with impatience. There was something approaching a stampede when the white khedivial train finally came to rest. Everyone wanted to be the first to kiss the august hand. British officers watched the scene moist-eyed with emotion.

Tewfiq Pasha was greeted on alighting from the train by General Wolseley and the Duke of Connaught, son of Queen Victoria, both in the warlike attire they had worn at the Battle of Tel al-Kebir. Together with Sir Edward Malet, the British consul-general, they boarded the khedive's carriage. I heard a pasha near me murmur, with tears in his eyes, "The khedive is returning to Cairo like a child to the arms of its nursemaid."

The procession was headed by a hundred British guardsmen in full-dress uniform. Soldiers lined the entire route from Bab al-Hadid station to the palace at Gezira. The bands played the khedivial anthem and God Save the Queen, turn and turn about.

The city is still illuminated tonight. Three days of celebrations, complete with fireworks, are planned.

Her Britannic Majesty's soldiers roam the city on their big English horses. Scarlet tunics predominate. Cairenes stare curiously at Scottish infantrymen with bare knees, pleated skirts, shiny boots, and little bonnets cocked over one ear.

It is hard to know how to describe these 20,000-odd armed men who are preparing to parade through the capital's streets on 30 September. They cannot be called soldiers of the khedive, not being subject to his authority, nor are they foreign troops summoned by the khedive, never having been summoned by him. They are forces of occupation, you will say. But Great Britain has firmly denied any intention of occupying Egypt! In that case, are they soldiers of a protecting power? No, London says it is resolutely opposed to the idea of a protectorate. We shall be forced to conclude, sir, that the presence of these soldiers is purely fortuitous. They must be straightforward visitors.

"Britain has no intention of annexing Egypt and recognizes no one's right to do so," we are continually assured by members of Sir Edward Malet's staff. "Neither annexation nor a protectorate. We shall evacuate Egypt as soon as her peace and security are guaranteed." But aren't they that already? Not a shot was fired on 14 September, when General Drury Lowe's cavalry entered Cairo. 'Arabi promptly surrendered to the victors and was imprisoned in the Citadel.

Sir Edward Malet's officials add, however, that Britain will not withdraw her troops from the banks of the Nile until she is assured that Egypt is "on the road to stability and progress". A laudable plan, sir, but nobody knows how long it will take to complete. We are confronted by a disguised protectorate of indeterminate extent and indefinite duration.

Of the French who have returned to Cairo in recent days, many bitterly regret that their government has not associated itself with Britain's military operations. "Egypt is becoming British," they say. "We have lost Egypt."

Would you permit me, sir, to venture a different interpretation? It may be that, by not landing troops at Alexandria, France has won Egypt — that is to say, the hearts of the Egyptians. Although political and economic power will probably elude her, she will — in even stronger measure — retain her schools, her language, and her cultural influence. Egypt may perhaps be British, but she will think in French.

Albin Balanvin

PS. This piece will be my last. My pen has never ceased to scratch paper since the birth of the Sémaphore in the spring of 1863. Farewell, dear readers. After twenty years on deck it is time for me to retire to my cabin. The new political era beginning in Egypt calls for new pens and, perhaps, a new form of journalism. I surrender the helm to Maxime Touta, wishing him a fair wind.

PART THREE

Summer Pleasures

I

May 1885

Yes, I love the early summer at Alexandria. Having got here before everyone else, I take possession of the sand and sea. The season stretches ahead of me. I think of all the little pleasures to come. The little pleasures and, perhaps, the great joys . . .

The sea is like glass this morning. I ran down the beach and plunged in under the petrified gaze of Mahmud, who finds the Mediterranean frightening. He mistakes it for some mysterious demon to be humoured at all costs. Last year I caught him throwing coins into the sea to purchase its good will.

Floating in that silent water with my arms extended, I shut my eyes and allow my thoughts to wander. Three months' leave of absence from the *Sémaphore* will allow me to take a real holiday. I need to break off and look at myself for a while, to suspend my avid observation of the world.

Mahmud is signalling furiously from an upstairs balcony, but I'm undeceived. He's perfectly capable of supervising the work of the two young Nubian decorators he engaged. My crucified body makes no sign of life. Mahmud's apprehensive expression amuses me, but there's no doubt I need it in order to hurl myself into the water. The sea scares me, too, in my heart of hearts. I wonder if I would brave it if no one was watching.

The two Nubians, brush in hand and almost naked, warble unidentifiable songs all day long. Their jet-black bodies are streaked in places with blue and pink paint. I chose blue for the balconies and pale pink for Nada's bedroom.

My father will be arriving in four days' time, and the work must be completed by then. I want to spare him any worries of that kind. He has aged in the last few months, with bouts of fatigue and slight losses of memory. I think he's more surprised than affected by them. Will he bathe in public this year?

I received a visit from the Bedouin who guard the villas from October to May. I offered them tea before handing them their annual fee. They told me than an Englishman had built a house behind the dunes, and that for part of the winter some stonemasons were working on it flat out.

If the English are also going to park themselves here instead of spending the summers in Europe . . . Ramlah is becoming more and more popular. At this rate the villa gardens will end up touching. When Papa had this house built we were almost alone in the midst of sand dunes and fields of wild figs. The idea of spending money at Ramlah seemed ludicrous to many members of the family. Today they're quite happy to be housed here. Eight bedrooms – eleven, even, counting the annexe where Alexandre and his family stayed last year – are not too many.

My father can boast of being one of the first Ramlahites, but who ever heard him boast about anything? Fortunately, Aunt Angéline is there to restore the balance: to hear her talk, "the Doctor" actually invented sea-bathing . . .

The balustrades of the balconies are finished. Next, the Nubians will repaint the shutters in the same blue. But Nada's bedroom isn't going well at all. I asked for a pastel colour, not that chocolate-box pink. They're going to repaint it tomorrow morning, and I shall supervise the mixing myself.

Where the other rooms are concerned, we'll see. It's impossible to repaint the whole place every year. The Falakis are to have the green room at the end of the passage. Angéline will be less audible that way, and the green will help to calm her nerves. It won't hurt Lolo to put a little distance between him and his mother. The cubby hole near the maids' room will suit him perfectly.

I passed the Englishman on the beach, accompanied by a big black bulldog. He's a thickset man of fifty-five or thereabouts. I nodded to him, but he didn't even return my nod and addressed his dog – which resembles him — instead. There was something sinister about the sight of those two bulldogs on the deserted beach.

I'm not one of those who nurse an obsessive hatred of the English, despite the *Sémaphore*'s troubles, but it has to be acknowledged that most of them find it impossible to disguise their contempt for us.

Officially, those gentlemen landed in Egypt solely to protect European residents and restore the khedive's authority. Well, three years have gone by since then, and there's no further talk of their withdrawing. The British control the army, the police, and the whole of the civil service. Each minister is flanked by a blue-eyed aide and "adviser". The humblest Egyptian corporal soon grasped where authority resided.

Nassif Bey's widow was the first to arrive. Mahmud sighted her on the platform, accompanied by her granddaughter and two other people. She sent word that she would expect us for tea in two days' time, when my father gets here.

A lively, cheerful Coptic Christian, Nassif's widow has always had a soft spot for Papa. She attaches even more importance to his friendship since her husband's death, as if he were the last surviving witness of a bygone era. But she's a very modern woman for her age, and doesn't hesitate to meet her women friends at the Miramare between five and eight in the evening.

"She's not very Coptic," says Aunt Angéline, under the impression that this is a handsome compliment.

2

I don't give a damn, not really, if the Englishman declines to say a word to me, but his failure to acknowledge the greeting of an old gentleman like my father was downright boorish. We were a few feet away from him on the path to the beach. His bulldog came up and sniffed our shoes, growling, but he didn't even call it off.

"In your place I'd have made a scene," said Nassif Bey's grandson. A brilliant youngster educated by the Jesuit Fathers, he professes a prickly kind of nationalism. At tea yesterday afternoon he had some very harsh things to say about the forces of occupation. According to him, the khedive forfeited all credibility in September 1882, when he returned to Cairo under the aegis of British bayonets. As for 'Arabi, he's a traitor:

"He shouldn't have been so quick to surrender, far less bargain with the judges in the course of his trial. That death sentence, which was promptly commuted to exile in Ceylon, was a disgrace. 'Arabi discredited himself forever by writing to *The Times* and saying he hoped the British would carry on his work."

My father, who was finding the atmosphere a trifle oppressive, quoted his mentor Clot Bey: "Egypt is too far away from all the empires that could aspire to possess her for them to retain her permanently. That's why she has belonged to so many people in succession, and why she'll never belong to anyone."

Then he adroitly changed the subject by regaling us with us some reminiscences of his time at medical school. I had no idea that, after Dr Clot's pupils had extracted the first bladder stones, he put them in a little box and presented it to Muhammad Ali. "I know of no stones more precious," declared the viceroy.

Nassif Bey's widow was delighted by this anecdote. Her granddaughter, who had been listening intently, opened her doe-like eyes wide. Eighteen or nineteen years old, she looked like a pharaonic statue.

"You're very beautiful, mademoiselle," my father had told her, knowing that it would please her grandmother. "I'm tempted to call you Nefertiti."

At his age he could afford to make such remarks.

Étienne Mancelle has written to inform us that he cannot leave Ismailia before 15 June. His new duties as Director of Operations (his precise title, apparently, is "Director of Operations of the Transit and Navigation Service of the Suez Canal Company") compel him to supervise certain operations on the spot. That accursed Canal! However, Nada added a few words to the effect that she was counting the days until her arrival. Those two lines have almost obliterated the bad news. The thought of them is a constant source of delight to me.

No one cared to spend the summer at Ramlah in 1883 — the previous year's events were too recent — so only a few of us christened the villa. Last year's season was delightful, however, and this year my father decided to invite the Mancelles.

I have not been myself since they accepted — I, who was trying to forget Nada and thought I had almost forgotten her. From time to time, excitement surges over me like a blast of hot air. It's as if I'm several years younger, watching and waiting for a letter written in that rounded, rather slanting hand.

Nobody knows that Nada saw the villa four years ago, when it was unfurnished and unpainted. I hope she'll like the pink I chose for her bedroom.

Albin Balanvin has been free as air since he retired. I went to see him at the Miramare, where he has taken a very quiet room overlooking the gardens. We're still on excellent terms, but our relations will never be entirely clear-cut. The *Sémaphore*'s Cairo correspondent was wise enough to surrender his pen in September 1882. Did he do so with good grace? The postscript to his last piece wounded me: I was expecting something better than his "fair wind" to Maxime Touta, not that I've ever said so to anyone.

Our relations have, in fact, been easier since the *Sémaphore* became a daily and transferred to Cairo. Readers have ceased to compare "the new correspondent" with the old. Balanvin himself has a hard time finding his way around the paper, which has taken on a more modern format. He speaks well of it, on the whole, but cannot refrain from occasionally firing off one of those lethal, velvet-encased darts of which he alone possesses the secret.

In any case, writing his memoirs is doing him a lot of good. He works on them every morning. In the afternoon he sometimes joins in the conversations on the terrace or goes for a stroll on the beach. Madame Buzel, the proprietress of the Miramare, adores him. The ladies leave him cold, but I've often noticed how he charms them.

Balanvin's memoirs promise to be fascinating. They will span five reigns, since our friend arrived in Egypt under Muhammad Ali, lived through the dark days of 'Abbaas, the laxity of Sa'id and the follies of Isma'il, and is now, despite his retirement, attentively observing the jejune activities of Tewfiq.

"It's the end of a reign I find most interesting," he says mischievously, knowing that a lot of people in Cairo and Alexandria are apprehensive of his project.

Muhammad Ali's illness, not to say madness, will occupy several pages of the book. Balanvin intends to reproduce some confidential information about the mental decline of the founder of the dynasty, hitherto unpublished but given to him at the time by Dr Clot Bey. My father cannot wait to compare these remarks with his own recollections.

The succeeding reign will not be the least interesting of the lot. 'Abbaas, who was hated by the French, may well find himself unexpectedly rehabilitated by Balanvin's book. I've heard him say, more than once, "At least 'Abbaas didn't throw the peasants' money out of the window."

He plans to include a detailed account of 'Abbaas's assassination by two young Mamelukes, and how his corpse was ensconced in a carriage and paraded around the streets of Cairo to hoodwink Sa'id, the crown prince.

The memoirs will doubtless make veiled allusions to the morals of Sa'id, the monarch who played soldiers and progressed from town to town with his entire army in tow. I'm curious to read Balanvin's account of Sa'id's death, having more or less witnessed his death throes in Palace No. 3.

I was unaware that certain members of his family declared it was poison and were convinced that the dying man had succumbed to a doctored cup of coffee.

Balanvin has promised me some unpublished details of the Xavier-Saillard affair, but doesn't want to talk about them for the moment.

The bulk of the book, I surmise, will be devoted to Isma'il's reign. The ex-khedive detested the *Sémaphore*'s correspondent, but, knowing the influence he wielded, granted him several private audiences. Balanvin's account of these interviews promises to be fascinating! He had a long talk with Isma'il during a recent trip to Constantinople. It appears that the Sultan's guests often see, seated at the end of the table, a man with a fair, dyed beard. Taciturn as a rule, he waxes voluble and sarcastic when questioned. The former khedive has lost none of his wit and vigour, it seems, and his rancour is as keen as ever, even though he no longer cherishes any hopes of regaining the throne.

I'm not too sure what our friend intends to write about the worthy Tewfiq. There's almost nothing – either good or bad – to be said about him. However, the British offer innumerable targets for mockery to a pen as talented as Balanvin's.

Three Parisian publishers are already vying for the manuscript, which the *Sémaphore* plans to serialize. It has been agreed with the author that, if certain passages prove too inflamatory, the newspaper will refrain from printing them so as not to court more trouble. Balanvin negotiated this with the editor direct. He didn't tell me until it had all been settled, not that I resent it. One must understand him . . .

This afternoon, just as I was leaving, he said casually, "My manuscript will require careful editing when the time comes. It's a job for a professional, someone with a good eye, if you know what I mean. Would you be willing to read it for me?"

The wretched man made me blush!

3

Mahmud is terrified of two things: the sea and Aunt Angéline. News of the Falakis' arrival sent him into a panic. He hitched up the carriage we hire for the season at dawn, having asked me a hundred times whether it would be proper to seat Lolo on the box beside him so as to leave more room for *Sitt Angelina* and her husband.

The Falaki family's arrival at the villa would have merited a photograph. Lolo was a priceless sight in his sola topi and the yellow-checked jacket he now wore in the belief that it made him look like an English tourist. Angéline, who had deposited two hatboxes on her husband's lap, was vigorously wielding her fan. Her complaints about the heat redoubled when the horse jibbed at climbing the last little dune. Mahmud hauled on the bridle while the two men got down and pushed. Fortunately, my aunt found the sea air soothing. Here at Ramlah she does not get breathless at siesta time, thanks to the "bath" she takes on the veranda. Lolo reminds her of it daily on leaving the lunch table: "*Ya mami*, it's time for your air bath."

If the bombardment of Alexandria had profited anyone, that person was Alfred Falaki. He was heavily compensated for the gutting of his jeweller's shop in the Rue des Sœurs. The British have been very open-handed – "By dipping into the local exchequer," as Nassif Bey's grandson emphasizes – in order to show that their era is commencing under the auspices of justice and prosperity. Uncle Alfred claimed to have lost a number of valuable items. However, according to several shopkeepers in the neighbourhood, he removed all his merchandise at the end of June, more than ten days before the looting and arson began. The delighted expression he wore during 'Arabi's trial was eloquent of this swindle.

Besides, would he have opened another shop at al-Mansoura the following year had he not pocketed a very substantial indemnity? Other people did worse things than Alfred, it is true. Only the other day Nassif Bey's widow was telling us about a neighbour of hers who holds dual nationality, Greek and French, and is a Spanish dependant as well. He took advantage of this to put in three separate claims for compensation.

That was three years ago — three years already. How quickly the time goes by! We have forgotten the treacheries of some and the minor cowardices of others.

"Everything gets blotted out by the rays of the Egyptian sun," as Balanvin says.

Alexandre's wife must find Uncle Alfred extremely vulgar, I imagine. Brought up in the lap of luxury, my sister-in-law never mentions money. It's difficult to resist her natural refinement. Alice dresses to perfection. I find her physically very attractive, with her silken skin and carmine lips. She reminds me of a flawless porcelain vase.

The birth of little Edmond a few weeks ago has left her unmarked. She has regained her girlish figure and resumed her sand baths. In spring-time, back in Cairo, she spends hours buried in the sand near the Pyramids. At Ramlah it's Alexandre who digs her a trench beside the sun umbrella, and she shields her head from the sun with a sort of pearl-encrusted skull cap. Her older children, Henri and Yolande, who play with little spades, sometimes scatter sand over that disturbing, half-buried body of hers.

My father watches all these activities with a puzzled expression. "What with my sister's air baths and my daughter-in-law's sand baths," he says, "we're a pampered bunch . . . "

The Austrian nanny, who never strays from the older children's side, schools them in good manners under my brother's approving eye. I sometimes wonder which is Alexandre's greater source of pride: being Alice's husband or employing an Austrian nanny. He has acquired an air of self-importance since going into his father-in-law's timber business. The bourgeois way of life seems to suit him to a tee. One could be forgiven for thinking he aspires to nothing more. And I used to imagine he was an original, or even a rebel . . .

Little Edmond had a fit the day after his arrival here. He was in his nursemaid's arms when his body suddenly stiffened and he turned his eyes up. His limbs jerked in all directions; then he lost consciousness.

As luck would have it, my father was not far away. He calmed the nursemaid and removed the baby's clothes before applying poultices to his legs and cold compresses to his head.

"The best thing in such cases," he said, "is to apply two or three leeches behind each ear."

The baby has had convulsions before, apparently. According to Papa, they could be symptomatic either of a cerebral disorder or of an overly precocious intelligence.

Aunt Angéline's version, broadcast on the terrace of the Miramare: "The Doctor thinks Edmond is a budding genius."

Alexandre's children are the best customers of the young donkey-driver on the beach. Each is entitled to one ride a day. My brother has obtained a discount from the boy in the blue *galabiya*, who charges him one piastre a ride instead of one-and-a-half. Only the wealthy know how to economize, it seems.

You should see how little Yolande, who has only just turned three, holds the donkey's reins! She sits up ramrod straight on the red velvet saddle and refuses to let anyone support her. The Austrian nanny runs after the donkey, getting tangled up in her skirts.

Lolo is very proud of the fact that the donkey-driver takes him for an Englishman. The youngster, who must be around twelve years old, sings out "Hello, Mister!" as he passes the Falakis' sun umbrella every morning. His eyes are alight with intelligence. Even if Lolo addressed him in Arabic, I suspect he would contrive to reply in English.

My cousin has been itching to emulate the children ever since he got here. This morning he mounted the little grey donkey, which made painfully slow progress despite being sworn at and belaboured with a stick by its youthful master. Lolo delightedly trotted along the shore, his long legs almost touching the ground.

Uncle Alfred, standing beside the sun umbrella, watched him through a pair of naval binoculars.

"We should take a photograph of him, we really should!" Aunt Angéline exclaimed admiringly.

"Maman's pet" will be forty-five in a few days' time. A cake has already been ordered from Alexandria, complete with candles, but the celebrations have been deferred until the arrival of Rose, Marguerite and Violette, who have rented the whole of a large house at Fleming Beach from 1 June. The Dabbour invasion is imminent.

I don't know how many of them there are. Over the years, the three Dabbour brothers have done their respective blossoms proud – more than proud, in fact. Each couple must have produced at least ten children. Even Uncle Alfred, their grandfather, seems to get mixed up between all the roses, daisies and violets, whereas he could give a detailed description of every pair of earrings in his three shops at Cairo, al-Mansoura, and Alexandria.

4

The events of last night have clearly been the main topic of conversation on the beach and, this evening, on the terrace of the Miramare.

It must have been nearly two in the morning when someone hammered loudly on our door. At first we failed to hear him over the sounds of the sea and the wind, which was rattling the windows. Mahmud, who sleeps beside the kitchen on the ground floor, was the first to wake. He was too scared to answer on the grounds that "the sea had come to claim its own", or some such nonsense, so I had to open the front door myself.

By the light of his flickering storm lantern, a man in a *galabiya* introduced himself as the servant of the Englishman beyond the dunes. He had been told to summon "the Doctor" to the bedside of a very sick young man. I was reluctant to wake my father, but he was already descending the stairs in search of his medical bag and his overcoat.

"No, no," he told me, "don't trouble to come with me, it's not worth it."

I didn't insist for fear of annoying him. Upstairs, the Falakis slumbered on, dead to the world.

A horse and trap were waiting at the garden gate. The servant cracked his whip, and they set off into the teeth of the gale. Ten minutes later they were greeted by the furious barking of the black bulldog, which was chained up. The Englishman silenced it with a kick in the ribs. Then, armed with an oil lamp, he wordlessly showed my father the way.

A woman with greying hair was standing at the head of the bed. The patient, a young man of about twenty, had a high fever and was suffering from rigors. He breathed with difficulty and coughed up phlegm from time to time.

"Is it serious?" the woman asked in French.

My father, who was taking the young man's pulse, didn't reply. He folded back the covers, sounded his chest, and discovered a particularly painful spot.

"Pneumonia," he said at length.

The Englishman was standing beside the bed, unflinching. Doubtless he was wondering if a "native" physician could be trusted.

My father applied vesicatories to the painful area, then waited for the congestion to diminish by degrees. The exhausted Englishwoman dozed off. As for the patient's father, he signalled his impatience with a muffled grunt and left the room.

Some time later it became necessary to administer a purgative and assist the young man to the commode. The servant lent a helping hand. Roused by the commotion, the Englishwoman awoke with a start. She uttered a little cry on seeing her son's gaunt face, but my father reassured her with a soothing gesture.

Later still, he asked for some tea to be brought to encourage the patient to perspire. This time it was the father himself who went to tell the servant to heat some water.

My father did not pack his bag and don his overcoat until dawn, by which time the young man was sleeping peacefully.

"Give him a spoonful of brandy and sugar every two hours," he told the woman with the greying hair, whose eyes were wet with tears.

I hadn't managed to get back to sleep. I blamed myself for having let an old man go off into the chilly night on his own, even if he was a doctor. Meantime, the Falakis were blissfully snoring along the passage.

When my father returned at five a.m., Mahmud greeted him sweating with apprehension and wearing all his lucky charms. I hurried downstairs to reassure myself that he was all right. My heart had thumped so often on hearing him come home in the old days. But that was in town, in Cairo, and he hadn't been a man of seventy-four.

The Englishman drove over in the trap to see us this morning. His son was much better. He thanked my father in very correct French but declined a coffee, saying that he was expected in town. We learned that his name was Elliot Bey, and that he was one of Alexandria's deputy directors of customs.

Aunt Angéline scored a great success on the terrace of the Miramare this afternoon. She recounted the story from start to finish, complete with a number of hitherto unknown details:

"The young man was at death's door. His father had been told there was only one physician in the whole of Ramlah who could save him, so he came and begged my brother the Doctor to turn out in the middle of the night. Well, he packed his medical bag, hitched up the trap, and drove there post-haste. I'll spare you a description of the gale that was blowing . . . "

5

The season is gradually coming to life. There were at least eight sun umbrellas on the beach this morning.

Eight sun umbrellas but not a single bather. I dived in despite the waves, which were quite choppy, and swam out to the buoy. Would I have done so without those anxious glances – from doe-eyed Mademoiselle Nefertiti among others? I find Nassif Bey's granddaughter more and more attractive. She reminds me a little of last winter's young Armenian girl, but she's prettier. Prettier by far.

Seated on a deckchair with her gown hitched up an inch or two, she's chatting with the young Dabbours. Her bare feet are half buried in the sand. Just now I made her laugh by describing my first experience of journalism. The khedive's sugar refinery, the pots of honey . . .

My profession may arouse the polite disdain of men of substance – men who know how to make money like Cousin Rizqallah or Uncle Alfred – but it fires the imagination of the young. How attentively the Dabbour boys listen to my stories of the newspaper office! If I've been playing this game for several days now, it's because of the "pharaonic statue". I like to see her lovely eyes light up.

I wonder what she thought of Uncle Boctor, who surprised us by turning up on the beach at eleven. He'd come to inspect the latest improvements to the villa his son is building fifteen minutes' walk from here. Rizqallah hasn't stinted himself, by all accounts. There's an immense terrace overlooking the sea, and the whole of the ground floor is paved with Carrara marble.

"Your cousin always tends to overdo things a bit," my father muttered.

I can't believe Rizqallah authorized Uncle Boctor to insult the workmen. To hear him fault their plastering, he must have given them a regular earful. He seems more vulgar the older he gets.

My cousin has always overdone things, it's true, but who would dare to criticize him these days? In our family circle his success is cited as an example to the younger generation. You should see the look of admiration on the young Dabbours' faces, whatever their flower of origin, whenever Rizqallah's name is mentioned!

My cousin's stroke of genius was to buy government securities on a massive scale in August 1882. National Debt Preferred Stock, quoted at 91.5 at the beginning of the year, had fallen to 80 after the insurrection. Rizqallah went wildly into debt to acquire some. He was called a madman, and several members of the family stepped in to make him see sense.

"That son of a dog will have us all in prison before he's through!" shouted Boctor, spitting out of the window.

Poor Bella was at her wits' end. Her own family was just as alarmed by her husband's business ventures. By the end of September, however, government stock had risen to 95.5. Rizqallah sold all his holdings, together with some big parcels of land at Daïra, discreetly acquired at the same time, which had also shot up in value. His triumph was complete.

The subject of Rizqallah cropped up again this afternoon, while we were strolling in the Place des Consuls. It was hardly possible to set foot in the square without mentioning his name.

Lolo had promised to show the children an amazing magician who cut a woman in pieces, so a whole party of them had decided to go into town for the occasion. The ladies wanted to go shopping, Uncle Alfred had to look in at his shop, and I took the opportunity to see how things were going at the *Sémaphore*'s offices.

The Alexandria bureau had forfeited much of its importance since the newspaper's transformation. Its editorial staff were only two in number, although they received three reinforcements during the hot season, when the entire court, followed by government ministers and a sizeable proportion of the diplomatic corps, took up its summer quarters in Alexandria.

The only journalist present confirmed that there was no news. In spite of various approaches, the authorities had not revoked their decision to suspend the *Sémaphore* for three months. This had at least earned us an immense amount of publicity – and a well-deserved holiday.

When I rejoined the party in the Place des Consuls, Lolo was looking as dismayed as the children by the sight of a woman's torso, deprived of its arms and legs, answering the spectators' questions in Italian. "It must be a trick," he kept saying.

The younger ones were delightedly wandering down the avenues of lebbek acacias and around the statue of Muhammad Ali, nibbling ears of grilled sweetcorn. We ended the afternoon idling in front of the bandstand. The Egyptian army band made a very respectable attempt at a Gounod waltz and the overture to *The Barber of Seville*, but the polkas that followed lacked verve. In conclusion we were treated to the khedivial anthem, and the children sang *"Salaam Afandina"*.

Every building in the Place des Consuls had been rebuilt. One looked in vain for a trace of the devastation of 1882. It was almost shameful. I never revisit the square without a tightening of the heart. No place reawakens so many memories, both delightful and distasteful.

I can still see us going into the French consulate, my father and me, then a boy of thirteen, to ask for Rizqallah. It was a sunny afternoon in January. The huge esplanade, with its two fountains, seemed to be taking a siesta. A few days later the square was black with people: Europeans on their balconies, Egyptian soldiers in chains, and a tearful young officer stripped of his lieutenant's insignia . . . I saw the square again in 1868, elaborately decorated to mark Khedive Isma'il's return from Constantinople. Monsieur Xavier-Saillard, who was supervising the adornment of his façade with Chinese lanterns, hardly spared us a glance . . . Then there was the grim day in July 1882, after the bombardment of Alexandria, when Walid al-Ahlawi rode around the square trying vainly to dissuade the looters. He had gone by the time the volley rang out, I could testify to that. I also committed my evidence to paper, and it was read out in full at the trial of 'Arabi's supporters . . .

Touta et Fils, Rizqallah's big department store, covers three floors. It sells just about everything in the way of men's, women's and children's attire, as well as various household appurtenances: Smyrna carpets, embroidered curtains, bedspreads. One of Rizqallah's brothers heads the flannel and drapery department, another is in charge of the lace counter.

The saleswomen, both Christian and Jewish, are all more or less distantly related to Rizqallah or Bella.

Boctor never fails to visit the shop when he's in Alexandria. He tours the counters, plays the boss — although he has no connection with the business — and utters an oath or two for form's sake. The salesgirls accuse him of making lewd advances, so I've heard. It's lucky he doesn't spit in the aisles as he did on the beach this morning!

Touta et Fils occupies the site of Xavier-Saillard's former headquarters. A big "T" is carved into the lintel over its doors, just as the celebrated "X-S" used to be. My cousin must have dreamed of this ever since he carried the Frenchman's briefcase.

Adolphe Xavier-Saillard never returned from Nice, whither he had fled before the bombardment. It seems that his eldest son's tragic death prompted him to wind up his business and bid Egypt farewell. Rizqallah worked like a maniac to secure his boss a generous sum in compensation. He then offered to buy the two ruined buildings. According to widespread rumours, Xavier-Saillard sold them to him on very favourable terms.

To see our family's name emblazoned in big letters in the Place des Consuls would no doubt have made me very proud ten years ago. Today, that *Touta et Fils* is more a source of embarrassment to me, as it is to my father. "Money always smells," he once observed, "don't you think?"

But there's a more personal reason for my embarrassment. I thought I was making something of a name for myself, thanks to journalism, but people more and more often ask me if I'm "connected with the department store". We pen-pushers count for little in this sad world!

6

We now get the four-page *Egyptian Gazette* every morning – or, to be more precise, half of it, because Elliot Bey tears off the front half, which is printed in English, and sends my father the other two pages, which are in French.

"No newspaper has ever been better utilized," was my father's smiling comment. He has agreed to share its cost with the bulldog-owner.

The *Egyptian Gazette* isn't the daily I myself would have chosen. Subsidized to the hilt, it abounds in useless information. One is told every other day that "the khedive left his residence at Ramlah by carriage at ten in the morning. He went for a drive along the banks of the Mahmudiya Canal and returned to the khedivial villa at about seven in the evening." Aunt Angéline revels in this kind of news item, which supplies her with ammunition for her evening conversations on the terrace of the Miramare.

My British-subsidized colleagues devote much attention to the crowded ships that sail for Europe daily. Not all the passengers fleeing the summer heat are foreign residents. They include many corpulent pashas bound for European spas, there to recoup the energy they expended during the latest theatre season. The *Egyptian Gazette* carefully prints the names of the first-and second-class passengers aboard every ship, generally adding " . . . and a number of third-class passengers." This spares us an over-long recital by Lolo, who reads the lists aloud to his mother on the beach. Aunt Angéline utters exclamations when he comes to certain names, not that she can number many of those wealthy passengers among her acquaintances.

This morning, after listening to Lolo's litany, my father could not resist describing, yet again, his departure aboard the *Masr*, commanded by Poisson

Bey, for the World Exhibition of 1867. He would never have repeated himself like that a few years ago, but the youngsters never tire of hearing about the Tuileries or Khedive Isma'il's innumerable purchases in the big Parisian boulevards. I must admit that I, too, am always happy to hear him reminisce about his talks with the astronomer Mahmud Bey. "Do you think it acceptable, doctor, that Egypt should have no less than seven different postal systems? Do we need an Egyptian, a French, a British, an Italian, an Austrian, a Greek, and a Russian postal system? A civilized country can't go on like this. I shall raise the matter with His Highness . . . ."

Wedged into a deckchair a trifle too narrow for her rump, Aunt Angéline generally complains that it's getting too hot and calls for air, air: *"Hawa, hawa!"*

Here at the seaside she doesn't hesitate to unbutton the top of her gown, even at the risk of revealing a voluminous bosom the colour of milk. Lolo, seated beside her on a campstool, deciphers the *Egyptian Gazette* with occasional cries of "Listen to this, *ya mami!* 'Yesterday the khedive left at ten o'clock . . . '"

Inevitably, I myself end by reading the two insipid pages that go the rounds of our sun umbrellas all morning. Is it really necessary to record the number of slaves freed last month? There were eighty-two of them in May, apparently, including twenty-one women. The British are very proud of this monthly tally, which is intended to testify to Egypt's progress along the road to civilization. Elliot Bey has ringed the information in red pencil to make sure we don't overlook it.

This afternoon Aunt Angéline managed to drag my father off to the Miramare. He found himself in the thick of a very heated argument about the effects of tobacco. Nestor Gianclis, the cigarette manufacturer, proudly exhibited the first prize for hygiene he recently won at the Spa Exhibition.

"Tobacco is not only harmless," he loudly declared. "It protects smokers against epidemics of all kinds."

"Prove it!" said my father.

Far from climbing down, Gianclis impressed his listeners by launching into a long tirade larded with medical terms.

"By permeating the whole organism, tobacco becomes a powerful antiseptic capable of resisting attack by all infectious and contagious diseases. It becomes a poison sufficiently attenuated to enable the body to resist the most virulent toxins."

"Not so, monsieur," my father retorted sharply. "Be advised that cigarettes stain the teeth, upset the digestion, and inhibit the salivary glands, thereby leading to emaciation. Be further advised that excessive smoking causes angina pectoris and strokes. It also creates a predisposition to apoplexy, lethargy, and insanity."

This did not dissuade a number of people from accepting the cigarettes generously offered them by Monsieur Gianclis and lighting up. My father returned to the villa in an extremely irritable mood, suffering from a bad headache. These outings don't suit him at all.

7

There was no reason why I shouldn't have attended that gala buffet at the palace. It would be an opportunity to meet all kinds of people, to show my face — as one has to do in this profession — and, perhaps, to help resolve the *Sémaphore*'s affairs.

"I'll pick you up in my carriage," said Rizqallah, who had moved into his luxurious villa nearby some days ago.

He wanted to show off his new conveyance, no doubt, but I never get bored with Rizqallah. His multifarious activities render him a well-informed man, a disseminator of all kinds of anecdotes. Yesterday, for instance, he called at his shop, the stock exchange and the French consulate in turn, and still found time to pay a flying visit to the harbour to say goodbye to a banker sailing for Europe in the *Sénégal*. The quayside was paved with flowers, it seems.

Tireless and ever on the alert, Rizqallah is interested in people as well as money. That's his great strength. He anticipates their wishes with surprising ease. Women are not immune to his charm. He is known to have at least two mistresses in Cairo and a third at Alexandria. He goes from one to the other, not forgetting his wife, and runs this little harem as expertly as he manages his business affairs. For a long time, Nada herself made me think she was seduced by Rizqallah's dynamism, but I was mistaken. Étienne's sincerity and loyalty counted for more in her eyes, but had she ever been truly in love with him?

I must admit that Rizqallah's luxuriously appointed landau, with its green leather seats and ebony handles, has wonderful springs. Heedless of bumps and potholes, we got to Ras at-Tin Palace without even realizing it, as if crossing a velvet carpet. All the khedive's many guests seemed to have arrived at the same moment. We had to queue up outside the massive gateway, which is flanked by columns of pink granite, for a good ten minutes. Rizqallah got out of the carriage three times to pay his respects to various people.

The palace's ceremonial courtyard, which overlooks the sea, was brilliantly illuminated. We were welcomed at the foot of the grand staircase by gentlemen ushers and conducted into the reception rooms. There I lost my cousin, who hurried from one person to another, shaking hands and exchanging formal embraces.

Senior officers of the army of occupation, looking very much at ease, strolled from room to room in their dazzling uniforms. I still couldn't get used to seeing Britishers wearing tarbooshes and hearing them addressed as *bimbashi*, *amiralai*, or *qa'imaqam*.

Old Nubar Pasha walked past without recognizing me. I was quite ready to concede that he might have forgotten the amateur journalist whom he had summoned to his office over ten years ago to discuss the mixed courts, but I'd had at least two interviews with him since his reappointment to the premiership. He was doubtless unwilling to be seen in public with a journalist from the *Sémaphore*. Balanvin, who hates him, has always resented his preference for Britain over France.

But France and Britain presented us with a charming spectacle that night. No one failed to notice Monsieur Camille Barrère chatting cordially with Sir Evelyn Baring. The two consuls-general were clearly intent on dispelling the rumour that they were on bad terms, especially after the polemics that had greeted the ban on the *Sémaphore*.

I had already spoken with a score of people when the doors of the buffet opened to reveal the great drawing room, which was hung with yellow silk.

"Don't you find the decoration of the ceilings a trifle ornate?" said a familiar voice. I hadn't expected to run into Nassif Bey's grandson at the palace.

"The ceilings may be a trifle ornate," I replied with a smile, "but the floors are exquisite. What do you expect, though? Palaces are like people: a mass of contradictions."

We had no time to pursue the subject because Rizqallah was swiftly bearing down on us. He simply had to leave, he said. He was expected at a reception in town. No matter, I replied, Nassif Bey's grandson could keep me company.

I was hailed in English-accented French.

"If it isn't my neighbour's son!"

Elliot Bey was standing at the entrance to the drawing room, unaccompanied by his bulldog and holding a glass of champagne. I hardly recognized him in his tarboosh and immaculate white tunic.

"So you're the *Sémaphore* correspondent," he went on. "You must explain to me why your paper doesn't like us."

"You said it, I didn't," I replied.

He assumed a spuriously dejected air. "The annoying thing about the *Sémaphore* is, one's obliged to read it to keep abreast of current affairs."

The compliment amused me. "You're absolved from that obligation for another few weeks," I replied, matching his tone. "The authorities have banned us."

"I know, that's why I've had to take the *Egyptian Gazette* instead."

We exchanged a look and then burst out laughing. Nassif Bey's grandson was not only puzzled but probably shocked.

"How can you expect the Egyptian people to love an occupying power?" he demanded fiercely, in English. "How can a nation consent to be deprived of control over its own country?"

Elliot Bey slowly sipped his champagne. "I seem to recall," he said, "that Egypt has always, ever since the time of the pharaohs, been governed by foreign powers or rulers of foreign blood."

"You're not being very kind to the khedive," I said ironically.

He saw his mistake. "Ever the journalist! You're right, I shouldn't have said that. No one can dispute the Egyptianness of Muhammad Ali's dynasty after four generations on the banks of the Nile. Besides, Tewfiq Pasha is an admirable man, God knows – a true patriot."

"Yes indeed," Nassif Bey's grandson said in an acid voice, "he meets your requirements in every respect."

The Englishman did not rise to this. "The Egyptian people," he went on, "can at least be grateful that their country has been at peace since 1882. The national finances have been restored and the fellahin are less heavily taxed. The use of the *kurbash* has been prohibited."

"That's a joke! People are being thrashed all day long, you know that perfectly well."

"But only, young man, because that kind of practice cannot be suppressed by decree. It will take time – far more time, incidentally, than we ourselves foresaw when assuming temporary charge of Egypt's affairs. The frightening extent of the task we've undertaken was not immediately apparent to us. There are limits to the means employed, too. I would remind you that we're merely British officials in the khedive's service. The British consul has no formal powers. Believe me, it would have been simpler for Britain to take over the government of the country lock, stock and barrel – to turn Egypt into a straightforward protectorate. However, we chose to respect the pride and independence of the Egyptian people."

Elliot Bey was interrupted by the applause that accompanied the khedive's withdrawal to his private apartments. Then he was borne off by a high-spirited bunch of officers who were comparing the merits of the various champagnes on offer.

"I could have told your English friend a thing or two!" the young Copt said regretfully.

"He's not my friend, he's my neighbour. Your neighbour, too. You can find him on the beach at about six in the evening, two days a week. But watch out for his bulldog."

Nassif Bey's grandson has his sister's glowing eyes, but he lacks the amused smile that sometimes lights up Nefertiti's beautiful face.

"Of course," he said in the carriage that was taking us back to Ramlah, "you *Shawam* have done well out of the British occupation. You hold some excellent posts in the new administration."

"I would point out," I retorted, "that my father's family has been settled in Egypt since 1740. Muhammad Ali wasn't even born then! What's more, the *Shawam* didn't wait for the British occupation to become involved in the economic life of the country, to found newspapers, and so on."

"It's a question of mentality. You keep yourselves to yourselves, you differentiate yourself from the Egyptian people."

"There are only some 10,000 of us. In order to survive, I'm sure we need to differentiate ourselves a little."

He shrugged his shoulders, clearly regretting the digression. The *Shawam* were not his main preoccupation. After a long pause, he said in a low, serious voice, "In spite of his age, my grandfather remained on the list of physicians accredited to the khedive until he died. Tewfiq Pasha, whom he had known since childhood, sometimes opened his heart to him. One day – it was just after the bombardment of Alexandria – he told my grandfather, 'We're incapable of governing ourselves. Rather than become Turkish again, we'd sooner be British.' Well, speaking for myself, I've never been Turkish and I'll never be British!"

8

My nerves had been on edge for three days. I was sleeping badly and eating little. The Mancelles' imminent arrival was even giving me a sporadic nervous tic, a fact that hadn't escaped my father's notice.

I asked Mahmud a dozen times if he was ready to hitch up the trap. We got to the station far too early, and, since the little Ramlah train was up to its usual tricks, we waited there for a good hour-and-a-half, desultorily chatting with the cabby from Bulkeley, whose services I had enlisted for the occasion.

Étienne got out first, and for a moment it seemed he was on his own. I was struck by his beaming face and thinning hair. His new title, "Director of Operations of the Transit and Navigation Service of the Suez Canal Company", had not gone to his head. His expression was as gentle and kindly as it had always been.

His three sons followed, wearing almost identical shirts. Then came Eugénie, accompanied by her young sister. Now sixteen, the Mancelles' eldest child had the self-assured, rather supercilious manner of a genuine Ismailia Frenchwoman. She surveyed the platform inquiringly, as if surprised not to find a porter at her instant beck and call. Mahmud hurried forwards, followed by the limping old cabby.

As for me, my heart was pounding as it had in the old days, or almost. Nada finally appeared, one tentative foot on the step. I'd expected to see a weary woman encumbered by her travelling outfit, but she was smiling radiantly, hair loose and fluttering in the wind. She caught sight of me halfway along the platform and blew me a little kiss.

The luggage was stowed aboard in wild confusion. The boys were keen to show off their muscles. Étienne, never one to stand on ceremony, rolled up his sleeves and helped to load a special package of substantial dimensions. I went from one conveyance to the other, hustling Mahmud and the cabby, while Nada watched the commotion with amusement.

"The children have dreamt of Ramlah almost every night," she told me when we were on our way.

"And you?" I longed to ask but didn't dare.

When we breasted the little dune and the sea came into view, and when a rather stronger breeze than usual nearly blew Eugénie's hat off, I saw Nada half-close her eyes and draw a deep breath. I was insanely happy at that moment. It was like a new beginning.

My father showed them round the house. I made myself scarce, not wanting to hear Nada's exclamations of delight, which would have sounded false. Play-acting wasn't her style, however. While anxious to please the old man, she would, I'm sure, have been as restrained as possible.

The Mancelles distributed little gifts among the villa's various inhabitants. Even Mahmud was presented with a Swiss pocket knife, which made him tremble with joy. My father was very touched to receive a volume of Clot Bey's unpublished memoirs bound in sumptuous tooled leather.

"And this is for you," said Nada, holding out a small parcel wrapped in pale pink paper.

"The wooden block was carved in our desert," Étienne felt called upon to add.

The inkwell was not the kind that would have been sold in the stationery department of *La Belle Jardinière*. I realized from the look of it that Nada had seen to the order herself, and I sensed that it would become my travelling companion for evermore, whatever the circumstances.

Once the presentations were over, Étienne and his sons proceeded to open the big, mysterious-looking package.

"A velocipede!" exclaimed Lolo.

"Yes," said the Director of Operations, "but mark this: a velocipede must be propelled at no more than twenty kilometres an hour by an experienced rider and fifteen by anyone else."

Lolo frowned, cudgelling his brains. Étienne continued to hold forth like a man who had done his homework before making such a purchase.

"You see," he went on, "while riding a velocipede you must breathe through your nose. The air gets forced back into your nostrils, so it's inadvisable for children under the age of twelve to engage in this activity."

Eugénie, who had gone off to change, created a sensation. Now attired in a short skirt and Zouave trousers, she went over to the contraption and prepared to mount it.

"What?" Aunt Angéline exclaimed in a strangled voice. "A young girl? Surely not!"

"Don't worry," Étienne told her. "We also have a ladies' saddle. It's broader, rounded, and slightly springy."

"But a young girl!" Angéline repeated.

Half amused, half embarrassed, Étienne went on, "I assure you, madame, that moderate exercise on a velocipede is an excellent sedative for the nervous system. According to our doctor in Ismailia, it's a sovereign remedy for gout and obesity."

"But a girl of sixteen!"

My father stepped in. "Yes, Angéline, exercise never hurt anyone, even a young girl. Riding a velocipede with the wind in one's face must be a refreshing experience."

Eugénie set off along the road.

"Not too fast!" called Étienne. "Not too fast, Ninette!"

Then, turning to us: "Girls must not exceed a speed of twelve kilometres an hour."

My father laughed heartily. I sometimes wonder if he isn't the most modern-minded of us all.

Nada liked the pink I'd chosen for her bedroom. *Their* bedroom, I should have said, but I can never endure the thought of her sharing that man's bed.

He has given her five children. Five times at least he has undressed her, caressed her, penetrated her. I hate to think of it. When associated with Étienne, it's as if there's something gross and abnormal about the act. She shouldn't have surrendered herself to *him* in that way. I like to believe that she retains no memory of those embraces, and that there's nothing between them any more. I like to believe that at night, before extinguishing the lamp, he has to content himself with planting a chaste kiss on the brow of the mother of his children . . .

9

Nada isn't one of those women who make a fuss when approaching the water, uttering little shrieks and fleeing at the first wavelet. She has been used to bathing in Lake Timsah for a long time now.

When we were all beneath our sun umbrellas I saw her walk slowly down to the sea, wade in thigh-deep, then bend to scoop up a little foam and moisten the back of her neck. She waded in still further. A moment or two later she slid into the water and performed a few strokes.

Étienne, standing at the water's edge, was already holding a towel open in conformity with a basic principle enunciated, no doubt, by his doctor in Ismailia:

"Sea-bathing must never be prolonged beyond the second shivering fit. As soon as this occurs you must leave the water, dry yourself promptly, and keep moving."

Nada invariably stayed in too long, according to the Director of Operations. He flapped the towel to remind her to come out, then cupped his hands and called, in a rather ridiculous way, "Na-da! Na-da!"

When she finally emerged I couldn't tear my eyes away from that alluring, rather full-hipped body under the wet bathing dress that moulded itself to every contour. I was terribly jealous of Étienne as he wrapped the towel around her, enveloped her, rubbed her down. Nada smiled at us, her eyebrows grey with salt, before retiring to the tent to change.

How could I stop thinking about the way we'd bathed together on the same beach four years ago? Our naked bodies in the water, brushing against each other, becoming entwined . . . My hands on Nada's hips, on her buttocks . . . In my dreams, God knows why, they became the swarthy hands of Walid al-Ahlawi . . . We must have stayed in the water far too long, *Monsieur le Directeur* – well beyond the second shivering fit. We never stopped shivering, truth to tell, but not with cold, and there was no towel waiting for us when we came out. We dried off in the first rays of the sun. It was warm – one of those September mornings when the sea, smooth as a lake and ever so slightly misty, decides to slumber on.

But rest assured, *Monsieur le Directeur*, we kept moving after all that rash self-indulgence. In the bedroom upstairs, stretched out on the three blankets that served us as a mattress, we never ceased to caress each other, hold each other close, taste the salt on each other's skin . . .

Ever since her arrival Nada has seemed, not to be avoiding my eye – that would be unlike her – but to be neutralizing the look in her own eyes as if nothing had ever happened between us in this house, or as if we mustn't think of it any more. Her attitude completely paralyses me. I've turned back into the youth who hardly dared look at her, but knew she was there beside him and heard her inimitable laugh. Nada is here, and her laughter hasn't changed.

"Thank you again for the inkwell," I said a little later. It was just before lunch, and she was alone on the veranda, gazing out to sea.

She didn't say, "Don't mention it." She smiled faintly, nothing more.

"However," she said after a pause, "if what I hear is true you won't be using it for several weeks because the *Sémaphore* has suspended publication."

"Don't you believe it, I never stop writing. Not just articles, either."

Instead of pursuing the matter, she changed the subject. "This is where Aunt Angéline takes her air baths, I gather."

"Yes," I said foolishly. As if this veranda were primarily associated in my mind with Aunt Angéline's daily bouts of asphyxia! Should I have reminded her that this was where we spent two hours together after making love – two hours of sipping tea and munching bread and cheese, two hours of idle talk and delicious fits of the giggles?

"Lunch!" called Angéline from the dining room. "The *sayaddeya* will get cold!"

I managed to sit on Nada's right, just as I did when I used to drop my napkin on the floor and brush against her while retrieving it. A couple of dozen Dabbours of all ages were present at this lunch in honour of Lolo's birthday. When the cake appeared, the hero of the day filled his lungs in an alarming manner so as to blow out all forty-five candles at once. He was duly applauded. Then Alfred Falaki fetched his present. Having feverishly unwrapped the parcel, "Maman's pet" discovered a fishing rod inside. He stared at it wide-eyed and almost inarticulate with surprise.

"It's just what I wanted!"

When lunch began the Mancelle children seemed rather bemused by all those exclamations and noisy bursts of laughter. Then they were carried away by the tide. Even Eugénie ended by thawing sufficiently to talk about the velocipede to two Dabbour girls of her own age. Roses, daisies, or violets — I'll never be able to tell one from another!

Eugénie is sixteen, exactly Nada's age when she arrived in Egypt. I still find it hard to believe that this French girl from Ismailia, with her prim manner and metallic voice, is Nada's daughter.

Over coffee Étienne spoke of his work. I learned in passing that Félix Percheron has at last become the freshwater canal's deputy director of stores. It's his marshal's baton, no doubt.

It appears that six million tons of traffic will pass through the Suez Canal this year.

"How much per ton?" asked Uncle Alfred.

"For laden vessels? Nine francs fifty."

"Very pretty!"

10

Our summer pleasures know no bounds. Last night, all Alexandria attended the execution of an itinerant musician condemned to death for murdering the Greek grocer in Nebi Danial Street. His appeal for clemency was rejected by the cabinet last week. Numerous Ramlahites went into town for the occasion, and I could kick myself for having been inveigled into joining them on such a sinister jaunt.

Originally due to take place in the Place des Consuls, the hanging had been transferred to Moharram Bey because – as the *Egyptian Gazette* explained – "it would have been too grim a sight for European eyes." What hypocrites!

At three in the morning, a big crowd made for the place of execution to be sure of getting a good view. There were as many straw boaters to be seen as tarbooshes, and plenty of ladies, both English and French, Greek and Italian, were anxious not to miss the spectacle. A special omnibus service had been organized.

On emerging from a pleasant but interminable dinner at the home of the *Sémaphore*'s editor, I bumped into a party from Ramlah including my brother Alexandre. I should have refused to come along, but some fool made a remark that touched a nerve:

"If journalists are scared of attending executions, who'll report them?"

I put myself in my father's place at medical school, balking at the prospect of inserting his scalpel in a patient's flesh. This execution was nothing compared to the ones I'd witnessed in the Place des Consuls in 1882, after all, but in some strange way it seemed more brutal.

When they came for him, the accused man asked for a drink. He was handed a pitcher of water, then loaded into a horse-drawn prison van, which set off at a trot. Halfway up a hill the van got stuck in the sand and had to be pushed with the help of a bunch of bystanders.

Amiralai George Harvey Bey, stationed beside the gallows in his capacity as Alexandria's police commissioner, was growing impatient. The condemned man asked to say his prayers, a request that could hardly be denied. Then he asked for another drink of water.

"What good will a drink do him now?" quipped Alexandre.

I was appalled by my brother's macabre little sally, but it was too late for me to leave this loathsome place, where a man convicted of a crime he might not have committed was about to die before our eyes.

The condemned man mounted the platform with his hands tied behind his back. The rope was too short, and the hangman clumsily endeavoured to pay out some more. Harvey Bey was showing increasing signs of impatience. Spectators near the scaffold claimed that the condemned man, being just as eager to get the business over and done with, had stood on tiptoe and even advised the hangman on how to arrange the noose round his neck. But these are the kind of details that Aunt Angéline makes a meal of after the event . . .

When the trapdoor finally opened, projecting the hapless man's body into space, I experienced a kind of vertigo. After a minute or two the physicians on duty approached the deceased to certify that he was dead. The body was left to hang there for an hour after the police had filed past on foot and on horseback.

This morning the sea is in a bad mood. So am I. I decided against showing my face to Nada at the breakfast table. If anyone is looking for our two pages of the *Egyptian Gazette*, they're in the dustbin at the bottom of the garden, torn into little strips.

The *Sémaphore*'s suspension suits Bartillat perfectly. I've never seen him as relaxed as he was at dinner last night.

"Actually, temporary bans are a hygienic measure," he said, eyes alight with mischief behind his pince-nez. "They could profitably be imposed on each newspaper in turn. All of us should be compelled to give our pens a rest and take an occasional break."

Bartillat doesn't think anything of the sort, of course. He's a newspaperman to the marrow — the *Sémaphore* is his daily drug. No woman could give him the same thrill as the unexpected wire that arrives just as the paper is going to press. Even on his deathbed, the *Sémaphore's* editor will ask to see the latest dispatch from Reuters or Havas.

His good humour derives from the fact that our advertising order book for the end of the summer is already full. Advertisers expect our circulation to rise as soon as the paper reappears, and they haven't balked at the increased rates we're charging. Only Uncle Alfred has been pestering me for the past two weeks to get him "a good rate", as he calls it.

At the palace the other night, Bartillat managed to have a quick word with the French consul-general, who had just been chatting with his British opposite number. According to him, the celebrated editorial of 8 May was merely an excuse to suspend the *Sémaphore*. In reality, Sir Evelyn Baring couldn't tolerate the amount of space the paper had for weeks been devoting to the reverses inflicted on the British expeditionary force in the Sudan after Gordon Pasha's murder by the Mahdists. He hadn't expected the *Sémaphore's* suspension to cause such a stir among the consulates. He couldn't revoke the ban without losing face, but he would be careful not to make another such mistake in the future.

"What article are you cooking up for our first issue?" Bartillat asked me in an aside.

I replied, in the vaguest terms, that I was thinking it over.

"You're right to relax beside the sea," he said with a smile. "But I hope you've brought a pen and an inkwell with you."

An inkwell . . .

II

Everyone was down on the beach by about eleven in the morning. The families of Rose, Marguerite and Violette had turned out in force, so we were quite a crowd. Some of the Dabbour boys were taking running dives into the waves, doubtless in the hope of catching Eugénie Mancelle's eye. The younger children were making a sand castle under the Austrian nanny's supervision, the older ones had gone to watch Lolo get entangled in his fishing line. Idle chatter was in progress under the sun umbrellas.

"Do you think Ismailia could accommodate another jeweller's shop?" Uncle Alfred asked Étienne. "It would be my fourth, you see, and that would solve the problems of inheritance when the time came. I'd leave one to Lucien and one to each of my blossoms . . . "

All at once my father got up and took off his dressing gown. He was wearing a bathing costume beneath it. We watched him walk down to the water's edge. Conversation died.

"What on earth are you doing, Boutros?" cried Aunt Angéline.

Thin as a rake, my father waded into the sea. Instinctively, I followed him and dived in too. We swam together a few metres out, streaming with water and smiling happily.

The old devil! He had caused a sensation last year by bathing in front of everyone like that, when all he'd done till then was to take a few surreptitious dips very early in the morning. It was his way of setting an example at the age of seventy-three – a very effective example, too, because the ensuing days saw some gentlemen – and even some ladies of a certain age – venture a few feet from the shore for the very first time. So here he was, repeating the demonstration this year as well. We would have to wait and see what effect it had.

"Where did you learn to swim?" I asked him.

"In the Nile, like everyone else at that time. We didn't worry too much about the purity of the water – not until some tiny leeches found their way into the mouth of one of my cousins and attached themselves to his palate. They had to be removed with pincers."

"What about the sea?"

"Oh, I didn't discover the sea until much later, when Nassif invited me to stay at Alexandria. He said I was insane. I was twenty-five when I bathed in salt water for the first time. That's nearly half a century ago . . . I found a charming little inlet near the Place des Consuls – a former parade ground. It's just been redeveloped in accordance with Mancini's plans."

We were swimming slowly, side by side, when I sensed that his strength was giving out.

"Help me ashore," he muttered.

I took his arm at once, then supported him around the waist. He was so thin, it added to my alarm. I hadn't imagined him to be so frail. Fortunately, we weren't out of our depth. After a while he wanted to swim on unaided.

"Let go, I'll be all right . . . "

No one had noticed. We came ashore together, escorted by a gaggle of children carrying spades. When we reached the sun umbrellas I suggested going back to the house, loudly enough for everyone to know it was my idea, not his. This time it was he who followed me. Meanwhile, tongues were briskly wagging on the subject of Dr Touta's latest swim.

He went upstairs to his room leaning on my arm. Having dried himself, he changed and lay down at once, not even bothering to brush the sand off his feet.

"Whatever you do, don't say anything to Angéline," he muttered feebly, closing his eyes.

I asked Mahmud to go and fetch my brother from the beach. In the meantime, Nada came into the room. She had guessed, when she saw us emerge from the sea, that something was wrong.

"Do you think I ought to inform the doctor at Bulkeley?" I asked her.

"Your father might be very annoyed."

"You're right. Let's wait awhile."

He was asleep already. I shut the door very quietly and joined her outside in the dim passage. The shutters were always closed before noon.

"Nada," I said softly, "do you remember that room?"

She looked startled.

"Nada, I –"

"No, Maxime, please don't." Then, a moment later, "You have your life ahead of you, Maxime."

I started to say something, but she stopped me by brushing my lips with her fingertips. We heard Alexandre's heavy footsteps on the stairs.

Lunch went ahead without my father. We told Aunt Angéline that he'd had a light meal as soon as he came in and was taking a siesta right away.

He'd improved a great deal by late afternoon, thank God, and played his usual evening game of whist with the Falakis as if nothing had happened.

Personally, I was out on my feet. The others went into town in search of entertainment. After much discussion, they split up into two groups: one went to the Zizinia Theatre to see an Italian vaudeville show, the other to the Debbane for an athletics display in the course of which Gunner Nicoll, a celebrated member of the British garrison in Cairo, was to perform prodigious feats with weights and dumbbells. If the *Egyptian Gazette* were to be believed – and why shouldn't I have believed such a respectable publication? – this giant of man issued a nightly challenge to all comers to take him on with the sabre.

"He provides the helmets and body armour," said Lolo, whose sole topic of conversation this had been for the past three days.

The day's emotional turmoil had tired me out. Now that my father's mortality had been brought home to me, I kept thinking of all we had never said to each other.

I also kept thinking of all I'd wanted to say to Nada that morning – all she might never again permit me to put into words.

12

Rizqallah proposed to christen his new seaside villa in style. Every member of the family had been invited to a masked ball for at least 300 guests. My father declined the invitation on grounds of age, as might have been expected. Aunt Angéline and Uncle Alfred hesitated briefly and then declined as well. This had made it possible to explain to Boctor Touta that his presence, too, was not required at his son's party.

I hate fancy dress, but it was difficult for me to refuse Rizqallah's invitation. Besides, Nada and her husband were looking forward to going. They must have been used to attending such functions in Ismailia. I eventually resigned myself to wearing a Bedouin costume, resolving to discard it as soon as possible in the course of the evening.

For three days on end the villa hummed with confabulations in which the three Dabbour teams took an active part. The young and not-so-young tried on costumes, changed their minds, conferred together. Alexandre and his wife were particularly excited by these preparations. These had necessitated several trips to the *Touta et Fils* department store to buy lengths of flannel and poplin, silk and velvet, ties, bows, hats, lace, and all manner of accessories.

"Your cousin makes money even when he invites people to his home," my father observed with a smile.

On the night of the ball I closeted myself in my room and waited for peace to be restored downstairs, determined to sneak out after everyone else had gone. As bad luck would have it, Lolo was still in the hallway attired as a British soldier in a ridiculous red tunic, gaiters, and a sola topi. Aunt Angéline, who had just finished adjusting the bottom of his trousers, stepped back to admire him.

There was nothing for it but to walk all the way along the dunes with "Maman's pet", he dressed up as a British soldier, I as a Bedouin. I prayed to heaven we didn't meet some belated passer-by, least of all a Bedouin! Halfway there I pleaded a call of nature and urged my cousin, with a vehemence that startled him, not to wait for me.

The entrance to Rizqallah's villa was illuminated from above by resinous torches that gave off thousands of sparks.

"This is even grander than Ras at-Tin Palace!" exclaimed a young marquis in a powdered wig. I recognized Nassif Bey's grandson under his mask.

There was a trace of sarcasm in his voice. He must have thought me grotesque in my *abaya*, *kufiya* and sandals, but I consoled myself by catching sight of someone at the far end of the second reception room: Étienne Mancelle attired as a green grasshopper. Everyone declared his costume a great success; I, to my great pleasure, found it absolutely ludicrous.

"He's the Suez Canal's director of operations," Rizqallah was explaining to several important guests, among whom I recognized the vice-president of the mixed courts' court of appeal, the Italian consul, and a leading member of the Jewish Benevolent Society.

My cousin had dressed up as Julius Caesar, so his wife had been obliged to wear a Cleopatra costume.

"At least she's got the nose for it," someone murmured spitefully as I was going out into the garden to look for Nada.

Designed by an Italian architect and built of the finest materials, the villa opened out on to a spacious terrace that overlooked the sea. The garden on the landward side was completely sheltered from the wind. The night was warm, and the temperature, augmented by a couple of hundred Chinese lanterns installed for the occasion, was extremely pleasant.

I was amused to see Nassif Bey's granddaughter dressed as a pharaonic princess.

"Nefertiti!" I called.

"No, Isis, if you don't mind . . . "

She looked superb in her close-fitting costume, and the swept-back hair accentuated her doe-eyed gaze. When a bunch of young musketeers and cavaliers bore her off towards the dance floor, I experienced a sudden pang of jealousy.

Rose, Marguerite and Violette had felt it incumbent on them to dress up as flowers, but they'd confused the issue by swapping identities. Their husbands, the three Dabbour brothers, had reproached them for recklessly squandering money at *Touta et Fils*. Their own black costumes were ill-defined – so much so that one wondered if they were wearing fancy dress at all.

I finally found Nada talking to some strangers at the end of the garden. Dressed as an Amazon, she wore a long, voluminous skirt that lent her a majestic appearance. She caught sight of me and gave a little wave but went on chatting. Rather put out, I returned to the reception rooms, where the band was playing a lively tune.

Sufragis in red livery were circulating among the dancers bearing silver salvers. Some Indians were performing a sarabande with a grotesque-looking British soldier in their midst.

The person who looked most at sea in all this revelry was Bella, the mistress of the house. Going up to her, I kissed her and congratulated her on the success of the evening. We had barely exchanged a few banalities when Caesar called her over to meet a Harlequin, alias the wife of the chairman of the Sanitary Committee.

The band struck up a quadrille. Isis and her group of young admirers took the floor. She removed her shoes to dance but retained the bangles around her ankles. I was captivated by those olive-skinned feet with the painted toenails, which made the silver bangles bounce at every step. Isis was certainly the first female pharaoh of all time to dance the diagonal quadrille as expertly.

I heard someone swear in Arabic behind my back. "The lavatories are permanently occupied," Uncle Boctor was remarking to a lady. "I'll end by doing it in my pants!"

"What!" I said. "You here, Uncle?"

"Not for long, you goddamned Bedouin! If you think I'm going to spend all night at this charade . . . "

While he was making for the exit I divested myself of my costume. More comfortable in a shirt, trousers, and the pair of shoes I'd been careful to bring with me, I asked Isis to dance. She held out her arms with a charming gesture and we were promptly carried away by the music. Everyone applauded when the music stopped, but it started again at once and we set off once more, rhythmically advancing and retreating, turning, beginning again. After twenty minutes, tired but in high spirits, we went to have some refreshments at the buffet.

"Did you know I stayed at your grandparents' house on my very first trip to Alexandria? I was thirteen at the time. Your grandfather impressed me immensely. He seemed to know everything about the world of politics."

"Politics don't interest me," Isis said simply. "It was medicine I persuaded my grandfather talk about whenever I saw him. I'd like to become a doctor myself, as a matter of fact."

My look of surprise made her smile.

"You don't think I'm up to it?"

"No," I said, "but I didn't know that women — "

We were interrupted by a cheerful voice.

"If it isn't my neighbour the journalist!" exclaimed a thickset Tyrolean in leather shorts.

Elliot Bey kissed Isis's hand and introduced his son, an extremely handsome young man who had turned up without a costume. Almost at death's door when my father saw him that night, he now looked the picture of health.

"It's your cousin's champagne that deserves to be in fancy dress," the deputy director of customs said roguishly. "An excellent vintage. We don't do ourselves as well, even in England."

Lolo was bearing down on us with a broad smile. He had affected an English accent as soon as he got to the party, which made him even more of a laughing-stock. Apprehensive of Elliot Bey's reaction, I hurriedly intercepted him.

"Go down to the beach at once," I told him in a low voice. "There's a surprise waiting for you."

"I don't understand," he said, looking puzzled.

"Exactly, there's nothing *to* understand. It's a surprise."

I turned to find myself alone. Elliot Bey had gone over to the buffet and his son had asked Isis to dance.

Ten minutes later the band stopped playing and Rizqallah, using his hands as a megaphone, invited everyone out on to the terrace. There I ran into my brother Alexandre, rather constricted by a jerkin with puffed sleeves and very disappointed to find another two Saint-Simonians among the guests.

"That'll teach me to take my wife's advice. I'd have made a splendid Mameluke."

Overhead, the first rocket exploded into an enormous red and blue bouquet. Caesar was even treating us to a firework display! That was when I caught sight of Lolo in his pith helmet. The fool was standing beside the pyrotechnists with his arms dangling. I hurried down to the beach, ran up to him, and hauled him away by the sleeve.

He thanked me most sincerely on the way back to the house, still in his English accent. "That *was* a nice surprise! I was right up close. I've always wanted to watch a rocket being lit."

Nada's smile when she saw us coming told me that she had guessed something. We looked at each other for a moment and burst out laughing while Lolo, with his eyes on stalks, gazed at the showers of sparks in the sky.

Dancing resumed as soon as the firework display ended. In the corner of the main reception room we overheard a rather heated exchange between Isis and her brother.

"I'll dance with anyone I please!" she was saying.

He must have reprimanded her for having danced twice in succession with the young Englishman. Several people including my cousin Violette were surreptitiously listening. In the end, Nassif Bey's grandson towed his sister towards the exit.

"It's late," he said curtly. "We're going home."

I asked Nada for one waltz, then another. I must have had a dozen dances with my Amazon. We didn't say anything of importance, but I encircled her waist, grasped her hands, savoured her smile and the way her eyes sought mine.

At three a.m., ever the grand seigneur, Rizqallah summoned several carriages for the benefit of those who had come on foot. Lolo had a bright idea: he not only came with me but seated himself between me and Nada.

13

I awoke rather late and slightly bemused, thinking back on the ball. I had a strange feeling of having deceived Nada with Isis and Isis with Nada.

In the afternoon Mahmud ferried us to the Miramare in several batches. The Mancelles wanted to say hello to Albin Balanvin. As for Aunt Angéline, she was dying to hear and comment on the latest tittle-tattle about Rizqallah's party.

"Nassif Bey's granddaughter danced twice with the young Englishman," she said, sugaring her tea. "I don't have to tell you what a scandal it caused. Apparently, the girl's brother made the band stop playing, strode out into the middle of the floor, and slapped her face with everyone watching."

A woman friend claimed to have heard two loud bangs issue from Nassif Bey's house that morning.

"*Ayou!*" exclaimed Aunt Angéline. "He probably tried to kill her."

I was seated at a neighbouring table with Balanvin and the Mancelles. Nada, who had caught the echoes of this conversation, couldn't help smiling.

"Your aunt should have been a journalist."

"A novelist, you mean."

Étienne and Albin were talking about Ferdinand de Lesseps' election to the Académie Française.

"We don't see him on the isthmus as often since he became president of the Panama Canal Company."

"Two canals are a lot for one man, even if he is an 'Immortal' . . . "

We chatted of this and that for a good hour. Occasionally Étienne would enlist his wife's confirmation of some point or other. "Now that the trees are getting steadily bigger, Ismailia is becoming lovelier every year, isn't that so, my little dove?"

That ridiculous nickname and its evocation of their life together filled me with bitter resentment.

Étienne and Nada went back to the villa with Aunt Angéline. I stayed behind with Balanvin, who suggested a walk on the beach.

His cane dug into the sand a little, but he was fond of these leisurely strolls in the late afternoon, when the sun was still reluctant to set.

"You're looking a trifle depressed, my young friend."

I was thirty-five. Balanvin will continue to call me "my young friend" until his dying day, I suspect.

"Depressed?" I said, forcing a smile. "Perhaps I'm worried about the *Sémaphore*'s future."

"Come, come, the *Sémaphore* has never been in better shape, you know that perfectly well." He paused, tapping the knob of his cane, then said casually, "She married Mancelle, but it's you she looks at. Would you sooner she married you and looked at Mancelle?"

I was taken aback. Nothing escaped him, the devil! It was the first time he had ever ventured to broach such an intimate subject, but his remark went straight to my heart. So Nada looked at me, did she? She looked at me so much that it showed. I was feeling much better already — very much better, almost euphoric.

We walked on in silence for a while. Then, in a cheerful voice, I said the first thing that came into my head:

"What about your chapter on the Xavier-Saillard affair?"

It was a stupid question, given that Balanvin had already told me more than once he didn't want to talk about it.

"The Xavier-Saillard affair? It's quite straightforward, my young friend." He punched some little holes in the sand with his cane. "Your eyes were riveted to Walid al-Ahlawi — I can understand that, incidentally — but I was interested in the real protagonist. I'm talking about the soldier who tried to strike poor Xavier-Saillard."

He walked on, talking as he went.

"The soldier in question had a brother who was employed on Xavier-Saillard's estates. He'd been whipped two weeks earlier, together with several other peasants, by order of my likeable compatriot, for some trivial matter concerning hours of work."

"I see, so his brother wanted to avenge him."

"Very astute of you. Do you recall that Étienne Mancelle witnessed the scene — that he saw Xavier-Saillard get to his feet and horsewhip his assailant several times?"

"Yes, and he went and told the French consul about it," I said.

"And the consul wouldn't listen. Well, young Mancelle was so distressed that he wrote a detailed description of the scene to his mother the same night. I recently got hold of that letter during a trip to France. Mancelle has authorized me to publish it without mentioning his name."

"It must be rather touching."

"Interesting, certainly. It states that the assailant and his victim not only exchanged blows; they had a violent argument."

"In Arabic?"

"Xavier-Saillard knew a little Arabic, but it was French he used when he shouted at the soldier that his punishment would be worse than his brother's."

"And Mancelle didn't say anything?"

"Indeed he did — he told the whole story, but the French consul declined to record his evidence. The young engineer was so shocked, he never spoke of it again, not to anyone."

Listening to Balanvin, I reflected that Étienne might well have mentioned it years later to Nada. His little dove . . .

"The French consul seized on the affair with suspicious alacrity," Balanvin continued. "He was looking for an opportunity to put the new viceroy in his place. Isma'il had recently dared to criticize the Suez Canal Company's use of forced labour in front of the entire diplomatic corps, so the Xavier-Saillard affair came at just the right moment. Isma'il was obliged to go to Alexandria in person and see his army publicly humiliated. It mortified him deeply, and he moved heaven and earth to get the consul replaced."

"So Walid al-Ahlawi had nothing to do with it?"

"I don't know if he was aware that several of his men had gone to the aid of Xavier-Saillard's assailant. All I know — because I also went to the barracks at Alexandria, like your father — is that the incident made him very popular, and that he vowed, in the presence of some other officers, to get his own back."

"Oh no," I said. "I can assure you that Walid had nothing to do with the burning of Xavier-Saillard's buildings. I even saw him trying to deter the looters."

"I never said he revenged himself in that way. What you may not know, my young friend, is that as soon as he was appointed colonel of the 5th, Walid called on Xavier-Saillard in full-dress uniform, accompanied by an interpreter. Not to demand money, but to list all the irregularities, large and small, committed by my unfortunate compatriot, down to and including the notorious matter of the toll fees for the lock on the Mahmudiya Canal. The police, who were currently controlled by the 'Arabists, knew all about this. The interpreter was really sweating, believe me, and he didn't dare translate even half of what Walid said. If the British hadn't landed, and if 'Arabi had come to power, Xavier-Saillard would undoubtedly have been brought to book."

"He lost a son in the bombardment."

"And found peace. He hurriedly sold his business and retired to Nice. Your cousin Rizqallah took advantage of this to buy his two ruined buildings – for a good price, I'm told."

"I hope my cousin didn't become involved in any, er . . . irregularities while working for the man."

Balanvin had paused once more and was punching holes in the sand.

"My young friend, in some occupations people get their hands dirty occasionally. We journalists aren't exempt from that kind of mishap, even if we claim it's only ink that stains our fingertips."

14

No one resisted the sea this morning. Limpid and unruffled by a breath
of wind, it attracted us all like a lover. At least fifteen bathers swam out
to the buoy, an unprecedented event in the annals of Ramlah.

Aunt Angéline, although complaining of lack of air, tore herself away
from her deckchair and walked down to the water's edge. Her heavy tread
left dents in the moist sand. Even Mahmud – armed, it is true, with
especially potent amulets – ended by venturing beyond the sun umbrellas.

Nada is looking at me. I hardly dare turn my head. Her gaze is like a
feather-light caress that makes me tremble, glides gently over my skin,
lingers and envelops me. I yield to its touch, surrender myself entirely.
Sometimes, when our eyes meet, that exchange is as good as the wildest
embrace. Everything else belongs to the past. From now on, Nada's gaze
must suffice me. But for that I shall need her physical presence, at least
from time to time.

Rose, Marguerite and Violette, surrounded by a swarm of young
Dabbours and Mancelles, braved the sea for the very first time. They held
hands, thigh-deep, giggling, caterwauling and uttering occasional shrieks.
My father, lying back in his deckchair, regarded them with amusement.
He was getting ready to take his second bathe of the season.

"Don't worry," he said in a low voice, when I saw him get up and take
off his dressing gown.

He slid gently into the water the way some women do, first bending
down with his bottom in the air. After a few slow breaststrokes he turned
over on his back and floated for a while. I couldn't resist swimming out to
the buoy to join him.

Clinging one-handed to the rings attached to the sides of the big white ball, we exchanged a few words.

"How beautiful the sea looks," I said tritely.

He didn't reply at once.

"It was the sea that transported all our families to Egypt. They came in search of peace, or prosperity. Sometimes just in search of a husband, like your poor mother. I said 'poor' because she's dead. Stupid of me . . . "

The white ball was bobbing gently. My father continued to muse aloud.

"Our families were right to come to Egypt. It suits us here. I don't think we'll ever leave, not now. Anyway, *I'll* be here for ever." He smiled. "Yes, for ever. When the time comes, you must bury me in that pretty graveyard on the Ramlah road, near the convent of the Dames de Sion. Whatever follies the human race commits, no one will disturb my slumbers there."

I almost protested that there was no reason for him to speak about that, but his tone was so serene, so cheerful, that I restrained myself. Swimming breaststroke side by side, we slowly made our way ashore.

Elegant Alice was taking a sand bath in her pearl-encrusted skullcap. We gave her a little wave, but she could only respond with a nod, the rest of her being imprisoned beneath the scorching surface. Yolande, armed with a miniature spade, continued to bury her mother under the Austrian nanny's vigilant eye. The latter hadn't let Yolande out of her sight since she got lost among the dunes the other day.

"We could put her on a sort of leash," the nanny had suggested, but my father immediately condemned that preposterous idea, and it was dropped.

He went off to dry himself. I took the opportunity to pause beside the sun umbrella of Nassif Bey's widow, who was temporarily on her own.

"Isn't your granddaughter on the beach today?"

"I'm expecting her. She was a little out of sorts this morning."

"Nothing serious, I hope?"

"No, no . . . Your father, who was kind enough to drop in earlier on, assures me she'll be perfectly all right. He even prescribed a swim in the sea."

"Papa has always been an advocate of natural therapies," I said with a smile.

'He's a true physician – and a true Egyptian,' she added, rather strangely.

Had they been talking about the graveyard? From Egypt, conversation turned to the British.

"Poor Nassif couldn't endure the occupation," she said. "It was no coincidence that he died only a few days after the British landed in Alexandria. We would have celebrated our fiftieth wedding anniversary this year. Imagine, my family didn't want me to marry him! But I'm boring you with my reminiscences . . . "

The Falakis had bought their rather ridiculous floral sun umbrella at *Touta et Fils*. Seated in its shade with his paunch propped on his thighs, Uncle Alfred tells his amber beads – or calculates his profits? – for hours on end. He asked me yet again this week to persuade the *Sémaphore's* advertising manager to give him a discount.

"Tell him I'm going to open a fourth shop. At Ismailia, this time."

Lolo, wearing his sola topi, was immersed in the *Egyptian Gazette*.

"Listen to this, *ya mami*! 'At ten yesterday morning the khedive left his residence at Ramlah by carriage and –'"

Angéline was suffocating despite the two fans she was flapping in front of her enormous breasts.

"Lolo, Maman's pet, pass me the pitcher. I must have a mouthful of water. This heat is killing me, I assure you!"

Nearby, Rizqallah was surrounded by half-a-dozen ladies who hung on his every word.

"This winter," he was telling them in his mellow voice, "you womenfolk will be regular chameleons. We've received a big consignment of watered velvet. The season's colours will be green, lily of the valley, plum, and beaver. Just wait, my dears, until you see those heavy fabrics and sables. No, no, wool is out! *Khalass!* I've ordered some batches of serge with self-colour patterns."

The ladies shivered with excitement. My cousin proceeded to kindle everyone's imagination by alluding, not for the first time, to the project in preparation at Alexandria – a scheme in which he himself hoped to participate.

"I tell you this: once it has been built, the Hôtel-Casino San Stefano will be *the* smart rendezvous, the high spot of Ramlah's summer season. People will go there to take tea, of course, but there'll also be attractions for all ages: balls, concerts, fencing matches, puppet shows, pantomimes . . . Yes, my dears, throughout the season! From May to September. And I can already tell you that all the rooms will be lit by electric light! At night, viewed from the sea, the San Stefano will resemble a glittering ocean liner . . . "

"What about the Miramare?" asked one of the Dabbour brothers.

"The Miramare will be small beer compared to the marvel I'm talking about. We're entering a new epoch, an era of prosperity such as Egypt has never known before. The San Stefano is going to cost millions."

"Very pretty!" said Alfred Falaki.

Nassif Bey's widow and her granddaughter had joined the circle. Isis, out of sorts? Not a bit of it! She had never looked more beautiful. Her eyes shone and she even burst out laughing when I described my first visit to the *Sémaphore d'Alexandrie*.

"I'm Maxime Touta."

"Never heard of you."

"I'm Armand de —"

"Make up your mind, monsieur!"

Rizqallah informed us that his villa was to be enlarged in the very near future. Apparently, his Italian architect had designed a pavilion, based on the one at Palace No. 3, to be erected at the end of the garden.

"So you'll be throwing another party, another masked ball, will you?" one of the three blossoms asked jokingly.

"Will I!" replied Caesar, who loved to brag. "And this time we'll have two bands, not one. Isn't that right, Bella?"

"Hello, Mister!" the donkey boy called to Lolo as he led his animal along the beach.

The Mancelle children address him in Arabic, and to think they couldn't rub two words together when they got here!

I was as happy as they when Étienne announced, in front of everyone, that he plans to build a villa here. This week my father will take him to see the Bedouin and negotiate a price for a plot of land.

"It was Nada's idea," the Director of Operations pointed out. "But I warn you, we won't be employing the same architect as Rizqallah!"

Nada smiled and said nothing. Our eyes met.

Everyone was irresistibly attracted to the sea once more. My father turned to Isis.

"You should go for a swim, mademoiselle. Out to the buoy, even."

"Oh, I'd never dare swim as far as the buoy."

"Perhaps Maxime would go with you," Nada suggested with a smile.